"W.E.B. Griffin is the best chronicler of the U.S. military ever to put pen to paper—and rates among the best storytellers in any genre."
—The Phoenix Gazette

HONOR BOUND

The high drama and real heroes of World War II . . .

"Rousing . . . An immensely entertaining adventure."
—Kirkus Reviews

"A tautly written story whose twists and turns will keep readers guessing until the last page." *—Publishers Weekly*

"A superior war story." *—Library Journal*

W.E.B. GRIFFIN'S CLASSIC SERIES

PRESIDENTIAL AGENT

Griffin's electrifying series of homeland security . . .

"Is Griffin our Homer or Tacitus? Those military experts wrote about real soldiers and what the world needs now is a real-life Charley Castillo, Griffin's smart and efficient Department of Homeland Security agent. Castillo and his team of tough and shrewd experts are just the kind of believable people we want in these situations. And if it takes a novelist like Griffin, who has honed his skills and weapons in five previous series, to bring them to life, at least their real counterparts will have some fictional role models to live up to." *—Publishers Weekly*

"Tough-fisted . . . hard-edged . . . Griffin's formula is straightforward: set up a bunch of obstacles, and let us watch Charley Castillo knock them down one at a time. His novels promise action, suspense, and rousing entertainment, and they never fail to deliver." *—Booklist*

"Punchy prose that connects like a right hook. Griffin should offer Castillo's services to Washington!"
—Chicago Tribune

THE CORPS

The bestselling saga of the heroes we call Marines . . .

"Great reading. A superb job of mingling fact and fiction . . . [Griffin's] characters come to life."

—*The Sunday Oklahoman*

"This man has really done his homework . . . I confess to impatiently awaiting the appearance of succeeding books in the series." —*The Washington Post*

"Action-packed . . . Difficult to put down."

—*Marine Corps Gazette*

BROTHERHOOD OF WAR

The series that launched W.E.B. Griffin's phenomenal career . . .

"An American epic." —Tom Clancy

"First-rate. Griffin, a former soldier, skillfully sets the stage, melding credible characters, a good eye for detail, and colorful gritty dialogue into a readable and entertaining story."

—*The Washington Post Book World*

"Absorbing, salted-peanuts reading filled with detailed and fascinating descriptions of weapons, tactics, Green Beret training, Army life, and battle."

—*The New York Times Book Review*

"A crackling good story. It gets into the hearts and minds of those who by choice or circumstance are called upon to fight our nation's wars."

—William R. Corson, Lt. Col. [Ret.], USMC, author of *The Betrayal* and *The Armies of Ignorance*

"A major work . . . Magnificent . . . Powerful . . . If books about warriors and the women who love them were given medals for authenticity, insight, and honesty, Brotherhood of War would be covered with them."

—William Bradford Huie, author of *The Klansmen* and *The Execution of Private Slovik*

BADGE OF HONOR

Griffin's electrifying epic series of a big-city police force . . .

"Damn effective . . . He captivates you with characters the way few authors can."
—Tom Clancy

"Tough, authentic . . . Police drama at its best . . . Readers will feel as if they're part of the investigation, and the true-to-life characters will soon feel like old friends. Excellent reading."
—Dale Brown

"Colorful . . . Gritty . . . Tense." —*The Philadelphia Inquirer*

"A real winner." —*New York Daily News*

MEN AT WAR

The legendary OSS—fighting a silent war of spies and assassins in the shadows of World War II . . .

"Written with a special flair for the military heart and mind." —*The Winfield Daily Courier* (KS)

"Shrewd, sharp, rousing entertainment." —*Kirkus Reviews*

CLANDESTINE OPERATIONS

A new kind of war demands a new kind of warrior . . .

"A thrilling new series has begun, opening doors to special ops and investigating the path to the Cold War. An incredible mix of intrigue and diplomacy from a literary team that ignites suspense lovers everywhere. Readers will be panting for the next novel." —*Suspense Magazine*

"A Griffin adventure to bring out the Walter Mitty in every red-white-and-blue-blooded American male."
—*Kirkus Reviews*

BOOKS BY W.E.B. GRIFFIN

HONOR BOUND

BOOK I: HONOR BOUND
BOOK II: BLOOD AND HONOR
BOOK III: SECRET HONOR
BOOK IV: DEATH AND HONOR
(and William E. Butterworth IV)
BOOK V: THE HONOR OF SPIES
(and William E. Butterworth IV)
BOOK VI: VICTORY AND HONOR
(and William E. Butterworth IV)
BOOK VII: EMPIRE AND HONOR
(and William E. Butterworth IV)

BROTHERHOOD OF WAR

BOOK I: THE LIEUTENANTS
BOOK II: THE CAPTAINS
BOOK III: THE MAJORS
BOOK IV: THE COLONELS
BOOK V: THE BERETS
BOOK VI: THE GENERALS
BOOK VII: THE NEW BREED
BOOK VIII: THE AVIATORS
BOOK IX: SPECIAL OPS

THE CORPS

BOOK I: SEMPER FI
BOOK II: CALL TO ARMS
BOOK III: COUNTERATTACK
BOOK IV: BATTLEGROUND
BOOK V: LINE OF FIRE
BOOK VI: CLOSE COMBAT
BOOK VII: BEHIND THE LINES
BOOK VIII: IN DANGER'S PATH
BOOK IX: UNDER FIRE
BOOK X: RETREAT, HELL!

BADGE OF HONOR

BOOK I: MEN IN BLUE
BOOK II: SPECIAL OPERATIONS
BOOK III: THE VICTIM
BOOK IV: THE WITNESS
BOOK V: THE ASSASSIN
BOOK VI: THE MURDERERS
BOOK VII: THE INVESTIGATORS
BOOK VIII: FINAL JUSTICE
BOOK IX: THE TRAFFICKERS
(and William E. Butterworth IV)
BOOK X: THE VIGILANTES
(and William E. Butterworth IV)
BOOK XI: THE LAST WITNESS
(and William E. Butterworth IV)
BOOK XII: DEADLY ASSETS
(and William E. Butterworth IV)
BOOK XIII: BROKEN TRUST
(and William E. Butterworth IV)

MEN AT WAR

BOOK I: THE LAST HEROES
BOOK II: THE SECRET WARRIORS
BOOK III: THE SOLDIER SPIES
BOOK IV: THE FIGHTING AGENTS
BOOK V: THE SABOTEURS
(and William E. Butterworth IV)
BOOK VI: THE DOUBLE AGENTS
(and William E. Butterworth IV)
BOOK VII: THE SPYMASTERS
(and William E. Butterworth IV)

PRESIDENTIAL AGENT

BOOK I: BY ORDER OF THE PRESIDENT
BOOK II: THE HOSTAGE
BOOK III: THE HUNTERS
BOOK IV: THE SHOOTERS
BOOK V: BLACK OPS
BOOK VI: THE OUTLAWS
(and William E. Butterworth IV)
BOOK VII: COVERT WARRIORS
(and William E. Butterworth IV)
BOOK VIII: HAZARDOUS DUTY
(and William E. Butterworth IV)

CLANDESTINE OPERATIONS

BOOK I: TOP SECRET
(and William E. Butterworth IV)
BOOK II: THE ASSASSINATION OPTION
(and William E. Butterworth IV)
BOOK III: CURTAIN OF DEATH
(and William E. Butterworth IV)

AS WILLIAM E. BUTTERWORTH III

THE HUNTING TRIP

VICTORY AND HONOR

W.E.B. GRIFFIN
AND WILLIAM E. BUTTERWORTH IV

G. P. Putnam's Sons
New York

G. P. PUTNAM'S SONS
Publishers Since 1838
An imprint of Penguin Random House LLC
375 Hudson Street
New York, New York 10014

First G. P. Putnam's Sons hardcover edition / August 2011
First Jove premium edition / June 2012
First G. P. Putnam's Sons premium edition / September 2017
G. P. Putnam's Sons premium edition ISBN: 9780515150988

Printed in the United States of America
11 13 15 17 19 20 18 16 14 12

Cover design by Sara Wood
Cover photograph from the National Archives
Cover typographic styling by Lawrence Ratzkin

IN LOVING MEMORY OF

Colonel José Manuel Menéndez

Cavalry, Argentine Army, Retired.
He spent his life fighting Communism and
Juan Domingo Perón.

VICTORY
✪ AND ✪
HONOR

PROLOGUE

There was little question by January 1945 that the Axis—Germany, Japan, and Italy—had lost the war. It was now just a matter of time.

In early 1942, just before the Japanese conquest of the Philippines was complete—the greatest defeat in American history—President Franklin Delano Roosevelt ordered the American commander in the Philippines, General Douglas MacArthur, to Australia.

On Corregidor Island, as MacArthur boarded a small patrol torpedo boat at a wharf in Manila Bay, he made the melodramatic promise to the Philippine people, "I shall return!"

On October 20, 1944, after he had waded ashore from one of the landing craft that had carried troops of the United States Sixth Army onto the beaches of Leyte, ignoring Japanese mortar and sniper fire, MacArthur melodramatically proclaimed, "I have returned!"

On January 17, 1945, Soviet troops forced the Germans out of Warsaw, and ten days later liberated the Auschwitz and Birkenau concentration camps, where they found the remains of more than a million people who had been murdered by the Germans.

On January 28, 1945, the Battle of the Bulge—Germany's last-ditch attempt to turn the tide of war in Western Europe—failed. The Americans suffered some 75,000 casualties, the Germans nearly 100,000. The Americans easily recovered from their losses. The Germans had thrown just about all of their reserves into the fight and had no means of recovery. Most historians agree that after the Battle of the Bulge, the Germans had absolutely no hope of winning the war.

On April 12, 1945, Franklin Delano Roosevelt, the thirty-second President of the United States, died suddenly at Warm Springs, Georgia. With him at the time was his mistress, Lucy Mercer, his wife's former social secretary.

Roosevelt was not quite four months into his fourth term as President. Vice President Harry S Truman—who had seen Roosevelt only twice since their inauguration; never for more than fifteen minutes, and he had never been alone with him during that time—was sworn in as the thirty-third president on the afternoon of Roosevelt's death.

The next morning, Lieutenant General Leslie Groves, a U.S. Army Corps of Engineers officer in charge of something called the "Manhattan Project," went to Truman in the Oval Office and said, "Mr. President, there is something you have to know."

He then went on to tell President Truman what President Roosevelt had felt the former U.S. senator from Missouri should not know: The Manhattan Project had secretly developed a new superweapon, called the "atomic bomb," and two of these devices were available for use.

On April 25, 1945, Major General Isaac Davis White's "Hell on Wheels" Second Armored Division, with its bridges across the Elbe River, was prepared to take Berlin. Ordered to halt in place so as to permit the Red Army to take Berlin, White—a direct descendant of Isaac Davis, the man who fired "the shot heard around the world" at Concord Green, thus starting the American Revolution—was reported to be so angry that he kicked the windows out of his truck-mounted command post.

On April 28, 1945, Benito Mussolini and his mistress were captured by antifascist Italian partisans, executed, and then hung upside down from a light pole.

On April 30, 1945, as Soviet troops came close to the "Führer Bunker" in Berlin, Adolf Hitler and Eva Braun—his ex-mistress and bride of mere days—committed suicide. As soon as Dr. Josef Goebbels had seen that their bodies had been burned, the Nazi propaganda minister stood by as his wife fed cyanide capsules to their six children, and then she and he bit into their own capsules.

On May 2, 1945, Red Army troops completed the capture of Berlin and the last German troops in Italy surrendered.

On May 7, 1945, Germany surrendered unconditionally.

I

[ONE]
Hotel Britania
Rua Rodrigues Sampaio 17
Lisbon, Portugal
3 May 1945

The younger man quickly stood when he saw the older man enter the restaurant and walk toward his table.

The older man was in his fifties, featured an ill-defined mustache and somewhat unkempt gray hair, and wore a black single-breasted garment with little or no padding in the shoulders—what members of his social class thought of as a "sack suit"—with a white button-down-collar shirt and bow tie.

He looked like a distinguished schoolteacher. Indeed, he always reminded the younger man of the Reverend Richard Cobbs Lacey, headmaster of Saint Mark's of Texas, an Episcopal preparatory school in Dallas at which, a decade earlier at age fourteen, the younger man had had a brief—five-month—and ultimately disastrous association.

The younger man wore the somewhat splendiferous

uniform of a South American Airways captain—SAA wings on a powder-blue tunic with four gold stripes on its cuffs and darker blue trousers with an inch-wide gold stripe down the hem.

Neither man was what he appeared to be.

The older one, whose name was Allen Welsh Dulles, was deputy director for Europe of the Office of Strategic Services. And the younger one, whose name was Cletus Howell Frade, was a Marine Corps Reserve lieutenant colonel detached for service in South America with the same U.S. spy organization.

They shook hands. Then Dulles motioned for Frade to sit, and found his seat.

A waiter appeared.

"A Johnnie Walker Black Label—a double, neat—for me," Dulles ordered, and then asked, "Cletus?"

Frade shook his head. "I'm flying. Or at least I think I am."

Dulles nodded, then looked at the waiter and said, "Just the one drink, please."

The waiter left.

"So, how goes the war?" Frade said.

"In one sense, rather well," Dulles began, then paused as he saw the waiter suddenly approaching with his drink.

When the waiter had left again, Dulles raised his glass in salute and solemnly said, "To victory in Europe."

He took a sip and then went on in explanation: "Just before I left Bern to come here, I learned that German forces in the Netherlands, Denmark, and northwestern Germany will surrender tomorrow to Field Marshal Bernard Montgomery at Lüneburg Heath, just southeast of Hamburg.

"Grand Admiral Karl Dönitz, now head of the German state, has sent Admiral von Friedeburg, his successor as commander in chief of the German navy, to General Eisenhower's headquarters in Reims to set up things. And Colonel-General Alfred Jodl—the chief of staff of OKW, who will actually sign the surrender documents—is on his way to Reims as we speak."

"And the other sense? What's that? The reason you're not in Reims?"

"I thought it more important—and so did Graham—that we had a talk before you went back to Argentina. The other sense, Clete, is that our war—Graham's, mine, and yours—is just about to begin."

Frade's eyebrows went up when he heard his name rolled in with those of Dulles and Colonel Alejandro F. Graham, USMCR, the deputy director for the Western Hemisphere of the Office of Strategic Services. Both men were equals in the OSS, reporting directly to—and on occasion directly defying—OSS director William "Wild Bill" Donovan.

"That sounds ominous," Frade said. "Who are we going to fight?"

"It's a long list of belligerents, I'm afraid, starting with those Germans you know are already in South America under the Nazis' Operation Phoenix and planning, at some point, to resurrect the Thousand-Year Reich. And the Soviet Union, of course. Josef Stalin really is not Friendly Uncle Joe, as Roosevelt and Eleanor have tried so hard to make us believe. But our immediate enemies are Admiral Leahy and General Marshall and others of their ilk. And possibly Harry Truman, although he may surprise us. And, of course, not to forget Henry Morgenthau."

"The secretary of the Treasury?"

"The secretary of the Treasury," Dulles confirmed.

"You don't really think anybody's going to go along with that nutty idea of his . . . what's it being called? 'The Pastoralization of Germany'?"

"Yes, Cletus, I'm afraid that I do. They want Germany powerless, and believe completely demolishing its industry will accomplish that. But what I actually was thinking about is Morgenthau finding out about the deal we quietly struck with Colonel Gehlen. Morgenthau's Jewish. He has every right in the world to loathe and detest the Germans for what they did to the Jews—and see that they're punished for it. He quite seriously proposed summarily executing the top one hundred Nazis as soon as they came into our hands. I shudder to think what Morgenthau would do if he knew we had arranged the movement of several hundred Nazis to sanctuary in Argentina."

"That's been a constant question in my mind from the beginning," Frade said, and his memory flashed with his initial *oh shit!* reaction to being told of the operation some sixteen months earlier in this same hotel.

Frade clearly recalled Dulles and Graham announcing that the plan was not only for American spies to smuggle German spies to South America—but for *Frade's* OSS spooks and SAA Lockheed Constellation aircraft to carry out the operation. They explained that they had made the secret agreement with Lieutenant Colonel Reinhard Gehlen, who was head of Germany's Abwehr Ost—Russian—intelligence. Gehlen believed (a) that Germany was losing the war—they said he in fact was involved with Count von Stauffenberg in Operation Valkyrie, the plan to assassinate Adolf Hitler—and (b) that after the war, Gehlen's agents faced firing squads or worse, particularly if Stalin had a say.

So Gehlen offered to the OSS all his assets, data, and agents in place in exchange for Gehlen and his officers and their families not falling into ruthless Russian hands.

Perhaps even more staggering—if protecting enemy agents at war's end wasn't outrageous enough—was the fact that Dulles and Graham were doing this specifically without anyone's knowledge or authority—including Wild Bill Donovan's. They explained that if they didn't tell the OSS chief, then he could honestly say he never knew. But more important, if they *did* tell Donovan, he'd likely feel duty bound to share it with his boss, FDR. And then—if against incredible odds they actually got approval—the secret soon would find its way to others—Morgenthau and Vice President Henry Wallace leapt to mind—who would act on their moral outrage over aid and comfort to the Nazis.

And the OSS—and America—would lose Gehlen's great wealth of intelligence on Communist spies, especially those who had infiltrated America's all-important atomic bomb program, the Manhattan Project.

Dulles and Graham further explained to Clete that

sharing this devout distrust of Communists were certain elements within the Roman Catholic Church hierarchy, influential ones who offered to readily supply Vatican-issued passports and other papers identifying Gehlen's men and their wives and children as, respectively, priests and nuns and orphans seeking safe passage to South America to perform God's work.

Having taken an oath to defend the United States against all enemies foreign and domestic, Cletus Frade came to agree with the position that Morgenthau and all others who simply sought retribution against the Germans would cause the United States even greater harm if they failed to secure Gehlen's intel.

And shortly thereafter, Frade's SAA Connie left Lisbon for Buenos Aires with the first load of Vatican-sponsored priests, nuns, and orphans among its passengers.

Now, sixteen months later, Frade asked, "Are we going to do any more of that, now that the war's over?"

Dulles nodded.

He sipped his scotch and then said, "There's another thirty-five or so of Gehlen's men still in Germany that we promised to get out. Which we are going to have to be even more careful about now with Germany's surrender; word is that Morgenthau has ordered the Secret Service—it being, of course, under the Treasury Department—to assign agents to track what happens with senior Nazis, particularly those top one hundred he'd like to see standing before a firing squad and mowed down with machine guns."

"Tracking every senior Nazi won't be easy for them to do."

"Agreed. But there are two things in play. One, Morgenthau is on a mission he devoutly believes in, and will not be deterred."

Frade nodded. "And the second?"

"That some Secret Service agent need only stumble across one of Gehlen's men we're smuggling for our whole operation to be blown."

Frade made a face, then said, "Well, if you and Graham are right about the Russians—and I think you are—then making the deal was the right thing to do. Why the hell wouldn't Morgenthau also see that?"

"If I were Jewish," Dulles said, "I don't think *I'd* be able to see it. Particularly after seeing the movies of the concentration camp ovens. And the bodies. And insofar as destroying German industry is concerned, I've always thought it had more to do with punishing the Germans than anything else."

"Colonel Graham told me he thought it had more to do with giving the Russians a license to steal what's left of German industry and move it to Russia. He said that the plan had been written by Morgenthau's deputy, a guy named Harry Dexter White, who he and J. Edgar Hoover were agreed was a Communist."

"I submit the possibility that we're both right," Dulles said.

"You said Admiral Leahy and General Marshall are our enemies, too," Frade said. "What did we do, change sides?"

"Clete, you know that the OSS has always been a thorn in the side of the Army and the Navy. I don't think it's too far off to say they've always hated us—them and especially Hoover's FBI—for any number of reasons, some of them valid but most simply visceral. We're not like they are. From the beginning, we had Wild Bill Donovan's friendship with Roosevelt to protect us.

"Roosevelt is gone. The military establishment is already telling Truman it's time to shut down the OSS. The war in Europe is over, and General MacArthur refuses to permit us to operate in the Pacific. What worries me is that Harry Truman won't—doesn't know how to—say no to the generals."

"I always thought generals and admirals were afraid of presidents, not the other way around."

"Harry Truman was a captain in the First World War. After it, he joined the reserves and stayed in. He's currently a reserve colonel. Colonels—with certain exceptions, such as Graham and you—don't argue with generals. It's not a question of whether the OSS will be shut down, but when. And whenever it happens, it will leave a vacuum that won't be good for the country."

"When do you think it will happen?"

"The Army, Navy, and State Department intelligence people will probably start to try to take us over—or try to take over individual operations, such as yours—possibly right about now. I don't think we'll be officially shut down for three, maybe four months."

"And what am I supposed to do when that happens?"

"That's what I came to tell you, Clete—that I don't

know what to tell you to do. You'll be on your own. If, for example, some would-be admiral in the Office of Naval Intelligence arrives in Buenos Aires and says, 'You now belong to me, so give me everything you know about everything here,' you could not be faulted for doing just that.

"But, on the other hand, if you decide that handing over information or assets to someone would not be good for the country . . ."

"What would I do with stuff—with the people, the assets, all of it—I decided not to turn over?"

"You could, as I intend to, go on the perhaps naïve premise that sooner or later—very likely later, much later—President Truman, or even his successor—they're already talking about General Eisenhower in that capacity—will see there is a need for an agency like the OSS and resurrect it."

"Jesus Christ!"

"My sentiments exactly. I believe that will happen, Clete. But in this agreement with Gehlen I *have* to believe that will happen, don't I?"

Frade met Dulles's eyes a long moment, then said, "If I turned over what I know about all of Gehlen's people I've gotten into South America, how long do you think it would take for Morgenthau to find out?"

Dulles considered the question as he sipped at the scotch. He finally said, "A week. Possibly as much as two. People have a tendency to present the misbehavior of others to their superiors as quickly as they can."

"The Gehlen operation was your decision. So, if I

opened my mouth about that, you'd be in trouble, right?"

"I don't want you to take that into consideration, Clete."

"And if I did roll over, a lot of people who don't need to know about the Gehlen operation get to know about it and the Russians get to know about it, right? Probably before Morgenthau does?"

"That seems a credible scenario."

"And the Russians learn everything about Gehlen's agents in place, right?"

Dulles looked Frade in the eyes but did not reply.

Frade went on: "Whereupon the Russians execute them. And I won't be responsible for that."

"That would have to be your decision, Clete, taking into account what it would mean for you. You'd be liable to find yourself in very hot water."

Frade shook his head in frustration.

"Well," he said, "I've been in hot water before, but if I declare that I don't know anything, then I don't know anything."

Dulles said, "To repeat myself, that would have to be your decision."

"What happens to von Wachtstein and Boltitz now?" Frade then said.

Major Hans-Peter von Wachtstein had been deputy military attaché for air—and Frade's mole—in the German Embassy in Buenos Aires. Frade had asked Dulles to have him and Kapitän zur See Karl Boltitz, the embassy's naval attaché, safely moved to the States. Both of their fathers had been in Hitler's High Command—and both targeted for execution for their participation in Operation Valkyrie. While the fate of Peter's father still was unknown, the OSS had evidence of Karl's father being killed—and it hadn't been a stretch of anyone's imagination to believe that Hitler would have ordered the sons hung from a meat hook, too.

"What do you mean?" Dulles said.

"I mean, do they get sent back to Germany? Or what?"

"That's the most likely scenario."

"You arranged to get them sent to Fort Hunt. Can't you arrange to get them sent back to Argentina? They could be a great help in dealing with the bad Germans there, starting with those involved with Operation Phoenix."

"I'll try. That would be the decent thing to do, and I will try. But right now I don't see how I could help."

Frade shook his head, then sarcastically said, "Whoopee!"

Dulles drained his drink.

"I am sorry, Clete. Unfortunately, that is the nature of our business."

Frade was silent a long moment, then sighed.

"Yeah, I know," he said, "but it damn well doesn't mean I have to like it. Thank you for leveling with me, Mr. Dulles."

"How many times have I asked you to call me by my Christian name?"

"I could no more call you 'Allen' than I could call Colonel Graham 'Alejandro.'"

"You could if you tried."

"And if that's all you have for me, Mr. Dulles, I'll get in my airplane and fly another load of Germans wearing clerical garb and carrying Vatican passports to sanctuary in Argentina."

Frade stood and put out his right hand. Dulles took it.

"We'll be in touch," Dulles said.

Clete nodded and walked out of the restaurant.

[TWO]
Washington National Airport
Arlington, Virginia
1310 10 May 1945

The four-engine, triple-tail Lockheed Constellation was the finest transport aircraft in the world. In 1939, Howard Hughes, the master aviator whose vast holdings included the majority of shares in Trans World Airlines, had ordered the superplane built to his specs. It was capable of flying forty passengers in its pressurized cabin higher (an altitude of thirty-five thousand feet) and faster (cruise speed was better than three hundred knots) and for a longer distance (forty-three hundred miles) than any other transport aircraft. Its wing design was nearly identical to that of the single-seat Lockheed P-38 Lightning fighter—although on a far grander scale.

South American Airways would have never received a single Connie if President Franklin D. Roosevelt had not had what Clete Frade thought of as a "hard-on" for Juan Trippe and his Pan American Airways. Actually, if Roosevelt had not been beyond pissed at Trippe—who had hired, then at first refused to fire, Colonel Charles "Lucky" Lindbergh after the world-famous aviator had dared to cross FDR—there never would have been a South American Airways at all.

But SAA did indeed exist, and it had not just one but a total of eleven Connies, setting it up to dominate trans-oceanic air travel postwar—and angering the volatile Juan Trippe no end.

Graham had told Clete: "FDR really knows how to carry one helluva grudge."

Four days earlier, when Clete had landed South American Airlines Constellation *Ciudad de Mendoza* at Buenos Aires's Coronel Jorge G. Frade airport—after a one-stop, Dakar-Senegal, flight from Lisbon—his wife had been waiting for him with a radiogram.

LOS ANGELES CAL 3 PM 5 MAY 1945

VIA MACKAY

CLETUS H FRADE

SOUTH AMERICAN AIRWAYS

BUENOS AIRES ARGENTINA

LITTLE CLETUS STOP THERE ARE FIVE CONNIES
IN THE USED CAR LOT STOP IF YOU CAN HAVE
YOUR BANK GUARANTEE PAYMENT AND GET THEM
FLOWN OUT OF HERE WITHIN FIVE DAYS THEY
ARE YOURS STOP REGARDS HOWARD

By the time Cletus broke ground at the controls of South American Airways Constellation *Ciudad de Córdoba* four hours later, he was absolutely convinced he was on a roll.

When he hadn't been considering all that Allen Dulles had told him about their new enemies, Frade had spent much of the time between Lisbon and Buenos Aires wondering what the hell he could do about Peter von Wachtstein and Karl Boltitz. He wanted them out of prisoner-of-war confinement at Fort Hunt, Virginia, and back to Argentina—or somewhere safe—yet hadn't come up with much of anything.

Howard Hughes's radiogram solved just about everything.

While Frade was genuinely delighted to be able to buy five more Connies for SAA, taking a dozen pilots and six flight engineers to Los Angeles to pick them up was the cherry on that cake. It gave him a reason for the flight that would satisfy the curiosity of the U.S. government.

And there was a cherry on that cherry, too. "Aunt Martha" Howell was the only mother Clete had ever known—his mother having died in childbirth when he was an infant—and Clete was about twelve before he realized that his sisters Beth and Maggie were really his cousins. They had not yet seen Cletus Howell Frade Jr., who was now five months old. He could pick up the women in Midland or Dallas and bring them to Buenos Aires now and worry about getting them back to the States later.

Most important—the cherry on top of the cherry-on-the-cherry—once Frade was in the States he could have a shot at getting Peter and Karl out of Fort Hunt.

He hadn't figured out exactly how he was going to do that, but he wasn't worried.

He was on a roll.

Clete made a very low approach in *Ciudad de Córdoba* along the Potomac River to the runway of what he thought of as "Gravelly Point"—the mudflats that in 1941 had been filled in to provide an airport near Washington.

Frade keyed his microphone and in Spanish said to his copilot, "I think, Gonzalo, that this would be a good time to dirty the bird up."

"Gear coming down, flaps to thirty," Gonzalo Delgano replied.

As chief pilot of South American Airways, Delgano wore a uniform—one even more colorful than Frade's SAA uniform—that had five gold stripes on the tunic cuffs, an inch-and-a-half-wide stripe down each hem of his trousers, and SAA wings topped with a circled star.

Somewhere over North Carolina, Clete had changed out of his SAA uniform. He now wore his Marine Corps uniform, the silver oak leaves of a lieutenant colonel on the epaulets and collar points, and it brought back the memory of the first time he'd landed here, in October 1942, as a first lieutenant. He'd been twenty-two, and recently returned from flying F4Fs of Marine Fighter Squadron VMF-221 off Fighter One on Guadalcanal—where he'd become an ace.

Sitting beside him in the Eastern Airlines Douglas DC-3 had been Colonel A. F. Graham. The previous day in Los Angeles, Graham had promised Frade immediate relief from a Pacific War Heroes War Bond Tour if he agreed to join something called the Office of Strategic Services. Frade had never heard of the OSS, but he would have volunteered for service in the New Orleans Girl Scouts if that guaranteed his ticket off the tour.

After Frade signed a document that made clear that the penalty for revealing anything about the OSS was castration by dull knife—and worse—Graham told him that he was being sent to Argentina: (a) to command a three-man team whose mission would be to destroy allegedly neutral Spanish and Portuguese merchant vessels resupplying German submarines, and (b) to establish contact with el Coronel Jorge G. Frade—his politically powerful father, quite probably the next president of the Argentine Republic—and attempt to tilt him toward the Allies. Clete knew next to nothing of his father, except that his grandfather, the legendary Texas oilman Cletus Marcus Howell, called him "an unmitigated three-star sonofabitch."

Against great odds, Clete had—more or less—accomplished both missions.

On Lieutenant Colonel Cletus H. Frade's uniform—above ribbons representing two Distinguished Flying Crosses and three Purple Hearts he had won on Guadalcanal—there was the ribbon representing the Navy Cross. His citation for the nation's second most senior award for valor mentioned nothing about his aid-ing in the destruction of a "neutral" ship and the German submarine it was resupplying in the River Plate. Doing so would've caused substantial diplomatic problems for the United States government.

And, as a son, Cletus had more than made peace with his father—shortly before the Schutzstaffel—the notorious "SS"—had had el Coronel Jorge Frade killed.

The SS's unlimited capacity for cold-blooded murder was now on Clete's mind as he brought the Constellation in on final at Washington National. He was going to do everything in his power to save Peter and Karl.

Frade hadn't talked to the Washington National control tower—if he had, they almost certainly would have denied him permission to land. He had filed a flight plan to the airport in Baltimore, and National had no idea he was coming until someone in the tower had seen the huge airplane, gear and flaps down, coming up the Potomac River lined up with the runway.

Furthermore, this clearly wasn't an American airliner coming in to land. *South American Airways* was lettered down the sides of the fuselage, and there were Argentine flags prominently displayed on each of the three vertical stabilizers.

Already Clete could see frantic activity on the field. There was a reception party assembling. It was riding in a FOLLOW ME jeep, a Ford pickup truck—and a second jeep festooned with flashing lights, siren, and the legend MILITARY POLICE. Heavily armed MPs rode standing up, keeping an eye on the huge aircraft.

Oh, shit!

But . . . that's to be expected.

Could this be the end of my being on a roll?

Frade touched down the Connie on the numbers marking the beginning of the runway and immediately put the propellers of the four Curtiss-Wright Cyclone engines into reverse.

And kept his hand on the throttle pitch levers.

He had landed here in a Connie once, though in the right seat. Howard Hughes had been the pilot. Clete knew that Hughes habitually did things with airplanes beyond the capabilities of lesser pilots, even including former Marine Corps fighter pilots.

Frade didn't have approach charts giving him the length of the runway, but he remembered Howard using up most of it. And now Frade knew it was very likely he would run out of runway and have to go around—take off and make another attempt at landing.

But when he finally got the aircraft stopped, he had about three hundred yards of runway left.

Yes! Still on a roll!

After being led by the FOLLOW ME jeep and other vehicles to a quiet part of the tarmac, Frade ordered the engines shut down. Chief Pilot Delgano glanced out the windscreen.

Everyone was looking up at the Constellation with surprise, awe, or anger—often in combination.

"Cletus," Delgano said, "I really think we should have gone into Baltimore."

"I should be back in about two hours," Frade said, unstrapping his harness. "I want to take off ten minutes after that. If I'm not back in three hours, go to Buenos Aires without me."

Frade left the cockpit and started walking through the just-about-empty passenger compartment. There were forty-one seats, only six of which were occupied. Among the passengers were two male South American Airways captains and three females. The women were Mrs. Martha Howell and her daughters, Elizabeth, twenty-one years old, and Marjorie, nineteen.

Beth Howell stopped Clete as he walked down the aisle.

"When you see Colonel Graham, ask him about Karl, please," she said.

To Clete's utter surprise—once again proving, he told himself, he could be blind to the obvious—he'd recently learned that Beth and Karl were romantically involved. They had been making the beast with two backs as recently as when they all had gathered for Jorge Howell Frade's christening and maybe going all the way back to when Beth and Karl met at Clete and Dorotea's wedding.

"Sure," Clete said to Beth—but he thought, *With a little bit of luck, Graham won't learn I've been anywhere near Washington until sometime tomorrow.*

The sixth passenger was a burly, middle-aged man wearing a suit. He was now carefully checking a rope ladder he'd tied to the aircraft's floor at the rear door. Frade had figured it was highly unlikely that Washington National would have a set of steps—or even a ladder—tall enough to reach the fuselage of the new aircraft.

"Ready, Don Cletus," the man said after he had hung the ladder out the door.

His name was Enrico Rodríguez. He was a retired *suboficial mayor*—a sergeant major—of the Húsares de Pueyrredón regiment of the Argentine Cavalry. All his adult life, he had served el Coronel Jorge Guillermo Frade, first as batman and chauffeur, then as bodyguard. He had been beside him—and left for dead—when el Coronel Frade had been assassinated, and now quite seriously believed God's mission in life for him was to protect el Coronel's only child.

Cletus went to the door and knelt to get on the ladder.

"Leave the shotgun, Enrico. And if you have a pistol, leave that, too."

Enrico looked very unhappy.

"Or stay on the airplane," Frade finished.

Rodríguez first took a Remington Model 11 twelve-gauge riot shotgun from where he had it suspended under his suit jacket and wrapped it in a woolen blanket on the aircraft floor.

He looked at Frade, who raised his eyebrows in question.

Rodríguez then reached under his jacket and came out with a Ballester Molina .45 ACP semiautomatic pistol, which was a variation of the 1911-A1 Colt pistol, manufactured in Argentina under license from Colt. He carefully added it to the blanket with the Remington and looked at Frade.

Frade's eyebrows rose higher.

Rodríguez met his eyes for a moment, then shrugged.

He raised the right leg of his trousers and took a snub-nosed Colt Police Positive .38 Special revolver from an ankle holster and hid it with the other weapons.

"This is America, Enrico. No one is going to shoot at us here."

"You are the one, Don Cletus, who says that one never needs a gun until one needs it badly."

Frade nodded, then quicky went down the rope ladder. Rodríguez followed.

[THREE]

On the tarmac, Frade and the welcoming committee examined each other.

Lieutenant Colonel Cletus H. Frade—one hundred ninety pounds on a trim six-foot frame—carried himself with the élan, some would say the arrogance, of a Marine fighter pilot.

The MPs—a captain, a sergeant, and a private first class—saluted when they saw his silver oak leaves. Frade returned the salute and handed the senior of the MPs a small leather wallet.

The MP captain examined it.

It contained a gold badge on one side and a sealed-in-plastic photo identification card in the other. The photo ID was clearly patterned after the Adjutant General's Office identification cards issued to commissioned officers. There was space for a photo, a thumbprint, and the individual's name, rank, and date of birth.

But this was not an AGO card. In its center was the

Great Seal of the United States. In two curved lines at the top was the legend THE UNITED STATES OF AMERICA, and under that, OFFICE OF STRATEGIC SERVICES. A rectangular block at the bottom, with space for the individual's name and rank, identified Cletus H. Frade as an area commander.

The credentials were not exactly bona fide—although they had been manufactured by the OSS's Document Section. A Princeton professor of psychology with three doctoral degrees recruited into the OSS thought it would be nice if OSS operators in the field had their own credentials.

Wild Bill Donovan had lost his famous Irish temper when he'd seen them.

Absolutely unbelievable! Who the hell does this academic think OSS agents would show these? They're spies, for christsake!

He tossed the sample credentials in his Shred and Burn wastebasket and tried to forget about them. But when Colonel A. F. Graham, his deputy director for the Western Hemisphere, showed up at his door, Donovan decided to share them for a laugh.

After inspecting them, Graham said, "May I have these, Bill?"

"You're serious, Alec?"

"Yeah. It's no secret in Argentina that Frade and his men are OSS. He may find a use for them. He's resourceful."

"He's a damn dangerous loose cannon," Donovan had replied, then pushed the credentials to Graham. "Get them out of here. Every time I see them, I get mad all over again."

Graham had been right. Frade had successfully used them a few times—once to dazzle the stubborn commander of the Army Air Corps base in Brazil. When he saw Frade identified as an OSS area commander, the chickenshit had become the poster child for cooperation and goodwill. That experience had made Frade think they just might work at Washington National now.

"How may I help you, Colonel?" the MP captain, looking appropriately impressed, said.

Well, Frade thought as he took back the wallet, *that worked.*

So far, so good. Still on a roll . . .

"Presumably, Captain, you're in charge of security?" Frade asked.

"Yes, sir."

"I will be here no more than three hours," Frade said. "I'll be loading five passengers. Three of them may already be here. I'll get the ones who are not. I don't want anyone to get near my aircraft."

"Yes, sir," the captain said. "I understand."

Frade gestured toward Enrico. "Sergeant Major Rodríguez here is under strict orders to keep the aircraft secure."

Clete noticed that Enrico read between the lines—that he was going to stay with the airplane and not accompany Clete—and was both surprised and glad that Enrico did not protest being left behind.

"Yes, sir," the captain repeated. "There won't be any problem."

"We didn't get any heads-up about this," one of the civilians, a starchy heavyset man in a cheap suit, charged in an officious tone.

"Of course you didn't," Frade said. "You're from the airport, right?"

"Yes, I am."

"We'll require fuel, of course. And enough food for a dozen people for a ten-hour flight. In Marmite cans. You can bill that to the OSS, right?"

"I'd have to have authorization."

"From whom?"

"From the OSS."

"Then you just got that authorization," Frade said. "Now, has anybody seen a chauffeur-driven 1940 Cadillac?"

"As a matter of fact," the MP captain said, "there's a car like that in the parking lot."

Frade turned to the civilian from the airport.

"See what you can do about a real ladder or stairs to get up there," he said, pointing to the Constellation's rear door. "I'm not sure my passengers will want to climb a rope ladder."

"I'm sure I can come up with something," the man said.

As Clete approached the custom-bodied Cadillac, his grandfather's chauffeur got out and opened the rear door. Tom, a silver-haired black man, had been driving Cletus

Marcus Howell around Washington for as long as Clete could remember.

The Cadillac had a gasoline ration sticker affixed to its windshield. The otherwise glistening door had stripes of dull black tape on it, obviously to cover something on the door. Until that morning, the door had shown a legend required by the Office of Price Administration.

There had been gasoline rationing in the United States since early 1942, not because there was any shortage of gas but because there was a critical shortage of rubber to make tires.

A fairly complicated distribution system had been set up. At the bottom end were ordinary citizens who received two gallons of gas a week. At the top were politicians, from local mayors to members of Congress, who got all the gasoline they said they needed. Ordinary citizens got an "A" sticker, whereas congressmen and other important politicians got an "X" sticker.

In between were those who were issued "B" or "C" or "D" stickers. "B" meant the car was being driven by someone essential to the war effort—somebody driving to work in a tank factory, for example. A "B" sticker was worth eight gallons a week. "C" stickers were worth as many gallons of gas as clergymen, doctors, and "others essential to the war effort" could convince the ration board to give them. "D" was for motorcycles, which got two gallons per week.

There was a "C" on the windshield of the custom-bodied Cadillac, which was registered in the name of the Howell Petroleum Corporation. Cletus Marcus Howell was chairman of the board of Howell Petroleum, and he had been more than a little annoyed that he had to go to a ration board and beg for gas so that he could conduct the business of Howell Petroleum, whose oil wells and refineries in Texas, Louisiana, and Venezuela were turning out many millions of gallons of gasoline every day.

But he had put up with the regulations of the Office of Price Administration because he thought of himself as a patriotic American, and because his only grandson, Cletus Howell Frade, a Marine hero of Guadalcanal, was still serving his country.

He had, however—almost literally—gone through the roof when the Office of Price Administration decreed that passenger vehicles enjoying the privilege of extra gasoline because they were being used for business had to paint the name of that business and its address on doors on both sides of said vehicle, so that the citizenry would know that no one was getting around the system. The Office of Price Administration had helpfully provided the size of the lettering and the color that had to be used.

The dull black stripes on the door of the Cadillac had been applied to conceal the legend painted in canary yellow that was prescribed by the Office of Price Administration:

Howell Petroleum Corp.

16th & H streets NW

Wash., DC

Sixteenth and H streets Northwest was the address of the Hay-Adams Hotel, where Cletus Marcus Howell kept an apartment—and the Cadillac—for use when he was in Washington. It was across from the White House.

The universally loathed gas rationing had ended almost immediately after the Germans had surrendered unconditionally on May 7, 1945. As soon as that news had reached Cletus Marcus Howell, at his home in New Orleans, he had telephoned Tom, the chauffeur, and told him to cover the goddamn door sign immediately, until the door could be repainted.

"Nice to see you again, Mr. Clete," Tom said.

"Nice to see you, too, Tom."

"Where we going?" Tom said as he got in behind the wheel.

"Fort Hunt," Clete replied from the backseat. "You know where it is?"

"Never heard of it."

"You weren't supposed to have heard of it, Tom."

"Where is it?"

"I haven't a clue. Somewhere around Alexandria."

[FOUR]
Fort Hunt
Alexandria, Virginia
1405 10 May 1945

Finding Fort Hunt, it turned out, wasn't at all difficult. Surprisingly, there had in fact been a highway sign with an arrow pointing the way.

Getting into Fort Hunt was another story.

One hundred yards off the highway, there had been another sign, this one very large:

STOP AND TURN AROUND NOW

RESTRICTED NATIONAL DEFENSE ESTABLISHMENT

ENTRANCE TO FORT HUNT STRICTLY FORBIDDEN WITHOUT PRIOR CLEARANCE

TRESPASSERS WILL BE PROSECUTED

BY ORDER OF THE COMMANDING GENERAL

MILITARY DISTRICT OF WASHINGTON

"What do I do, Mr. Clete?" Tom asked.

"Let's see what happens if we ignore that," Clete said.

What happened a half-mile down the road was the appearance of two MPs, both sergeants and both armed with Thompson submachine guns. They stood in the middle of the road. One of them held out his hand in an unmistakable *Stop Right Damn There!* gesture and the other looked as if he would be happy to finally be able to shoot the Thompson at somebody.

Tom stopped the Cadillac. Almost immediately, an

Army ton-and-a-half truck, commonly called a weapons carrier, appeared behind the Cadillac. An MP jumped from the passenger seat, and two more MPs from the truck bed. They all had Thompsons, and they were clearly determined to do their duty to keep interlopers not only from getting into Fort Hunt, but also from escaping now that they had been captured.

The sergeant who had made the *Stop Right Damn There!* gesture now marched toward the Cadillac, with the other covering his back.

He had almost reached the car when he saw that the passenger was in uniform, and that the insignia of a lieutenant colonel was on his collar points and epaulets.

He went to the rear door and saluted. Clete returned it as the window rolled down.

The MP said, "Sir, may I have your prior clearance?"

"Take me to the commanding officer, Sergeant," Clete replied, then nodded at the MP standing behind him. "And tell the sergeant there that if he intends to fire that Thompson, he'd better work the action."

That didn't have to be repeated. The sergeant immediately looked down at his weapon and clearly recalled that the Thompson submachine gun fired from an open bolt. Looking more than a little chagrined, he pulled back the bolt, thus rendering it operable.

Frade met the eyes of the MP at his window, smiled, then said, "Have you a vehicle we can follow, or would you rather ride with us?"

"Just a moment, Colonel, please, sir," the sergeant said.

After consultation with the others, the sergeant returned to the Cadillac and got in the front seat. The sergeant with the now-functioning weapon walked to the weapons carrier, got in the front seat, and signaled for all but two of the others to get in the back. The two exceptions started walking in the direction of a guard post mostly hidden in the heavily treed roadside.

The weapons carrier moved to the front of the Cadillac.

"If you'll just follow the truck, please?" the sergeant sitting beside Tom said.

Frade knew the highly secret mission of Fort Hunt—the interrogation of very senior enemy officer prisoners, predominantly German, but including a few Italians and even, Colonel Graham had told him, two Japanese—but he had never been here before.

It was not an imposing military installation, just a collection of built-in-a-hurry-to-last-four-years single- and two-story frame, tarpaper-roofed buildings. Clete wondered why it was called a fort. Most for-the-duration military installations—like the senior officer POW Camp Clinton he had visited in Mississippi—were called camps.

The two-vehicle convoy stopped at one of the two-story frame buildings. It bore the sign HEADQUARTERS, FORT HUNT. Standing in front were two U.S. Army soldiers, a slight, slim, bespectacled lieutenant colonel in a somewhat mussed uniform, and a stocky, crisply uniformed master sergeant. Both wore MP brassards on their sleeves and carried 1911-A1 pistols in holsters dangling cowboy-like from web belts, instead of the white Sam Browne belts that MPs usually wore.

Both looked with frank curiosity at the little convoy.

"Wait here, please, Colonel," the MP sergeant sitting beside Tom said as he opened his door.

Screw you, Clete thought. *I want to hear what you tell those two.*

Frade was out of the Cadillac before the MP had reached the soldiers standing in front of Headquarters, Fort Hunt.

The two looked curiously at him. The master sergeant, apparently having spotted Frade's silver oak leaves, said something behind his hand to the lieutenant colonel, whereupon both saluted.

"Good afternoon," Clete said cheerfully as he returned the salute. "Why do they call this place a fort? It looks as if it was built yesterday."

The question was obviously unexpected.

Clete saw on the Army lieutenant colonel's uniform his name: KELLOGG.

After a moment, Kellogg said: "Actually, it was a fort. It was built for the Coast Artillery just before the Spanish-American War."

"No kidding?"

"And the land once was part of George Washington's farm," Kellogg added.

"I'll be damned!"

"How can we help you, Colonel?" Kellogg then said cordially but with authority.

"My boss wants to chat with a couple of your guests," Frade replied.

"Colonel, may I see some identification?" Kellogg said.

Frade handed him the leather wallet holding his spurious credentials.

The lieutenant colonel examined them carefully, then handed them to the master sergeant, who did the same before handing them back to Frade.

"We don't see many credentials like those," Kellogg admitted.

"Well, so far we've managed to keep them off the cover of *Time*," Frade said.

"And your . . . *boss* . . . your boss is who?"

"Colonel Alejandro F. Graham, USMCR—"

"I know Colonel Graham," Kellogg interrupted.

"—sometimes known as the Terrible Tiger of Texas A&M," Frade finished. "Whose bite is far more deadly than his growl."

Kellogg smiled somewhat uncomfortably.

"And you say Colonel Graham sent you out here to chat with two of our prisoners?"

"No. What I said was that *he* wants to chat with two of them, and sent me out here to fetch them."

Frade went into a pocket on his tunic and came out with a sheet of paper.

"One of them is a Kapitän zur See Karl Boltitz and the other is Major Freiherr Hans-Peter Baron von Wachtstein. Now, that's what I call a mouthful! I wonder how they get all that on his identification card?"

The master sergeant smiled.

"It's not easy, Colonel," he said. "And some of these Krauts have names that are even worse than that."

"Colonel, this is more than a little unusual," Kellogg said. "We didn't even know you were coming. Do you have any kind of authority—written authority?"

"You mean, you want me to sign for them? Sure. Be happy to."

"No, I meant a document authorizing you to take these officers with you."

Frade sighed. "Colonel, let me explain how I came to be here. I got to Washington two days ago. I can't tell you . . . Hell, why can't I? The Germans have surrendered. I was in Portugal . . .

That's true. I was in Lisbon not long ago, smuggling even more Nazis out of Europe.

". . . as area commander . . .

Now I'm lying again. I've done so much of that it comes as natural to me as it did to Baron Munchausen.

". . . I haven't worn a uniform in years. Anyway, I got to Washington two days ago. Good Marine and fellow Aggie that I am, I immediately reported to the Terrible Tiger of A&M. Colonel Graham showed me a chair, handed me copies of *Time* and *Life*, and said to read them while he looked around for something for me to do. An hour ago, he handed me the names of these two Krauts and told me to go fetch them."

"Colonel, how do I know that's true?" Kellogg asked.

"Well, you could trust my honest face. Or you could ask yourself, 'If Colonel Graham didn't send this guy, how come he's riding in the colonel's chauffeur-driven

Cadillac?' Or you could call the Terrible Tiger and ask him. I would recommend Options One and/or Two."

Kellogg considered that a moment, then said, "Excuse us a moment, will you, please, Colonel?"

"Certainly."

The lieutenant colonel and the master sergeant went inside the headquarters building.

If they're calling Graham, I'm screwed.

But why do I think they won't call him?

Because, with a little bit of luck, one or both of them has been on the receiving end of one of Graham's fits of temper.

The fits are rare but spectacular, and usually triggered by someone insisting on complete compliance with a petty bureaucratic regulation.

Never wake a sleeping tiger!

And I'm on a roll!

Not quite two minutes after the pair had walked into the headquarters building, the master sergeant came out.

"Sir, Colonel Kellogg suggests you go inside and have a cup of coffee with him while I go fetch the Krauts for you."

"Fine. Thank you very much."

"What we're going to do is send an MP escort with you to the Institutes of Health, in case the Krauts try to escape or anything."

Oh, shit! Frade thought.

He nodded. "Good idea."

The Office of Strategic Services had taken over the National Institutes of Health building in the District of Columbia "for the duration."

In the headquarters building, Frade quickly found the light bird's office. It had a sign hanging over the door: LTCOL D. G. KELLOGG. PROVOST MARSHAL.

Several minutes later, about the time Kellogg had poured coffee into a chipped but clean china mug for Frade, Kapitän zur See Karl Boltitz and Major Freiherr Hans-Peter Baron von Wachtstein were escorted into the office by two military policemen.

They marched up to Lieutenant Colonel Kellogg's desk and came to attention and clicked their heels.

Boltitz—a tall, rather good-looking, blond young man—was dressed in the white uniform worn by officers of the German navy at sea. He paid little attention to the officer in the Marine Corps uniform. Von Wachtstein, also blond, was smaller and stockier. He was wearing U.S. Army khakis, to which had been affixed the insignia of a Luftwaffe major and his pilot's wings. When he saw the Marine Corps officer, he gave what could have been a double take, but quickly cut it off to stand at attention.

Kellogg began: "Gentlemen, this is Colonel—"

"Cletus Frade," Clete interrupted in a commanding tone, "lieutenant colonel, U.S. Marine Corps. We're going to take a little ride. And if you're even thinking of trying to get away from me, don't. I'd like nothing better than the chance to shoot either or both of you Nazi bastards."

To add visual support to his statement, he took a Model 1911-Al Colt from the small of his back.

"I always carry this with a round in the chamber."

"Colonel Frade," Colonel Kellogg said quickly and nervously, "I can assure you that both of these officers have been very cooperative and . . ."

Frade snorted his disbelief.

". . . I'm sure they will give you no problems."

"Their choice," Frade said. "They either behave or they're dead men."

Neither German officer said a word.

[FIVE]
The Office of Strategic Services
2340 E Street NW, Washington, D.C.
1535 10 May 1945

Preceded by an MP jeep and trailed by an MP weapons carrier, the Cadillac turned off E Street and stopped before a Colonial-style building that would have been quite at home on a college campus. Frade was in the front with the chauffeur; Boltitz and von Wachtstein rode in the back.

Frade surveyed the area and thought, *What the hell do I do now? I never wanted to be here in the first place—and damn sure not with POWs I just broke out of the slam.*

I've got to get rid of these MPs. . . .

Frade rolled down his window and commanded the driver of the lead jeep, "Drive around to the rear."

In the back of the building were parking spaces. One

of the two nearest the door was empty. It had a neatly lettered sign: RESERVED FOR THE DIRECTOR.

Frade pointed to it and ordered, "Pull in there, Tom."

After Tom parked, Clete told Peter and Karl to wait in the car and then got out.

Two men in police-type uniforms came quickly—almost ran—from the building.

Clete intercepted them and announced, "Colonel Frade to see Colonel Graham."

He did not offer his credentials. The security officers would know they weren't bona fide.

"That's General Donovan's parking spot, Colonel," the shorter of the security officers said. "You—"

"He told me to use it," Frade cut him off, and started walking toward the building entrance.

Then he had a sudden idea.

He stopped, turned, and pointed to the jeep and weapons carrier.

"Have those escort vehicles moved to the front of the building," he ordered the security men.

Frade heard them barking orders to the drivers of the MP vehicles as he entered the building. He came to two other security officers who were sitting behind a curved reception desk.

"Colonel Frade to see Colonel Graham," Frade announced. "I do not have an appointment."

One of the security guards automatically reached for a telephone and dialed a number.

With a little bit of luck, Frade thought, *Graham won't be here.*

Then I will make sure the MPs have moved, and go back outside and see if there's another way to get out of that parking lot.

Frade could quite clearly hear the voice of the male who answered the call snap: "What?"

Dammit—he's here!

"Who is this, please?" the security guard said into the phone.

"Who did you expect to get when you called this number?" the voice on the phone demanded incredulously.

"Colonel Graham, sir."

"Okay. You got him. *What?*"

"There's a Marine officer here, Colonel. Lieutenant Colonel Frade. He says he doesn't have an appointment—"

"He damn sure doesn't!" the voice said, then before hanging up added: "Send him up."

Colonel Alejandro Federico Graham, USMCR, the deputy director of the OSS for Western Hemisphere Operations, was standing in the corridor when Frade got off the elevator. He wore his usual immaculate uniform.

"Well, look what the tide floated in!" Graham said in Spanish.

"Mi coronel," Frade said, and saluted.

Graham returned the salute, shook his head, and said, still in Spanish, "We are Marines. Naval custom proscribes the exchange of hand salutes indoors unless under arms. Try to remember that in the future."

Then he gestured for Frade to follow him into his office.

"I'm almost afraid to ask what you're doing here," he said, waving Frade into an inner office and then into a chair.

"A personnel matter, *mi coronel.* A *personal* personnel matter."

"What kind of a personnel matter?"

"I am in receipt, *mi coronel,* of a letter from the Finance Officer, Headquarters, USMC, informing me that inasmuch as I have not provided the appropriate proof that I have flown any aircraft the required four hours per month for the past twenty months, I am therefore not entitled to flight pay, and it will therefore be necessary for them to deduct the appropriate amount from my next check."

"*¡Jesúcristo!*"

"And since I have not received any paycheck at all for the past twenty-some months, I thought I'd come and see if I couldn't clear the matter up."

"Well, I'd probably be more sympathetic if I didn't know how far removed from the welfare rolls you are, Colonel. What's that phrase, 'Rich as an Argentine'?"

"That, *mi coronel*, is what they call the pot calling the kettle black."

Graham shook his head.

"So, what really brings you up here, Clete?"

"On the way back from Portugal with yet another load of Teutonic people carrying Vatican passports, as I sat there watching the needles on the fuel gauges drop, I wondered what was going to happen to Boltitz and von Wachtstein once the Germans surrendered."

"And?"

"I thought that they would probably be loaded onto a troopship, returned to the former German Thousand-Year Reich, and then locked up in a POW enclosure until somebody decided their fate. If they survived that long."

"And that's probably what will happen."

"So I figured I'd better come up here and get them."

"The injustice of the Nazis getting to go to Argentina, and the good guys getting locked up—and possibly worse—is that, more or less, what you were thinking?"

"That's exactly what I was thinking. We owe them, and you know it."

"You did give just a little thought to their being locked up at Fort Hunt and getting them out of there would be impossible?"

"*Next* to impossible, *mi coronel.*"

Graham raised an eyebrow. "Meaning what?"

"Meaning that at this moment, they're sitting in my grandfather's Cadillac, which is waiting in General Donovan's reserved parking spot."

"You got them out of Fort Hunt?" Graham asked incredulously.

Clete nodded.

"I told them you wanted to talk to them; had sent me out there to fetch them."

"And what the hell do you plan to do with them now?"

Graham said. But before Frade could reply, he asked, "Why the hell did you bring them here? To me?"

"Well, the guy at Fort Hunt didn't entirely believe me. So he took the path of least resistance."

"Explain that to me."

"He was afraid I was telling the truth, so that made him afraid to call you and check. And he was afraid I was a phony. So he sent a jeep and a weapons carrier loaded with MPs with me, to make sure I came here."

"And now what, Clete? Now that you've painted yourself into one hell of a corner?"

"Well, I had the security guards order the MPs to the front of the building. If there's another way to get out of the parking lot behind the building, I get in my car and we're gone."

"To where?"

"Gravelly Point."

"What did you do, fly your Red Lodestar into there?"

"No. What I have is a South American Airways Constellation."

"You flew a *Constellation* into National Airport?"

Clete nodded.

"*¡Jesúcristo!*"

"I've now got about fifteen hundred hours in Connies. I'm getting pretty good at it."

"And what do you want me to do? Bring you cigarettes and magazines when you're in the Portsmouth Navy Prison?"

"I want you to do what you know is the right thing," Frade said seriously. "Help me get to the airport."

Graham exhaled audibly.

He met Frade's eyes, then spun around in his chair. Then he turned so that he was facing Frade again.

"You're way ahead of me, aren't you, you clever bastard?" he said icily. "You know that if Donovan himself walked in right now, the chances of you being court-martialed—which you richly deserve—are damned slim. You know too much. And the same applies to me."

"I wouldn't have come here if that light bird at Fort Hunt hadn't sent the MPs with me. I had no intention of involving you in this at all."

"And what did you think was going to happen when you got away with it? *If* you got away with it?"

"I'm going to drop off my resignation from the Corps at the embassy in Buenos Aires the day I get back. Then I'm going to disappear in Argentina. I saw Mr. Dulles in Lisbon. He said I'm going to have to decide what to do, and what I've decided is to disappear. I'm getting pretty good about helping other people disappear there."

"You can't just resign from the Corps, you goddamned fool! You'll get out of the Corps only when the Corps permits you to get out of the Corps!"

Frade stared at Graham and thought, *I wondered about that. He's probably right—if I wasn't also an Argentine citizen.*

Graham picked up one of the telephones on his desk and dialed a single number.

"Security chief, please," he said, then looked at Frade and added, "Sit there, Colonel, and don't say one goddamn word."

Well, Frade thought, *I tried.*

At least I didn't tell Beth I was going to get Karl.

"This is Graham. There are two MP vehicles from Fort Hunt in front of the building. Go out there and find whoever's in charge and bring him up here."

He hung up the phone.

He turned to Frade and said, "Continue to sit there with your mouth shut, Colonel. I have no interest in hearing anything you might be tempted to say."

He waited ten seconds, then said, "The proper Marine officer's response to that, Colonel, is 'Aye, aye, sir.' And for the moment at least, you are still a serving officer in the Corps."

"Aye, aye, sir."

An MP captain, this one festooned with all the proper MP accoutrements, came into the office three minutes later. He saluted.

"Captain," Graham said, almost cordially, "I'll see to it that the prisoners get back to Fort Hunt. I can see no need for you to wait around here."

"Yes, sir."

"That's all, Captain," Graham said. "You are dismissed."

"Yes, sir."

The captain left and closed the door.

"That's all, Colonel Frade," Graham said. "You are dismissed."

Clete stood, and, remembering what Graham had said about Naval custom proscribing the exchange of hand salutes indoors unless under arms, didn't.

He met Graham's eyes for a moment, then marched toward the door.

"Clete," Graham called.

Frade turned.

"You were right, Clete. Wild Bill will throw one of his famous Irish fits when he hears about this, but that'll be the end of it. We both know too much, and he is fully aware that we do."

"I hope that's the case, sir."

"Please present my compliments to Kapitän Boltitz and Major von Wachtstein. And my best regards to Doña Dorotea."

"I'll do that, sir. Thank you."

"Maybe we'll see one another one day. Strange things happen in this business we're in. Belay that. *Were* in."

"*Were* in, sir?"

"The reason Donovan's parking spot was so conveniently open for you is that he's over in the Pentagon begging General Marshall not to shut down the OSS this afternoon."

"But if they shut down the OSS right now, what about . . ."

"All the ongoing projects? Several of which you're running?"

"Yes, sir."

"God only knows, Colonel Frade. Have a nice flight. *Vaya con Dios.*"

[SIX]

Washington National Airport
Arlington, Virginia
1705 10 May 1945

The public address loudspeakers of South American Airways Constellation *Ciudad de Córdoba* blared in the passenger compartment: "Passenger von Wachtstein to the cockpit. Passenger von Wachtstein to the cockpit."

Hans-Peter Baron von Wachtstein made his way up the aisle and entered the cockpit.

"Sit there, Hansel," Frade said in German, pointing to a jump seat. "Don't touch anything, and pay attention. You might learn something."

Von Wachtstein sat down and strapped in.

"National," Frade said in English into his microphone, "South American Double Zero Two rolling."

Frade advanced the throttles to takeoff power.

"Gear up and locked. Flaps to zero," Chief Pilot Gonzalo Delgano reported a few minutes later.

Frade pointed out the window, and von Wachtstein looked, then nodded. They were passing over the White House.

Then Frade looked at von Wachtstein and said, "This ends your flight-deck familiarization of the Connie for now."

As Peter unbuckled his harness, Clete gestured with his thumb toward the passenger compartment.

"Karl and Beth . . ."

"What about them?" von Wachtstein said.

"Go back there, Hansel, and throw ice water on Romeo and Juliet before they embarrass my aunt Martha and everybody else with a shameless exhibition of their mutual lust."

"Ah," von Wachtstein said. "Too late."

II

[ONE]
Aeropuerto Coronel Jorge G. Frade
Morón, Buenos Aires Province, Argentina
1235 11 May 1945

Washington, D.C., was a long way—just over five thousand miles—from Buenos Aires. It had been necessary for South American Airways Double Zero Two *Ciudad de Córdoba* to refuel at Belém, Brazil, after a nine-hour flight from Washington. Refueling had taken two hours. Then it had been a just-over-eight-hour flight to Buenos Aires.

The *Ciudad de Córdoba* completed its landing roll and turned off the runway onto a taxiway. A tug—it had been surprisingly easy to convert John Deere tractors, ones fitted with enormous double tires for use in rice fields, into aircraft tugs powerful enough to move Constellations—painted in SAA's powder blue and gold color scheme came down the taxiway toward the Constellation.

The Connie stopped, then shut down its engines as the ground crew backed up the tug to it and connected to the front landing gear.

The tug dragged the airplane to the tarmac, past three

enormous hangars, and then pushed the Connie, tail first, into the center hangar.

"It would seem, Gonzalo," the pilot said solemnly to his first officer, "that we have once again cheated death."

"Cletus, you know damned well I don't like it when you say that," Delgano said as he unfastened his harness, stretched in his seat, and then stood.

"Well, you may be happy with near-empty tanks—maybe ten minutes left—but I'm always concerned."

Delgano snapped his head around to examine the fuel gauges.

They showed there was considerably more fuel remaining than ten minutes.

"Gotcha!" Frade cried happily.

Delgano shook his head and left the cockpit.

Frade looked out the window. The Connie was the only airplane in the hangar, but there were a number of automobiles, most of them large and chauffeur driven.

Frade waited until the REAR DOOR light glowed red and then he killed the MASTER POWER switch and left his seat.

By the time he walked through the passenger compartment he was the last person in it.

When he stood on the platform at the head of the ladder, the first thing he looked for was the couple he often in the past called—to their great annoyance—*Hansel und Gretel.*

When he found them, his throat tightened and his eyes teared.

Hansel—Hans-Peter Baron von Wachtstein—had his arms around Gretel—the former Alicia Carzino-

Cormano—in a bear hug that suggested neither had the slightest intention of ever breaking the embrace in their lifetimes.

His thoughts were interrupted by a shrill whistle. He knew it well, including the time it had brought three taxis to a dead halt at once during rush hour on Avenida 9 de Julio. His wife made it by squeezing her tongue tip with two fingertips, then quickly exhaling. It was a skill Clete had never mastered, either as a Boy Scout when all the other members of Troop 36, Midland, Texas, could do it with ease, or after his marriage, when he had tried even harder to learn how.

He found her standing near the foot of the stairway.

Doña Dorotea Mallín de Frade, who had just turned twenty-two, was the image that came to mind when one heard the phrase "classic English beauty." She was tall and lithe, blond, and had startlingly blue eyes and a marvelous milky-smooth complexion.

Standing off to the right was Enrico Rodríguez and another man who looked very much like him. They both cradled Remington Model 11 twelve-gauge riot shotguns in their arms as they kept a wary eye on everybody in the hangar. The other man, former Sargento Rodolfo Gómez, had, like Rodríguez, retired from the Húsares de Pueyrredón. He now was rarely more than fifty feet from Doña Dorotea and her children—and usually closer.

Clete was not wearing his Marine Corps uniform, nor his SAA captain's uniform. He was far less formally attired in khaki trousers, a yellow polo shirt, battered Western boots, and a wide-brimmed Stetson hat—once the property of his late uncle James Fitzhugh Howell, who for almost all of Clete's life was the only father Clete had known.

Frade went quickly down the stairs and embraced his wife.

Dorotea put her mouth close to his ear and whispered: "You done good, my darling. And do I have a reward for you in mind!"

"You mean maybe two empanadas and a beer?" he asked, teasing.

"Maybe afterward," Dorotea said, flicked her tongue in his ear, and broke their embrace.

Then something caught his eye. Three men were walking up to them.

One of the men wore a clerical collar and was fond of referring to himself as a simple priest. This was not precisely the truth, the whole truth, and nothing but the truth. Clete had once thought of the Reverend Kurt Welner, S.J.—a bespectacled, slim, fair-skinned man who'd lost most of his light brown hair and looked to be in his forties—as the *éminence grise* behind the throne of the Cardinal Archbishop of Argentina and the official chair of the president of the Argentine Republic, whose confessor he was.

Events over the last twenty-odd months had caused Frade to add to that the throne of the Papal Nuncio to Argentina, and to conclude that if Welner was not de jure Pope Pius XII's man in Argentina, he held that role de facto. Well, maybe not directly, but through one or more of the most senior cardinals in Pius XII's inner circle.

At dinner one night in Lisbon, Allen W. Dulles had told Frade that when dealing with Welner—or any other Roman Catholic clergyman of importance—the thing to keep in mind was that he understood his first priority was to preserve the Roman Catholic Church and always acted accordingly.

Welner had been el Coronel Jorge G. Frade's best friend, as well as his confessor, and as soon as Clete had arrived in Buenos Aires, Welner had appointed himself to that role for Cletus Frade. He had been very helpful in several difficult situations, and would doubtless be helpful in the future. But after his dinner with Dulles, Clete had never been able to look at Welner without remembering what Dulles had said about the highest priority of powerful, influential Roman Catholic clergymen.

The second man was General de Brigada Alejandro Bernardo Martín, a tall, fair-haired, light-skinned thirty-nine-year-old. Frade was about as surprised to see Martín in uniform as he was to see either him or Father Welner in the hangar, and wondered who had had the big mouth announcing the Connie's arrival.

Martín was chief of the Ethical Standards Office of the Argentine Ministry of Defense's Bureau of Internal Security, the official euphemism for the Argentine Intelligence and Counterintelligence Service, and usually wore civilian clothing.

Also in the last twenty-odd months, Frade and Martín

had become close friends. Before that, they had been adversaries, which caused Clete to consider that Martín's first priority still was the Argentine Republic—and that the priorities of the Argentine Republic were most often not the same as those of the Office of Strategic Services.

The third man was an American officer, Major Anthony J. Pelosi, whose pink and green uniform was adorned with the golden aiguillette of a military attaché, parachutist's wings, and the ribbon of the Silver Star medal, the nation's third-highest award for gallantry. His citation was as vague vis-à-vis exactly what he had done, and where, as was Frade's Navy Cross citation, and for the same reasons.

"Gentlemen," Clete said, "may I say I'm dazzled by your military sartorial splendor? Alejandro, I don't think I've ever seen you in your general's suit."

Martín said: "Surely you've heard, Colonel Frade, that Argentina is now at war and we are allies?"

Frade had indeed been told that Argentina had declared war on the Axis powers on March 27, about six weeks earlier.

He said: "I do remember hearing something about that, now that you mention it. It looks like our side is winning, doesn't it?"

"In Europe, Colonel, it seems we have won," Martín said.

He handed Frade a copy of the *Buenos Aires Herald*, an English-language newspaper.

"This is today's edition," Martín said.

Splashed across the front page was a photograph of an immaculately turned-out German officer sitting at a desk.

His marshal's baton lay on the desk beside his upside-down uniform cap, which held one of his gloves.

The caption beneath the photograph read:

> German Field Marshal Wilhelm Keitel signs a surrender document at Soviet headquarters in Berlin, May 9, 1945. The Soviets insisted that a second ceremonial signing take place in Soviet-occupied Berlin.

"Interesting," Clete said. "I heard the Krauts surrendered to General Eisenhower in Reims, France, on May seventh."

"It says the Russians demanded that there be a second signing in Berlin," Martín pointed out unnecessarily.

"Well, wherever it happened, it certainly calls for a celebration drink, wouldn't you say, Alejandro?"

"I would say that what calls for a celebration," Father Welner said, "is that you pulled it off."

"Pulled what off?" Clete asked.

"Bringing Karl and Peter here, of course," Welner said. "I really didn't think you stood much of a chance."

"Oh, ye of little faith!" Clete said. "What I'm wondering, Father, is who had the big mouth and told you—and the general—about it. I just don't think your being here is a coincidence."

"I did," Dorotea said simply. "I told both of them. I thought they might be able to help."

Clete looked at his wife. She was not only more intimately involved with his OSS activities than anyone suspected—except perhaps Martín and Welner—but she was very good at it.

If she told them not only that I had gone to Washington, but why, she had her reasons. What the hell could they be?

"How the hell could they have helped?" Frade asked, more confused than annoyed or angry.

"Perhaps she had this in mind, Cletus," the priest said, handing him an envelope. "There was no question in Dorotea's mind that you would succeed."

Clete opened the envelope. It held two booklets called *libretas de enrolamiento.* One was in the name of Kurt Boltitz and the other in that of Peter von Wachtstein, both of whom, according to the LE, had immigrated to Argentina in 1938.

"Karl," Frade called out, "make Hansel stop forcing himself on that poor woman, and the both of you come over here."

When they had, Clete handed them the identity documents.

"Say 'thank you' to Dorotea," Clete said. "But not to either of these two, for I'm sure neither of them would break the—at least—ten laws of the Argentine Republic somebody had to break to get these."

Boltitz and von Wachtstein had known Martín officially when they had been respectively the naval attaché and the assistant military attaché for air of the embassy of the German Reich.

Martín offered his hand to Boltitz and said, "Karl."

Boltitz replied, "Alejandro."

Martín then did the same thing to von Wachtstein.

Neither said "thank you," but profound gratitude could be seen in the eyes of the Germans.

"How good are those, Alejandro?" Frade asked.

"They will withstand all but the most diligent scrutiny," Martín said, and then added: "We'll get into that when we talk."

"Okay."

"It would be better if we talked now," the priest said.

Clete looked between the two Argentines and his wife.

"Here?"

"Why don't we go to the house on Libertador San Martín?" Dorotea suggested. "The men could have a shower, and then we could talk over lunch. Everyone else can go to Doña Claudia's house and we can all get together later."

Clete looked at his wife and thought: *Why do I think this has been the plan all along?*

Beth Howell was visibly—and vocally—distressed at being separated from Boltitz. But aside from her exception, Dorotea's plan went unchallenged.

The men, plus Dorotea, went to what Cletus thought of as "Uncle Willy's house by the racetrack"—it was across Avenida Libertador General San Martín from the Hipódromo de Palermo—in a four-car convoy. Martín's official Mercedes led the way, followed by Tony Pelosi's U.S. Embassy 1941 Chevrolet, then by Father Welner's 1940 Packard 280 convertible—a gift from el Coronel Jorge G. Frade—and finally by the enormous Horch touring car that had been el Coronel Frade's joy in life and in which he had been assassinated.

Their route took them past the German Embassy on Avenida Córdoba, causing Clete to wonder if Martín had done so intentionally. There were two soldiers standing in front of the gate. They were wearing German-style steel helmets and German-style gray uniforms and were holding German 7mm Mauser rifles in what the Marine Corps would call the Parade Rest position.

But they were not Germans. They were Argentines. And flying from atop the pole just inside the fence was the blue and white flag of Argentina, not the red swastika-centered flag of Nazi Germany that had flown there for so long.

Clete wondered what Boltitz and von Wachtstein were thinking about that.

[TWO]
4730 Avenida Libertador General San Martín
Buenos Aires, Argentina
1405 11 May 1945

When the parade of vehicles from the airport reached Uncle Guillermo's turn-of-the-century mansion, Cletus saw proof that it had been no accident that everybody had come there for a talk over lunch. Dorotea indeed had set it up—and made sure they were expected.

The first suggestion of that was the 1940 Ford station wagon parked at the curb. A legend painted on its doors read FRIGORÍFICO MORÓN. That, Frade thought, could be considered disinformation—*maybe even a cover*—as the Frigorífico Morón—or Morón Slaughterhouse and Feeding Pens—no longer existed to process the cattle from his estancia. The property in Morón was now the site of Aeropuerto Coronel Jorge G. Frade.

Two men were sitting in the Ford. Clete knew that they were armed with Remington Model 11 twelve-gauge riot shotguns, .45 ACP Thompson submachine guns, and Argentine versions of the U.S. 1911-A1 .45 ACP pistol. He was certain, too, that on the street behind the mansion there could be found another vehicle, maybe not another station wagon, but one also carrying the FRIGORÍFICO MORÓN legend on its doors, and also holding at least two well-armed men.

The armed men were all ex–troopers of the Húsares de Pueyrredón. And they had been born—as had their parents and their parents' parents, as far back as anyone could remember—on Estancia San Pedro y San Pablo.

Clete's father had versed him well in their distinguished history, to which he now was deeply connected.

Back in 1806, Estancia San Pedro y San Pablo had been owned by Juan Martín de Pueyrredón. When the British occupied Buenos Aires, he escaped to the estancia, which encompassed some eighty-four thousand hectares, or a little more than three hundred twenty-five square miles. He turned several hundred of its gauchos—*his* gauchos—into a cavalry force, and returned to Buenos Aires and recaptured the city. Not overwhelmed with modesty, Pueyrredón named his force of ferocious cowboys the Húsares de Pueyrredón. The title was made official in 1810, and the regiment was the most senior unit of the Argentine army.

From the beginning, gauchos of Estancia San Pedro y San Pablo had done their military service with the Húsares and then returned to the estancia, either after completion of their required national service or on their retirement.

As the estancia, under the Napoleonic Code, passed from one descendant of Juan Martín de Pueyrredón to another, many of the *patrónes* of Estancia San Pedro y San Pablo—after starting their careers fresh from the military academy as *subtenientes*—in time became colonels commanding the Húsares de Pueyrredón. Two of the most recent colonels commanding, el Coronel Jorge G. Frade and his father, el Coronel Guillermo Alejandro Frade, had done so.

El Coronel Jorge G. Frade would have preferred that his only son, Cletus, follow in the footsteps of his ancestors. But he'd taken what solace he could from knowing that Cletus had served with great distinction in the United States Corps of Marines, which el Coronel Frade had considered to be a military organization very nearly as prestigious as the Húsares de Pueyrredón.

On el Coronel Frade's assassination, the gauchos of Estancia San Pedro y San Pablo—the ex-troopers of the Húsares de Pueyrredón—had no trouble at all passing their loyalty to the new *patrón.*

First Lieutenant Cletus H. Frade, USMCR, had been more than a little discomfited to be crisply saluted by the estancia's gauchos. More recently, he had been even more discomfited when Enrico Rodríguez spread the news all over the estancia of Clete's promotion to lieutenant colonel—and the ex-troopers began addressing him as *"mi coronel."*

But he had grown used to it, and had come to think, perhaps immodestly, of the gauchos/ex–Húsares de Pueyrredón troopers as his private army. They were deployed all over Argentina, protecting the vast properties that he'd inherited after his father's murder. As here at Uncle Willy's house, they stood guard over Clete's immediate and extended families, as well as at the various places where he had, as he thought of it, stashed people who needed either protection or confinement.

Frade thought of all this when the massive iron gate to the mansion was opened to them by a tough-looking man cradling a Thompson in his arms and then when they had driven into the underground garage and another heavily armed man had opened the Horch's door, smiled, and said, "Doña Dorotea," and then come to attention and said, *"Mi coronel."*

Everyone exited their vehicles and followed Dorotea into the house itself. They were greeted by a small army of servants standing behind a distinguished-looking elderly man wearing a nicely tailored butler's suit and tie. Antonio Lavalle had been Jorge Frade's butler. Now he was head of Dorotea's crews running everything for her everywhere.

Dorotea turned to the newly arrived group of men and announced, "For those of you gentlemen who have not met our butler, this is Antonio Lavalle. He and his staff will assist those of you who would like to perhaps freshen up. Or who would simply prefer to relax. Please make yourself at home."

She then turned to Antonio Lavalle and said loud enough for everyone to hear, "And you may please start serving any of our guests in the library."

As Clete walked with his bride up the staircase to the mansion's master bedroom, which took up most of the third floor, he thought—as he often did—that he had many memories of Uncle Guillermo's house, many of them very private and very touching—and too many of them of vicious murder.

Clete's father had been born here, and had insisted on turning over the mansion to him the first day that father and son had, over many drinks and emotional moments, reconnected.

Not long after, Clete had been in the master bedroom when la Señora Marianna Rodríguez de Pellano—Enrico's sister, who had cared for Clete from birth until his mother had gone to the States and died in childbirth—had had her throat cut in the kitchen. Assassins had killed her in order to get to Clete. But, when they'd come upstairs after him, he had shot them both dead with an Argentine .45—wounding one first in the leg before putting a round in his forehead.

Three days later, as Clete lay in the bed, an angry la Señorita Dorotea Mallín burst in and gave him hell for not calling her after the attack. What happened next caused Clete's first son to be conceived—and for Clete to no longer be able to lovingly refer to Dorotea as "the Virgin Princess."

And, late one December night, it had been in Uncle Willy's house that Clete had first come across a young man in the library. The stranger, slumped in the armchair, had worn a quilted, dark-red dressing gown. There'd been a cognac snifter resting on his chest, a lit cigar in the ashtray on the table beside him, and Beethoven's Third Symphony coming from the phonograph.

That night First Lieutenant Cletus H. Frade, USMCR, met Kapitän Hans-Peter Baron von Wachtstein of the Luftwaffe. Peter had accompanied to Argentina the body of Clete's cousin, who'd been killed at Stalingrad flying as an observer in a German Storch. While Clete and Peter immediately understood that they were enemies, they also learned they were fighter pilots—and more. "Suppose," Peter had suggested, "that as officers and gentlemen, we might pretend it's Christmas Eve? We'd only be off by a couple of weeks." They had—and over time had become close friends.

[THREE]
4730 Avenida Libertador General San Martín
Buenos Aires, Argentina
1500 11 May 1945

Hors d'oeuvres and cocktails were being served when Clete and Dorotea entered the enormous, richly appointed library. The Frades looked as satisfied—maybe as satiated—as if fresh from the shower.

Clete saw the look Peter von Wachtstein was giving him and had an epiphany.

I know what you're thinking, Hansel!

"How come you and Dorotea, who you last saw only a week ago, just got to enjoy the splendors of the nuptial couch, while I—without the opportunity to do the same since last July—sit here sucking on a glass of wine and a black olive with my equally sex-starved wife but two kilometers away?"

Or words to that effect.

Clete and Dorotea walked across the polished hardwood floor toward von Wachtstein.

"I have several things to say to you, Hansel," Clete said as he took two glasses of Cabernet Sauvignon from a maid, handing one to his wife.

"Really?" von Wachtstein said.

"'Life is unfair,'" Clete intoned solemnly.

"Is it?"

"'Fortune favors the pure in heart.'"

"You don't say?"

"'Patience is a virtue, and all things come to he who waits.'"

"What the hell are you talking about?" Dorotea asked, confused.

"Hansel, you may wish to write some, or all, of that down," Clete concluded.

Clete looked around the room. With the exception of Father Welner, who was smiling and shaking his head, everyone looked baffled.

"Why don't we go in and have our lunch?" Clete went on. "I'm sure that everyone—Peter especially—is anxious to get this over and move on to other things."

Frade stood at the large double doors between the library and the ornate dining room and waited politely as his guests passed through.

When the last of them had done so, Clete looked around the library.

With a couple of exceptions, he thought, *it's just like it was the night I found Peter here listening to the phonograph. Then there was only one leather armchair and footstool. Now there's two, because Dorotea wanted her own.*

And, of course, when this was my father's library, there was no hobbyhorse or baby blue prison pen to keep the kids from crawling around—or any other accoutrements of toddlers and infants.

My father never had anything to do with kids.

Would he have liked it—or not given a damn?

His reverie was interrupted by Lavalle.

"*Mi coronel,*" the butler said, "there is a telephone call."

"When did you start calling me '*mi coronel,*' Antonio?"

Both Dorotea and Lavalle had told Clete—many times—that gentlemen referred to their butlers by their surnames. Clete thought it was not only rude but also insisted that gentlemen referred to their friends by their given names, and Antonio Lavalle often had proved just how good a friend he was.

"When you were promoted, *mi coronel,*" Lavalle said with a smile.

Clete smiled and shook his head.

"Tell whoever it is that we're having lunch and I'll call back."

"It is el Señor Dulles."

Clete gave that a long moment's consideration, then

said: "Start feeding the hungry, Antonio. Tell Doña Dorotea I had to take a call."

Clete walked to one of the large, brown-leather-upholstered armchairs. As he settled into it, his mind went back to the first time he'd met Allen Welsh Dulles.

It had been a remarkable meeting—one in which some staggering pieces of the greater espionage puzzle that affected Clete began to fall into place. It had taken place at Canoas Air Base, Puerto Alegre, Brazil, in the commanding officer's Mediterranean-style red-tile-roof cottage in July of '43, days after "Aggie"—Colonel Graham—had sent "Tex"—Frade—a cryptic radio message that he was to see the CO at "Bird Cage"—Canoas, where the first Lockheed Lodestars destined for the newly formed South American Airways had been sent for final delivery to el Señor Cletus Frade, managing director of SAA.

Frade, of course, had expected to see the commanding officer. Instead, the cottage held only a stranger.

"Allen Welsh Dulles," he introduced himself, then made them drinks, then casually announced that they had mutual friends. "My brother—John Foster Dulles—has a law firm in New York City; among his clients are Cletus Marcus Howell and Howell Petroleum. And, of course, I have been friends with Alejandro Graham a long time—and not just our time working for Wild Bill Donovan."

Frade, not knowing what to believe of the stranger's story, didn't reply.

Then Dulles really surprised him by naming Frade's mole in the German Embassy: "Galahad is Major Hans-Peter Baron von Wachtstein."

Frade, who refused to reveal that to anyone in or out of the OSS, professed ignorance.

Dulles answered: "The FBI, the Office of Naval Intelligence, the Army's Chief of Intelligence, and of course SS-Brigadeführer Ritter Manfred von Deitzberg—among others—would dearly like to know that, too."

And that got Frade's attention, too.

He knew that the Germans had at least two secret programs in Argentina. Von Deitzberg—Reichsführer-SS Heinrich Himmler's deputy—was running one, an unnamed operation in which senior SS officers were ransoming Jews to be released from concentration camps and moved to Argentina. The other was Operation Phoenix—senior members of the Nazi hierarchy purchasing property in South America, primarily in Argentina but also in Paraguay, Brazil, and other countries, to which they could flee when Germany fell, and from which they could later rise, Phoenix-like, to bring Nazism back.

Then Dulles described the private dinner in the Hotel Washington he'd had only nights earlier—"Just me, Graham, Donovan, the President, and Putzi Hanfstaengl."

Frade again professed ignorance—this time truthfully. "Am I supposed to know who Putzi Haf-whatever is?"

Dulles explained that the wealthy Ernst "Putzi" Hanfstaengl, who had attended Columbia with Roosevelt and Donovan, had been in Hitler's inner circle before he got smart and fled to the United States—just prior to the SS's plan for Putzi to suffer a fatal accident. FDR prized Putzi's insider perspective of the mind-set of Hitler's high command. And, as Dulles related to Frade, it was Putzi's belief that most if not all senior Nazis knew the war was lost, that Hitler was psychologically unable to face that, and that no one dared suggest it to him.

"Which explains the existence of such secret operations as Phoenix and Valkyrie," Dulles said.

Then, finally convincing Frade that Dulles was who he said he was, Dulles said: "I am privy to a secret about Valkyrie known to no more than nine Americans, one of whom is you. Through Admiral Wilhelm Canaris"—he paused to see if Frade recognized the chief of the German military intelligence service, the Abwehr, then went on after he'd nodded—"I am in communication with General von Wachtstein, who in fact intends to assassinate Adolf Hitler. One of his other co-conspirators—Lieutenant Colonel Claus von Stauffenberg, *Count* von Stauffenberg—is a close friend of young von Wachtstein . . . your Galahad."

Clete felt the hair on the back of his neck stand up.

Peter had told Clete that he'd seen von Stauffenberg in Munich and that the subject of regicide had been discussed.

Then, making Frade's head really spin, Dulles broached the biggest secret: the Manhattan Project. He explained that the Americans were racing the Germans to develop an enormously powerful atom bomb from an element known as uranium.

"Whoever creates this bomb first is going to win the war. It's as simple as that," he said. Then, saying Graham shortly would TOP SECRET message him the same, he laid out Frade's marching orders: "So your first priority is the immediate reporting of anything you hear about uranium or a superbomb."

The next priorities, Dulles went on, were of equal importance: allowing the ransoming and Phoenix operations to continue while learning everything about them.

"As morally despicable as the ransoming is," Dulles explained, "FDR says the bigger issue is saving lives wherever and however possible. If we were to expose the ransoming, the real result would be the extermination of all the Jews in concentration camps. And if we expose Phoenix, the Nazis will simply deny its existence. Letting it continue, however, allows us to trace the money from the moment it arrives in Argentina. You'll create a paper trail of what was bought with it, and from whom. Plus the names of the officials—Argentine, Paraguayan, Uruguayan—who are being bought. Everything.

"The thinking is that if we went to General Ramírez or General Rawson now with what we have, or what you might dig up, they would tell us to mind our own business. The Argentines are not convinced the Germans have lost the war. But, while the Germans will hang on as long as possible, ultimately they will surrender unconditionally, as demanded by Roosevelt at the Casablanca Conference. And what *that* means, under international law, is that the moment the Germans sign the surrender document, everything the German government owns falls under the control of the victors. Things like embassy buildings, other real estate, bank accounts.

"Our ambassador will then call upon the Argentine

foreign minister, present him with a detailed list of all German property in Argentina—which you will have prepared, to include bank account numbers, descriptions of real estate, et cetera—and inform him that we're taking possession of it.

"The Argentine government may not like it, but it's a well-established principle of international law, and it really would be unwise of them to defy that law. I rather doubt they will. Nations, like people, tend to try to curry favor with whoever has just won a fight."

Cletus Frade then admitted that his head was indeed spinning, and suggested that he was way out of his depth, that starting up South American Airways was proving challenging enough.

Dulles replied: "Alec Graham said, vis-à-vis you, something to the effect that the first impression you give is of a dangerously irresponsible individual who should not be trusted out of your sight. And then, depending on how much experience one has with really good covert intelligence officers, one comes to the realization that one is in the company of a rare person who seems to be born for this sort of thing."

Frade had considered that, wondered how much of it was smoke being blown up his ass, then said: "Does that mean you're going to tell me what this airline business is all about?"

"Alec and I talked about that, and General Donovan told me he'd asked the President. No one knows anything except that Franklin Delano Roosevelt thinks it's a good idea, and that he was pleased to learn of your remarkable progress in getting one going."

Two years later, Frade—who now knew a helluva lot more than he wanted about the usefulness of South American Airways and about the secret German operations—picked up the telephone from the lower shelf of the table next to his chair. He crisply announced, "Area Commander Frade speaking, sir."

He heard Allen W. Dulles chuckle.

"How was your flight from Washington, Area Commander?" Dulles asked.

"How did you hear about that?"

"I spoke with someone who began the conversation along the lines of 'I'm glad you're there. You won't believe what Alec's loose cannon just did with a pair of POWs at Fort Hunt.'"

"From that I infer 'there' is 'here,' right?" Frade said.

"I'm in the Alvear Palace."

"And you're here because of what allegedly happened in Washington? I don't understand . . ."

"In part that. I thought we—you, me, and those *allegedly* sprung from Fort Hunt—need to discuss some new developments, ones that have come up in the week since you and I last spoke in Lisbon—"

"Oh, do we absolutely have to talk!" Frade announced.

"—and so," Dulles went on, "believing that because you had just flown the Atlantic you probably would spend at least a day or two in the bosom of your family, I went back to Lisbon and caught the very next South American Airways flight to Buenos Aires."

He paused, chuckled, then went on: "Tangentially, an observation or two about that: Your airline must be making money, Cletus. I was lucky to get a seat. Every one got sold, despite the outrageous prices you're charging for a ticket. Many of the seats were occupied by Roman Catholic clergy of one affiliation or another. I decided that Buenos Aires must be overflowing with sinners for the Pope to spend so much money rushing all those priests, brothers, and nuns over here to save souls."

Clete laughed.

"I'll tell Father Welner what you said," he said.

"Have you seen the good Father lately?"

"He met the airplane and he's here now. Having his lunch. He and General Martín—they met the plane and said we had to talk."

"Do they know about von Wachtstein and Boltitz?" Dulles said.

"Welner handed them—in front of Martín—Argentine identity documents stating that they'd immigrated to Argentina in 1938."

"Then what Martín probably wants to talk about is what should be done with them in the immediate future. So far as a great many Germans in Argentina are concerned, both are traitors to the Thousand-Year Reich."

"Not only Argentine Germans," Frade said, "but I'd say at least half of the newly converted *clergy*—of the sort you said were on your flight—also think they're traitors.

I don't mind the good Germans, but I've about had enough of these Kraut bastards."

Dulles didn't reply immediately. Then he said, "Understood. We need to discuss that, too."

"So," Frade said, "can you tell me about these new developments you just mentioned?"

And why they are so important that you came all the way here to tell me about them?

"When can we get together?" Dulles said. "I don't want to talk about them on the phone."

"I don't think you want to come here to Uncle Willy's house."

"Not if Martín and Father Welner are there, Cletus."

"Okay. Well, what I'm planning now—and, unless I'm given a good reason not to, what I'm indeed going to do—is spend the night here, then load everybody on the Red Lodestar and fly them out to Estancia San Pedro y San Pablo. From there, I don't know."

"Okay."

"So then why don't you drop by Jorge Frade about nine tomorrow morning and fly out to the estancia with us? Martín and Welner aren't going."

"Very well. I'll see you at the airport at nine," Dulles said, and hung up.

[FOUR]
Estancia San Pedro y San Pablo
Near Pila, Buenos Aires Province, Argentina
1005 12 May 1945

Cletus Frade brought the Lodestar in low over the pampas and smoothly touched down on the runway. The first time he'd flown here, the runway had been grass. Now, three years later, it was pebble and lined with lights. And the tarmac was now cobblestones, and there was another hangar, this one large enough for two Lodestars.

During the landing, he had seen that there was a welcoming party. It wasn't until he had taxied up to the hangars and stopped the aircraft that he really realized how large the group was.

"It looks like the Turtles have come out to welcome us," Frade said, turning to look at his wife in the copilot seat.

When I met you, he thought, *you'd never even been in an airplane.*

And look at you now, Amelia Earhart!

"Darling," his copilot said resignedly, as she shut down the engines and then took off her headset, "I've told you time and again that they don't like being called the Turtles."

A Top Secret personnel roster filed in Colonel Alec Graham's office at OSS Headquarters in Washington, D.C., listed the members of OSS Western Hemisphere Team 17, which was code-named Team Turtle. A sunken ship was sometimes said to have "turned turtle"—and the original mission of the team had been to cause the sinking of the *Reine de la Mer* to stop its replenishments of German U-boats.

The roster listed, under one Lieutenant Colonel Cletus Frade, USMCR, Majors Maxwell Ashton III and Anthony J. Pelosi (now assistant military attachés at the U.S. Embassy); Captain Madison R. Sawyer III; Navy Lieutenant Oscar J. Schultz, the team's radioman; Master Sergeant William Ferris, their weapons and parachute expert; and Technical Sergeant Jerry O'Sullivan, who operated the team's highly secret radar.

Ferris, Ashton, and Sawyer all came from wealthy, socially prominent families, thus meeting the criteria for the—possibly a little jealous—critics of the OSS who suggested the abbreviation actually stood for "Oh, So Social."

The only Turtles missing from the reception party—or not on the Lodestar—were Captain Sawyer and newly promoted Master Sergeant Sigfried Stein, the team's explosives expert, who was a refugee from Nazi Germany. Both were at Frade's Estancia Don Guillermo, near Mendoza in the foothills of the Andes, holding down the fort of what Frade thought of as the lunatic asylum, and his wife thought of as her little house in the mountains, more formally known as Casa Montagna.

There were also four gauchos on horseback by the hangars, all armed with either rifles or submachine guns, and there were, Clete knew, at least six or eight more out of sight, keeping watch on the Big House.

There were also a half dozen servants of both sexes

from the Big House and as many mechanics/ground handlers.

"I really hate to go out there," Clete said to Dorotea. "Signing autographs for fans is so tiring."

"My father was right about you. You're bonkers, absolutely bonkers. I should have listened to him."

"You were deaf with uncontrollable lust."

"You bah-stud!"

"I love it when you talk dirty."

"My God!" Dorotea exclaimed as she opened the door to the passenger compartment. Clete saw that she was smiling.

After disembarking from the Lodestar, the women saw that the children were placed in baby carriages for the ride to the Big House that would pass through over a hectare of English garden. Then the women—with the exception of Dorotea—walked after the servants who pushed the baby carriages. Other servants trailed them with everyone's luggage.

The men, meantime, pushed the Lodestar into the hangar. Moving the big airplane took grunting effort from all of them.

When the Lodestar had been arranged to Clete's satisfaction, Allen Dulles cleaned his hands with a handkerchief. Then, pointing, Dulles asked, "What's that under the tarpaulin?"

"The last time Hansel was here, he left in a hurry and forgot it," Frade said. "Being the wonderful fellow that I am, I've been taking care of it for him."

Von Wachtstein, having heard his name, walked up as two mechanics responded to Clete's gesture and started removing the tarpaulin.

When they had finished, von Wachtstein said, "My God!"

The Fieseler Storch—a small, high-wing, single-engine aircraft—was painted in the Luftwaffe spring and summer camouflage scheme of random-shaped patches in three shades of green and two of brown. Black crosses identifying it as a German military aircraft were on both sides of the fuselage aft of the cockpit, and the red Hakenkreuz of Nazi Germany was painted in white circles on both sides of the vertical stabilizer.

"It looks like it could be flown right now," von Wachtstein said.

Frade glanced at his wife, then said, "Dorotea and I flew it to your mother-in-law's house for dinner last week."

"How did Peter come to 'forget it' the last time he was here?" Dulles asked.

"Well," Frade said by way of explanation, "Peter can't be accused of being a military genius, but he did set up an emergency get-out-of-Dodge plan. Which worked."

"When we got word," von Wachtstein furnished, "Ambassador von Lutzenberger called me at four A.M. with the joyous news that God had saved our beloved Führer from Claus's bomb at Wolfsschanze. I then picked up Karl Boltitz at his apartment, went out to El Palomar Airfield, filed a flight plan to Montevideo, and, as soon as it was light, took off in the Storch. And flew here. Cletus then flew us—no flight plan—to Canoas in the Red Lodestar. Thirty-six hours later, Karl and I were officially POWs at Fort Hunt."

"Von Lutzenberger," Dulles said, "the German ambassador in Buenos Aires?"

Von Wachtstein nodded.

"He knew what you were doing?" Dulles pursued.

Von Wachtstein nodded again, then looked at Frade and said, "What happened to him after the unconditional surrender?"

"I don't know," Frade said. "I should have asked Martín."

"I did ask General Martín," Dorotea said. "The ambassador and his wife are either in Villa General Belgrano or will be shortly. Just about everybody else from the embassy was taken to the Club Hotel de la Ventana in the south of Buenos Aires Province."

"What's that, a house?" Major Ashton asked. "'Villa General Belgrano'?"

"It's actually a place," von Wachtstein said, "a little village in Córdoba. It looks like it's in Bavaria. It was started by German immigrants, and when the Argentine government had to put the interned survivors of the *Graf Spee* somewhere, the most dedicated Nazis were sent there. I used to fly that"—he pointed to the Storch—"up there once a month with the payroll and their mail."

"And the less dedicated Nazis?" Dulles asked.

"Some of them went to an Argentine army base near Rosario," Boltitz chimed in, "and the rest to the Ventana Club Hotel."

"I used to go there, too," von Wachtstein said. "Usually, I had a message or a package for the Bishop of Rosario, a man named Salvador Lombardi. You know what they say about converts to Catholicism becoming more Catholic than the Pope? Well, that sonofabitch was a convert to National Socialism and was more of a Nazi than Hitler. He told me one time that anyone who opposed der Führer would suffer eternal damnation. And he meant it."

"I believe the bishop is a close friend of my Tío Juan," Frade said. "I wonder why that doesn't surprise me."

There were many reasons for Frade's deep distrust of el Coronel Juan Domingo Perón—his godfather, "Uncle" Juan—who was vice president, secretary of War, and secretary of Labor and Welfare of the Argentine Republic. Chief among them was that Perón, very sympathetic to Germany's socialist political ideals, was too friendly with the Nazis in Argentina. And, Frade had discovered, Perón's ultimate ambition wasn't to become president of Argentina—he instead aspired to be ruler of a Greater Argentina, which the Nazis had intended to create by combining Uruguay, Paraguay, and even parts of Chile and Brazil.

All of which supported Frade's strong suspicion that Perón had been complicit in the Nazis' ordering the assassination of el Coronel Jorge Frade and the attempted assassination of Cletus Frade.

And when Clete—who embraced Sun Tzu's philosophy of keeping one's friends close and one's enemies closer—finally ordered his Tío Juan to move out of Uncle

Willy's Avenida Libertador mansion—calling him a degenerate sonofabitch for his lust for thirteen-year-old girls—Perón had actually pulled a pistol on him. It had taken Frade considerable restraint not to let Enrico's riot shotgun accidentally discharge double-ought buckshot in Perón's direction.

"Some of those messages for Bishop Lombardi were from Perón," von Wachtstein confirmed.

Allen Dulles suddenly put in: "Getting off the subject of Colonel Perón and with the caveat that there's never a good time to say something like this, Peter and Karl, I want you to know both personally and on behalf of the OSS how very sorry we are about what Hitler did to Admiral Boltitz and General von Wachtstein."

"Thank you," von Wachtstein said simply.

"Thank you," Boltitz said, then added: "But I have to tell you—fully aware that this is probably what we sailors call 'pissing into the wind'—that I haven't completely given up hope about my father. One of the later arrivals at Fort Hunt told me he had heard that when the word came that the bomb at Wolfsschanze failed to kill Hitler, my father, who was in Norway, in Narvik, simply disappeared."

Frade had a sudden cold-blooded thought: *He knew what was going to happen to any of the conspirators.*

Jumping into those icy waters was preferable to what the SS would do to him—starting with torture and ending by getting hung from a butcher's hook—if they got their hands on him.

"It's possible, of course, that he took his own life," Boltitz went on.

Jesus, he's reading my mind!

"But I don't think he would do that. He had Norwegian friends."

Sorry, Karl, but I'm afraid you really are pissing into the wind.

"I'll see if I can find out anything for you," Dulles said.

"Thank you."

"I'd love to say let's go get something to drink," Frade said. "But that'll have to wait. Let's go to the *quincho.* At least we can get some coffee."

"You don't need me in there," Dorotea said. "And I have our lady guests to attend to. Clete can tell me what happened later." She saw the look of surprise on Allen Dulles's face and added: "He always tells me everything, Mr. Dulles. I thought you knew that."

She then walked briskly toward the Big House.

III

[ONE]
Estancia San Pedro y San Pablo
Near Pila, Buenos Aires Province
Republic of Argentina
1050 12 May 1945

"When this is over," Clete announced after everybody had filed into the *quincho*, "the bar will open. In the meantime, sit down, have a cup of coffee, and pay attention to our boss."

There are all sorts of *quinchos*, structures originally built of poles supporting a thatched roof, designed to keep people out of the sun and rain while watching meat grill on the wood-fueled parrilla. The Big House's *quincho* was somewhat more elaborate. At least three generations of Frades had used it to entertain not only their friends but the senior employees of the Estancia San Pedro y San Pablo. There was a large number of the latter.

This *quincho* was a substantial brick building large enough to seat fifty people at what in America would be called picnic tables. The roof was covered with red Spanish tiles, and there was a complete restaurant-size kitchen to complement the twenty-foot-long parrilla. And there was a well-stocked bar.

"Thank you, Colonel Frade, for that enthusiastic introduction," Dulles said dryly, and sat down on one of the wooden plank tables.

"There's good news and there's bad news," Dulles began. "As you're aware, the very good news is that the Germans have surrendered unconditionally, and as soon as we're finished here, we'll have a drink to celebrate that.

"The bad news is that the end of any war is a dangerous time. Some argue that it can be more dangerous than during the war, because on the losing side there can be breaks in chains of command and in discipline, and lawful orders can either be lost in the chaos or be outright ignored—or both. Nor is it unusual among those on the losing side for there to be instances of every man for himself. I'll get more into that in a moment.

"While Germany has surrendered, the fact is the war is not over for us. You won't be sent to the Pacific. But you won't be going home, either, because you're needed here. And concerning that, the other bad news—there's so much of it I hardly know where to begin—is that the OSS shortly will cease to exist."

That announcement caused a sudden anxious energy in the *quincho*. Some of the Turtles suddenly sat upright, causing the wooden legs of their seating to screech across the tile floor. Others blurted a mix of "What?" and "I'll be damned!"

Clete Frade popped to his feet and extended his right

arm over his head, the palm of his hand out. "Hold it down. Let Mr. Dulles continue."

There then came some audible sighs, but the room turned quiet again. Frade returned to his seat.

Dulles went on: "Believe me, I don't like it any better than you men. But I'm afraid that we—the OSS—had it coming. Let me go off on that tangent. I'm sure you will all be shocked to hear that the Army, the Navy, the State Department, and the FBI have never liked the OSS. They've had to put up with us because the OSS enjoyed the protection of President Roosevelt. The OSS was his idea. The moment Roosevelt died, the pressure on President Truman to disband us began. It increased with the German surrender. It isn't a question of whether the OSS will be shut down, but when.

"So far as the OSS in Argentina is concerned, organizationally Team Turtle is de jure subordinate to the OSS station chief, Colonel Richmond C. Flowers, USA, who is the military attaché at our embassy in Buenos Aires.

"De facto, Team Turtle is directly subordinate to Colonel Graham and, to a lesser degree, myself. While Majors Ashton and Pelosi, who have been accredited to the embassy, are de jure subordinate to Colonel Flowers, de facto Colonel Flowers has been told that he does not have either the authority to tell them what to do or the ability to question them as to what they are doing.

"In a manner of speaking, Flowers is Marshall's man in the OSS. His allegiance is to General Marshall, not to General Donovan. You understand, of course, that when I refer to the chief of staff of the Army, I am not referring to General George Catlett Marshall personally, but to one or more of his subordinates who know his desires and will try hard to satisfy them. That would include his deputy chief of staff or someone even lower on that chain of command. Or—almost certainly—the assistant chief of staff for intelligence, and others lower on that chain of command.

"Everyone still with me? If there are questions, please ask them. Because what I'm about to tell you concerns not only some of your fine work being completely destroyed, but also what you may well face in the very near future."

He paused and looked around the room.

There were more than a few expressions of curiosity. But no questions.

"Okay," Dulles said with a nod, then went on: "Shortly after Colonel Flowers was named OSS station chief for Argentina and told that he had no control over Team Turtle, he complained to General Marshall that, because of all the things Team Turtle was doing, he had nothing to do. Marshall—or, as I said before, one of his loyal underlings—complained to General Donovan. In an attempt to spread oil upon the troubled waters, Donovan threw Marshall a bone."

He paused, then said with a smile, "How's that for a masterful double cliché?"

That got him chuckles, and Master Sergeant William Ferris applauded and called, "Hear! Hear!"

Dulles then said: "That bone being the care and maintenance of the files Team Turtle had been keeping that listed in which banks and which safety-deposit boxes resided all the money and precious stones, et cetera, that Herr Doktor Goebbels and other National Socialist officials had been sending to Argentina to fund their Operation Phoenix. The release of the intel was done, I must say, over Colonel Frade's most strenuous objections. But when ordered by General Donovan to turn over said files to Colonel Flowers, Colonel Frade dutifully did so."

"How's that for a masterful stupid decision?" Frade asked bitterly.

"You had no choice, Clete," Dulles said evenly. "It was an order."

"I could have given Flowers half of the files, a quarter of them," Frade argued. "He wouldn't have known the difference, and we would have had at least some of that money and those valuables left to grab. But, no, I gave the bastard everything we had on Phoenix."

"As you were ordered to do," Dulles repeated, and then stopped. "I am about to talk out of the other side of my mouth on the subject of obeying orders. When Colonel Flowers made an unwise decision vis-à-vis those files—"

"'Unwise decision'?" Frade parroted. "How about a masterful *double* stupid decision?"

Dulles smiled at him.

"If you like," Dulles said, "I will rephrase: When Colonel Flowers, to ensure those files would not fall into the wrong hands, made his masterful double stupid decision to take the files out of the embassy and place them in the safe in his home, he thus unwittingly permitted parties unknown—"

"Otherwise known as el Coronel Juan Domingo Perón," Frade interrupted again.

"—to gain surreptitious access to them and photograph them, thus permitting the holders of the various bank accounts and safety-deposit boxes to move the assets elsewhere before they could be seized by the Argentine government on Germany's unconditional surrender.

"On learning that there were no assets to be seized, Colonel Flowers suspected that Colonel Frade had not only intentionally given him false data when ordered to turn over the files to him but had given the bona fide data to, quote, some of his Argentine friends, close quote. And then reported his suspicions as fact to the assistant chief of staff for intelligence.

"Flowers, of course, had no way of knowing that, in addition to turning over the files to him, what Colonel Frade had actually done was make copies of everything and given those copies to the legal attaché of the U.S. Embassy, Mr. Milton Leibermann, and informed General Donovan that he had done so.

"Mr. Leibermann notified the FBI that he had come into possession of the files, the accuracy of which he had verified, from Colonel Frade.

"On receipt of this communication, J. Edgar Hoover called General Donovan and asked why Colonel Frade had been so obliging, inasmuch as officers of the OSS and the FBI in Argentina were forbidden to communicate with one another. General Donovan told him that Frade had been so concerned the files would be compromised once they were in the hands of Colonel Flowers that he felt justified to place a copy of them into the hands of the FBI.

"And so it came to pass, as it says so often in the Bible, that when the assistant chief of staff for intelligence, in righteous indignation, called upon General Donovan with Colonel Flowers's suspicions vis-à-vis Colonel Frade, General Donovan was able to tell him they were unfounded. 'General, the data Frade furnished Colonel Flowers was accurate. Ask J. Edgar Hoover, who has a copy.'

"The assistant chief of staff for intelligence apparently contacted Director Hoover, for that was the last either Donovan or the OSS heard of the matter.

"I think it reasonable to assume, however, that the assistant chief of staff for intelligence did indeed discuss the matter with Colonel Flowers. I also think it reasonable to assume that they refused to relieve Colonel Flowers for cause because that would have been tantamount to admitting the officer forced upon the OSS was grossly incompetent.

"Getting back to what I said at the beginning, the bad news here is that when the OSS is inevitably disbanded, Team Turtle personnel will be reassigned. That almost certainly means everyone will be assigned to the Office of the Military Attaché—in other words, to Colonel Flowers.

"And as soon as the OSS is disbanded—and probably

before, possibly as soon as tomorrow—Colonel Flowers is going to try to assume authority over all of you."

"Fuck him," Tony Pelosi blurted.

"Please permit me to associate myself with Major Pelosi's position," Major Ashton said.

That earned them some chuckles.

"While orders are orders," Dulles said, "there is a loophole here: Until the OSS is formally disbanded, and until Colonel Flowers is ordered to assume command, so to speak, the status quo will prevail. He will not have the legal authority to issue orders to any of you.

"I think, however, that he will try. If he fails, he will have lost nothing. If he succeeds, the advantages to him are obvious. Victors write history. He will write the history of why the plan to have Operation Phoenix assets seized failed, and Colonel Frade's gross incompetence—and perhaps his disloyalty—will be the reason."

"Mr. Dulles," Lieutenant Oscar Schultz asked, "two questions."

"Shoot, Jefe," Dulles said.

Jefe—"chief" in Spanish—made reference both to the Brooklyn-born Schultz's former status as a Navy chief radioman and to what he was called by the workers of Estancia San Pedro y San Pablo. Fluent in Spanish, Schultz often could be found in what he called his gaucho outfit—a broad-brimmed black hat, loose white shirt with billowing sleeves, billowing black *bombachas* tucked into calf-high soft black leather boots, and a wide silver-studded and buckled leather belt carrying a fourteen-inch knife in a silver scabbard.

"Make that three questions," the old sailor said. "But if I get the right answer to question one, I won't have to ask the other two."

Dulles, Frade, and Ashton immediately took Jefe's meaning.

Frade and Dulles laughed.

Ashton said, "Good thought!"

Schultz pulled his wicked knife from its scabbard, looked at it admiringly, then began, "A quick and simple fix for this problem—"

"Sorry, Jefe," Dulles interrupted. "As General of the Army Eisenhower was denied permission by President Roosevelt to remove a problem named Charles de Gaulle by shooting him, this deputy director of the OSS herewith denies you permission to remove a problem named Colonel Richmond C. Flowers by shooting or any other lethal means."

"I was afraid you'd say that," Schultz said, his tone genuinely disappointed, and slipped his blade back into the scabbard.

That caused general laughter.

"Even though," Dulles added, "the gentleman in question clearly deserves it."

More laughter.

"And your other two questions?" Dulles asked.

"How much time do we have before they shut down the OSS?"

"I really don't know," Dulles replied. "Much depends on what happens in the Pacific. Or, more precisely, President Truman's perception of what will happen there. If he thinks that the war will continue for some time, he may decide that the OSS might prove useful and not shut us down immediately. On the other hand, if he thinks the Emperor will surrender—or seek an armistice, or something unexpected happens . . ."

Dulles met Frade's eyes for a moment.

Clete thought: *He's talking about that superbomb, that "atomic" bomb!*

". . . in the near term, he may decide the OSS is no longer needed."

Schultz was not satisfied with that answer.

"Time frame?" he pursued.

"From tomorrow to possibly as late as October or November. Sorry, Jefe, that's really the best I can do."

"And what are our priorities during that time?"

"Right now there are two. I'm not sure which priority is most important; both could be. Immediately, I would lean toward protecting the Gehlen operation. Because if President Truman hears about it—especially via Treasury Secretary Morgenthau—he will very likely order that the OSS be shut down that instant. And then probably order the arrest of everybody concerned with the Gehlen operation.

"I think that alone explains the absolute necessity for keeping it a secret. But let me express further how important it is: A moment ago, I said that you could not take out Colonel Flowers despite his having proven to be a danger to the OSS. That said, if Colonel Flowers were to learn of the Gehlen operation, and was about to pass what he had learned, or even thinks he had learned, on to anyone—"

"Then we could shoot him?" Schultz interrupted.

"That's a very tough call to make, Jefe, and we would have to be absolutely sure the Gehlen operation was in imminent danger of being compromised. But . . ."

"Understood," Schultz said, nodding.

Dulles added, "Colonel Frade, I think it important that you understand that."

"I understand," Clete said. "And what I want everyone else to understand is that we are not going to take out Colonel Flowers until I am sure we have to. I'll make that decision. Everybody got that?"

There were nods and mumbles of "Got it" and "Okay."

"Not good enough," Clete said. "You will respond, Mr. Schultz, by saying, 'Aye, aye, sir.' Army personnel will respond by saying, 'Yes, sir. I understand the order.'"

There was something in the tone of his voice that discouraged either wisecracks or insubordination.

"Aye, aye, sir," Schultz said.

This was followed by multiple, overlapping, replies of "Yes, sir, I understand the order."

"Thank you," Frade said. "Please continue, Mr. Dulles."

"The second problem falls under what I mentioned earlier," Dulles said, "about the dangers unique to the end of a war. There has been a great deal of confusion—and, at times, outright chaos—leading up to the Germans agreeing to surrender unconditionally. And now afterward. Accordingly, the intelligence that we have, and continue to gather, is all over the chart. Some of it is solid and reliable. And some is so wild that it boggles the mind."

"Let's hear the wild stuff," Pelosi said.

Schultz, sitting next to Pelosi, looked at him and chimed in: "Yeah, I'd like to hear something worse than the news that we're being disbanded and taken over by our worst nightmare."

There were a couple chuckles.

"I'll save the outrageous for later," Dulles said. "But I will say now that it fits with some of what you've already dealt with—specifically the Phoenix program, which of course we know existed and therefore lends some credibility to the wildest of scenarios. And it shares the common thread of U-boats still at sea—possibly as many as sixty submarines, but maybe only twenty. Our intelligence, as I said, is all over the chart. We know a great deal about some of these subs, almost nothing about others. And knowing nothing means we haven't the first idea if their crews plan to follow orders to surrender their vessels and crews—or if they have their own plans, either missions meant to be executed at war's end, or perhaps instances of every man for himself—or, in this case, every vessel for itself. Of all these U-boats, however, we are particularly interested in two, U-234 and U-977."

"Excuse me, Mr. Dulles," Boltitz interrupted. "With regard to U-234, if memory serves, she's a Type XB *U-boot*, a minelayer pressed into service as a cargo carrier—long range, able to cover more than eighteen thousand nautical miles if running on the surface. And I know that U-977 is a Type VIIC."

Dulles grinned. "I take it you have a connection with submarines, Karl?"

Boltitz nodded. "Peter and I. We know Kapitänleutnant Wilhelm von Dattenberg well. He was master of U-405, also a VIIC."

"The last information I have," Dulles said, "is that von Dattenberg still is her captain. How do you two know him?"

Von Wachtstein offered: "Karl and I were together in school at Philipps University in Marburg an der Lahn."

"And," Boltitz added, "I served five patrols under von Dattenberg."

"I wasn't aware that you had been a submarine officer, Karl," Dulles said.

"I went from *U-boots* to Admiral Canaris's staff. I thought at the time that my father was responsible. I now believe Willi von Dattenberg was. I found out that he was—he and his father were—close to Canaris. But if that's the case, how did Willi escape the SS after the failure at Wolfsschanze?"

"Karl," Dulles said, his tone almost that of a kindly schoolmaster, "the SS isn't—*wasn't*—nearly as infallible as they would have people believe."

"I've had that thought, too, sir," Boltitz said. "It's what permits me to think that the possibility my father may have escaped their net isn't for certain pissing into the wind."

"We all devoutly pray the same, and that you're standing at the rail with your back to the wind," Dulles said.

"I think your submarine experience may prove to be quite valuable. It might well be something Colonel Frade's defense counsel can use when he is court-martialed for breaking you out of Fort Hunt."

This produced a round of chuckles and laughter.

"All right," Dulles went on, "I was about to say, 'Talking about submarines, starting at the beginning,' but I just realized I don't know where the beginning is. So, starting with what we do know: We know with some certainty that when Grand Admiral Dönitz issued the cease hostilities order on May fourth, sixty-three U-boats were at sea. Five of them complied with their orders to hoist a black flag and proceed to an enemy port to surrender, or to a neutral port to be interned.

"We have unreliable information that forty-one of them have been scuttled by their crews, possibly to prevent the capture of whatever may be onboard in something called Operation Deadlight. We don't know how many were actually sunk, and we have no boat identification.

"Assuming these subs were either surrendered and/or sunk, that means forty-six from sixty-three leaves us seventeen U-boats unaccounted for.

"These could be part of another intel report—one of somewhat dubious reliability—that says a total of *twenty* submarines sailed from ports in Norway, primarily Bergen, *for Argentina*, between May first and May sixth."

"That many?" Frade said. "And we know nothing about them?"

Dulles shook his head. "Not really. We have no identification of which boats are supposed to have done this. And if true, that's quite a sizable operation.

"But what we *do* know with some certainty is that U-234 sailed from Narvik on April sixteenth, two weeks before these twenty are supposed to have headed for Argentina. The mission of U-234 was a special one"—he glanced at Karl—"and I think it may explain the presence of Vizeadmiral Boltitz in Norway."

"Mr. Dulles, can you elaborate on that?" Karl said.

"We suspect your father may have gone there to take control of the U-boat—and particularly its cargo—to keep her from sailing after the bomb took out Hitler."

"What the hell is aboard that sub?" Frade said.

"According to our information, U-234 was bound for Japan with a varied and very interesting cargo, some of which was either not listed on the manifest at all or listed under a false description. That is to say, in addition to a ton of mail—which, of course, almost certainly includes cash and diamonds—we're told that U-234 took aboard five hundred sixty kilograms of uranium oxide. And passengers included both Nazi and Japanese officers, as well as certain scientists, two of whom the OSS was actively pursuing prior to the German surrender."

"What's that about?" Ashton asked. "That uranium?"

Dulles met Frade's eyes for a moment before replying, "German scientists have been working on what might be called 'an explosives amplifier.' I don't know much more than that about it . . ."

The hell you don't! Frade thought.

You told me that uranium is what's in the atom bomb.

". . . except that we really don't want the Japanese to get their hands on it. What I do know is that we can't permit U-234 to get to Japan. And General Smith and I are agreed that it can't get there."

"General Smith?" Ashton asked.

"General Walter Bedell Smith, Eisenhower's chief of staff," Dulles clarified, and then saw something on Ashton's face. "Why did you just nod understandingly, Ashton? Who else did you think I might be talking about?"

Ashton looked mildly uncomfortable, glanced at Frade, then shrugged. "Actually, until just now, I was wondering why the OSS deputy director for European operations had come to this backwater of the war. *'He must certainly have more important things on his plate right now.'*"

"And now you think you understand?" Dulles said.

"At first, I thought your purpose, sir, forgive the vulgarism, was to cover Eisenhower's ass vis-à-vis the Gehlen operation. He's privy to it, isn't he?"

"Is that what you understood?" Dulles asked softly, ignoring the question. "That was your analysis?"

"Yes, sir. That is, until you mentioned that half ton of uranium oxide and then General Smith. I would guess that General Smith is one of the very few officers privy to the secret of the atomic bomb. That's really why we have to take out U-234, isn't it?"

Dulles glanced at Cletus Frade, then said, "Major Ashton, tell me what you know about—what did you say?—an 'atomic' bomb."

"I know the Germans were trying to build one, and I know that we are."

"And how did you come into this information, Major Ashton?" Dulles asked softly.

Dulles locked eyes momentarily with Frade again.

Frade shook his head to deny responsibility.

"Clete didn't tell me, sir," Ashton said.

"Clete didn't even come close to it," Technical Sergeant Jerry O'Sullivan offered. "All he told any of us was to keep our eyes and ears open to any mention of uranium, and to tell him immediately if we heard anything at all."

"And, except for this one instance with Niedermeyer, we didn't hear anything," Ashton said.

"Niedermeyer?" Dulles said.

"Oberstleutnant Otto Niedermeyer—the first of two of Oberstleutnant Gehlen's officers to arrive in Argentina—is the source of my information, sir."

Ashton looked from Dulles to Frade, then back to Dulles, and went on: "Clete sent Jerry and me to San Martín de los Andes to see what, if anything, we might get Niedermeyer to tell us. Cutting to the chase, after we'd had a couple of drinks—more than a couple; *in vino veritas*, so to speak—I asked him why he thought you, sir, had trusted Colonel Gehlen. He replied, words to this effect, because Gehlen had given you the names of the Russian spies operating in the Manhattan Project, which he told me was the code name for our attempt to build an atomic bomb."

"And once in possession of this information, what did you do with it?" Dulles asked evenly.

"I took it to Clete."

"And?"

"Clete told me I was not to mention it to anyone, and then he sent me back to San Martín de los Andes to tell Niedermeyer that if Clete ever heard Niedermeyer had told this story—or anything at all about the Manhattan Project—to anyone else, Clete personally would shoot him."

Dulles locked eyes with Frade again. Frade's face showed that he was pleased with Ashton's report of his "atomic bomb" behavior.

Dulles shrugged, shook his head, and exhaled audibly.

He then said: "Another masterful double cliché has suddenly popped into my brain: As no secret is safe if more than one person knows it, I guess we have to accept that the cow has escaped through the open door of the barn and there is no point in trying to get it back in.

"The truth is that Argentina is no longer a backwater of this war. As I started to say a moment ago, General Smith—and, yes, he is privy to the Manhattan Project—and I are agreed that we simply cannot permit U-234 to reach Japan. There are other reasons for me being here—despite other important things on my plate—but based on what credible information we have, sinking or, in an ideal world, capturing U-234 is perhaps the most important reason of all.

"And the reason Argentina is no longer a backwater is because General Smith and I agree again that U-234 cannot reach Japan without refueling at least once and that any refueling will have an Argentine connection.

"Naval experts at Eisenhower's headquarters have suggested a scenario involving those twenty submarines that are alleged to have sailed for Argentina from Norway during the period from May first to May sixth.

"This scenario proposes that the subs are tankers. Manned by as few people as possible, they would rendezvous with U-234 at either a planned location or one determined by radio contact with her. The fuel would be transferred, the crew of the tanker submarine would transfer to U-234, and then the tanker submarine would be scuttled."

Dulles looked at Boltitz.

"Karl, your opinion of this?"

Boltitz looked at Dulles, nodded, and after a moment's thought said: "I'm not saying it couldn't be done. But I can see a number of problems with it. As you would expect, refueling a submarine at sea is not anywhere near the same thing as an automobile pulling up to a service station. There would have to be large-capacity pumps and a substantial quantity of hose aboard either U-234—which, considering how much cargo she is carrying, seems unlikely—or on each of the tanker submarines. Are that many pumps available, that many hoses, in Norway? I rather think not.

"Further, transfer at sea between submarines is hazardous. There would be considerable risk that U-234 would be damaged in the process—by collision or fire or explosion.

"U-234 does have aboard enough fuel to bring her from Norway to Argentina—a distance of some seven thousand nautical miles—presuming she cruised at best speed to conserve fuel, which means quite slowly.

"That problem, the great distance between Europe and here, is what made the replenishment ship program necessary. And, as we well know, replenishment ships are no longer available, thanks to parties who shall remain nameless."

Those members of Team Turtle who did not grin either grunted or made some other sound of acknowledgment.

Boltitz continued: "A scenario that occurs to me as more feasible is that U-234 may be slowly making her way here at best speed for fuel efficiency. Meanwhile, the tanker submarines are making their way here at a higher rate of speed. They might be traveling in pairs, but more likely alone, to lower the chance of loss in case they were detected.

"In either event, either sailing together or rendezvousing at some prearranged point, one of them would transfer its fuel to a second, and then be scuttled, with her crew moving to the other.

"This could be repeated with other pairs of submarines, with the ultimate result being that, say, two hundred miles off the Argentine coast, there would be four—possibly more—submarines with full tanks, ready to fill the tanks of U-234. After doing so, they again would scuttle whatever empty vessels and the remainders would accompany U-234 to Japan."

"That does make sense," Frade thought out loud.

After a moment, Dulles said: "All right, then. Let's put this line of thought on the back burner for the moment and discuss U-977. Most of what we have heard about her sounds like the product of fevered imaginations. About the only thing we know with absolute certainty—as Karl has confirmed—is that she is a Type VIIC—"

"Which is the same *U-boot* type as U-405," Karl Boltitz offered.

Dulles motioned for him to continue.

"She's sixty-seven meters in length," Boltitz then said. He paused. "My apology. That's two hundred and twenty *feet*. She draws fifteen feet. She carries a crew of approximately fifty, and is armed with fifteen torpedoes—four tubes forward, one aft—and a small 8.8cm deck gun. Her surface range, at twelve miles per hour, is more than eight thousand miles. *Untersee*—submerged, if you will—she can run only eighty miles. And to avoid detection, she would certainly run most of the distance submerged to *schnorchel* depth—only surfacing for a couple hours a night—meaning it could possibly take U-977 months to reach here. The snort is not strong, and thus the captain must limit her speed to six knots."

"Schnorchel?" Frade repeated.

Boltitz nodded. "'Snort' for short. You would call it a snorkel. It is a tall tube that rises from the conning tower to above the surface so that the *U-boot* can take in fresh air while running submerged."

"Thank you, Karl," Dulles then said. "Okay, our information is that U-977, under command of twenty-four-year-old Oberleutnant Heinz Schäffer, left Kristiansand, Norway, to begin a routine patrol on May second. She had arrived there on April thirtieth."

"That sounds suspicious," Boltitz said. "It takes more than two or three days to prepare a boat for patrol. Could it be that she was made ready for sea elsewhere and went to Kristiansand to pick up something?"

Dulles looked at Boltitz, then turned to Clete Frade.

"Colonel Frade, this is where the outrageous part begins. I'm afraid that I've already gone on long enough, to the point where everyone not only needs a libation but, I believe, deserves one—"

"I thought you'd never ask," Frade said.

"—but just *one*," Dulles continued, "until after we have finished with the business. Which I promise won't take long."

[TWO]

All the men in the *quincho* stood at their wood-plank tables, all holding their drinks aloft in their right hand.

"In the words of Aristotle, 'We make war that we may live in peace,'" Allen W. Dulles solemnly intoned. "To victory in Europe!"

The room filled with the parroting of "To victory in Europe!" and the chanting of "Hear, hear!"

After everyone had taken a sip of their drinks, Dulles motioned for them to take their seats.

"Drink up, gentlemen," Dulles then said. "The alcohol should help make what I'm about to share with you seem at least a little plausible."

"Great!" Oscar Schultz said. "Now we get the outrageous stuff."

"I'll drink to that," Tony Pelosi put in, and tapped his glass to el Jefe's.

Dulles then glanced at Karl Boltitz and said: "I take it that everyone recalls what our U-boat expert said about the short period of time that U-977 spent in dock at Kristiansand before heading to sea?"

"That she was made ready for sea elsewhere," Pelosi offered, "and went to Norway to pick up something?"

"Yes, except not 'something.' Rather, 'someone.'"

"Who?" Clete Frade said.

"What fevered imaginations have come up with is that U-977 went to Norway to pick up Adolf Hitler and his new wife, to transport them to safety in Argentina."

"That's ridiculous!" Jerry O'Sullivan blurted. "Everybody knows they committed suicide. Hitler married her, then shot her, then bit on a cyanide capsule."

"On May one," Dulles said, "Grand Admiral Dönitz went on the radio and announced that Hitler had met a hero's death on the battlefield."

"Oh, bullshit," Tony Pelosi said.

"That suggests," Dulles went on, "that Hitler died—or that Admiral Dönitz wants us to believe he died—on April thirtieth, or even earlier. We've heard he took his life on April twenty-eighth. Timewise, there would have been plenty of time for him to fly to Norway and get aboard U-977."

"Presuming he wasn't dead," O'Sullivan said with some sarcasm.

"According to Zhukov," Dulles said, "he isn't dead, and neither are Frau Hitler, Martin Bormann, Herr Doktor Goebbels, and a half dozen other important Nazis. Suggesting, if true of course, that Operation Phoenix was indeed known all the way to the top."

"According to who did you say, Mr. Dulles?" Clete asked.

"Marshal of the Soviet Union Georgi Konstantinovich Zhukov," Dulles said. "The victor of the Battle for Berlin. Eisenhower's counterpart."

"He actually said that?" Peter von Wachtstein asked.

"His interpreter told Ike he said just that, and that most of them, including Mr. and Mrs. Hitler, are on their way to a safe haven in Argentina. If nothing else, this bit of what my gut tells me is disinformation is a classic example of why our having Gehlen's intel about the Russians is absolutely critical. They are not to be trusted."

"Jesus!" Frade said. "It's incredible. Ike can't believe him, can he?"

"Ike thinks it has something to do with General I. D. White," Dulles said.

"Who's he?"

"The commanding general of our Second Armored Division. General White not only moved into what will be the American sector of Berlin without asking Ike, but he also ignored Zhukov's order that he was required to wait for permission. The rape of Berlin—which has been ghastly—bothered General White. He ordered the Russians out of the American sector. When they refused to go, he issued a proclamation stating that anyone but Americans found with a weapon in the American sector would be presumed to be Germans refusing to obey the surrender order and would be shot on sight. As would rapists, armed or not."

"Good man!" Ashton said, raising his glass in salute. "Here's to General White." He took a sip, then looked at Frade and added, "Colonel, no disrespect intended, but can I go work for him when we're disbanded?"

That earned him a couple chuckles and at least one grunt of agreement.

Dulles went on: "White could have started World War Three right there, but after a half dozen of Zhukov's troops had in fact been shot, the Russian caved in and ordered all his troops out of the American zone. Eisenhower believes, not with a great deal of conviction, that what Zhukov is up to, in case there is anything to the inevitable rumors that Hitler did not commit suicide and escaped Berlin, is to blame it on General White. In any event, Eisenhower has ordered the OSS to look into it as a high priority, and David Bruce is doing just that."

"The OSS guy in London?" Frade asked.

Dulles nodded.

"I'm surprised Bruce didn't turn that wild-goose chase over to you," Frade said.

"It was the other way around, Clete. Unfortunately for poor David, he takes his orders from me."

"I'm afraid to open this can of worms," Schultz said, "but how the hell was Hitler supposed to get out of Berlin? It was surrounded, right?"

"Yes, it was, Jefe," Dulles said. "But we've heard that Hanna Reitsch flew into Berlin on April twenty-eighth, just before Hitler's suicide, and then supposedly flew out with the newly appointed chief of the Luftwaffe, General Robert Ritter von Greim, a day or two later."

"I thought," Ashton said, "that we had total air superiority over Berlin. How did this Hanna Reitsch manage to do that?"

"The story is that a Fieseler Storch landed on the Unter den Linden," Dulles said. "Is that possible? Who do I ask, von Wachtstein or Frade, if that's possible?"

"It's possible," von Wachtstein immediately replied. "No problem whatsoever."

"What's the Unter den Linden?" Clete asked.

"A wide boulevard near the Reichschancellery," von Wachtstein explained. "It used to be lined with linden trees. You could get in and out of there in a Storch without much trouble at all."

"Presuming," Dulles said, "that there were not perhaps fifty or so Russian fighters in the area supporting the Red Army who would welcome the opportunity to shoot down such an airplane."

"Who's this Hanna Reitsch flying the Storch?" Frade said. "How good a pilot is he?"

Von Wachtstein laughed.

He then explained: "Hanna Reitsch is a *woman*, Clete. And *she's* a much better pilot than you or me."

Clete raised his eyebrows and nodded. After a moment's thought, he offered: "And Russian fighters wouldn't be a problem for the Storch if the pilot knew what she was doing."

"What?" Ashton challenged. "You think a fighter couldn't shoot down that little observation plane?"

"Once upon a time, Bacardi," Clete said by way of explanation, "on an island far, far away called Guadalcanal, a Marine pilot was flying around over the jungle in a Piper Cub that he 'borrowed' from the Army. He was directing artillery fire and suddenly became aware of a string of tracers coming his way. He looked over his shoulder and saw that he had two Zeros on his tail. Not knowing what to do, he made a sharp right turn and went down on the deck. The Zeros made a three-sixty and had another go at him.

"The Marine went even lower in his humble Cub, then made another right turn. The first Zero flew over him, and the second tried to make a right turn and flew into the trees. The first Zero made two more passes at the little Piper Cub and then gave up. I tried to claim the Zero that went into the trees as a kill, but they said no dice. For one thing, you can't claim a kill if the enemy plane went down because of pilot error, and for another, you can't claim a kill if you are flying a Piper Cub stolen from the U.S. Army.

"So, to answer your question, Major Ashton, a female who is a better pilot than Hansel or me, flying a Storch—which stalls at about thirty miles an hour—would have no trouble avoiding Russian fighters."

Dulles said, "You're agreed that it's possible that Hanna Reitsch could have flown Hitler—for that matter, any two people—from Berlin to Norway. Is that so, Peter?"

"Yes, sir. It's possible," von Wachtstein replied. "I submit, however, that the real question is: Is it plausible?"

Dulles looked at him a long moment. He said: "We have to proceed on that possibility. The mission obviously is to locate U-977. How nice it would be if we could capture her. And even if the outrageous tale proves to be exactly that—the Hitlers and others are not aboard—then she most certainly will be carrying other valuables."

"How the hell can we possibly do that?" Frade said. "Definitely not with SAA's aircraft or certainly not Peter's Storch. We'd need heavily armed military assets in order to actually capture a sub—and certainly to sink one, if it came to that."

"Right, Cletus. What's been discussed is that there are enormous numbers of long-range aircraft—bombers, B-17s and B-24s—now available in Europe to search for submarines. But I don't think that's going to be of much help except in the waters between Norway and the English Channel. Once the submarines get into the Atlantic—as some of them probably have already—they will head southwest for the Atlantic and soon be beyond the range of any aircraft looking for them.

"Similarly, although a bomb group has already been ordered to Sidi Slimane in Morocco, I don't think it will be of much use. As soon as they can get there, the submarines will be deep into the Atlantic, beyond the reach of aircraft.

"At some point west of Europe and North Africa, Eisenhower's—SHAEF's—authority ends, and the military command is that of the Navy. They will be ordered—as soon as I can get to Washington and convince Admiral Leahy of the necessity to do so—to begin searching for these submarines. I don't think they'll have much luck, but the effort will have to be made.

"Insofar as sending B-17s and/or B-24s here to Argentina or Brazil, that has been considered and decided against. Brazil has asked for such aircraft in the past and, in the probably justified belief that they would use them against Argentina, their request was denied. And obviously we couldn't send them to Argentina and not to Brazil.

"So, what happens now is that when I get to Washington, I am going to try to get you authority to call upon the B-24s we presently have at Canoas should you need them to deal with any enemy submarines you find, either offshore or within Argentine waters.

"That brings us back to that basic premise. The best—indeed almost the only—hope we have to either sink or capture the submarines in question is Team Turtle. And in doing so, you will not only be up against the Nazis involved in Operation Phoenix but against substantial numbers of our countrymen, in and out of uniform."

Dulles stopped, looked thoughtful as he sipped his drink, then went on:

"Considering how everyone now has the OSS in their crosshairs, I was about to make an attempt at giving you a stirring pep talk about overcoming great obstacles. Then I remembered the best pep talk I ever heard. How many of you have seen the movie *Knute Rockne, All American*? With Pat O'Brien playing Rockne?"

I don't believe this! Clete thought.

Our distinguished OSS deputy director is going to inspire us by quoting from a movie?

Is that the booze talking?

Everybody indicated that they had seen the motion picture, and Clete now saw some of the men showing curious expressions.

"All right then," Dulles went on. "There was a scene in that motion picture where Coach Rockne went to the hospital bed of one of his players who was terminally ill. At the moment, I can't think of his name, either in the film or in real life—"

"Gipp," Master Sergeant William Ferris furnished. "They called him the Gipper."

"Right," Dulles said.

"The actor's name was Richard Reagan," Frade said. "He's now the only aerial gunner in the Air Force who's a captain."

"His name is *Ronald* Reagan," Ashton quickly corrected him. "And he's a *first lieutenant* in the *Signal Corps* making those venereal disease movies they make everybody watch."

"You know," Schultz chimed in, "you pick up some dame in a bar, diddle her, and two weeks later your dick drops off."

That produced laughter.

"*Clark Gable* is the only commissioned officer aerial gunner in the Air Forces," Ferris said. He then quoted Gable's most famous line: "'Frankly, my dear, I don't give a damn!'"

"You would if it was your dick about to drop off," Schultz said.

More laughter.

Clete saw the look on Dulles's face.

"Silence on deck!" Frade barked.

And when he had it, Clete said, "Please go on, Mr. Dulles."

"I don't think that would be a very good idea," Dulles said. "And it was my mistake to open the bar so soon."

Frade said, "Inasmuch, sir, as we obviously need a pep talk, I really wish you would. Please, sir."

After a long moment, Dulles shrugged.

"Very well," he said. "I think I should make the point that not all motion-picture actors in uniform find safe sinecures for themselves. Jimmy Stewart is also in the Air Forces. He has led his B-17 group on twenty-odd missions over Germany and was recently promoted colonel. Closer to home, Captain Sterling Hayden, a Marine, has been infiltrating fellow members of the OSS into—and out of—Albania for some time."

He paused to let that sink in.

Ashton then popped to his feet, stood at attention, and said, "Sir, I started that unfortunate silliness. I hope you will accept my apology."

"We are all under something of a strain, Major," Dulles said after a moment. "No apology is necessary. Please take your seat."

Ashton did, and after a moment, Dulles said: "Now, where was I? Oh, yes, in the film Rockne goes to the bed of the terminally ill football player known as the Gipper.

As difficult as this will obviously be, try to think of me as the character, the Gipper, that Lieutenant Ronald Reagan played.

"This is what he said to Coach Rockne: 'Rock, sometime when the team is up against it and the breaks are beating the boys, tell them to go out there with all they've got and win one for the Gipper. I don't know where I'll be then, but I'll know about it and I'll be happy.'"

There was silence in the *quincho.*

Frade thought: *The silence of embarrassment.*

"The point I had hoped to make," Dulles said, "and obviously failed so completely to make, was that I know that Team Turtle is really up against it. But I haven't seen a suggestion that any of you are thinking of throwing in the towel. And I wanted you to know how much I appreciate that. I'm proud to be associated with all of you."

There was a moment's silence.

Then O'Sullivan stood up.

"And I want you to know, Mr. Dulles, that this Irishman will be proud for the rest of his life that he was privileged to work for you."

Ashton stood and said, "Hear, hear!" and began to applaud.

Five seconds later, everyone was on his feet and applauding.

I'll be goddamned, Clete thought. *Mister deputy director of the OSS looks like he's going to blubber.*

Dulles finally found his voice.

"Colonel Frade," he said, "I would suggest that these

proceedings are at the point where you may reopen the bar."

That caused the applause to increase in volume.

"Thank you, all," Dulles said, then drained his glass. "Now, let us really celebrate victory in Europe."

[THREE]
Aeropuerto Coronel Jorge G. Frade
Morón, Buenos Aires Province, Argentina
0905 13 May 1945

As the Red Lodestar turned onto a taxiway, Clete Frade saw that two of the Constellations he'd arranged to have brought down from Los Angeles were already painted in the South American Airways color scheme. Another was in a hangar being painted, and the other two were parked waiting for their new paint jobs.

And then he saw two familiar men walk out onto the tarmac from the passenger terminal. One was his uncle, Humberto Duarte, managing director of the Anglo-Argentine Bank and director for finance of South American Airways. The other was the vice president, secretary of War, and secretary of Labor and Welfare of the Argentine Republic, el Coronel Juan Domingo Perón.

Shit! Tío Juan!

What's that sonofabitch want?

"Do you see what I see?" Peter von Wachtstein asked from the copilot's seat as he turned the aircraft from the taxiway to the tarmac.

"Don't let anyone off the plane until I say so," Clete said, and quickly unstrapped his seat belt and shoulder harness. He was at the fuselage door in the passenger compartment before von Wachtstein had stopped the plane in front of the passenger terminal.

The original idea the previous day—that after the meeting and lunch Clete would fly Dulles in one of the estancia's Piper Cubs to Jorge Frade, where he would board South American Airways Flight 717 to Canoas—had failed by increments. First, Clete flying anybody anywhere was obviously out of the question once the bar had been reopened.

The alternative plan—that a South American Airways pilot would fly an Estancia San Pedro y San Pablo Piper Cub conveniently at Jorge Frade to the estancia, pick up Dulles, and fly him back to Jorge Frade so he could catch a plane to start flying to Washington—went out the window during lunch.

There had still been a great deal to talk about with Dulles:

How was the current status of Boltitz and von Wachtstein going to be affected by the German surrender?

What was to be done with the Germans who had been brought to Argentina in the deal with Oberstleutnant Gehlen? They were divided into three groups—the Good Gehlen Germans, Good Germans, and Nazi Germans—and one answer to that question obviously would not fit all.

There had been no satisfactory answers to these questions. Dulles said that he was either going to have to look into the problem, or they would just have to wait and see what developed, or Clete would just have to use his best judgment.

About three in the afternoon, Clete had realized the discussions were getting nowhere.

"All we're doing here is kicking a dead horse," Frade announced. "Or, to quote the distinguished Kapitän zur See Boltitz, 'All we're doing here is pissing into the wind.' I suggest we knock it off. In the morning, on the way to Mendoza, we'll drop Mr. Dulles off at Jorge Frade in time for him to catch SAA's oh-nine-thirty Flight 701, nonstop Lodestar service to Rio de Janeiro."

At that point, Dulles had raised his hand, and when he had everyone's attention said, "One final thought, Colonel Frade. I am aware that circumstances beyond my control are leaving everyone here—and especially you, as commanding officer—out on a limb. The only thing I can do—and do herewith—is order that any orders you consider it necessary to give will be presumed to be based on my authority.

"In other words, Clete, do what you think should be done. I'll take responsibility for any action of yours."

Frade approached Perón and Duarte on the tarmac at Aeropuerto Jorge Frade. Argentine social protocol dictated that Frade wrap his arms around his uncle and make kissing noises with their faces in close proximity. That was fine with Clete; he really liked his uncle.

But the same protocol applied to his godfather, which wasn't quite the same thing. And Clete had hated every second of their greeting.

That faint tinkling sound is drops of ice falling to the tarmac after a less-than-warm embrace with my Tío Juan.

"When I called San Pedro y San Pablo," Humberto Duarte then announced, "Dorotea said you were on your way here. So Juan Domingo and I came to intercept you."

"So I see. What's up, Humberto?"

Perón cleared his throat, then answered for him: "President Farrell is aware that I am a director of SAA, Cletus, and he called me to see how soon a special flight could be set up to go to Germany. I naturally called Humberto."

"The President himself did, did he?" Clete said in an unimpressed tone that Perón could not mistake.

Clete felt all of Argentina's recent presidents—Rawson, Ramírez, Farrell—were flawed, but especially Edelmiro Julián Farrell.

Farrell had overthrown Ramírez in a bloodless coup d'état, masterminded—Clete was sure, but could not prove—by el Coronel Juan Domingo Perón. Because one of General Farrell's first acts as president of the Provisional Government of Argentina was to name Labor Secretary Perón to the additional posts of vice president and secretary of War.

Farrell had also summoned Clete to the Pink House, where he told him that "as a dear friend of your father from our days at the military academy" he had been pleased that Clete had been wise enough not to accept a position in General Ramírez's government.

Farrell added that he had deeply regretted having to depose Ramírez.

"But P.P. simply seems unable to understand that Germany and Italy are fighting our fight—Christian civilization against the Antichrist, the Russian Communists."

That shortsightedness had confirmed to Clete that Farrell was not to be trusted. And his opinion hadn't changed when a year later, almost to the day, President Farrell conveniently announced that the Argentine Republic was now in a state of war with Germany, Italy, and Japan.

It all caused Clete to wonder: *What would've happened had my father indeed become president? Would he have shown similar deficiencies?*

"Yes, Cletus," el Coronel Juan Domingo Perón now replied arrogantly, "el Presidente himself."

Clete said: "Exactly what kind of a special flight?"

Clete watched Perón mentally consider his answer.

Just what are you really up to now, you sonofabitch?

"In military terms," Perón then replied officiously, "a reinforcement and replacement flight. Our diplomatic personnel in Germany not only have been under an enormous strain lately, but may not even have enough to eat or adequate shelter."

"You want me to fly some diplomats to Germany?" Frade asked incredulously.

"President Farrell and Foreign Minister César Ameghino do. You would take some diplomatic personnel there, to replace the diplomats whom you would then bring home. Plus some supplies—food and medical supplies, that sort of thing—to support our embassy."

"I'm sure the Americans and the British would be

happy to see that food and medical attention would be made available to the embassy personnel," Clete said. "And, for that matter, see that they got safely to Sweden or Switzerland. Now that I think of it, that's probably already been done."

"I'm sure that Minister Ameghino has considered his options," Perón said, "and concluded that sending a plane is the thing to do."

Frade looked between Perón and Duarte, and thought:

Whatever this is all about, it has nothing to do with rushing aid to a clutch of abused diplomats.

Damn it! What is *this sonofabitch up to?*

My God! Has he got Hitler stashed somewhere? And he wants me to go over there so the sonofabitch can fly to sanctuary here in comfort?

That's more absurd than Hitler on a U-boat!

I didn't believe that bullshit—and neither did Dulles—about Hitler and his girlfriend taking off from some tree-lined street in Berlin and flying to Norway in a Storch to board the sub.

Perón looked toward the new Constellations, then went off on a tangent: "I presume those are the new aircraft you acquired?"

"That's them, five Connies," Clete said.

"I wasn't aware until this morning, when we got here, that we were even contemplating such an investment," Perón said.

"The executive board approved the purchase, Juan Domingo," Duarte offered. "I'm sure that you were sent a copy of the minutes of that meeting."

"Presumably, these five new aircraft would solve the problem of not having enough aircraft?" Perón said.

Frade shook his head and said, "Having aircraft available is not the problem. What is a problem is that I can't fly into Germany without clearance. You do know what's going on over there, right?"

"You think it's necessary for you to personally fly the relief mission?" Perón asked.

You don't like that? Fuck you, Tío Juan!

"If an SAA aircraft is going to be flown into Germany, I'll fly it."

"You have a reason?" Perón pursued.

"Let's say I want to protect my investment in SAA," Clete said.

"Perhaps, with your contacts, your information about conditions in Germany is better than mine," Perón said.

Does he know Dulles is here?

"Germany will be—probably already has been—divided into four zones," Clete said. "Russian, English, French, and American. Berlin itself will be sort of an island in the Russian zone, and also divided into four zones. We would need permission from either Eisenhower's headquarters or the French, whoever is controlling the airspace, to fly across France into Germany—as a matter of fact, it would probably be better to have permission from the Spaniards to fly across Spain into France—and I don't know if we can get it."

"Request has been made for whatever permissions are required from the appropriate ambassadors in Madrid and Paris," Perón said regally. "I cannot imagine their denying it."

Frade held his gaze a long moment, then said: "You get me the clearances and I'll do it. I'll be back from Mendoza tomorrow. Say, anytime twenty-four hours after that."

"Why are you going to Mendoza?" Perón asked.

That's none of your fucking business, Tío Juan!

"I have business there, Tío Juan."

"You know, Cletus, if I didn't know better, I'd say Major von Wachtstein was sitting in your airplane. That fellow looks just like him."

No use trying to deny it.

"That's Peter," Clete said. "Now that he's been released from his POW camp, he needed a job. SAA hired him."

"That was unusually quick for him to be released from POW status, wasn't it?"

"What I heard was that the Americans released him as soon as the surrender was signed. Sort of a reward for his contributions to the war effort."

"Please give him my regards," Perón said.

"I'll do that."

"I'll tell President Farrell and Foreign Minister Ameghino that you see no problems with the relief flight."

"None but getting the clearances," Clete said.

"Thank you," Perón said.

After another icy embrace, Perón marched into the passenger terminal.

Humberto then embraced Clete and looked into his eyes.

"Whatever you're thinking of saying, don't," Clete said.

"You do have a very strange relationship with your godfather, don't you?"

Clete laughed, then punched Duarte fondly on the arm.

As he turned to walk toward the Red Lodestar, he saw Dulles, Boltitz, and von Wachtstein at the foot of the stairs and starting toward him.

Damn it, Hansel! So much for keeping everyone on the aircraft.

[FOUR]

"Trouble?" Allen Dulles asked Clete when they'd stopped near the nose of the Red Lodestar.

"I don't know exactly. It's damn sure out of left field. The president and the foreign minister—with how much input from Perón, I don't know—want me to take a Connie into Germany, presumably Berlin, ostensibly to take a replacement diplomatic crew in, and bring the diplomats that are there back here. And to take supplies of food, medicine, et cetera, with me."

"Interesting," Dulles said.

"I thought so," Clete said. "And it's just what we don't need—another diversion."

"So, what are you going to do?"

Frade shrugged. "I guess I'm going to take a Connie into Germany."

"Is that wise?"

"It looks like I don't have much of a choice," Clete said. And then he had another thought, and said it aloud: "But, yeah, I do think it's wise. Maybe I can meet Colonel Gehlen, since we're agreed that getting him and his people out still is our priority."

"I'd like to go with Clete," von Wachtstein suddenly said.

Dulles and Frade looked at him in surprise.

Peter explained: "I'd like to see that my father's body, presuming I can find it, is taken to Schloss Wachtstein and buried with my mother and my brothers."

Dulles said: "Peter, I appreciate your feelings, but—"

"I'd like to go, too," Boltitz put in. "I want to see if I can find out what happened to my father."

"And I can appreciate that, too," Dulles said, "but—"

"Perhaps I also could learn something about the *U-boots* we're interested in," Boltitz argued.

"I'm not sure that any of you going over there is a good idea," Dulles announced. "And there is a simple solution to the problem. When I get to Washington, I'll call David Bruce—he's with Eisenhower, wherever that might be—and tell him to tell Ike to have SHAEF deny SAA permission to enter occupied Germany."

Frade grunted, then looked past Dulles and saw Enrico Rodríguez coming toward them, and the women milling on the tarmac near the foot of the stairs.

"What did that sound mean?" Dulles challenged.

Frade turned to look at him and said, "That policy didn't last long, did it?"

"Excuse me?"

"I seem to recall you telling me that since I was out on a limb, I was free to do what I think should be done."

Dulles studied Frade for a long moment.

"Touché, Colonel Frade," he said finally. "I also recall saying I would take responsibility for any action of yours. So, what I'll do when I get to Washington is call David Bruce, tell him I'm sending you over there, and tell him to do what he can for you."

"Thank you," Frade said.

"One final comment, Clete," Dulles said. "Please consider that when General Donovan, as he so often does, refers to you as 'our loose cannon,' he's unfortunately often right."

"Ouch!" Frade said.

Dulles put out his hand. Clete took it, then ordered, "Enrico, see that Mr. Dulles gets on his plane."

"*Sí*, Don Cletus."

Dulles was barely out of earshot when von Wachtstein asked, "Was that a polite way of making it easier for you to tell Karl and me that we cannot go to Germany?"

"Probably, Hansel," Clete said, "but the problem for you and Karl is not Dulles. It's those two." He nodded toward the back of the Lodestar, where Alicia von Wachtstein was sitting with Miss Beth Howell. "As far as I'm concerned, you guys need their permission, not Dulles's."

Clete knew that neither woman was going to be remotely thrilled to hear that the men they loved—and had just been reunited with—were about to leave them for war-torn Germany.

"I would suggest, Karl," Clete said as they stood on the tarmac, "based on my long experience with a live-in woman, that you not broach the subject of you going to Germany with me until we're on our way back from Mendoza. Unless you really meant that vow of celibacy you took."

Von Wachtstein laughed.

Boltitz's face turned red.

"Clete," Karl said, "I have been meaning to discuss my relationship with Beth with you."

"Yeah, I'll bet you have, Karl. Confession is good for the soul!"

Von Wachtstein laughed again, this time louder.

"What are you three laughing about?" the baroness called.

"I don't think you really want to know, Alicia," Clete called back. "In case anybody needs to 'freshen up,' do it now. As soon as Dulles's plane takes off, we go wheels-up for Mendoza."

IV

[ONE]
Casa Montagna
Estancia Don Guillermo
Km 40.4, Provincial Route 60
Mendoza Province, Argentina
1550 14 May 1945

Casa Montagna had been built by Clete's Granduncle Guillermo after he returned from a tour of Tuscany and had had an out-of-character very good year at both the Hipódromo and the poker tables at the Jockey Club.

"In other words, damn the expense!"

Casa Montagna had been built on a natural plateau two thousand feet above the vineyards of the estancia. Carving a road up to it out of the granite of the foothills of the Andes had taken two years. The last—upper—kilometer of the road was so steep it had to be taken in a vehicle's lowest gear.

The plateau was perhaps three hundred meters wide and two hundred meters long. A low stone wall on three sides kept people and animals from falling off the mountain.

The main house was built of natural stone and stood three stories tall. The third floor had dormer windows, and the red tile roof extended over a verandah whose pillars were covered with roses. From the front of the house, there was an unobstructed view of the Andes Mountains. The rear of the house was against what anywhere else would be called "the mountain" but here was referred to as "the hill."

Enrico Rodríguez had told Clete that Clete's mother had loved Casa Montagna, and also that it had been her last home in Argentina. It was from Casa Montagna that his parents had left to catch the train in Mendoza for Buenos Aires, and from there the ship that took them to New Orleans, where she had died in childbirth.

El Coronel Frade had never set foot in Casa Montagna again.

Clete Frade led Peter and Alicia von Wachtstein, Karl Boltitz, Beth Howell, and Enrico Rodríguez into the bar.

They found—sitting around tables holding a collection of bottles of various intoxicants and plates of cheese and sausage—Captain Madison R. Sawyer III, Master Sergeant Siggie Stein, the Reverend Francisco Silva, S.J., Wilhelm Fischer, Otto Körtig, Ludwig Stoll, and el Subinspector General Pedro Nolasco. Pouring wine at the bar was the estancia's manager, el Señor Pablo Alvarez.

"I was under the impression that cocktail hour began at seventeen hundred," Cletus Frade announced sternly, hoping he sounded like an indignant lieutenant colonel who had just caught his subordinates at the sauce when they should have been about their duties.

Except for a few smiles and chuckles, he was ignored.

Sawyer, Stein, and Fischer quickly rose and, their hands extended, went to von Wachtstein and Boltitz. That civilized gesture quickly degenerated into hugs and embraces.

"I now believe it," Körtig said. "I never thought you'd get away with getting them. Clete, you are truly an amazing man."

"Please tell that to my wife, Otto," Clete said.

Frade sat down beside Körtig, offered his hand to Pedro Nolasco and then to Stoll.

"If you would be so good, Ludwig," he said. "Hand me that bottle of Cabernet Sauvignon before Pedro gets into it again."

When the hugs and back-patting were over—as if suddenly remembering their manners—Boltitz and von Wachtstein, with their women following them, came to the table where Clete sat with Körtig.

Körtig and Stoll stood up.

"I know who you are, of course," Körtig said. "But not which is who."

Peter came to attention, clicked his heels, nodded, and said, "Peter von Wachtstein, Herr Oberstleutnant."

Pedro Nolasco's eyebrows rose.

Clete thought: *I wonder how long it's going to take to get Peter to get that Pavlovian reaction out of his system.*

Körtig put out his hand. "I was privileged to be a friend of both your father and Claus von Stauffenberg, von Wachtstein. I'm very glad to see you here." He paused and added, "Where we rarely come to attention and click our heels."

Otto, Clete thought, *you're reading my mind.*

"And where I am known as el Señor Körtig," Niedermeyer finished.

"That was stupid of me, wasn't it?" von Wachtstein asked after a moment's reflection.

After pausing long enough to make it clear that he agreed with von Wachtstein's assessment of his own behavior, Körtig then gestured at Stoll. "My deputy at Abwehr Ost, the former Hauptmann Ludwig Wertz, now known as el Señor Stoll." Körtig paused, then asked, "And by what name are you now known?"

God, Clete thought admiringly, *you're a good officer!*

"His own," Clete answered for him. "When he and Boltitz got off the plane from the United States, Father Silva's boss—the Black Pope's nuncio to Argentina, otherwise known as Father Welner—"

Subinspector General Nolasco laughed. He had told Clete the head of the Society of Jesus was known as "The Black Pope."

"—handed them *libretas de enrolamiento* in their own names, stating they'd immigrated here before the war," Clete finished.

"How do you do, Señor Körtig?" Boltitz asked.

"And I knew your father, too. I presume this charming young woman is la Señora Boltitz?"

"The *charming* young woman is the Baroness von Wachtstein," Clete said, then pointed. "*That* one is my sister, Beth, who has high hopes that Boltitz will eventually make an honest woman of her."

"I can't believe you said that!" Beth said. And then added, "You sonofabitch!"

Nolasco laughed again.

All the Germans—especially Boltitz—looked uncomfortable.

"She loves me unconditionally, as you may have just heard," Clete said. "Beth, see if you can say 'hello' nicely to the gentlemen."

When the handshaking was over, Frade announced: "Before we get down to serious drinking, I think we have to get into how the surrender in Europe is going to affect things here. There have been some interesting developments, some concerning U-boats that may or may not be headed here. Karl and Peter have already heard all this; there's no reason for them to hear it again. Enrico, why don't you give them a tour of the place and show them what's changed while they were in Fort Hunt? Give us two hours or so."

Frade exchanged glances with Boltitz.

That should be enough time for you and Beth to figure out how to be alone.

[TWO]
Casa Montagna
Estancia Don Guillermo
Mendoza Province, Argentina
1810 14 May 1945

It had taken all of the two hours that Frade had guessed it would, but the conclusion drawn by all was essentially that nothing, for the moment, was really changed by the unconditional surrender of the Thousand-Year Reich. Until they heard from Colonel Gehlen and learned what was going to happen to what they now called the "Gehlen organization," they would have to wait and see what happened next. And the U-boats were a wild card that they could do nothing about—even if they did exist—until more intel could be collected.

For now at Casa Montagna, the Gehlen Nazis would remain in their comfortable imprisonment. Father Silva would continue his efforts to see that the wives and their children who didn't wish to be eventually returned to Germany were absorbed into the society of Argentina. And Subinspector General Nolasco would continue to ensure that the Gehlen Nazis didn't try to vanish into Argentine society.

Clete found himself at the bar with a glass of Don Guillermo Cabernet Sauvignon in hand, wondering about the moral implications of his having arranged for Beth to finally jump into bed with Karl Boltitz. And wondering what was going to happen to them.

It's a given that they will get married, probably as soon as Cletus Marcus Howell can get down here from the States.

But then what?

Unlike Peter von Wachtstein, who had a marketable skill—he would go to work for SAA as a pilot—and had successfully moved to Argentina most of his family's portable assets, Karl Boltitz had neither marketable skills nor a nest egg. Karl was a naval intelligence officer, and not only were the vessels of the Kriegsmarine—what was left of them—almost certainly going to be scuttled, but the Kriegsmarine no longer would need an intelligence officer.

Clete knew that, while Boltitz didn't have a dime, money itself wasn't a problem. Beth was independently wealthy, although he didn't think her mother had told her just how wealthy.

The problem was Karl's honor. He was a proud man. It had never entered Clete's mind that Karl had considered Beth's finances when making his first pass at her—or, perhaps more correctly, when she, which seemed entirely likely, had made her first pass at him. But he was entirely capable of being able to refuse to enter a marriage in his penniless status. And even if Beth could get him to the altar, Karl would feel ashamed.

While Boltitz was a very good intelligence officer, the only places where he could use those skills now would be in something like the Gehlen organization or the OSS. But the OSS was going down the toilet, very possibly taking the Gehlen organization with it.

Especially if Secretary of the Treasury Morgenthau hears about the Gehlen organization.

Frade had just decided that about the only thing that could be done was for him to talk to Otto Körtig and see if he had any ideas when he became aware that Siggie Stein had joined him at the bar.

Stein came right to the point.

"Colonel, can I go to Germany with you?"

"Why the hell would you want to do that?" Frade said.

"I'll tell you, sir. But it doesn't make much sense, even to me."

"Give it a shot, Siggie."

"I started to think about Germany a couple of weeks ago, after I saw that picture of General Patton taking a leak in the Rhine."

And now you want to take a piss in the Rhine?

Well, why the hell not?

You're certainly entitled to a little revenge.

"And then Mother Superior told me a story about Nazis in Chile," Stein said.

"Go over that again, Siggie?"

"Truth being stranger than fiction, we've become pretty close. She comes up here a couple of nights a week and we kill a couple of bottles of wine."

"A couple of bottles of wine? In here?"

"Yeah, Colonel, a couple of bottles of wine. But not here in the bar; we go to the radio room. I moved in there . . ."

The radio room was a small apartment on the upper floor of the Big House.

Frade raised an eyebrow and said, "I didn't know that you moved out of the BOQ."

"I think the officers were glad when I did."

"Polo included?"

Frade sipped his wine and thought, *If he's been looking down his commissioned officer's nose at Stein, I'll ream him a new asshole.*

"No. Not Captain Sawyer. When I moved out of the BOQ, he even asked me if I had a problem. I told him no, that I moved out because I wanted to."

"Any Kraut officer in particular?"

"It's not what you're suggesting, Colonel. Nothing overt. They were just as uncomfortable as officers having me in there as I was as a sergeant being in the BOQ."

Stein saw the angry look on Frade's face.

"Let it go, Colonel, please," he said.

"You were telling me about Mother Superior's drinking problem," Frade said.

Stein laughed. "Her problem is that she thinks it sets a bad example for the nuns if they see her having a couple of glasses of wine. So she's been doing it alone in her room at the convent. Drinking alone is no fun."

"The officers didn't like drinking with you, either? Is that where you're going, Siggie?"

"I didn't like drinking with the officers, so I did most of my drinking in the radio room. Then, one time she came to see me and I was having a little sip. Nice polite Jewish boy that I am, I offered her one. She took it, then took another one. The next time she came to the radio room, she brought some cheese and salami. We had another couple of belts together. That's the way it started."

"You said she said something about Nazis in Chile?"

"According to her, she was working at the Little Sisters' Hospital in Santiago when this happened."

"When what happened?"

"They call it the Seguro Obrero Massacre," Stein said. "That's the building that houses the health insurance ministry, or something like that."

"What kind of a massacre?" Frade asked as he pulled the cork from another bottle of Cabernet Sauvignon.

"Nazis."

"Who did the Nazis massacre?"

"The Nazis *got* massacred. She said what happened was that a Chilean Nazi—they called themselves 'Nazistas'—named Jorge González von Marées got a bunch of college kids, and people that age, all fired up about National Socialism and Adolf Hitler, and they tried to stage a putsch."

"When did this happen?"

"In 1938. Mother Superior was there filling in as a doctor in the emergency room at the Little Sisters' Hospital in Santiago. Same order of nuns as here."

Frade nodded as he topped off his glass and then slid the bottle to Stein.

"So," Siggie said as he poured himself a glass, "what happened when this Nazi zealot did that . . . Wait. 'Zealot' is a really bad choice of word. The Zealots were Jewish warriors in Judea trying to throw the Romans out in the first century; they killed a lot of Romans because they just wouldn't give up."

They tapped glasses and took sips.

"Really nice wine," Stein said, and went on: "Anyway,

what this Chilean Nazi *idiot* did was convince about sixty of these young guys that all they had to do was take over a building at the university and the Seguro Obrero building and the people would rush to support them and National Socialism would come to Chile.

"According to Mother Superior, they could have caused real trouble, but while they probably didn't stand a chance of taking over the country, they would have become heroic martyrs."

"Exactly what did these Chilean Nazi lunatics do?"

"About half of them took over a building at the university, and the other half took over the health insurance building. The cops—they call them 'carabineros'; they carry carbines—surrounded both buildings. Then the army sent a couple of cannons to the university building and fired a couple of rounds.

"The lunatics at the university surrendered. The cops—or maybe the army—then told them that what was going to happen now was that the lunatics were going to go to the health insurance building and convince the lunatics there that what they should do is surrender before anybody else got hurt.

"This made sense to the lunatics—they could see themselves being marched off to the slam while people cheered them, where they would be tried, jailed for a couple of months, and then be remembered all their lives as the heroes who brought Nazism to Chile with their bravery.

"So off they went to the health insurance building, where they talked the other lunatics into surrendering. When the others put down their weapons, the lunatics from the university were marched into the building, chased up the stairways, and then shot and/or bayoneted."

"All of them?"

"Mother Superior was there with the ambulances from the hospital. She saw officers going around making sure they were all dead." Stein mimed someone holding a pistol. "*Pop.* You're dead."

"After they surrendered, they were killed?" Frade said.

"Somebody with power—I'd like to think it was a Jew, but there's no telling—thought, 'Now, wait a minute. If we just arrest these people, they'll be back. On the other hand, if they resist and they all die, that would be unfortunate, but that would mean they won't be causing any more trouble.'"

"Mother Superior agrees with that theory?"

"She knows that's what happened. What she can't understand is why I think it was a good idea."

"Neither can I. That sounds like cold-blooded murder."

"Colonel, what were you thinking when you turned your Thompson on Colonel—whatsisname? Schmidt?—and his officers?"

"I was thinking if any one of them managed to get their pistols out, they were going to shoot me."

"That's all?"

"Look, later, when I was trying to justify to myself shooting Schmidt, I managed to convince myself that I had also saved General Farrell's life, and Pedro Nolasco's."

"And that's all?" Stein pursued.

It took Frade a moment to reply.

"Okay, Siggie. I'm apparently very good when it comes to justifying what I've done that I'm not especially proud of. I told myself that I was responsible for turning the Tenth Mountain Regiment around, which meant they would not get into a firefight with the Húsares de Pueyrredón and that meant a lot of Schmidt's troops and a lot of Húsares would not get killed. And that—I just said I'm really good at coming up with justifications—there wouldn't be a civil war where a lot of innocent people would get killed. By the time I was finished, I had just about convinced myself that I was really Saint George and Schmidt was the evil dragon."

Stein nodded. "Don't be hard on yourself, Colonel. You did the right thing, and so did whoever ordered that the Chilean Nazis be killed. That stopped the Nazi movement in its tracks in Chile. God knows how many people would have been killed if the Nazis had taken over the country."

"Why does this massacre make you want to go to Germany?"

"I told you, Colonel, I don't understand it, but it does."

"You're not thinking of doing something more than pissing in the Rhine?"

"Say, shooting Nazis so they can't rise Phoenix-like from the ashes?"

"That thought did run through my mind, Siggie."

"No, sir," Stein said, then went on: "Don't look for

some nice explanation why I can't go with you, Colonel. All you have to say is 'No way.'"

"Whatever happened to that Leica camera you used at Tandil?"

"I've still got it. You want it?"

"I don't know who Perón is sending to Germany with me, and I don't know who I'm going to bring back from Germany. And he's not going to tell me. But if I had photographs I could show Nolasco, Martín, and as far as that goes, Körtig . . ."

"I'll go get the camera."

"No. You can just bring it with you when we go to Germany. You'll go as the radio operator. In an SAA uniform."

"Yes, sir. And thank you."

"When we finish this bottle of wine, Sergeant, get on the radio to Estancia San Pedro y San Pablo. Tell Schultz what's going on. Tell him to get blank OSS ID cards out of the safe and have them made out for von Wachtstein and Boltitz by the time we get there tomorrow. You still have yours, right?"

"Yes, sir. But you told me those IDs are not real . . ."

"They're not. But people don't know that. And in our business, Sergeant Stein, what people don't know usually hurts them."

[THREE]

Estancia San Pedro y San Pablo

Near Pila, Buenos Aires Province, Argentina

1305 15 May 1945

As the Red Lodestar, with Peter von Wachtstein at the controls, made its approach to the airfield, then smoothly touched down, Clete thought, *There are some people born to be pilots, and ol' Hansel is one of them.*

"Don't worry," Clete said, "with a little practice—four, five hours shooting touch-and-gos, you'll eventually get the hang of it. I'll show you the tricks."

It went right over von Wachtstein's head.

His face showed he thought he'd been caught with his hand in the cookie jar.

"Just kidding, Hansel."

"Alicia and I are going to Doña Claudia's," von Wachtstein then said. "What about Karl and Beth?"

"That depends on where Beth's mother is," Clete said. "That's where they'll go."

One of the drivers of the cars waiting for them told them that *"las señoras"* were all at Estancia Santa Catalina.

"Karl," Frade said, "your call. When we get there, you and Beth can try to look innocent, or hang your heads in shame. Doesn't matter. Martha Howell will see through it and make you both pay for your lewd and lascivious behavior."

"Screw you!" Beth said.

There was a 1942 Chevrolet Master Deluxe sedan with diplomatic license plates parked in front of the Big House when Clete and Siggie Stein rolled up in one of the estancia's station wagons.

Probably Tony Pelosi and/or Max Ashton, Clete decided, just before he decided, *I guess Doña Alicia has been dropped from the roll of* las señoras.

His wife was sitting on the side verandah with the U.S. Embassy "military attachés" Pelosi and Ashton, and someone he was surprised to see—Milton Leibermann, the "legal attaché" of the embassy. Their children were nowhere in sight.

"I thought you'd be with *las señoras,*" Clete said to his wife when all the handshaking and kissing were done.

"I didn't think Milt came all the way out here from Buenos Aires just for the hell of it," Dorotea said matter-of-factly.

Leibermann laughed.

"She's good, Clete," he said. "I didn't. And neither did these two."

"Excuse me?"

"When I asked Tony if I could borrow his embassy car to come out here, he said he'd drive me. And then Max sniffed something was up and found the time in his busy schedule to join us."

"So, what's up, Milt?"

"I got a letter from an old pal, a fellow Gangbuster, that I thought might be of interest to you."

"A fellow Gangbuster?" Clete asked.

"That's what we called ourselves when we were going through the FBI Academy," Leibermann said. "There was a radio program at the time called *Gangbusters*. Allegedly based on the exploits of the New Jersey State Police under Colonel H. Norman Schwarzkopf."

"I don't understand," Clete confessed.

"Read this," Leibermann said, handing Frade a sheaf of typewriter paper. "I will then entertain questions."

Dear Milt:

For reasons which will become apparent as you read this, I really wish that instead of writing this in some haste, we were sitting – two old friends – across a table from one another. But that's simply not possible under the circumstances.

Let me start with the good news: You will shortly learn through normal channels that the Bureau's Operation in Buenos Aires has been upgraded by Director Hoover from Foreign Station to Overseas Division, and that the Director has named you Chief thereof.

That appointment comes with a substantial pay increase, of course, but this has all happened so suddenly that I just don't know the details. When I have them, I will get them to you as soon as I can.

The appointment also carries with it both much greater responsibility and authority than you were charged with as Special Agent in Charge Buenos Aires Station. The Section Chief, South America, is being informed today that effective immediately, Overseas Division, Argentina, will report directly to the Assistant Director for South America. Who just happens to be yours truly.

While your outstanding performance of your duties certainly merits a promotion like this for you, I must in candor tell you that another reason for it was the Director's realization that for you to be able to deal with the responsibilities you will now have you will require both more authority than you had as Special Agent in Charge and the appropriate senior title to go with them.

"Well, congratulations, Chief Leibermann," Clete said when he had read the first page. "Who's this from?"

"Clyde Holmes, the deputy director of FBI Operations," Leibermann answered. "He's probably number four in the Bureau hierarchy."

"I'm impressed, and I think I may say, without fear of objection, that your promotion merits a celebratory libation. What would please you in that connection, Chief Leibermann?"

"A Johnnie Walker Black on the rocks, thank you, Colonel. But you better hold off on the congratulations until you have read the whole thing."

Clete signaled for a maid and ordered her to bring the rolling bar onto the verandah.

"I presume, Chief, that I have your permission to share this bulletin of good fortune with my wife?"

"I think you all better read it," Leibermann said matter-of-factly.

Clete handed the page he had read to Dorotea and started on the second page:

> In the conversation with the Director that set all this in motion, he said, "The end of the war in Germany means not that our work will be lessened, but rather increased, especially with regard to Soviet espionage in the United States." Or words to that effect.
>
> Much of this centers around the past, present, and future operations of the Office of Strategic Services, which, the

Director feels, will shortly be disbanded.

The Director also stated that when the OSS is disbanded, he feels there will be an attempt by the Army, the Navy, and the State Department to absorb the OSS and its assets, and that doing so would be inimical to the Bureau's ability to carry out its responsibilities, especially with regard to Soviet espionage.

If you'll give this a moment's thought, Milt, you will see that the Director is again right on the money. The Army and the Navy are rightly concentrated on taking the war to Japan. In that connection, the Soviets are regarded as our allies. The State Department is trying very hard to get the Soviets to declare war on the Japanese.

But the Director understands that the Bureau, in the discharge of its responsibilities, must look beyond the obvious and consider the realities.

The Director feels that the most unpleasant of these realities is that the most dangerous enemy the United

States is facing is the Soviet Union, closely followed by very senior officers in the government who are unable, or unwilling, to face this fact and act accordingly.

The Bureau knows that our "Soviet allies" have been conducting intensive espionage activities with regard to the Manhattan Project. The reason we know is twofold. First, we have of course for some time been conducting our own counterintelligence efforts. Secondly, parties unknown passed to us, quite literally under the door, an envelope containing the names of Soviet agents within the Manhattan Project.

Some of these spies and traitors were already known to us, but six others were not. Further investigation by the Bureau revealed the six others are in fact Soviet espionage agents.

Who slipped the envelope under the door?

The Director believes the envelope came from Allen W. Dulles, the Deputy Director of the OSS for European Operations. Why the anonymous, surreptitious delivery?

"This guy seems to know what he's talking about," Clete said as he handed the second page to Dorotea.

"He generally does," Leibermann said. "He's a Mormon."

"Excuse me?"

"A priest of the Church of Jesus Christ of Latter-Day Saints," Leibermann explained. "They don't drink or smoke, and while they bend the truth sometimes, they never lie. There's a lot of them around J. Edgar Hoover."

"I never heard that," Clete said, and resumed reading the third page:

> The Director's – and my – scenario here is that if Dulles had followed normal channels for the dissemination of intelligence such as this – in other words, if it had gone to OSS Director Donovan, who would then have made President Roosevelt privy to it – the results would have almost certainly been disastrous.
>
> It is impossible to say exactly what President Roosevelt would have done with the intelligence, or what President Truman would do with it now, except that once either had become privy to it, word would certainly have immediately reached the KGB First Directorate, via one or

more of their subordinates, in a matter of days, even hours, and the Soviets would learn we were aware of their espionage activities and take the appropriate steps.

Director Donovan would have been fully aware of this, but would have been duty bound to pass this intelligence to the President.

It is entirely possible that Dulles decided that since passing the intelligence to Donovan would result in Donovan's passing it to the President, the thing for him to do was simply not pass it to Donovan.

But what to do with it?

Slip it under the FBI's door and place the burden of deciding whether or not to pass it to the President on the Director's shoulders.

This brings us to the point of this.

The Director is not about to pass to the President any intelligence as significant as this without knowing both how accurate it is and where it came from. What he has done is to go unofficially to President Roosevelt and, now, President Truman and tell them he has unconfirmed intelligence he believes is accurate that the KGB First Directorate has successfully penetrated the Manhattan Project.

President Roosevelt's reaction was disbelief that our Soviet allies would do something like that.

I'm sure, Milt, that you have heard how ill President Roosevelt was in the last months of his life.

The Director informed President Truman of the strong possibility that the Manhattan Project has been penetrated by the KGB First Directorate immediately after General Groves informed the President of the purpose of the Manhattan Project, that is, the day after President Roosevelt expired. The President responded by saying the Director should confirm what intelligence he has.

Obviously, therefore, the Bureau has to determine the source of the intelligence slipped under the door.

One strong possibility is that it came from German sources; Mr. Dulles is strongly suspected to have been in contact with enemy officials and officers before the surrender. If this is true, and if it became known to senior officials of the administration, Secretary Morgenthau in particular, they would have demanded to know the details of the meetings. If Director Donovan was not informed of all, or some, of these meetings, he could not answer such questions.

"This guy really does know what he's talking about," Clete said as he handed Dorotea that page. He saw that Dorotea had handed what she had read to Siggie Stein, and that Tony Pelosi was anxiously waiting for his turn.

"He usually does," Leibermann said.

"Why did you say he was a priest?" Clete asked as he took his first look at the next page.

"All adult male saints are priests," Leibermann said.

Clete nodded, then looked at the next sheet. "And here I am!"

This brings us back to Mr. Dulles and more particularly to Lieutenant Colonel Frade of the OSS. Although OSS Director Donovan has more than once referred to Frade in unofficial conversations with the Director and yours truly as "my loose cannon in Argentina" and other similarly derogatory terms, both the Director and I feel he's more important than this; that General Donovan may have been indulging in a little disinformation.

"J. Edgar Hoover and your priest buddy," Clete said, "seem to feel I'm more than a loose cannon. Should I be flattered or worried?"

"Both," Leibermann said with a chuckle.

The Director and I began to connect the dots. The process intensified when we heard that the President had ordered the sale of a fleet of Constellation aircraft to South American Airways, and that Frade was Managing Director of SAA.

We learned further that the business arrangements for the financing of this sale were handled by the New York law firm of Sullivan & Cromwell, specifically by John Foster Dulles, whose brother is OSS Deputy Director Allen W. Dulles.

The Bureau's learning that Lieutenant Colonel Frade's SAA had established commercial air service between Buenos Aires and Lisbon roughly coincided with an informal request by Treasury Secretary Morgenthau that the Director look into what he described as "credible rumors" that large numbers of Nazis were already leaving Germany for sanctuary in Argentina, in some cases with the assistance of the Vatican.

From other sources, the Director has learned that in the last months of the war, a number of officers of Abwehr Ost, the section of German intelligence dealing with the Soviet Union, had mysteriously disappeared from their posts and were rumored to be, together with their families, headed for sanctuary in Argentina. There has been no report – and the Army's Counter-Intelligence Corps has been on special alert to look for anyone connected with Abwehr Ost – of anyone so connected being taken as a POW or found, including the Abwehr Ost commander General Reinhard Gehlen.

Jesus H. Christ! Frade thought. *Has Morgenthau actually sniffed out the Gehlen op? If so, it's our worst nightmare come true.*

How soon before his sword falls on our necks?

He said, "I wonder who these 'other sources' who told him about Abwehr Ost are."

"Write this down, Clete," Leibermann said. "Never underestimate the FBI. Where is Gehlen, Clete?"

This is not the time to wonder whose side Leibermann is on.

"I don't know. I suppose the OSS has him somewhere in Germany. If Dulles knows, he didn't tell me. I guess I'll find out when I get to Germany."

"Which will be when?"

"We leave tomorrow. The Argentine Foreign Ministry has chartered an SAA plane to take a replacement diplomatic crew over there and to bring the diplomats there back. I think that's bullshit, and there is another purpose, probably including sneaking some more Nazis back here."

"And what about the rumor that some of this General Gehlen's people are already here in Argentina?"

"I've got about twenty of the Nazi element thereof comfortably locked up at Casa Montagna."

"And the non-Nazi element?"

"Some of them want to stay; they're being integrated into Argentine society. The ones that want to go back—or go somewhere else—are in hotels and ski lodges."

"How do you tell the difference between the Nazis and the others?"

"The good Gehlen Germans shoot the Nazis on sight."

"Is that what happened to von Deitzberg?"

Clete nodded. Niedermeyer, carrying an identity document in the name of Otto Körtig, had shot SS-Brigadeführer von Deitzberg in the men's room of the

Edelweiss Hotel in San Carlos de Bariloche—an act that both removed a severe threat to the OSS and proved whose side Niedermeyer/Körtig was on.

Leibermann said: "I was about to ask why the OSS is being so good to General Gehlen, but why don't I hold off until you've read some more?"

Clete's eyes went back to the message:

> And finally there is the May tenth "escape" from the Fort Hunt Senior POW Interrogation Center of two German officers who had been attached to the German embassy in Buenos Aires. When informally approached by the Director, who had learned that the two had been taken from the facility by a Marine Lieutenant Colonel named Frade, General Donovan replied that while the OSS had nothing to do with it, he was not surprised or even especially upset by what had happened. He said that both officers had not only been "turned" by Frade, but that both had been closely associated with the bomb plot to kill Hitler. He said that the father of one of them, a German general, had been hung with piano wire from a butcher's hook for

his role in the failed assassination plot.

General Donovan also told the Director that he doubted Colonel Frade would obey an order to come to the United States to answer for his actions. Donovan told the Director that Frade has had some "unfortunate experiences," which he did specify, with officers of the OSS and trusts "only Colonel Graham." Donovan said, "It is much harder to get a young bull back into the barn than it is a cow."

Donovan says Frade enjoys dual citizenship, and under Argentine law, its citizens may not be extradited. And General Donovan suggested there would probably be reluctance to court-martial Frade on any charge but murder, as he's been awarded the Navy Cross and became an ace on Guadalcanal.

The Director found it interesting that Donovan included neither Mr. Dulles nor himself with regard to those whom Frade trusts, and feels this suggests Donovan is not aware of the close relationship between Mr. Dulles and Frade.

> General Donovan also told the Director he knows of no OSS activities by anyone involving the Gehlen organization. The Director often says that while he and General Donovan often disagree, they never lie to one another.

"Your Gangbuster pal is right about that, too, Milt. Donovan does not know about the deal Dulles struck with Gehlen," Clete said.

"Which is?"

"Gehlen turns over everything Abwehr Ost has—including agents in place in the Kremlin—to the OSS in exchange for keeping his people, and their families, out of the hands of the Russians."

"Read on, Clete," Leibermann said, and nodded once at the sheets of paper.

> I'm sure I don't have to connect the dots for you, Milt, but let me tell you the scenario the Director has reached, with these very important caveats. First, the patriotism of Mr. Dulles and Lieutenant Colonel Frade is beyond question. Second, the interest of the Bureau is solely to protect the United States from Soviet espionage, with the

emphasis here on absolutely ensuring the Soviets do not gain access to the secrets of the Manhattan Project.

The Director believes we can proceed on the following premises:

That for the reason given – that any information General Donovan passed to President Roosevelt or President Truman now would soon be known to the Soviets – both Colonel Graham and Mr. Dulles (most likely together) decided that their oath to protect the Constitution from all enemies, foreign and domestic, gave them the authority to not give to General Donovan certain information.

The Director believes this was a very difficult decision for them to make, as he knows both of them hold General Donovan in the highest possible personal and professional regard. The Director personally feels that if General Donovan were in the shoes of either Dulles or Graham, he would have done as they did.

The damage to the OSS and to Mr. Dulles and Colonel Graham if any of this came out would be cataclysmic and would spill over to the Bureau and the Director personally. There are powerful figures in the government who would hold that if the Bureau or the Director personally even suspected anything like this, it would be the FBI's duty to bring it to the attention of the President.

The Director believes there is a strong possibility that Mr. Dulles has established a relationship with General Gehlen. This would neatly explain where he got the names of the Soviet agents who have infiltrated the Manhattan Project, and why they were "slipped under the door" to the Bureau. It would also explain the disappearance of Gehlen's officers in the latter months of the war. The rumor that they have found sanctuary in Argentina becomes a credible scenario if one considers they may have been flown there from Lisbon on Frade's SAA aircraft.

The question then becomes, "Why would Dulles do something like that?"

Gehlen had something Dulles wanted, and offered to exchange it for Dulles arranging to have his officers and their families taken to sanctuary FROM THE

SOVIETS in Argentina. That has to be intelligence, possibly even assets, German agents in place in the Soviet Union. Gehlen knew the war was lost and that when inevitably Abwehr Ost fell into the hands of the Soviets he and his people – including their families – would be interrogated under torture and then eliminated.

He knew that somewhere in the United States there was a person or persons who regarded the Soviet Union as a serious threat to the United States, and who would accordingly place a high value on Gehlen's intelligence assets, and who could arrange the sanctuary he was after in exchange for them.

It is also possible, of course, and an equally credible scenario that Mr. Dulles went to Gehlen and made the advance himself. If this was the case, he was the man Gehlen was looking for.

The Director, who is fully aware of the furor that would erupt in the United States if such a deal became known, nevertheless feels that Mr. Dulles has acted in a courageous, patriotic manner.

"At the risk of repeating myself, Milt, this Mormon pal of yours is very good," Clete said as he handed another page of the letter to Dorotea.

"At the risk of repeating myself, never underestimate the FBI. Read on—you're almost through."

> The question now becomes, "What's going to happen to the Gehlen assets?" Compounding this question, "Especially since the OSS is about to go out of existence?"
>
> This brings us to your mission, Milt, my old friend, something we would have considered a fantasy, if we ever considered it at all, in our days at the Academy.
>
> You are to get to Mr. Dulles, obviously through Frade, and convince him first that if we know what he's been up to, eventually, sooner or later, probably later, but inevitably, so will the Army Intelligence, Naval Intelligence, and the State Department.
>
> And when that happens - and/or when the OSS is incorporated into one of the above on its dissolution - the Gehlen data and personnel will be compromised.
>
> This doesn't even get into what will

happen to Mr. Dulles or Lieutenant Colonel Frade when their activities become known. The Director is sure they have considered at length all the many unpleasant scenarios of what will happen to them.

The obvious place to put the Gehlen assets is with the Bureau.

For that matter, the obvious thing to do with the OSS on its dissolution is to incorporate it into the Bureau, but that's a subject that can be dealt with later.

The Director would like Mr. Dulles to consider that the Director is far better equipped to refuse to divulge the sources of his information than Mr. Dulles is. And more importantly, the Director is better equipped than anyone else to keep them from falling into the hands of the Soviets.

The Director is willing – more precisely, eager – to meet with Mr. Dulles or Lieutenant Colonel Frade at any place of their choosing to discuss this personally.

Obviously, the less about this matter committed to paper, the better. Your reports on this matter will be relayed verbally to Bureau special agents visiting the Embassy in Buenos Aires covertly as diplomatic couriers, et cetera, who will identify themselves to you by introducing the phrase "loose cannon" into their conversation.

In consideration of the above, old buddy, when you've read this several times, you'd better put a match to it.

Looking forward to seeing you soon, Fellow Gangbuster.

Best,

Clyde

Frade looked at Leibermann, sighed audibly, then said, "Milt, you didn't have to show us this letter; you could have just come out here and told me Hoover wants to meet with Dulles. So far as that goes, there must be a 'legal attaché' in Bern who could have gone to Dulles directly. What's going on?"

"Multiple question," Leibermann said. "Where to start? Let me start by saying that Clyde Holmes and I are not old buddies. And that I think he thinks I'm even more stupid than is the case. Which sort of annoys me. That promotion is bullshit. I don't suppose you know how the FBI works?"

"I don't have a clue."

"Well, for one thing, they don't pay a hell of a lot of attention to civil service rules."

"I don't know what you're talking about."

"Well, just about everybody is a special agent, except for a favored few like inspectors and the directors. Special Agents in Charge are what it sounds like. But that's a position title, not a rank. They get extra money—how much depending on the circumstances, which are determined by the assistant directors. A SAC in charge of an office with fifty agents gets paid more than a SAC in an office with five—as long as they hold that office. If they screw up, they are reassigned to another office as a special agent and get paid as a special agent with so many years of service."

"And if they don't screw up?

"Then they're transferred from being a SAC of a five-man office to being SAC of one with, say, fifteen agents. That raises their pay. Knowing that they can get transferred at the whim of a deputy director upward, or downward, tends to keep people in line. You getting the picture?"

"I always thought the FBI was like the post office, cradle-to-grave security under civil service rules. How does the FBI get out from under the civil service?"

"First of all, no one complains. In large measure, the FBI system is basically fair; it rewards good work and punishes bad. Second, if some special agent decides he has been treated unfairly and goes to the Civil Service Commission, the investigator is shown pictures of him with some hooker and the suggestion is made that they will not be shown to his wife because he is known to be a friend of the FBI. Getting the picture?"

"I'm shocked. Really shocked. I've always thought of the FBI as Boy Scouts with guns."

"A great many of them fit that description, Clete."

"What you're saying is that if your buddy found out you didn't tell them the whole truth, you would have stopped being the SAC here and become . . ."

"A special agent in the Bullfrog Falls, Kansas, office, with a corresponding reduction in pay. Which would also have happened if my old buddy even knew I had been talking to you. And which will happen, I strongly suspect, however this thing turns out. I will be transferred to the Bullfrog, Kansas, office and encouraged to take my well-earned retirement. Retired special agents, like dead men, tell no tales."

"Jesus, Milt!" Stein said.

"So, why are you here?" Frade asked.

Leibermann held up his hand and moved it back and forth.

Frade looked at him curiously.

"I'm waving the flag," Leibermann said. "The last refuge of the scoundrel."

"Explain that."

"There's a lot in Holmes's letter that I agree with. Especially the threat the Russians pose. I don't like them any more than I like the Germans. Even with what we hear about German concentration camps, the Russians have probably killed more Jews over the years."

"My father used to say that," Stein said softly. "When

the Germans started in on the Jews, he said, 'Germany is getting to be no better than Russia.'"

"I think the Russians have to be stopped, and it looks to me as if the only people who understand that, and are in a position to do anything about it, are J. Edgar Hoover and Allen Dulles."

He waved his hand again.

"So, Clete, that explains why I'm here. Questions for you. Are you willing to go to Dulles with this?"

"Of course."

"The first thing Dulles is going to think—correctly—is that Hoover, in addition to wanting everything Dulles has gotten, or is going to get, from Gehlen, wants to take over the OSS. How's he going to react to that?"

"I dunno," Clete said. "Why doesn't Hoover just make a play to take over the OSS himself? If they're going to shut it down, the FBI would seem to me a logical place to put it."

"I don't think you understand that the reason the Army and the Navy want to take over the OSS is because that when it's in their tent, they can really kill it. They don't want it ever to come back. The OSS, running loose, has been a nightmare for them."

"But Hoover doesn't think it would be?"

"Hoover, rightly or wrongly, believes he could control it. And he thinks it would be useful. The Army and the Navy believe—I think they're wrong—that they could have done whatever the OSS has done, and done it more efficiently, and under the wise thumb of the chief of staff and/or the chief of naval operations."

"I don't know when I'll see Dulles again," Clete said. "And I can't go to Washington—he's in Washington—because I have to go to Germany tomorrow. When I get there, I'll get word to him that I'd like to see him. That's the best I can do right now."

"Well, if that's it, that's it," Leibermann said.

"What are you going to tell this Holmes guy?" Clete asked.

"That when I went to see you tomorrow, I just missed you. That I was told you were flying to Lisbon and would be back in a week or ten days."

"Okay," Clete said.

"Max, are you about through doing that?" Leibermann asked.

Ashton was making a nice stack of all the pages of the letter from Deputy Director Holmes. After he had tapped it a final time on the arm of his chair, he carefully handed the stack to Leibermann.

Leibermann took one page, held it up, and then set it on fire with a Zippo lighter. When it was almost consumed, he took a second page from the stack and lit it from the first.

He continued this process until all the pages had been burned. No one on the verandah said a word while this was going on.

Then Leibermann turned to Frade.

"I will now have that Johnnie Walker Black on the rocks that you offered a while ago," he said.

[ONE]

Executive Suite, South American Airlines
Aeropuerto Coronel Jorge G. Frade
Morón, Buenos Aires Province, Argentina
1725 16 May 1945

When the telephone on the desk of the managing director of South American Airways rang, Don Cletus Frade, with a grunt and some difficulty, took his feet from the desk and reached for it.

"Why do I think our diplomats may have finally decided to show up?" he asked of no one in particular.

There were six men in the room. Moments before the telephone rang, Frade had idly thought he couldn't remember ever having seen so many people in his office. All but one of them were wearing some variation of the SAA flight crew uniform.

Chief Pilot Delgano was there, in the most spectacular version thereof. Frade was wearing the uniform of an SAA captain. Hans-Peter von Wachtstein and Karl Boltitz were wearing the only slightly less spectacular uniforms of

SAA first officers. And Master Sergeant Siggie Stein was wearing the uniform of an SAA radio officer/navigator.

The man not in uniform was retired Sergeant Major Enrico Rodríguez, who, Clete had decided—after going so far as to put him in a steward's uniform—was just not going to look like a member of an SAA flight crew no matter how he was dressed.

And Rodríguez could not be left behind. To the usual arguments he made when not taking him along somewhere came up for discussion he had added a new one: "Don Cletus, I spent a year in Germany when el Coronel, may he be resting in peace with your sainted mother and all the angels, was at the Kriegsschule. You, however, have never been there."

Enrico Rodríguez was listed on the flight manifest as a "security officer."

They had been waiting since one o'clock for the "Foreign Minister's Relief Party" to show up, the last three hours of that time in the executive offices as a result of an executive decision by the managing director, who was in something of a pique at the time.

"Fuck it!" he said. "I'm not going to stand around here with my thumb up my ass waiting for these clowns any longer. We'll go to the executive offices and have them send up coffee and something to eat."

The executive offices were not quite the center of executive activity they sounded like. Managing Director Frade was now willing to admit he had been a little derelict in the execution of his duties when examining the architect's drawings of the buildings to be erected at

Aeropuerto Coronel Jorge G. Frade. Concerned primarily with the hangars, the control tower, and the maintenance and cargo-handling facilities, Frade had not realized until everything had been constructed and equipped that about half of the third floor of the terminal building was devoted to something called the "Executive Suite."

The Executive Suite was further divided into an office for the managing director, an office for the chief pilot, a conference room, an office for their secretaries, a small kitchen, separate restrooms, and a reception area.

SAA also maintained offices in downtown Buenos Aires—two floors in the Anglo-Argentine Bank, the managing director of which was el Señor Humberto Valdez Duarte. El Señor Duarte was also Cletus Frade's uncle and SAA's financial director. Duarte supervised the day-to-day business activities of SAA from his office in the bank.

The result of this was that the Executive Suite of the SAA terminal was, in corporate parlance, "underutilized." Neither Cletus Frade nor Chief Pilot Gonzalo Delgano had secretaries, and moreover Delgano had a small but adequate office off the flight-planning room in Hangar Two. He almost never went to the Executive Suite. Frade went there rarely, usually only when he wanted to change into—or out of—his SAA captain's uniform. The company had issued him three uniforms, and he kept them in the Executive Suite.

It was in the Executive Suite that von Wachtstein, Boltitz, and Stein had been hastily outfitted with SAA uniforms. Clete had sensed that all three shared his opinion of the garish outfits, but they were too polite to say anything, and he hadn't said anything either because he thought it would only serve to make a bad situation worse.

The truth was that while SAA pilots, from Chief Pilot Delgano down, thought their uniforms properly reflected their important role as dashing fliers, when Frade put on his uniform and looked into the mirror, he thought he looked like a tuba player in the Ringling Brothers, Barnum & Bailey Circus band—or maybe the guy driving the wagon holding the caged snarling tigers in the circus parade.

There were times, of course, when he had to wear it. Today, for one example. And, for another, when he was combining a scheduled Constellation flight with a training flight for pilots being upgraded from the left seat of a Lodestar to the right seat of a Connie, which meant passengers were aboard. And he wore it when flying to Lisbon, putting it on only after all other preflight activities had been accomplished and taking it off just as soon as he could when he had returned to Aeropuerto Jorge Frade.

"Who's down there?" Frade said into his telephone, his tone incredulous, and, after there was a reply, said, "Send them up."

He put the handset in the base and turned to the men in the room.

"Get your feet off the coffee table, Gonzalo. Your boss is on the way up. And so is the guy who thinks he's mine."

It was an open secret to those in the room that in addition to his role as SAA chief pilot, Gonzalo Delgano was a colonel of the Bureau of Internal Security. He had been keeping an eye on el Coronel Frade from the time he was a captain and ostensibly the pilot of el Coronel's Beechcraft Staggerwing. Now he kept an eye on Cletus Frade and SAA.

The other reference was obviously to Richmond C. Flowers, USA, the military attaché at the American Embassy who was de jure but not de facto the senior OSS officer in Argentina.

The same question ran through both Frade's and Delgano's minds: *I wonder what the hell this is all about.*

El General de Brigada Martín, in civilian clothing, came into the office first, followed by Colonel Flowers and two muscular young men, also in civilian clothing, one of them carrying a bulging leather briefcase that clearly was stuffed full.

Frade thought: *Clever fellow that I am, I suspect that those two are Marine guards.*

How do I know? They're muscular, bright-eyed—and nobody else in Buenos Aires has haircuts like that.

I wonder what the hell this is all about. . . .

"Good afternoon," Martín said.

"Bernardo, if you'll tell me who told you we were up here," Frade said as he stood up, "I'll have him dragged down Runway 28—that's the long one—by his testicles."

"Actually, it was a rather good-looking young woman," Martín said, smiling.

"Then by her ears," Frade said. He turned to Colonel Flowers. "Good afternoon, sir. I believe you know everybody?" Then, looking at the two muscular young Marines, he added, "Semper fi, guys."

The younger of the two smiled back and said, "Semper fi, sir."

Colonel Flowers raised his eyebrows.

Clete shrugged. "You know what we say, Colonel. Once a Marine, always a Marine."

Colonel Flowers looked uncomfortable. He had known Kapitän zur See Boltitz and Major von Wachtstein when they had been respectively the naval attaché and the deputy military attaché for air of the German Embassy.

Clete thought: *And by now you've heard that I plucked them from durance vile at Fort Hunt.*

"What's going on?" Martín asked.

"Actually, we were just talking about you," Frade said.

"Really?" Martín said as he walked around the room, shaking hands and exchanging embraces.

Flowers shook hands wordlessly with everyone.

"I said something to the effect that if *el General* was here we could ask him what this swap-the-diplomats mission is really all about," Frade said.

"I was hoping you could tell me," Martín said, walking finally to Clete, where he hugged his shoulder.

"May I say how elegant you all look in your uniforms?" Martín asked.

"Only if you say it without smirking," Clete said, then added: "You really don't know what's going on? Or where our passengers are? I told Humberto to tell my Tío Juan we wanted to leave no later than four-thirty."

"Colonel Frade, may I have a moment with you?" Colonel Flowers asked.

"Certainly. May we use your office, Gonzalo?"

"Certainly."

When they had gone into the adjacent office, Flowers said, "Sergeant, leave the briefcase, please, and wait for me in the corridor."

One of the Marines handed Flowers the briefcase, then both Marines left the office, closing the door behind them.

Flowers put the briefcase on the desk, then sat down in an armchair before it.

He looked at Clete and said, "May I ask where you're going?"

Why not tell him?

"The Foreign Ministry has chartered a Connie to take a crew of Argentine diplomats to Germany and bring back the ones who are there."

"Sort of a rescue mission?"

"I suppose you could say that. They were in Berlin while the Russians took it. That couldn't have been much fun."

"You're going to Berlin?"

Frade nodded. "I'm flying the airplane. The mission will be led by someone from the Foreign Ministry."

"And you're taking the two Germans with you?"

"If you're talking about von Wachtstein and Boltitz, Colonel, you're getting into areas I'm not at liberty to discuss with you."

That earned Frade the cold, tight-lipped expression he expected, but Flowers did not respond directly.

"I have half a million dollars for you," Flowers said.

Half a million bucks? Frade thought. *No shit?*

Oh! Talk about government efficiency! It's been damn near a year since I sent that invoice to Washington.

The actual idea of billing the OSS had been triggered by Doña Dorotea, who had been dealing with managers of various Frade enterprises going over their bills. She'd asked Clete, "Who's going to pay for all the money we're spending on the OSS? Us?"

After a moment's hesitation, he had replied, "Who else?"

Then he'd realized that Dorotea's question was one he had not previously considered. It had not taken him long at all, after his father had been assassinated and he had inherited everything he thought of as "el Coronel, Incorporated," to stop thinking about money. He had other things on his mind, for one thing, and for another, the well of Frade cash seemed to be as inexhaustible as the pool of water at the bottom of Niagara Falls.

What happened next started out the next day as simple curiosity: *How much am I spending on various things of interest to the OSS? And why the hell am I?*

He had been astonished with his first, really rough partial estimate.

Over the next week or so, he prepared a more thorough listing of his expenses and losses on behalf of the OSS. The latter started with what it had cost him to repair—actually rebuild—the house at Tandil, which had been machine-gunned literally to rubble by troops of Colonel Schmidt's Tenth Mountain Regiment.

When he had a more or less complete listing of things

the OSS should have paid for but hadn't, it was twenty-six pages in length.

In it, he had tried to err on the side of frugality—for example, he billed the OSS two hundred fifty dollars an hour for the "business use" of the Red Lodestar. That was half the ballpark figure SAA used for estimating the per-hour cost of flying SAA Lodestars on their routes.

He also had decided that ten dollars a day was a more than fair price for the OSS to pay for each "contract security operative"—the pressed-into-service ex-troopers of the Húsares de Pueyrredón.

Then, just as he had been genuinely surprised to see how often he'd used the Red Lodestar for OSS business, he really had been surprised to see how large his private army had grown. And how much it had cost to feed it and move it around.

At least a dozen times during the preparation of the invoice, he told himself that he was just wasting his time.

All this is going to do is piss off Donovan and Graham.

But, on the other hand, what if I didn't have access to the overstuffed cash box of el Coronel, Incorporated?

It isn't fair for the OSS to expect me to spend my own money doing things for the OSS—especially since doing things for them usually results in people trying to kill me.

When he was ready to hand the invoice to Tony Pelosi to be sent to Washington, he had second—or perhaps fiftieth—thoughts about actually sending it. But finally—*What the hell, why not?*—he typed a brief note, then signed it:

16 Jun 1944

Dear General Donovan:

Detailed invoice enclosed.

Please remit sum of $503,508.35 at earliest convenience.

Respectfully,

Clete Frade

Cletus H. Frade

Major, USMCR

And he handed the note and the invoice to Pelosi, who saw that they were put in the next possible diplomatic pouch.

When there had been no reply of any kind in two weeks, Clete had decided that Donovan or Graham, or both, were either really pissed at him or were ignoring him, or both, and that he'd simply made a fool of himself. Again.

He'd had no regrets. It had been interesting to see how much being a spy was costing him. The invoice showed he had dipped into el Coronel's cash box on behalf of the OSS for a little more than half a million dollars.

Now, Frade glanced at the briefcase on the desk and thought, *Better late than never!*

Frade then looked at Flowers. "I thought that might have money in it."

"Of course you did," Flowers said stiffly, handing Frade an envelope.

Frade opened it. It contained a single sheet of paper that read:

The Embassy of the United States of America — Buenos Aires, Argentina

Colonel Richmond C. Flowers

Military Attaché

16 MAY 1945

The undersigned acknowledges receipt of $500,000 (Five Hundred Thousand Dollars Exactly) in lawful currency of the United States from Colonel Richmond C. Flowers, USA.

____

Cletus H. Frade

Lieutenant Colonel, USMCR

Frade thought, *And more fucking government efficiency!*

They shorted me almost four thousand dollars!

Oh, well. Better the bulk of it than nothing at all.

Flowers then extended his fountain pen.

"Please sign that," he said.

Frade did so, handed pen and paper back, then, nodding at the briefcase, asked, "It all fit in there? Half a million dollars?"

"You may count it if you wish, but I assure you it's all there."

Frade nodded, opened the briefcase, and looked into it. It held five bricks of bills, each about the size of a shoe box, wrapped in some sort of oiled paper, which was translucent enough so that he could see stacks of one-hundred-dollar bills.

"Where'd you get it?" Frade said. "The Bank of Boston?"

"It came by diplomatic pouch," Flowers said.

Frade said nothing.

"You of course may keep the briefcase," Flowers went on, "until it's convenient for you to drop it off at the embassy."

"Thank you," Frade said, then had an irreverent thought and said it aloud: "It would be really bad form for me to walk out of here carrying all that money in my arms like so much Kleenex."

"I think I have the right to an explanation, Colonel Frade," Flowers said. "That's a great deal of money. What are you going to do with it?"

"Sorry, Colonel, you just don't have the need to know."

Did I say that because I didn't want to get into a long explanation of where and how I've been spending the OSS's money?

Or because I really dislike him?

"Sooner or later, Colonel Frade, you're simply going to have to accept that as the senior OSS officer down here, I do have the need to know about whatever you're doing."

Frade shrugged and in an agreeable tone said, "I hope you understand that I'm just obeying my orders, Colonel. It's nothing personal."

Flowers met Frade's eyes, and Frade thought he could actually see steam coming out of Flowers's ears.

Then Flowers cleared his throat and changed subjects.

"There is something else I would like to discuss with you, Colonel Frade."

"Yes, sir?"

"As you know, I wear several hats. I am both the military attaché here as well as the senior OSS officer in Argentina. While that latter role is, of course, known to the assistant chief of staff for intelligence, it is not known by any of the other military attachés in South America. They don't have, as you like to say, the need to know."

Why do I think he's rehearsed this speech?

No. What Colonel Pompous has done is to write it down and then nearly memorize it.

Which makes it important to him.

So where the hell is he going with it?

"Periodically, once every three months or so, the assistant chief of staff, intelligence—ACofS G-2—convenes a conference of military attachés in South America. My absence from such conferences would raise questions, obviously, so I attend.

"I have just returned from such a conference, this time held in Rio de Janeiro. The ACofS G-2 personally presided. The subject was our role now that Germany has surrendered. And, as part of this, the role of the OSS for the rest of the war and afterward was discussed."

Aha! Question answered.

This might be interesting.

Frade said: "And what did you and the ACofS G-2 conclude?"

Flowers's face showed that he hadn't expected questions during his speech. He almost visibly thought about answering the question and then decided to go with the rehearsed speech.

"It is the opinion of the ACofS G-2 that (a) General Marshall will order the dissolution of the OSS in the time frame between today and the successful termination of the war against the Empire of Japan and (b) that it would be in the national interest for the OSS simply to be folded, so to speak, into Army Intelligence."

"How long do you think it will be before we can successfully terminate the war against the Empire of Japan?" Frade asked.

There was an element of sarcasm in Frade's parroting of the "successful termination" phrase. It went right past Flowers.

"A number of factors affect that, actually," Flowers said. "For example, the main Japanese islands are under daily bombardment by B-29 aircraft."

"Germany also was under daily aerial bombardment," Clete replied. "We still had to cross the Rhine and take Berlin before they surrendered."

"There are other factors," Flowers said almost condescendingly.

Does that mean he knows about the atomic bomb?

The ACofS G-2 certainly does—Army Intelligence must have counterintelligence agents swarming all over the Manhattan Project—but I can't believe ACofS G-2 would tell Flowers anything about it.

If there's anyone who doesn't have a need to know his name is Flowers.

Let's find out.

Frade said: "You're talking about the Los Angeles Project? Right?"

Flowers's face showed that the Los Angeles Project—which Frade, of course, had just invented—was news to him.

"Or maybe the Manhattan Project?" Frade pursued.

"One or the other," Flowers said. "Probably both."

Colonel, you've never heard of the Manhattan Project until just now, Clete thought, and was still—with difficulty—resisting the temptation to ask Colonel Flowers whether he thought the New Orleans Project—or maybe the Sioux Falls Project—was also going to affect the successful termination of the war against the Empire of Japan.

But then Flowers asked: "So, do you agree?"

What?

"With what?"

Flowers went on: "That it would be in the national interest for the OSS to be simply folded into Army Intelligence."

"After the successful termination of the war against the Empire of Japan, you mean?"

The sarcasm again sailed right over Flowers's head.

"Then or now," Flowers replied. "Would you agree that the OSS should be folded into Army Intelligence? Surely, you've thought about that."

"Not until just now. You're sure, Colonel, that the OSS is about to be—what?—dissolved?"

"Well, Frade. I got that, I told you, directly from the ACofS G-2. And he would certainly know, wouldn't you agree?"

"Did the ACofS G-2 say why they're going to abolish the OSS?"

It took Flowers a moment to come up with a reply, but finally he said, "Because it will not be needed."

"Then why fold it into Army Intelligence?" Frade asked innocently.

Flowers started to reply—his mouth was actually open—and then he had an epiphany and it caused him to lose his temper.

"You arrogant sonofabitch!" Flowers blurted, spittle flying from his lips. "If you think you can make a fool of me, you've got another think coming!"

"Did I say something that offended you, Colonel?"

"You knew all about this, didn't you? And don't lie to me, Frade. Colonel Donovan told you, didn't he?"

"Told me what?"

"That the OSS is to be dissolved."

Frade held up his right hand, pinkie and thumb touching, three fingers extended.

"Boy Scout's Honor, I have never discussed this with Wild Bill."

Flowers glared at him, his face flushed with anger.

Frade went on: "And with respect, sir. It's not Colonel Donovan. It's *General* Donovan. Wild Bill's a major general now. I'm surprised you didn't know that."

Flowers was red-faced, and Frade could see steam coming out of his ears again.

"You ever hear, Frade, that he who laughs last laughs best? I'm going to have your ass sooner or later. Count on it!"

"Yes, sir. I'll tell General Donovan you said that, when I tell him you told me the ACofS G-2 told you that the OSS is going to be dissolved and that you and he are agreed that it should be folded into Army Intelligence." Frade paused, then gave in to temptation: "With the help of the Los Angeles Project, and maybe even the New Orleans Project."

Flowers took a moment to take control of himself.

"The war is about over, Colonel Frade. We'll all eventually go home. But when you get off the ship, or the airplane, or whatever returns you to the Zone of the Interior, you will be in handcuffs, on your way to a general court-martial and the Army prison at Fort Leavenworth!"

"Maybe I can get General Donovan to represent me at the court-martial. I understand he's a pretty good lawyer."

Flowers wordlessly turned and marched out of the office, slamming the door after him.

Frade was still looking thoughtfully at the door—*I*

don't think pissing him off was the smart thing to do— when Enrico came through it.

"The diplomats are arriving, *mi coronel.*"

"Whatever happened to 'Don Cletus,' Enrico?"

"The diplomats are arriving, Don Cletus, *mi coronel.*"

"Now, in German. If you don't get it right, you can't go."

Enrico got it right.

"Well, I guess you get to go."

"Danke, Herr Oberst."

[TWO]

General Martín, Chief Pilot Delgano, and Master Sergeant Stein were all at the Executive Suite windows with Leica C-II 35mm cameras and snapping pictures of the diplomats climbing the stairs to the *Ciudad de Rosario.*

"Anybody interesting?" Clete asked as he looked down at the tarmac.

"One man," Martín said. "Rodolfo Nulder."

"Who is he?" Frade asked.

"He was at the military academy with el Coronel and el Coronel Perón, and later at the Kriegsschule with your father," Enrico announced, and matter-of-factly added: "Then he was cashiered for being a pervert and a liar."

"What was that all about?" Clete asked.

"Young girls on the estancia," Enrico said. "Your father told el Coronel Perón that he never wanted to hear the name Rodolfo Nulder spoken again, and that if Nulder ever put foot on Estancia San Pedro y San Pablo again he would kill him."

"Bernardo?" Frade asked.

"I think Rodríguez summed it up pretty well," Martín said dryly.

Frade thought: *Wonder what my father thought of Tío Juan's taste for young girls?*

Would he have approved of me calling my godfather a degenerate sonofabitch and then throwing him out of Uncle Willy's—my—house?

Martín added: "El Señor Nulder is now the director of security at the Secretariat of Labor and Retirement Plans."

"And this lying pervert is going to Germany with the diplomats why?" Frade said.

Martín shrugged. "I have no idea, but that may be why they were so late getting here. They didn't want anyone to see Nulder getting on the airplane, so they waited until it was dark."

"And you have no idea why this sterling character is going to Germany?" Frade pursued.

Martín shook his head. "Not long ago, over drinks at the officers' casino at Campo de Mayo, I had a chat with el Coronel Sánchez of General Ramírez's staff. He just happened to mention that he'd had a conversation with *el General* in which *el General* mentioned that with so much on my plate, he was sure I was wasting my time and assets on investigating things at the Secretariat of Labor and Retirement Plans. 'Perón and his people are perfectly able to take care of that sort of thing themselves.'"

"You were told to back off?" Clete asked more than a little incredulously.

Martín repeated: "I was told that it was General Ramírez who had mentioned he hoped I wasn't wasting my time and assets on the Secretariat of Labor and Retirement Plans."

"You never happened to mention that to me."

Martín smiled. "I like you, Cletus. And I love my wife. But there are some things I never mention to either one of you."

"Taking pictures of this guy is backing off?" Clete said.

"Don Cletus Frade, master of the indelicate observation," Martín said with a smile.

"And I don't suppose you would be heartbroken if we kept an eye on him for you while we're over there, would you?"

"You know I'm always interested in anything you have to tell me."

"If this guy went to the Kriegsschule with my father . . ."

"He probably knows a good number of senior German officers," Martín finished for him. "Some of whom might wish to come here now that their services are no longer required."

"So this whole thing is an excuse to bring a planeload of Nazis here?" Clete wondered aloud.

"*Another* planeload of Nazis, you mean?" Martín asked.

"I have no idea what you're talking about, *mi general*," Clete said. "Unless you're suggesting that some of the priests, brothers, and nuns who SAA has ferried here for the Vatican—and traveling on Vatican passports—weren't who they claimed to be."

Martín said: "One thought that occurred to me is that if there was an important Nazi—or Nazis, plural—who wished to spare themselves a long and hazardous trip on a submarine to come here . . ."

"They could come in the comfort that SAA offers to all its passengers?" Clete finished for him.

"It's a thought," Martín said.

"Bernardo, did you hear the rumor that Hitler did not kill himself and his wife, but was flown out of Berlin in a Fieseler Storch?"

"Delgano mentioned that he'd heard that," Martín said. "Do you believe it?"

"No, I don't. But this thought of yours makes sense."

"Are you going to try to see General Gehlen while you're in Germany?" Martín asked, and then, before Clete could answer, went on: "Maybe he would have some thoughts on all this."

"No one seems to know where he is, but I'm going to try to find him."

"To what end?"

"I'll play that card when someone deals it," Clete said. "We made a deal with him. Nobody's told me the deal is off."

"Bring him here?"

"If that's the only option to keep him out of the hands of the Russians."

"He'd have a Vatican passport?"

"The others traveled that way."

"Clete," Delgano said, "Peralta just showed up; looks like he's headed here."

Captain Mario Peralta was a member of the second crew. If he had had any questions about First Officers von Wachtstein and Boltitz replacing the SAA pilots originally scheduled for the flight, Clete hadn't heard about them. That suggested to Clete that Peralta was taking his orders from Gonzalo Delgano both as an SAA pilot and as somebody else who also worked covertly for Martín.

"It would appear that your mission of mercy and compassion is ready to go," Martín said.

"You told me one time you had a man in Berlin," Frade said.

Martín nodded.

"José Ruiz," he said. "We were at the Academy together."

"He's the military attaché?"

"The financial counselor," Martín said.

"And he'll be coming back with us?"

Martín nodded again.

"He might be useful," Frade said.

"So I told Gonzalo," Martín said. "Anything else I can do?"

"As a matter of fact," Frade said, and handed him the briefcase he'd gotten from Colonel Flowers. "I forgot to leave my wife her allowance. Would you get this to her, please?"

Martín took the briefcase. It was much heavier than he expected.

"What's in here besides her allowance—bricks?"

"Nothing. I'm probably more generous to my wife than you are to yours."

Martín looked at the briefcase suspiciously but didn't reply.

"Go on. Have a look. You were going to anyway, the first chance you had. If you look now, you can apologize for doubting me."

After a moment's hesitation, Martín lifted the flap of the briefcase and looked inside.

"*¡Madre de Dios!*" he softly exclaimed a moment later.

"Gotcha! Now you can apologize."

"What's this for?" Martín asked.

"El General Bernardo Martín, master of the outrageous personal question. One man should never ask another why he is giving his wife a little pocket change for her purse."

"Forgive me," Martín said sarcastically.

The two looked at each other and smiled.

"Clete, be careful," Martín said. "I don't think the most dangerous part of this will be flying across the Atlantic Ocean."

"Great minds walk the same paths," Frade said, then shook Martín's hand and walked out of the Executive Suite of South American Airways.

[THREE]
Aboard *Ciudad de Rosario*
Approaching Val de Cans Airfield
Belém do Pará, Brazil
0135 17 May 1945

Captain Cletus Frade had been at the controls of the Constellation *Ciudad de Rosario* as she took off from Aeropuerto Coronel Jorge G. Frade, breaking ground at 1832. Mario Peralta was in the right seat.

As soon as the aircraft reached cruising altitude, he had turned the plane over to Peralta and sent another SAA backup pilot to the cockpit. Then he crawled into one of the two crew bunks and closed his eyes.

Three minutes later, Siggie Stein shook his shoulder.

"Don't shoot the messenger, Colonel. Your Collins is out."

A dozen Collins Radio Corporation Model 7.2 transceivers and SIGABA encryption systems had been acquired for Team Turtle at Stein's suggestion—"Trust me, they're six months ahead of state of the art"—from the Army Security Agency at Vint Hill Farms Station in Virginia. They were to provide secure communication with the ASA—and thus with the OSS—from anywhere in Argentina.

They were "installation systems," which translated to mean they were designed for use in a communications center, rather than "mobile," which would have meant installation in a truck.

One day at Estancia Don Guillermo, Clete had idly commented that he wished he could have the communications capability in the Red Lodestar.

"If you want to take a chance on me really blowing one up, I can have a shot at it," Stein had replied matter-of-factly. "Maybe el Jefe will have some ideas on how to do it."

Clete had remembered then—and only then, which embarrassed him—that Colonel Graham had told him that when being interviewed by OSS experts to see if he was qualified to be the radar man on Team Turtle, they had reported that Stein knew more about the transmission of radio waves than they did.

And that Stein and former Chief Radioman Oscar Schultz, USN, had become instant buddies when they started talking about communications equipment in a cant only the two of them understood.

Two weeks later, a SIGABA and Collins 7.2 were up and running in the Red Lodestar. Clete had not been surprised when a similar installation in SAA's first Constellation had worked well in Argentina. But he had been surprised—perhaps awed—when the system had worked in the middle of the South Atlantic Ocean and later on the ground at Lisbon.

Frade sat up in the crew bunk and said, "Siggie, I don't want to go to Germany without it. I won't go to Germany without it. What's wrong with it? Belay that. I wouldn't understand. Can you fix it, or are we going to have to go back to Buenos Aires for another one?"

"I *think* I can fix it if you can get me into the radio shop at Belém. Your call. It'll take me a couple of hours to get another system out of the warehouse at Jorge Frade."

"And to fix it at Belém?"

"Thirty minutes, if I'm right about what's wrong."

"Did Mother Superior teach you how to pray, Sergeant Stein?"

"She didn't have to. I'm a Jew. We pray a lot."

"Start now," Frade ordered.

He had then lain back down and closed his eyes.

Ten minutes after that, he opened them again, sat up, pushed himself off the bunk, and went looking for Stein, Boltitz, and von Wachtstein. He found them sitting in the seats for the backup crew, trying to doze.

He beckoned for them to follow him back into the sleeping section, motioned for the doors to the cockpit and the seating area to be closed, and then began, "We have a small problem. Belay that. We have a few small problems, plural.

"The Collins 7.2 is out. We can't do without it. Siggie thinks he can fix it if he can get into the Army Air Forces' radio maintenance facility at Val de Cans. The problem there is they may not let him in. The only reason we're going in there is because the Argentine Foreign Ministry leaned on somebody. The Collins 7.2 is a classified American radio, and they're going to wonder what the hell SAA is doing with one."

"Show them the phony OSS credentials," Stein suggested.

"The problem there—the problems—are that they *are* phony and that after I used them to get Karl and Hansel out of Fort Hunt, there's a good chance that the Army has spread the word to be prepared to arrest on sight Area Commander C. Frade of the OSS."

"So, what are you going to do?" von Wachtstein asked.

"Hansel, when you were a little boy back in the Schloss, did you ever act in a play?"

"What are you talking about?"

"You know, in a play, like *Hansel und Gretel*?"

"Yeah. Why?"

"Try to remember what your teacher taught you. You're going back on the stage when we get to Val de Cans. The play is called 'Here come the mysterious, all-powerful heroes of the Office of Strategic Services.' Starring Cletus Frade, All-American Boy. Now here's how it's going to work."

He told them.

Karl Boltitz asked dubiously, "Cletus, do you really think that's going to work?"

"It'll either work or we'll add new meaning to the Army Air Corps' song."

He then sang, *"We live in fame or go down in flames, nothing can stop the OSS Air Corps . . ."*

Frade now was standing between the pilot and copilot seats. The lights of the huge Brazilian airfield were in sight.

Mario Peralta had been in the pilot's seat during the seven-hour flight from Buenos Aires, as Clete had instructed, and another SAA backup pilot was flying as copilot.

"Give it to him, Mario," Frade ordered, "and then let me sit there."

Peralta did as ordered, but it was obvious he had been looking forward to making the approach and landing himself.

When Frade had strapped himself in and put on the headset, he gave another order, this time to the copilot: "I'll take it. You go back and send von Wachtstein up here."

"Sí, señor," the copilot said, his tone making it clear that he also had been looking forward to the approach and landing.

I knew that was going to piss them off. So why did I do it?

Because Peter needs more landing practice, and I'm the most qualified person to sit in the left seat to keep him out of trouble while he does it.

So fuck the both of you.

"Sit down, Hansel, and strap yourself in."

Von Wachtstein complied.

"You feel qualified to land this?"

Von Wachtstein considered the question and then nodded.

"Got the checklist?"

Von Wachtstein nodded again.

Frade keyed the microphone.

"Val de Cans tower, this is South American Airways

Double Zero Four. This is a Lockheed Constellation. I am ten miles south, at five thousand feet, indicating Two Nine Zero. Request approach and landing."

"SAA Double Zero Four, I have you on radar. Descend on present course reporting when at three thousand feet."

"You have the aircraft, First Officer," Clete said, and took his hands off the yoke.

"He sounded like an American," von Wachtstein said.

"This is an American air base," Frade replied. "One of our smaller ones."

After they touched down, von Wachtstein looked around in awe, and said, "One of your smaller airfields?"

They were trailing a FOLLOW ME jeep down a taxiway lined on both sides as far as they could see with far-too-many-to-count four-engined Consolidated B-24 bombers parked wingtip to wingtip.

"The larger ones are really crowded," Clete replied.

"What's going on here?"

"This base served two major roles," Clete said. "One, as a home base for B-24s looking for submarines and German—or allegedly neutral—merchant vessels, and, two, as a jump-off point for aircraft headed for Europe via Sierra Leone in West Africa."

"There's another Connie," von Wachtstein said as they came close to the transient aircraft tarmac.

The airplane bore the markings of the U.S. Army Air Forces.

Frade thought: *I wonder what the hell that's doing here?*

Did Graham or Dulles—or even Donovan—come down here to see me?

If that's the case, the odds are I'm not going to like what they have to say.

As ground handlers wanded the *Ciudad de Rosario* into a parking spot beside the other Connie, Frade picked up his microphone again.

"Val de Cans tower, this is South American Airways Double Zero Four. I'm sitting on the transient tarmac. Can you get a ladder out here to the cockpit door before, repeat before, you put a ladder up to the passenger door?"

"No problem, South American Double Zero Four. Where'd you get the American accent?"

[FOUR]

The flight-planning room was deserted except for an Air Forces lieutenant and a plump sergeant. They were sitting at sort of a counter. A weather map and a flight schedule chart were mounted on the wall behind them.

"Sorry," the sergeant greeted them, more or less courteously, "but this is for Americans only."

"Not a problem," Frade said, then looked at the officer. "Are you the AOD, Lieutenant?"

Frade was wearing the red-striped powder-blue trousers of an SAA captain, but had replaced the SAA tunic with a fur-collared leather jacket on which was a leather patch with Naval Aviator Wings and the legend FRADE, C H 1LT, USMCR. He also had replaced the ornate, high-crowned SAA uniform cap with the Stetson hat his uncle

Jim had been wearing when he dropped dead in the Midland Petroleum Club.

The lieutenant, whose face showed his confusion at what stood before him, shook his head and then asked, "You're from that Argentine airliner?"

"Figured that out, did you?" Clete said. "How about getting the AOD down here for me?"

Clete, who had done many tours as an AOD—aerodrome officer of the day—understood that at a little after two in the morning most AODs would be curled up on a cot and would tend to be annoyed if awakened to deal with anything less than the field being attacked by Martians. And AODs were usually senior to the officer in charge of the flight-planning room.

One of the stage directions Director Frade had issued to his cast was that when he issued an order, the reply would be in the same language used to issue the order. So, when he next said in German, "Hansel, you and Karl take a look at the weather map," von Wachtstein replied, *"Jawohl, Herr Oberst."* Then both headed for the weather map behind the counter.

This tended to further confuse the lieutenant and the sergeant. But the latter retained enough of his composure to proclaim, "Hey, you can't go back there!"

"Don't be absurd, Sergeant," Frade said.

"The colonel told you to get the AOD down here, Lieutenant," Siggie Stein snapped. "Do it."

"Easy, Siggie," Frade said.

Frade then extended to the lieutenant the credentials identifying him as an OSS area commander.

"Not only weren't we here, but I didn't show you that," Frade said. "Understood, Lieutenant?"

The lieutenant was clearly dazzled by the spurious credentials.

"Yes, sir," the lieutenant said. "Sergeant, go get Major Cronin."

Frade impatiently gestured for the lieutenant to return his credentials. The lieutenant hastily did so.

Major Cronin, a nice-looking young officer wearing pilot's wings, appeared two minutes later, looking somewhat sleepy eyed.

"You're off that Argentine Constellation, right?" he said.

"Correct," Frade said. He extended his credentials. "Take a quick look at that, please, Major, and then forget you ever saw it or us."

Major Cronin looked, then said, "Yes, sir. And what can Val de Cans do for the OSS?"

"You can start, Major, first things first, by getting someone from your radio maintenance section familiar with the Collins 7.2 transceiver up here to assist my communications officer. The 7.2 in my Connie needs service."

Major Cronin looked confused. "Excuse me, sir . . . what do I call you?"

"'Sir' will do just fine," Frade said.

"Sir, I'm a little confused. The Collins 7.2 is a fixed-station communications device. Are you sure that's what you have in your aircraft?"

"Trust the colonel, Major, when he says we have one in our airplane," Stein said.

"Yes, sir," the major said, and then turned to the lieutenant. "Charley, why don't you run over to the radio shack and get someone familiar with the 7.2 over here."

"Better yet, Lieutenant," Stein said, "why don't I go with you to the radio shack?"

"Yes, sir," the major and the lieutenant said in chorus.

"All right, sir?" Stein asked.

"Carry on, Stein," Frade ordered.

Von Wachtstein and Boltitz returned from the weather map.

"Looks pretty good, Clete," von Wachtstein announced in German. "A couple of minor storms to the south. The winds aloft will be on our tail."

"Danke schön," Frade replied.

Von Wachtstein and Boltitz then moved behind Frade and took up positions roughly like that of Parade Rest.

The major and the lieutenant looked intently at them.

"I presume you have been officially informed," Frade said, "that the SAA Constellation is bound for Germany to relieve the Argentine diplomatic staff in Berlin."

"We've been expecting you, Colonel," the major said.

"Please do not use my rank," Frade said.

"Sorry, sir."

"That mission of compassion and mercy, however, is not the only reason I and these members of my staff are going to Germany. The second mission is unknown, as is my association with the OSS, to the Argentine diplomats, and I wish it kept that way. Understood?"

"Yes, sir," the major and the lieutenant again said together.

"I wish to discuss the second mission with the officer,

or officers, commanding the B-24 submarine hunting group. Is that one officer or two?"

"Actually, sir, it's four. In the wing, there are two antisubmarine groups here, and a third, the 480th, at Port Lyautey, in Morocco. Three group commanders, colonels, and the brigadier general who commands the wing, sir."

"The general is where?" Clete asked.

"Here, sir. In his quarters."

"Let's start with him. Would you get him on the phone, Major, offer my apologies for waking him up, and ask him to come down here?"

"Yes, sir. And who do I say, sir, wishes to see him?"

"Tell him anything you wish, so long as you don't mention the OSS."

"Can I mention South American Airways?"

"Why not?"

VI

[ONE]
Val de Cans Airfield
Belém do Pará, Brazil
0218 17 May 1945

Brigadier General Robert G. Bendick, U.S. Army Air Forces, walked into the flight-planning room five minutes later, trailed by his aide-de-camp. He was a trim, intelligent-looking man in his midthirties; the aide looked like he had just finished high school.

"Good morning," General Bendick said. "I'm afraid my Spanish is awful."

"Not a problem, General," Frade said. "I speak English. Thank you for coming so quickly. We're a little pressed for time."

Frade handed him the spurious credentials.

"Oh," the general said.

"I never showed you those, sir. This is an out-of-school meeting."

"To what end?"

"We're headed for Berlin to relieve the Argentine diplomatic staff there. The aircraft has been chartered by the Argentine Foreign Ministry."

"I saw the notification of that," General Bendick said. "And?"

"Before we get into 'and,' why don't you tell me about the other Constellation on the tarmac?"

"Before we get into 'the other Constellation,' why don't you tell me about those Naval Aviator Wings you're sporting?"

Their eyes locked. Frade had a sudden epiphany.

I am not going to get away with bullshitting this guy.

So, what do I do now?

"In another, happier life, I was a Marine fighter pilot," Clete said.

Bendick's eyes remained on his.

"Oh, really? And where exactly were you a Marine fighter pilot?"

He doesn't believe me.

"They called it the Cactus Air Force, General."

"In another, happier life, I was a B-17 pilot," General Bendick said. "On one memorable day, I was saved from winding up in the drink off Guadalcanal by three Marine Grumman F4F Wildcats of VMF-221. Half a dozen very skilled Zero pilots had already taken out two of my engines and most of my vertical stabilizer when the Marines showed up. After dealing with the Zeros—the Marine F4Fs shot two down and scattered the others—the Marines then led me to Guadalcanal."

He's calling my bluff.

And he didn't just make up that yarn.

"The name Dawkins mean anything to you?" General Bendick then asked.

Clete nodded. "If the general is referring to Lieutenant Colonel Clyde W. Dawkins, I had the privilege of being under his command."

"At Fighter One? VMF-221?"

"Yes, sir," Clete said.

"You were then a what?"

"A first lieutenant, sir."

"And now?"

"I'm a lieutenant colonel, sir."

"So, what's this, Colonel?" Bendick asked, holding up the spurious OSS credentials. "I never saw anything like this before. What's an OSS area commander? And this makes you area commander of exactly what area?"

"Argentina and Uruguay, primarily."

Bendick's eyes showed he wasn't satisfied with that answer.

Bendick said: "Let's go back down Memory Lane, Colonel. What did Colonel Dawkins's officers call him?"

"'Sir,'" Clete blurted.

Clete thought he saw the hint of a smile on Bendick's lips.

"And behind his back?"

"'The Dawk,' sir."

"And so they did," Bendick said, "something that would be known only to his officers."

He handed Frade the spurious OSS credentials.

"We had been briefed, of course," he said, "on using Henderson Field in an emergency. We had also been briefed on Fighter One, and told it was not suitable for emergency landings of B-17 aircraft. As I approached Guadalcanal, I came to the reluctant conclusion that I had neither the altitude nor the controls to make Henderson, so I put it down on Fighter One.

"I was a pretty good B-17 pilot, but not good enough to land on only one main gear, so shortly thereafter I found myself sitting at the side of the runway with, thank God, all of my crew. We were watching my aircraft burn when a feisty tall drink of water showed up. He was wearing shorts and shoes—no shirt, no cap—and in each hand he had four of those little bottles of medicinal bourbon."

Bendick met Frade's eyes. Frade nodded.

Bendick went on: "I shall never forget what he said to me on that memorable occasion: 'When we saw you coming in, son, the odds were ten-to-one that nobody was going to walk away from your landing. You do know this isn't Henderson Field?'"

"That sounds like The Dawk," Clete said, smiling. "And *fists full* of medicinal bourbon bottles? Getting more than one little bottle from Colonel Dawkins meant he thought you had done good."

"So I later learned," General Bendick said. "So, welcome, welcome to Val de Cans. What do I call you?"

Colonel Dawkins, wherever you are, you have just saved my ass again.

How many times does that make?

"My name is Cletus Frade. My friends call me Clete. I wish you would."

The general offered his hand. "Bob Bendick, Clete."

Clete, pointing to them as he did so, said, "Peter von Wachtstein, Karl Boltitz, Enrico Rodríguez. My commo guy, Siggie Stein, is already in your radio shack; we have a Collins 7.2 aboard that needs fixing."

"An *airborne* Collins 7.2?"

"Siggie Stein is an amazing commo guy," Clete said.

"So, what can I do for you?"

"Tell me about the other Connie."

"It's classified Top Secret," General Bendick replied.

"Manhattan Project?"

"Excuse me?"

"Excuse me, but are you saying 'Excuse me' because you don't want to admit knowledge of the Manhattan Project?" Clete asked with a smile.

"I never heard of it," General Bendick said. "What is it?"

"I can't tell you. But it's the only thing I know that would justify classifying a passenger flight Top Secret."

General Bendick looked at Frade for a long moment.

"How about a planeload of Secret Service agents bound for Frankfurt?" he asked finally.

"Is that what it is?"

Bendick nodded.

"What would be so secret about that?" Clete asked.

"President Truman going to Germany?"

"I don't think that's very likely," Clete said. "Why?"

Bendick shrugged.

"The Secret Service is under the Treasury Department," Clete then said. "And the secretary of the Treasury suspects that Nazis are being smuggled out of Germany to Argentina."

"I know," Bendick said.

"You know that Nazis are being smuggled out of Germany, or that Morgenthau thinks they are?"

"These Secret Service agents have been nosing around the base flashing their badges and asking my junior officers and enlisted men if they know anything about Nazis being smuggled through here. Or even of mysterious airplanes passing through here. They are even threatening them with what happens when you lie to a Secret Service agent." He chuckled, and added: "I wonder what they're going to think about your mysterious airplane."

"If they ask, what will they be told?"

"Same that we were told. That it's a charter flight to rescue Argentine diplomats from Germany. Unless . . ."

"No. That's fine. And it has the advantage of being the truth. Did these Secret Service people talk to you, tell you what they're looking for?"

"No. I must look like somebody who would smuggle Nazis."

"If they had asked you, General—"

"I thought we were on a first-name basis."

"Sorry. *Bob*, if they had asked you . . ."

"What would I have told them? The truth. I've heard the rumors, and I think there's something to them, but I don't have any personal knowledge, and my counterintelligence people haven't come up with anything concrete."

"The rumors are true. One of my jobs is to try to stop fleeing Nazis trying to get to South America from getting there, or catch them. That's what I wanted to talk to you about. But before I get into that, how long has this planeload of Secret Service agents been here?"

"About forty-eight hours. All they were supposed to do was take on fuel, but there was a message saying 'delay departure until further notice.'"

"Which conveniently provided time for their people to ask questions of your people."

"That thought ran through my mind. What the hell is that all about?"

"I don't know," Clete said. "Maybe we'll find out when we get to Germany. Let's get back to the reason I wanted to see you. We have some pretty good intelligence that a number of German submarines are headed for Argentina. The number ranges from three we're very sure about, to a fleet—as many as twenty-odd. A fleet seems unlikely but can't be dismissed out of hand. The Nazis have a program called Operation Phoenix—"

"That's real?" Bendick asked.

"I don't know what you heard about it, so let me tell you what I know about it. Starting in 1943, the Nazis started sending money and things that can be easily converted to money—gold, diamonds, other precious stones, et cetera—to Argentina. The idea was to set up sanctuaries in Argentina, Paraguay, Uruguay, and Brazil to which senior officers could flee, both escaping the trials we plan for them and using their new home as a base from which they can rise, rested and with large amounts of money, Phoenix-like, and keep National Socialism going. Or bring it back to life."

"That's pretty much what I heard, but it sounded like the plot for a bad movie," Bendick said.

"They sent a lot of money—hundreds of millions of dollars—to Argentina, plus some senior SS officers to run the program. We've managed to stop a lot of it, but by no means all."

"What kind of senior SS officers?"

"Himmler's adjutant, for one. Actually, the Reichsführer-SS's First Deputy Adjutant. SS-Brigadeführer Ritter Manfred von Deitzberg. He came by submarine."

"And this guy is already in Argentina?" Bendick asked incredulously.

"Yeah, but he's no longer a problem," Clete said.

"How so?"

"He was taking a leak in the men's room of a charming little hotel in the charming little village of San Martín de los Andes when someone blew his brains all over the urinal with a Ballester-Molina—an Argentine copy of our .45."

"You wouldn't happen to know who did that, would you, Clete?"

"Of course not," Clete replied not very convincingly.

"And what are the Argentines doing about all these Nazis running loose in Argentina? Looking the other way?"

"You ever hear that money talks, Bob?"

"Is that what it is?"

"There is also an element—perfectly serious people—who feel the Nazis were a Christian bulwark against the Communist Antichrist. Unfortunately, to some odd degree, I'm afraid they may be right."

"You think the Communists are going to be a threat?"

It took Clete a moment to consider the wisdom of what he wanted to say. In the end, he decided to say it.

"I'm reliably informed that J. Edgar Hoover thinks they're the new enemy."

"And you agree with Hoover?"

"Yeah, I guess I do. I never was able to regard Stalin as Friendly Uncle Joe, and I know for a fact the Russians are trying very hard to break into the . . . one of our most important secrets."

"Which secret would that be?"

"Sorry, I just can't tell you."

"Which brings us back, I suppose, to why you wanted to see me."

"I don't know this for sure, but I have the feeling that just as soon as I get to Germany, there will be a meeting about the submarines headed this way."

"A meeting between whom?" Bendick asked.

"It will be under Eisenhower—probably under his G-2—but it won't all be under SHAEF. Someone from General Marshall's staff will probably be there, and certainly someone from Army Intelligence. And the Office of Naval Intelligence. And, of course, the OSS. And probably, come to think of it, the Secret Service agents here."

Clete then said: "Whatever intelligence is available about the German submarines will be presented, discussed, and it will be agreed that something has to be done about them. And, finally, it will be decided who exactly will have to do something about them.

"The one thing senior brass hates to do is take on a mission that will probably end in failure. Or about which they know very little, which would cause them to fail. So they will look around for someone who is an expert in the area of dealing with German submarines in South America. There are only two people who meet that criterion, Bob. You and me."

"I think I know where you're going, Clete," Bendick said, "but there is one flaw in your argument. I don't have any idea how to find these German submarines."

"You and I have something else in common," Frade said. "If we can't find the submarines, that's not the fault of G-2, or Naval Intelligence—it's our fault. 'What do you expect? While we've been fighting the Wehrmacht across Europe, Bendick and Frade have been sitting in beautiful South America drinking rum and Coca-Cola and chasing senoritas.'"

"Do you know how many aircraft we've lost over the South Atlantic?" Bendick asked.

"How many were actually shot down?"

"I take your point," Bendick said after a moment.

"I think they call that 'pilot error,'" Clete said. "You don't get no Air Medals or Distinguished Flying Crosses for pilot error."

Bendick shook his head.

"Here's how I see it," Frade went on. "OSS will be

given the mission, and your wing will be among our many assets."

"As I said, this particular asset doesn't have a clue where to look for these submarines."

"Maybe we can give you a little help there. Out of school."

"Out of school? I don't understand."

"I have some intel that I know is reliable, and when we get to Germany and start to talk to the crews of U-boats, I think we're going to have some more intel, maybe a good deal more. The problem is I can't tell G-2, or Naval Intelligence, and certainly not the Secret Service, about it, because they will want to know where it came from, and I can't do that."

"Why not?" Bendick asked almost automatically, and then, before Frade had a chance to answer, said, "You have spies in Germany, is that what you're saying?"

"Not spies, General," Boltitz offered. "One is an anti-Nazi former U-boat officer."

Bendick looked at Boltitz, then back at Frade. "And you're going to see this anti-Nazi U-boat officer in Germany? Is that what you're saying? And he's going to help you find these submarines?"

"What this anti-Nazi U-boat officer is going to do, Bob, is tell you all he knows about how U-boat crews are trained to cross the South Atlantic, what courses they followed in the past and presumably will follow now, their schedules of on-the-surface and submerged operations—that sort of thing. And then, when we get to Germany, he'll see what he can find out from U-boat crews now in POW cages."

"I'm a little slow sometimes," Bendick said. Then he looked at Boltitz. "Why should I trust you?"

Frade answered for him: "You've heard of the failed attempt by Colonel Graf von Stauffenberg to kill Adolf Hitler?"

Bendick looked at Frade, nodded, but said nothing.

"At the time, Kapitän zur See Boltitz was the German naval attaché in Buenos Aires and"—he gestured at Peter—"Major von Wachtstein was the assistant military attaché for air. The day after the bomb failed to kill Hitler, the embassy got a radio message ordering their arrest for high treason."

"They were involved in the bombing?"

"In the plot of the bombing," Frade explained, "as were Peter's father, Generalleutnant Graf Karl-Friedrich von Wachtstein, and Karl's father, Vizeadmiral Kurt Boltitz. General von Wachtstein was arrested, tried by a people's court, and hung from a butcher's hook."

"My God!"

"Vizeadmiral Boltitz, who worked for Admiral Wilhelm Canaris, the chief of German Military Intelligence, was not immediately arrested, nor was Admiral Canaris. We don't know where Vizeadmiral Boltitz is, only that the SS was looking for him until the last day of the war."

"He ran?" Bendick asked.

Frade nodded.

"On April twenty-third—just over three weeks ago—

the 97th Infantry Division of the Third U.S. Army liberated the Flossenberg Concentration Camp in Bavaria. They found Admiral Canaris's naked, decomposing body hanging from a gallows. It had been left there as a gesture of contempt following the admiral's execution on April ninth for his role in the failed attempt to kill Hitler."

"Jesus Christ!" Bendick said, then asked, "And these two German officers ran from the arrest order to Argentina?"

"No. What happened—both had been working for me—was that I flew them to Canoas, where they surrendered to the commanding officer. They were then flown to the senior enemy officer interrogation facility at Fort Hunt, outside Washington."

"If they had been working for you, why didn't you just keep them in Argentina?"

"Argentina was then neutral. Leaning strongly toward the Axis, but neutral. If von Wachtstein and Boltitz had stayed there, there was a good chance that some Argentine Nazi would learn where they were, tell the German Embassy, and the SS would go after them. Try to kill them."

"They'd actually do something like that?"

"They already had done something like that. They tried to kill the commercial attaché of the German Embassy, who had deserted his post. Boltitz and von Wachtstein were no longer of any use to me inside the German Embassy, so getting them into a POW enclosure in the States seemed to be the right thing to do."

"But they're not in a POW enclosure, are they?"

"No. They are now OSS special agents—show him your ID, Hansel."

Peter did.

Bendick nodded his acceptance.

Frade went on: "I knew I was going to need them, so last week—on May tenth—I flew to Washington and got them."

General Bendick looked at von Wachtstein and, shaking his head in disbelief, asked, "And you were the air attaché of the German Embassy?"

"Tell him, Hansel," Frade ordered.

"Before that," von Wachtstein said, "I was commanding officer of Jagdstaffel 232—Focke-Wulf 190s—defending Berlin against B-17s."

Bendick shook his head again and then asked Frade, "They were turned over to you—is that what you're saying?"

"No, what I said was that I needed them, so I went and got them. I didn't have the time to deal with the bureaucracy."

"You just took them from a POW camp on your own authority?"

Frade nodded.

Bendick again shook his head in disbelief.

Frade said: "Your original question, Bob, was something like 'Why should I trust Boltitz?'"

Bendick met Frade's eyes. "Has it occurred to you, Colonel Frade, that the smart thing for me to do is pick up that telephone and tell my provost marshal to come running? That two escaped German POWs and the guy who helped them escape are in flight planning?"

Frade held the gaze and said, "You could do that, General. It's known as 'covering your ass.' But you won't."

"And why won't I?"

"Two reasons. One is that you know that if you did, you'd be helping the Nazis get away with sending their submarines to South America, and you don't want to do that. Two, you're not that kind—the CYA kind—of an officer."

"How do you know? Was telling me all this smart?"

"Probably not. But in my business, every once in a while you have to take a chance. I took it. I'd take it again."

"Taking a chance like putting a shot-up B-17 down on a fighter strip? Because it wasn't really an option?"

"Yes, sir."

General Bendick turned to his aide-de-camp.

"Jimmy," he ordered, "get on the horn and get Colonel DuBois and Colonel Nathan down here. Tell them I'm running a middle-of-the-night training program in how to find submarines."

[TWO]
Transient Mess
Val de Cans Airfield
Belém do Pará, Brazil
0405 17 May 1945

SAA Chief Pilot Gonzalo Delgano, Captain Mario Peralta, and a flight engineer whose name Clete could never remember—he thought of him as "the chubby flight engineer, who, three-to-one, also works for the BIS"—were sitting over coffee at a table near the door when Clete and the others walked in.

The diplomats were sitting at various tables around the nearly empty mess.

"We wondered where you were," Delgano greeted them.

"We all set to go?" Clete replied.

"Anytime you are. Weather looks good, and we may even get that tailwind."

"Just as soon as we have some breakfast," Clete said.

"You haven't eaten?" Delgano asked.

"No. That's why we're going to eat now," Clete said.

If you'd have come out and just asked, "What have you been up to?" I probably would have told you.

"El Señor Nulder wondered what had happened to you," Delgano said.

"And asked you?"

Delgano nodded.

"What did you tell him?"

"The truth. I didn't know."

Clete ordered: "Enrico, why don't you go ask Señor Nulder if he can spare a moment for me?"

It was the first time that Frade had gotten a good look at Rodolfo Nulder, the director of security at the Secretariat of Labor and Retirement Plans. He thought there was something about him—his carriage, a hint of arrogance—that suggested a military background.

Nulder smiled and put out his hand as he approached the table.

"I'm Rodolfo Nulder, Señor Frade," he announced with a charming smile.

"So Capitán Delgano has been telling me."

"Did he also tell you that I was at both the military academy and the Kriegsschule with your father?"

"No, as a matter of fact, he didn't," Frade lied, somewhat deflating Nulder's arrogance, if only for a moment. "But he did tell me, when I asked him who was in charge of our cargo of diplomats, that you probably were. True?"

"When I left the army, I became involved with governmental security. I'm presently the director of security for the Secretariat of Labor and Retirement Plans—"

"The Secretariat of Labor and Retirement Plans?" Frade interrupted. "Or the Secretary of Labor and Retirement Plans?"

Nulder raised his eyebrows, then said, "Actually, I suppose one could say that both are true. I sometimes assist el Coronel Perón in security matters outside the Secretariat of Labor and Retirement Plans. This is one of those occasions. Actually, Señor Frade, I was hoping to have a word with you, to explain my role in this mission, when we arrived here. But then no one seemed to know where you were."

"No one did," Frade said.

Nulder's charming smile flickered off and then came back on.

He said: "I was going to tell you that in his role as vice president, el Coronel Perón thought, because I know Germany, that I would be useful in carrying out the mission President Farrell had assigned to the Foreign Ministry, and asked me to participate."

"Does that mean you're the man in charge?" Frade asked, not very pleasantly.

"Let me put it this way. Think of me as the liaison officer between yourself, as the managing director of SAA, and the senior Foreign Ministry officer, Ambassador Giménez, on this mission."

Frade considered that, nodded, and said: "Then I guess you're the man I'm looking for. You can pass this on to Ambassador Giménez. . . . Wait. I just thought of something: How can you be an ambassador to a country that no longer exists? What used to be Germany is now territory held by force of arms by the Allied Powers and under martial law. Can you accredit an ambassador to a military headquarters?"

Nulder's face showed both that he had not expected the question and that he had no answer to it.

"I really don't know," he confessed. "Why don't we leave such questions to the Foreign Ministry?"

"Okay. But the reason I wanted to see the man in charge—and the reason I'm just now having my breakfast—is that the commanding general of this base sent for me. When I got to his office, he had several officers of the United States Secret Service with him. Are you familiar with the Secret Service?"

"Somewhat," Nulder said.

"Well, their primary duty is to protect the President. I knew that. But what I remembered just now is that they're under the secretary of the Treasury."

"I don't understand what that means," Nulder admitted.

"Well, the secretary of the Treasury is a man named Morgenthau. He's Jewish. He doesn't like Nazis. He's heard that some Nazis are going to try to avoid trial for war crimes by escaping to South America. So he's put the Secret Service on it."

"I don't quite follow you," Nulder said.

"They were subtle, if you know what I mean," Frade said. "They didn't come right out and say they suspect the Foreign Ministry of doing anything they shouldn't, like smuggling Nazis into Argentina, but they did tell me that *any* diplomats going into occupied Germany could forget diplomatic immunity. Anybody caught trying to help Nazis get out of Germany will find themselves standing in front of a court-martial."

"I don't think they can do that," Nulder said.

"I don't know if they could or not, Señor Nulder. But that's what they told me. It was sort of a word to the wise, if you know what I mean."

Nulder did not reply.

"They also told me the Secret Service has authority on any U.S. base—like this one, and Canoas. Which means, if they wanted to, they could search the airplane and check everybody's identity.

"What they were saying, without coming right out and saying it, was that we can expect to be searched pretty carefully on our way home."

After a long moment, Nulder said: "Interesting. Have you any idea when we'll be taking off?"

"Ten minutes after I finish my breakfast."

"Well, then, I'll see you aboard," Nulder said, offered his hand, and then began walking away.

"Pass that on to Ambassador Whatsisname, will you, Señor Nulder?" Clete called after him.

Nulder acknowledged the call with an impatient wave of his hand, but neither replied nor turned around.

Clete looked at Delgano.

"Gonzo, why do I think I just ruined Señor Nulder's day? And why doesn't that bother me?"

"You're crazy, Cletus, that's why," Delgano said.

But Delgano was smiling.

And when Frade looked at Captain Peralta and the chubby flight engineer and saw their smiles, he knew it wasn't probable they were officers of the BIS—but certain.

[THREE]
Portela Airport
Lisbon, Portugal
1850 17 May 1945

The weather had not been good. And there had been no tailwind. There had been turbulence—some of it severe—several times.

Delgano had flown the entire leg with Peralta as his copilot. Frade knew that the smart thing for him to do was take over from Delgano to give him a rest. He also knew—although it wasn't true—that Delgano would take being relieved as proof that Frade found his piloting wanting. And so would the other SAA pilots and flight engineers.

So he had let him fly.

There was also some electrical disturbance; they didn't pick up Portela's Radio Direction Finding signal until thirty-five minutes after the dead-reckoning flight plan said they should. Worse, when they finally heard it, it showed them to be about one hundred miles south of where they should have been.

They had been in no unusual danger. They had a little more than an hour's fuel remaining when they touched down at Portela Airport in a driving rain.

Still, it had been anything but a pleasant flight, and Delgano's face showed his fatigue when he looked up at Clete.

"Nice job, Gonzo," Clete said.

The grateful look Delgano then made told Clete

he had made the right decision in not trying to relieve him.

A FOLLOW ME pickup truck led them to the passenger terminal.

It was raining so hard that Clete ordered that they leave the cockpit door closed and exit the aircraft by the passenger door, up to which had been rolled a covered stairway.

When they walked into the terminal, Frade immediately saw Fernando Aragão—ostensibly the SAA director in Portugal but, more important, the Lisbon OSS station chief. He was in his fifties and chubby, with slicked-back black hair and a neatly kept pencil mustache.

With Aragão was a well-dressed, tall, slender, olive-skinned man with an arrogant air about him.

Frade disliked him on sight.

Aragão began: "Señor de Hernández, this is—"

"I am Claudio de Hernández, the ambassador," the man cut him off. "Who's in charge of the charter aircraft?"

Frade pointed to Delgano.

Delgano pointed to Frade.

"Well," the ambassador immediately and more than a little arrogantly demanded, "which is it?"

Then, before anyone could reply, he demanded of Frade, who was wearing his Naval Aviator's leather jacket, "Who are you, señor?"

"Who did you say you were?" Frade replied.

"I am Claudio de Hernández, the Argentine ambassador."

"Good. I was wondering how I was going to find you."

"Excuse me?"

"Have you got something that says you're the ambassador? A diplomatic passport, a carnet, something like that?"

"I don't think I like your attitude or tone of voice, señor."

"I don't like yours much, either," Frade said. "We're back to how do I know you're who you say you are?"

"Señor Aragão has told you who I am."

"He's told me who he *thinks* you are." Frade looked at Aragão. "Has this fellow ever shown you his identification, Fernando?"

"Actually, no," Aragão replied. "But—"

"There you go," Frade said.

Coldly furious, de Hernández said, "I asked you before, señor. Who are you?"

"If you can show me something that says you're the Argentine ambassador, I'll tell you. Otherwise, I'm going to get in a taxi and go to the hotel. It's been a long flight, and I'm tired."

The ambassador came up with a diplomatic carnet and shoved it at Frade.

Frade examined it.

"This is in Portuguese," he said. "I don't speak Portuguese. You don't have a passport?"

The ambassador produced his diplomatic passport. "I hope you find that satisfactory, señor," he said sarcastically.

"Well, it's a step in the right direction. Have you got our overflight clearances, Mr. Ambassador?"

After a moment's hesitation, he said, "There is a problem. A small problem—"

"In other words, you don't have them?"

"You said that once I established my bona fides you would identify yourself."

"My name is Frade. General Farrell sent word to me that you—the Argentine Foreign Ministry anyway; I don't recall that he specifically mentioned the Argentine ambassador to Portugal—would have the necessary overflight permission waiting for me when we arrived in Lisbon. And now you're telling me you don't have them. I can't believe that General Farrell would tell me something he didn't believe. Exactly what's going on here, Mr. Ambassador?"

"Would you be so kind, Señor Frade, to tell me your function in this mission?"

"I'm the managing director of South American Airways. When General Farrell asked me to set this up, I was of course, as a patriotic Argentine, anxious to do what I could to rescue our diplomats from Germany, and I decided the best way I could do that was to fly the mission myself."

"You're a pilot?"

"How could I possibly fly this mission if I wasn't a pilot, Mr. Ambassador?"

"I wasn't told any of this," the ambassador said.

"Why should you have been? And there is another problem, Mr. Ambassador. When we were at the North American Val de Cans Airfield in Brazil, I was summoned by the general in command. He made two things clear to me. First, that he suspects this flight is a cover under which senior former German officials—Nazis, to put a point on it—will be allowed to escape Germany under Argentine diplomatic protection—"

"That's outrageous!"

"That's what the North American general suspects. Second, he told me that if we are caught smuggling Nazis out of Germany, not only will we be tried by a U.S. Military Tribunal and put in prison for at least ten years, but they will confiscate the airplane."

"They couldn't do that," Ambassador Hernández said. "We have diplomatic immunity!"

"I tried to tell him that. In effect, he said, 'He who has the power to grant immunity has the power to take it away.' I believe him. He was very serious. Now, I told Señor Nulder all this, and I told him to tell Ambassador Giménez, and now I'm telling you."

"The whole idea is preposterous!"

"Be that as it may, I am not going to risk arrest by the Americans, nor the loss of an SAA aircraft by confiscation. Not only did it cost SAA right at half a million dollars—*half a million dollars*, Mr. Ambassador!—but if they caught us trying to smuggle Nazis out of Germany on an airplane they sold us, they certainly wouldn't sell us another one."

"I give you my word of honor, Señor Frade, that I know nothing about any of this," Ambassador Claudio de Hernández said, his tone suggesting that he really hoped Frade would take his word.

Gotcha!

"What I would like you to do, Mr. Ambassador, is send a cable to the foreign minister in Buenos Aires, telling him that absent any clear denial from him that this rescue mission has absolutely nothing to do with rescuing Nazis from the wholly justified outrage of the Allies—and I will point out to you that Argentina has now become one of the Allies—that I intend to return to Argentina, flyover clearances or not."

"I'm not sure I can do that," Ambassador Hernández said.

"That, of course, is your decision. I can no more tell you what to do than you can tell me what to do." He turned to Aragão. "Fernando, where's the station wagon?"

"Just outside, Señor Frade."

"Then let's go to the hotel," Frade said. "Nice to meet you, Mr. Ambassador."

[FOUR]
The Bar, Hotel Britania
Rua Rodrigues Sampaio 17
Lisbon, Portugal
1935 17 May 1945

"Why do I think you're planning something evil?" Gonzalo Delgano asked Cletus Frade even before the bartender came to serve them. They were seated with Mario Peralta and Pedro Vega, the chubby flight engineer, as Fernando Aragão caught up to them.

"Did you see the dirty looks we got from our passengers as they were getting on that bus?" Frade replied.

"That's probably because that bus has been in service since the First World War and we were getting into Fernando's nice, nearly new American station wagon," Delgano said.

"Glad to be of some service," Aragão said.

The bartender approached them.

Frade gasped and otherwise mimed that he was dying of dehydration.

"Welcome back to Lisbon, Señor Frade," the bartender said, and without orders set two glasses, a siphon bottle of water, and a wine bottle on the bar.

As the barman pulled the cork from the wine bottle, Frade poured and drank two glasses of the soda water.

"I was thinking," Frade said, "that if there is one thing diplomats really need and seldom get it's a lesson in humility." He paused, went through the ritual of testing the wine, then said to the bartender, "Very nice. After you fill my glass, give small quantities to my friends."

"Humility? Such as getting on the ancient bus?" Peralta asked.

"That was a start, but what I'm thinking right now is to ask Fernando to have a word with the hotel manager, which will result in all of them being placed in no more than three or four rooms."

Peralta laughed.

"Don't laugh, Mario," Delgano said. "He's serious."

"Moot point," Pedro Vega, who Clete was now sure

was a BIS agent, said. He pointed to the lobby. "Too late. They're here."

"Damn!" Clete said. "Well, I guess we could ask Fernando to forget re-icing the food containers."

"Don't do that, Clete," Delgano said. "José Ruiz is the exception to the rule about diplomats, and it's been a long time since he's had a decent *bife de chorizo*."

"You're running me out of ideas, Gonzo," Frade said. "But . . . how about having Fernando tell the headwaiter they're all lousy tippers?"

"Maybe they could forget to put towels in those three rooms," Peralta offered.

"Better yet," Pedro Vega said, "have them pour water on the rolls of toilet paper in their *baños*. We used to do that at the Academy, remember?"

"Pedro, you're as evil as Cletus," Delgano said.

"I consider that a compliment, *mi coronel*," Vega said.

"Or we could have Mario fly the next leg, presuming we get clearances. That way they would be airsick all the way," Frade said.

"And I was just starting to like you," Peralta said.

"Speaking of clearances," Frade said. "Fernando, what's with the no clearances?"

"What's interesting," Aragão replied, "is that there were—yesterday—clearances. But five hours ago they were canceled. I asked London about it, and they said it was probably the Russians being difficult, but that's all they knew."

"The Russians?" Delgano asked incredulously.

Aragão looked at Clete for permission to answer the question.

"Tell them," Clete said. "They're friends."

Aragão nodded and said: "The story I got is that the Russians, after talking Eisenhower into letting them take Berlin, had no intention of allowing anybody else in, the agreements dividing Berlin into American, English, French, and Russian zones to the contrary notwithstanding.

"General White screwed that up for the Russians when he (a) took the Second Armored Division into Berlin without Russian permission—or Eisenhower's—and (b) threw the Red Army out of what was agreed to be the American zone. Our guy in London suspects the Russians don't want us to have any control over the airports, or even fly into Berlin unless we ask for permission. Eisenhower, finally realizing the Russians are trying to screw him, has no intention of asking their permission, as that would imply they have the right to say no."

If Delgano, Peralta, or Vega was curious how it was that the Portuguese station chief for SAA could call London and come up with that sort of information, they were too prudent to ask.

"Is there an airport in our zone?" Frade asked.

Aragão nodded. "Tempelhof."

"The Americans have Tempelhof?" von Wachtstein asked.

"London told me General White has it surrounded by

tanks and has been flying his Piper Cubs into it from his Division Rear, which is still at the other side of the Elbe River. You know something about Tempelhof?"

"It's—*it used to be*—Lufthansa's terminal. Good airport. I could get the Connie into it with no trouble."

If Aragão was curious to know how an SAA pilot knew so much about Tempelhof, he was too prudent to ask. But von Wachtstein saw the look on his face. And so did Frade.

"Fernando," Clete said, "say hello to Special Agent Peter von Wachtstein of the OSS, formerly major of the Luftwaffe. Peter, Fernando is the OSS station chief here."

Aragão didn't reply but looked at Boltitz.

Clete went on: "And Special Agent Karl Boltitz used to be Kapitän zur See of the Kriegsmarine. When we get to Germany, he's going to see what his U-boat buddies can tell us about all these submarines that Mr. Dulles tells us are supposed to be headed for Argentina."

"Damn it," Aragão suddenly exclaimed.

Clete looked on curiously as Aragão stabbed his right hand into his suit coat and came out with a sealed envelope.

"This came for you earlier, Clete. There've been fifty different stories making the rounds about those subs, each harder to swallow than the other. And I'm not sure this helps."

Frade took the envelope, opened it, and extracted the single page inside. His eyes fell to it:

PRIORITY

TOP SECRET

DUPLICATION FORBIDDEN

FROM AGGIE

TO TEX

VIA OSS LISBON STATION

MSG NO 412 1805 GREENWICH 16 MAY 1945

LAST NIGHT – 15 MAY – DAVID BRUCE DISPATCHED FOUR AGENTS FROM OSS LONDON STATION TO BERGEN NORWAY TO INTERVIEW SIXTEEN (16) GERMAN POWS BEING HELD THERE. OUR INFORMATION IS THAT CAPTAIN SCHAFFER OF U-977 GAVE HIS MARRIED CREWMEN THE OPTION OF CONTINUING ABOARD OR BEING PUT ASHORE IN EUROPE TO REJOIN THEIR FAMILIES. ON 10 MAY THE TOTAL OF NINETEEN (19) WHO TOOK HIM UP ON THE OFFER WENT ASHORE BY DINGHY AT HOLSENOY ISLAND NORWAY. SIXTEEN (16) SURRENDERED TO BE REPATRIATED. THREE (3) REMAIN AT LARGE.

IN INITIAL INTERVEWS NONE OF THE POWS SAID THEY HAD SEEN ANYBODY ONBOARD OTHER THAN FELLOW SUBMARINERS.

FURTHER, MARSHAL ZHUKOV IN BERLIN REPORTS THAT RUSSIAN AGENTS HAVE THE CHARRED REMAINS OF HITLER AND HIS BRIDE AS WELL AS THE GOEBBELS FAMILY AND OTHERS. ZHUKOV SAID THE REMAINS WERE RECOVERED OUTSIDE THE FUHRERBUNKER, IN THE REICH CHANCELLERY GARDEN. WHILE THE RUSSIANS ARE NOT EXACTLY BEING PARAGONS OF HONESTY WE HAVE NO REASON NOT TO BELIEVE THEM IN THIS INSTANCE.

MEANTIME SCORES OF ATTACK U-BOATS HAVE FOLLOWED THE ORDER OF ADMIRAL DONITZ TO STAND DOWN AND SURRENDER WITH THEIR CREWS. OPERATION DEADLIGHT WILL SEE THESE VESSELS SCUTTLED. U-977 AND U-234 ARE NOT AMONG THOSE HAVING SURRENDERED AND THEIR WHEREABOUTS AND ANY POSSIBLE TANKER U-BOATS REMAIN UNKNOWN. WE CAN ONLY PRESUME THEY CONTINUE EN ROUTE TO ARGENTINA. GEN BENDICK HAS BEEN ALERTED.

WILL LET YOU KNOW WHAT WE LEARN FROM U-977 POWS IN NORWAY. LET ME KNOW WHAT IF ANYTHING YOUR U-BOAT EXPERT LEARNS THERE. THAT SAID, IT MAY OR MAY NOT MATTER – WILD BILL SUSPECTS OUR LITTLE ORGANIZATION COULD BE OUT OF BUSINESS SOONER THAN EXPECTED.

AGGIE

END

TOP SECRET

DUPLICATION FORBIDDEN

Frade shook his head, then folded the sheet and stuffed it in his pocket.

"When the hell is 'sooner than expected'?" he said. He shook his head, then looked at Aragão and added, "Well, the only thing we know for sure now is that at least one U-boat is headed for Argentina. I never believed that Hitler was aboard. I also don't buy the story that there's a fleet of U-boats. Maybe one or two, and some tankers. Then again, maybe not. Karl should be able to get us some answers."

Aragão nodded. He said: "Where did the general at Val de Cans get his intel about this 'rescue the diplomats' operation you're on being a cover to get Nazis out of Germany?"

"From me," Clete said. "I wasn't being exactly truthful with the ambassador. Something about this smells, starting with why are these Argentine diplomats still in Berlin? Argentina declared war on Germany on March twenty-seventh—that's almost two months ago. They could have been in neutral Sweden that night, or the next day. Or in Spain the day after that. They stayed because they wanted to, and I don't mean for the joy of watching Russian T-34 tanks roll down . . . what's the wonderful name of that street? The Unter den Linden. They stayed for a reason."

"What kind of a reason?" Delgano asked.

"Any of a number of reasons. For example, suppose you were Heinrich Himmler and you had a couple of kilograms of diamonds you wanted to get to Argentina. Wouldn't it make more sense to give a quarter of them, or even half, to some friendly Argentine diplomat in exchange for his taking them to Argentina for you? Submarines get sunk."

"You think that's what it is?"

"I don't know, but if the secretary of Labor and Retirement Plans—my beloved Tío Juan—is involved, it's entirely likely. And we know he's involved because his good friend Nulder is in charge of the rescue mission."

"But you implied," Aragão said, "that they were going to try to smuggle Nazis back on your airplane."

"They may have had that in mind. Maybe just one or two really big Nazis. Who's going to count heads on a mercy flight? But I don't think so, now that I've led Nulder and Ambassador Hernández to believe the Americans are onto them. But precious stones, or something else? That wouldn't surprise me at all. Who's going to search the luggage of a rescued diplomat?"

"So that's what that was all about," Delgano said.

"I'm an evil man, Gonzo. You've said so yourself."

"So, what happens now?" Delgano asked.

"First, we finish this bottle of wine, and then maybe

another, and then we have dinner and a bath, not necessarily in that order."

"I meant tomorrow, Cletus," Delgano said, shaking his head in resignation.

"We wait for the flyover clearances. We can't go to Berlin without them."

VII

[ONE]
Hotel Britania
Rua Rodrigues Sampaio 17
Lisbon, Portugal
1705 18 May 1945

Ambassador Claudio de Hernández was sitting at the hotel's bar with Fernando Aragão when Frade, Delgano, Stein, Vega, and Peralta walked in.

Stein deposited a heavy, dripping burlap sack on the bar.

The barman appeared, looking askance at the burlap bag.

"Where have you been all day?" Ambassador de Hernández asked. "We've been looking all over for you."

"Have a sniff of the bag and take a guess," Frade said.

"I beg your pardon?"

Frade sniffed loudly and pointed at the burlap sack.

"After you pour us a little of that splendid Altano Douro 1942," Frade ordered the barman, "please ask the chef to join us."

Aragão sniffed the bag and smiled.

"I really thought you were kidding," he said.

"I never kid about whisky, women, or fishing," Frade said. "Aside from Vega getting a little seasick, everything went . . . *swimmingly.*"

"You have been fishing?" Ambassador de Hernández asked incredulously. "In the ocean?"

"That's where the fish usually are, Mr. Ambassador." Frade then added, "You're in luck, Fernando. There's even enough for the ambassador and the diplomats."

The chef, an enormous fat man in stained kitchen whites, appeared.

"Slide Siggie that tray, Mario," Frade ordered, pointing down the bar. "Siggie, put a sample of our fruits of the sea on the tray for the chef's edification."

Stein dipped into the bag, came out with three large fish fillets, and arranged them on the tray.

The chef bent over and sniffed them, then punched them with his index finger.

"Caballa," he said.

"Yes," Frade said. "In English, they say 'mackerel.' These are from what a *norteamericano* would call a 'king mackerel.'"

"And fresh," the chef said approvingly.

"Mere hours ago, they were swimming. Into your capable hands, my friend, I entrust them."

"I usually bake the whole fish," the chef said.

"Indulge me," Frade said. "I am Argentine, and the whole world knows we're crazy. For now, I want you to dribble a little olive oil on the fillets, lay some lemon slices on top, and grill them. Serve them with some fried potatoes and a small salad. Can do?"

The chef nodded. "Can do."

"After first selecting the best-looking fillets," Frade then ordered, "which you will serve to us just as soon as you can, serve the leftovers to the diplomats traveling with South American Airways with the compliments of Chief Pilot Delgano."

The chef nodded again.

Then Frade said: "They will taste much better if you drink a little Altano Douro as you grill them. Put a bottle for the chef on Señor Aragão's bill, Señor Barman."

Ambassador de Hernández's face showed that he believed Frade was either crazy or drunk. Or both.

The chef smiled, picked up the burlap sack, and disappeared in the direction of the kitchen.

Frade looked at de Hernández. "You were looking for me, Mr. Ambassador? Why?"

"The overfly permission has come, Señor Frade. But only as far as Frankfurt am Main."

"We are supposed to go to Berlin," Frade challenged.

"I know," the ambassador said more than a little lamely.

"What does Buenos Aires have to say about this?"

"About this specifically, nothing."

"And about things in general?" Frade pursued. "What about the assurance of either the Foreign Ministry or the President that no attempt will be made to smuggle Nazis to Argentina on SAA's airplane?"

"There has been no response to that specifically, Señor Frade."

"Then we're not going," Frade said.

"There was a message from el Coronel Perón, routed via the embassy, to Señor Nulder, which Señor Nulder shared with me."

"And are you going to tell me what it said?"

"It said that the Foreign Minister was doing everything he can to get the necessary overfly permissions, as the president is very anxious to relieve the diplomatic contingent in Berlin as soon as possible."

"We already knew that, didn't we?" Frade said.

Frade then took an appreciative sip of the Altano Douro, sighed audibly, and announced: "Well, if the secretary of Labor and Retirement Plans tells us that General Farrell is anxious to relieve the diplomatic contingent in Berlin as soon as possible, I don't see that we, as patriotic Argentines, have any choice. Have the passengers at the airfield no later than five-thirty tomorrow morning, Mr. Ambassador."

"That early, Señor Frade?"

"We have already lost more than a full day, haven't we, Mr. Ambassador, waiting for you to come up with the flyover permissions? I don't want to lose any more time."

"I'll pass that to Señor Nulder right away," Ambassador de Hernández said. He then stood and excused himself.

When the ambassador had gone, Delgano softly asked, "Half past five in the morning, Cletus?"

"I didn't say *we* would be there at that unholy hour. I think we should try to get off the ground at, say, nine."

[TWO]
Aboard *Ciudad de Rosario*
Approaching Frankfurt am Main, Germany
1235 19 May 1945

When Clete Frade had announced that Peter von Wachtstein would fly *Ciudad de Rosario* from Lisbon to Frankfurt am Main in the left seat, and that he would fly as copilot, the faces of the three SAA pilots showed they didn't like it at all.

Frade remembered what he had learned in the Marine Corps: *When there is dissension in the ranks, try explaining your reasons.*

He told them: "Von Wachtstein has flown all over Spain, France, and Germany. None of us has. And we don't have reliable charts. We're going to have to fly by the seat of our pants, looking out the window to see where we are. And Peter is the only one of us who'll know what the hell he's looking at."

"But, Cletus," Gonzalo Delgano protested, "von Wachtstein has less time at the controls of a Constellation than anybody else."

Rule Two: If reasoning doesn't work, apply a two-by-four with great force to the temples of the dissenters.

"Actually, Gonzalo, there's an even more important reason von Wachtstein will fly in the left seat."

"Which is?"

"I said so. Any further questions?"

Delgano's face reddened, but he didn't argue further.

Once they were in the cockpit, von Wachtstein suggested that while crossing Spain they take advantage of the Constellation's capabilities to become inconspicuous. The Connie could cruise at twenty thousand feet at better than three hundred miles per hour. At that altitude they would be hard to see from the ground, and even if there were contrails, the natural presumption would be that they were an Allied bomber. Further, von Wachtstein said, the Spanish had no aircraft capable of climbing that high to investigate, and even if they tried, any Spanish aircraft would have trouble catching up with the Connie.

"What the Spaniards have are Luftwaffe rejects," von Wachtstein said. "Nothing as fast as the Connie."

You just lucked out again, Cletus Frade.

You put Hansel in the left seat impulsively. And he just showed you it was the right thing to do.

"Let's do it," Frade ordered.

On takeoff, they navigated by dead reckoning, flying southeast across Portugal toward Spain while climbing to an altitude of twenty-two thousand feet. The weather was clear, and there were only a few isolated clouds.

They had been airborne just about an hour when von Wachtstein said, "Take a look at three o'clock, Clete. That's Madrid. Now, let's see if we can find the Pyrenees."

"Clete," von Wachtstein said, "did you ever see pictures, or maybe a newsreel, of crazy Spaniards running away from bulls down a narrow street?"

Clete thought a moment, then said, "Yeah."

"They do that in Pamplona," he said, and pointed. "Which means that we're about to fly over the Pyrenees. The last time I was here, I was flying an Me-210 and the oxygen wasn't working. So, I had to fly through them. Very interesting experience."

"Welcome to France," von Wachtstein announced, pointing downward at the snowcapped Pyrenees mountains. "Now, let's see if we can find Lyon."

"God, I hope that isn't what I think it is," von Wachtstein said.

"What do you hope it isn't?"

"Köln. You know, where the aftershave lotion comes from."

"You mean Cologne."

"That's what I said," von Wachtstein said. "If it is Köln, we're too far north." He shoved the yoke forward. "I guess there's only one way to find out."

"Please keep in mind this aircraft is not a fighter plane. Try not to tear the wings off."

"That's Köln, all right. That's the cathedral. Christ, the whole city is destroyed!"

"My God!" Clete said, looking at square miles of utter destruction.

"Welcome to the Thousand-Year Reich, Herr Oberstleutnant," von Wachtstein said.

"It's hard to believe," Clete said.

"Well, now that we've found the Rhine, I suppose we better go the rest of the way close to the ground."

"Well, there's what's left of Frankfurt am Main," Peter announced. "The airport is to the south."

"That looks as bad as Cologne," Clete said. "Jesus, there's hardly a building left standing." He paused. "There's one. A great big building."

"The I.G. Farben building," von Wachtstein said.

He pointed the Constellation toward it.

Clete saw the altimeter was indicating fifteen hundred feet.

They dropped another five hundred feet before flashing over the huge building that stood unscathed in the rubble.

"You're going to give our passengers heart failure," Clete said. "Jesus, there's an American flag on that building!"

"The Americans must have decided they were going to need it and did not bomb it," von Wachtstein said matter-of-factly. "Now, let's see if we can find the airport. You have the tower frequency?"

Von Wachtstein shoved the throttles forward and raised the nose of the Constellation as Clete dialed in the radio.

"Frankfurt Air Base, this is South American Airways Double Zero Four."

There was no response after several calls.

"Take us to five thousand feet, Peter. I'll try another frequency."

"Going to five thousand."

"Frankfurt, South American Double Zero Four."

There was no answer on the new frequency.

"Clete, we have company," von Wachtstein announced.

Clete looked past von Wachtstein and saw a twin-tailed Lockheed P-38 fighter.

It was so close that Frade could count seven swastikas—signifying seven kills—painted on the nose. Next to those was a picture, a drawing, the image of something else. It looked like an automobile with crossed lines going through it.

What the hell is that?

He shot down seven German airplanes and a convertible?

The pilot was holding up a piece of cardboard with numbers lettered on it with a grease pencil.

Clete tuned the radio to the frequency on the piece of cardboard.

He keyed the microphone: "Hello there, Little Brother. You're our welcoming committee?"

"Constellation aircraft, make an immediate, repeat, immediate one-hundred-eighty-degree turn to the right, maintaining altitude."

"Why should we do that?"

"Because I said so, goddammit! Commence one-eighty now!"

"Do it, Peter," Clete ordered.

Von Wachtstein cranked the yoke hard to the right.

"If one of our diplomats was taking a leak," Clete said, "he just pissed all over the wall. Or himself."

"Constellation, maintain course and altitude."

"Little Brother, could you point us toward the Frankfurt Air Base? And give me the tower frequency?"

"You are on a course for Rhein-Main," the P-38 pilot announced. "Do not deviate from this course."

"And the tower frequency?"

The P-38 pilot gave it.

"Frankfurt Rhein-Main, this is South American Double Zero Four."

"South American Double Zero Four, Rhein-Main. Be advised that there is a flight of four P-38 aircraft in your vicinity. They will guide you to the field. Begin descent to three thousand now."

"South American Double Zero Four commencing descent to three thousand."

There was a four-lane divided highway running close to the airport. Two lanes were empty, save for a few trucks and jeeps. The other two were crowded as far south as Clete could see with lines of gray-uniformed soldiers.

"What the hell is that?" Clete asked.

"The Frankfurt/Heidelberg autobahn," von Wachtstein said.

"I meant the soldiers."

"Prisoners, I suppose, being marched to POW compounds."

The runway was clear, but down its length were half a dozen obviously freshly and hurriedly repaired bomb craters. There were crashed or abandoned German aircraft all over the field.

Two U.S. Army bulldozers were pushing damaged aircraft away from the grassy area next to the runway, moving them into a pile.

As von Wachtstein completed the landing roll and then stopped, waiting for the promised FOLLOW ME vehicle to show up, he started pointing at various damaged aircraft and softly reported:

"That's a Focke-Wulf Fw-190. Good fighter. I used to have a squadron of them—

"That's a Messerschmitt Bf-109. I also used to have a squadron of them—

"The one with three engines, the transport, is a Junkers Ju-52. We called them 'Tante Ju,' for Auntie Ju. Not much like the Connie, is it?—

"My God, there's a Messerschmitt Me-323 Gigant!"

Clete then said, "There's the FOLLOW ME," as a Jeep with black-and-white checkered flags flying from its backseat drove onto the runway in front of them.

It led the *Ciudad de Rosario* down taxiways, on either side of which were still more abandoned Luftwaffe aircraft—some of them looking completely intact and ready to fly—to what was left of a three-story, concrete-block building.

There was a wooden sign: WELCOME TO RHEIN-MAIN AIR BASE.

"And there's our welcoming party," Clete said.

"And look what somebody's driving," von Wachtstein said.

"I'll be goddamned," Clete said.

There were ten vehicles waiting for them. Two buses—German ones, obviously just requisitioned from the fallen enemy—two U.S. Army six-by-six trucks, two three-quarter-ton weapons carriers, and three Chevrolet staff cars. Plus, parked a short distance from them, a Horch convertible sedan identical to the one at Estancia San Pedro y San Pablo, except this one was entirely black.

Leaning against the door was a tall, startlingly handsome U.S. Army officer, a yellow scarf around his neck. His sharply creased trousers were tucked into a pair of highly shined boots of a type Clete had never seen before. He carried a 1911-A1 Colt .45 ACP semiautomatic pistol in a shoulder holster. The eagles of a full colonel were pinned to his epaulets and the triangular insignia of an armored division was sewn onto his sleeve.

"Why do I think he's in charge?" von Wachtstein asked.

"Because he looks like General Patton?" Clete replied.

"*Mi coronel*, I think this is one of the times you should wear your SAA uniform," von Wachtstein said as a truck-mounted stairway was being backed up to the Connie's passenger door.

There was another full bull colonel waiting for them when Clete, the last to debark, jumped to the ground from the bed of the stair truck. He saw that the last of their passengers was boarding one of the buses and that their luggage was being loaded onto one of the six-by-six trucks by soldiers.

The rest of the crew—all the pilots but Gonzalo Delgano—plus both stewards, and even Enrico Rodríguez, were being loaded onto one of the three-quarter-ton weapons carriers.

The colonel waiting for them was short and pudgy. He wore glasses. His uniform, which had the flaming sword insignia of SHAEF on the sleeve, needed pressing.

Clete thought he and the other colonel, who was still leaning on the Horch, looked as if they were in different armies.

"Welcome to Germany," the pudgy colonel said in flawless Spanish. "My name is Colonel Albert Stevens, and at the moment, I'm the senior officer of SHAEF Military Government in Frankfurt. SHAEF has just begun moving from France into the I.G. Farben building. I've been assigned to look after you. And you are, sir?"

"Gonzalo Delgano, *mi coronel.* I am chief pilot of SAA."

The colonel offered his hand, then looked at Clete and von Wachtstein.

"I am Captain Frade," Clete said, "and this is Captain von Wachtstein."

"Von Wachtstein?" Colonel Stevens said. "That sounds pretty German."

"There are a great many Germans in Argentina, Colonel," Peter said.

"Well, you won't be flying to Berlin today. The Russians are being difficult. We're working on the problem, and by tomorrow I'm sure everything will be settled. So, what we're going to do is take your passengers into Frankfurt, to the Park Hotel, which is near the railroad station. Because there's just not room for everybody at the Park, we're going to put your crew up here, in what used to be the Luftwaffe officers' quarters. There's a mess hall—not fancy, but adequate—and I think you'll be comfortable.

"We'll leave your aircraft right where it is and service it, and of course place it under guard. I recommend that you not leave the air base. That seems to cover everything. Is there something you need?"

"We've got fresh meat aboard," Frade said. "We're going to need several hundred pounds of ice to keep it from going bad."

"That may pose a problem," Colonel Stevens said.

"Which I'm sure you can solve, Colonel," the natty colonel suddenly said.

Frade had not seen him walk up. Now that the natty colonel was standing beside Colonel Stevens, their sartorial difference was even more striking. And Frade now saw that the natty colonel's uniform had pinned to the breast parachutist's wings with three stars on them.

"I think the Argentine diplomats have been counting on their countrymen bringing them some decent meat, don't you?" the natty colonel went on.

"You think it's important obviously," Colonel Stevens said, his tone making it clear he had just received an order he didn't like.

"Yes, I do."

"Then we'll get some ice," Colonel Stevens said.

"Thank you," the natty colonel said, and started to walk back to the Horch.

Who the hell is this guy? Frade wondered, then decided that it was a question an SAA captain should not ask.

"If you'll get into the three-quarter, gentlemen," Colonel Stevens said, "you'll be taken to your quarters. I'll see you in the morning."

[THREE]

The Luftwaffe officers' quarters building was half destroyed, but the rooms to which an Air Forces sergeant took them were just about intact, except all the windows and the mirrors in the bathrooms were cracked or missing.

Frade had just sat on his bed—there were no chairs—when the natty colonel walked in.

The colonel greeted him: "I love your uniform, Captain—or should I say 'Colonel'?—it looks like something General Patton would design."

He put out his right hand.

His left hand held a bottle of Haig & Haig Pinch scotch whisky.

As Frade shook hands, he was reminded of the story General Bendick had told about The Dawk showing up at Fighter One with two fistfuls of medicinal bourbon bottles.

"Sir, who are you?"

"Bob Mattingly, Colonel. We both work for Allen Dulles. And to set the ambience for our relationship, when no one senior to me is around, you may call me Bob. And with your permission, I will call you Clete."

"Fine," Frade said. "Bob, did you think of glasses to go with the scotch?"

"As a member of Oh, So Social, how could I forget a social amenity like that? The Air Forces sergeant who brought you here is getting us some as we speak."

"Where'd you get the Horch, Bob?"

"The what? Oh, the car. It belongs to the Prince of Hesse. I pressed it into service. Magnificent machine, but I learned on my way here that it won't go faster than fifty. Fifty *kilometers*. I finally decided it's a parade car, designed to pass through hordes of screaming Nazis"—he paused and mockingly mimed Nazis giving the straight-armed salute—"but not designed to be used on the road."

Clete laughed.

He said: "You've got it in low range, four-wheel drive. There's a lever on the floor, next to the gearshift."

"You know the car?"

"As a fellow member of Oh, So Social, I of course know everything about such social amenities as fine motorcars."

Enrico Rodríguez stuck his head in the doorway.

Frade motioned for him to come in. He did, followed by Stein, Boltitz, von Wachtstein, and Delgano.

"I know who you are, Sergeant Major," Mattingly said in fluent Spanish. "Mr. Dulles told me Colonel Frade is never far from a man with a shotgun looking for someone to shoot."

"A sus órdenes, mi coronel," Rodríguez said.

"But these gentlemen—"

"SAA's chief pilot, Gonzalo Delgano," Frade said, pointing, "who is also a colonel in the Bureau of Internal Security. Karl Boltitz, former—"

"Trusted associate of Admiral Canaris," Mattingly interrupted. "We're working on finding your father, Kapitän. The last word we have is that he's not dead. We just don't know where he is."

"Thank you," Boltitz said.

"And that must make you Major von Wachtstein?" Mattingly asked.

"Yes, sir."

Frade added: "And that's Siggie Stein, our commo expert."

Stein and Mattingly were shaking hands when the Air Forces sergeant appeared with a tray of glasses.

Mattingly was pouring generous drinks into them when another face appeared at the door.

It was an Air Forces lieutenant colonel. He wore a pink Ike jacket, pink trousers, a battered cap with a crushed crown, and half Wellington boots. A certain swagger—and the way he wore his uniform cap—

identified him as a fighter pilot. He didn't look as if he was old enough to vote, and in fact had been eligible to do so for only the past three weeks.

"And who, Colonel, might you be?" Colonel Mattingly inquired.

"My name is Dooley," the very young officer said.

"Archer W. Dooley Jr., commanding the 26th Fighter Group?" Mattingly inquired.

"*Deputy* commander," Dooley corrected him. "How did you know that?"

"As Colonel Frade and I were just discussing, Colonel, we are members of an organization that knows everything. Sergeant, does that telephone communicate?"

"Yes, sir."

"Would you see if you can get General Halebury on it for me?"

"Yes, sir," the Air Forces sergeant said.

"Colonel, what—"

"Colonel Dooley," Mattingly interrupted him, "patience is a virtue right up there with chastity. I'm surprised you don't know that."

He took the telephone the Air Forces sergeant was holding out to him.

"Bob Mattingly, General," he said into it. "I have Colonel Dooley with me. I wonder if you could give the colonel his marching orders over the telephone?" He paused to listen, then added, "Thank you, sir. Doing so will save a good deal of time."

He handed the telephone to Dooley.

"Colonel Dooley, sir," Dooley said, then listened for no more than thirty seconds and concluded the conversation: "Yes, sir, that's perfectly clear."

Then he took the handset from his ear and looked at it.

"And what did General Halebury have to say, Colonel Dooley?" Mattingly asked.

"He said that until I hear differently from either you or him, I am assigned to you; that I am to do whatever I'm ordered to do and not ask questions."

"With a few minor exceptions, that's it. How did you come here, Colonel? How, not why?"

"I came in a staff car, if that's what you mean, sir."

"Which has a driver? Or did you drive it yourself?"

"I've got a driver. There's a group regulation that says majors and above have to have a driver."

"And what kind of a staff car is it, Colonel?"

"A requisitioned Mercedes—a convertible sedan."

"And is it adequately fueled for a round-trip to a destination some forty miles from here?"

"I just filled it up, sir."

"Sergeant, if you would be good enough to pour Colonel Dooley a drink, you may then leave us."

"Yes, sir."

When the sergeant was gone, Mattingly said, "Now, Colonel, you may tell us why you came here."

Dooley looked at the drink in his hand.

"Can I ask what's going on around here, Colonel?"

Mattingly nodded. "After you tell us why you came here."

"I wanted to see who was flying that Argentine Connie that I kept from flying into East Germany," Dooley said.

"That was you in the P-38?" Frade said.

"You were flying the Constellation?" Dooley replied.

"He was," Clete said, pointing at von Wachtstein.

"'*East* Germany'?" von Wachtstein parroted. "What's that?"

"Technically, it is the Soviet zone of occupied Germany," Mattingly said.

"And in another couple of minutes," Dooley said, "you'd have been over it, Captain—and probably got your ass shot down."

"By the Russians?" von Wachtstein asked.

"Why would the Russians shoot down an unarmed Argentine passenger aircraft?" Siggie Stein asked.

"Maybe they don't like Argentines," Frade offered.

"Unfortunately, Clete," Mattingly said, "there is a slight but real chance—one in three, or four, I would judge—that you would've been taken under fire by Russian aircraft had not Colonel Dooley here caused you to alter course. Or have been ordered—this is my most likely scenario—to land at Leipzig and interned. You were east of Fulda when Colonel Dooley turned you."

"Now I want to know what the hell's going on," Frade said.

"I recognize that voice. You're the guy on the radio," Dooley accused. "You're the wiseass who called me Little Brother!"

"I plead guilty to both charges and throw myself on the mercy of the court," Frade said.

"I wondered what that Little Brother business was all about," von Wachtstein said.

"As a fighter pilot, Colonel Dooley," Frade said, "I'm surprised you don't know that the wings of your P-38 are a minor design variant of the wings of a Constellation. Hence 'Little Brother.'"

"What do you know about what fighter pilots should know, wiseass?" Dooley exploded.

"Well, I agree with those who say most of them should not be allowed in public without their psychiatric nurses," Frade said, smiled, and sipped his whisky.

"With certain exceptions, of course," von Wachtstein chimed in.

"Fuck you, too!" Dooley exploded.

Frade and von Wachtstein laughed.

"Before this gets any further out of hand, Colonel Dooley," Mattingly said, "for your general fund of knowledge, I think I should tell you that these gentlemen are pulling your chain."

Dooley was Irish. Once his ire was ignited, it did not go out easily.

"Meaning what?" Dooley demanded.

"They are—or were—fighter pilots."

"And then we grew up and they let us fly real airplanes," Frade said.

He and von Wachtstein laughed again.

"That one," Mattingly said, pointing to von Wachtstein, "received the Knight's Cross of the Iron Cross from the Führer himself for his services as a fighter pilot. And that one"—he pointed to Frade—"had seven, I believe they're called 'meatballs,' painted on the nose of his Grumman Wildcat."

Dooley looked at Frade.

"No shit?" he asked. "Seven Jap kills?"

Frade nodded, then said, "But no convertibles. What the hell was that on your nose?"

"None of your fucking business," Dooley flared anew.

"What did you do, pop some poor bastard out for a Sunday drive?" Frade pursued.

"Go fuck yourself," Dooley said.

"All right, enough!" Mattingly said. "I'll stand you all to attention, if that's what I have to do."

Dooley looked at von Wachtstein and said, "You're telling me he was a Kraut fighter pilot? What the fuck . . . ?"

"Stand to attention, Colonel!" Mattingly ordered. "I said enough."

"I'd like to know about the convertible," von Wachtstein said, his tone of voice no longer joking or mocking.

"Go fuck yourself," Dooley said.

"You're at attention, Colonel!" Mattingly said, coldly furious. "You say one more word without permission and I'll send you back to General Halebury under arrest pending trial for insubordination!"

Dooley stood to attention.

After sixty seconds, which seemed much longer, Mattingly asked, "Is your temper and foul mouth under control, Colonel Dooley?"

"Yes, sir."

"Stand at ease," Mattingly said, then turned to von Wachtstein. "Was your question about the convertible serious, von Wachtstein, or more of this sophomoric bantering?"

"It was serious, sir. I had a reason for asking."

"Answer von Wachtstein's question, Colonel Dooley," Mattingly said.

Dooley shook his head, exhaled audibly, and with visible reluctance said, "When we were in Tunisia, we were flying interdiction missions—shoot anything that's moving—and I shot up a Kraut staff car on the desert."

"And then had it painted on your nose?" Frade asked disgustedly. "Jesus Christ!"

"That's enough out of you, Clete," Mattingly said.

Dooley went on: "I didn't have it painted on my plane until General Halebury made it mandatory. That was much later, after we came to Europe. He said painting swastikas on the noses inspired junior officers."

"And you didn't?" Mattingly asked.

"When General Halebury issued the order, I had four kills. What they were was that powered glider, the ME-323—"

"The Gigant," von Wachtstein said and, when he saw Clete's look, added, "We saw one just now. Very large aircraft, originally designed as a glider. Then they added four engines. It carries a great deal, very slowly."

Clete, remembering, nodded.

"I got my four kills on one day," Dooley said. "They were flying low across the Mediterranean at maybe one hundred twenty-five miles an hour. It wasn't aerial combat; it was murder. So I never painted swastikas for them on my nose. And then we're getting ready for the invasion, in England, and Halebury issues the order to paint kills on the nose. Still, I don't. And he sees my plane and eats my ass out. So then I painted four swastikas and the staff car on my nose."

"I saw seven swastikas," Clete said.

"I got two Messerschmitt Bf-109s and a Focke-Wulf Fw-190 after the invasion."

"Do you remember where you strafed the staff car?" von Wachtstein asked softly. "And when?"

Dooley looked at him curiously, but after a moment answered: "About half past three on the afternoon of April seventh, 1943. Right outside Sidi Mansour, Tunisia. I remember that because when I got back, my squadron CO and the exec didn't—and I got the squadron and my railroad tracks. Why do you want to know? Is it important?"

"You made just the one pass?" von Wachtstein asked. "You didn't go back to make sure everybody was dead?"

"There were just two people in the car," Dooley replied. "Both in the front seat. I saw the car go off the road and turn over. There was no need to make a second pass. Why do you need the details?"

"On the afternoon of seven April 1943, near Sidi Mansour, while riding in a staff car, a friend of mine serving in the Afrikakorps was attacked by an American P-51 Mustang. His car went off the road and overturned. Were you flying a P-51, Colonel?"

Dooley nodded. "You knew this guy?" he asked.

Von Wachtstein nodded. "Quite well. We were good friends. He told me what had happened to him. His name was Claus von Stauffenberg. Oberstleutnant Graf Claus von Stauffenberg—the officer who later saw it as his duty to try to kill Hitler."

"The guy with the bomb under the table that didn't go off?" Dooley asked.

"The bomb went off," Mattingly said. "But the force was deflected from Hitler by the massive leg supporting the table. Hitler lived, and later that day the SS stood Colonel von Stauffenberg against a wall on Bendlerstrasse in Berlin and executed him with Schmeisser submachine-gun fire."

"I don't know how to handle something like this," Dooley said. "If I'm supposed to say I'm sorry, I'm sorry. Hell, I was sorry when I did it."

"Colonel, for what it's worth," von Wachtstein said, "I can assure you Claus would bear you no hard feelings. You were doing your duty, as he did his."

"The details match too closely for this to be a coincidence," Mattingly said, as if to himself. "I would say it is what happened."

"Yeah," Dooley said. "His version of what happened and mine match too closely."

"There is one detail von Wachtstein didn't tell you, Colonel Dooley," Mattingly said. "Some time later, Peter's father was executed, in a very cruel manner, for his role in the bomb plot."

Mattingly poured a half inch of scotch in his glass and tossed it down.

"Well, I hope that everybody is now very sorry for all the cruel things you've been saying to one another, and that we can now play nice and maybe even get on with the business at hand."

The comment—and the tone of his voice—made everyone smile or chuckle.

"Which is?" Frade asked.

"First, I tell Colonel Dooley that everything he sees or hears from now on is top secret, and that if he ever—now or ever—breathes a word of it to anyone, he will be soundly spanked, or castrated with a chain saw, or both."

That earned him more smiles and chuckles.

"And to answer Colonel Frade's question about what happens now, what happens now is that we drive out into the countryside, to Kronberg im Taunus, where after we get something to eat I will tell you what happens now. You know Kronberg im Taunus, von Wachtstein?"

"The Schlosshotel, Colonel?"

Mattingly nodded.

"It used to be a club for senior officers," von Wachtstein said.

"It has been requisitioned as the headquarters of the Forward Element of OSS SHAEF," Mattingly said.

"Is that what you guys are?" Dooley asked. "OSS? I knew it had to be something like that."

"Colonel, I told you before that patience is a virtue right up there with chastity. This time, write it down. Von Wachtstein, can you find the Schlosshotel?"

"Yes, sir."

"Then why don't you lead the way in Dooley's car? We will follow you in the Horch, presuming Frade can show me how to get it out of low gear."

"I know the Schlosshotel," Enrico Rodríguez said. "And how to get there."

"And he also knows how to get a Horch out of low range," Frade said. "I suggest you let him drive."

"Splendid idea," Mattingly said. "That will permit you and me to ride in the backseat and acknowledge the roar of the party faithful."

Mattingly then mimed waving regally at an imaginary crowd.

[FOUR]
Frankfurt am Main, Germany
1815 19 May 1945

"Not very pretty, is it, Clete?" Mattingly asked as Enrico drove them down what was a narrow alley through the rubble of what had been a suburban area of Frankfurt am Main.

Only some walls of a few buildings were left standing. Here and there, gray-faced men and women searched the rubble for whatever they could salvage.

"It's unbelievable," Frade said.

"And you ain't seen nuttin' yet. Berlin is worse."

"You've been to Berlin?"

"I flew over it in a puddle jumper," Mattingly said, "as the Russians were taking it."

He saw the look on Frade's face and went on: "In North Africa, before I was called to the priesthood of the OSS, I was a tank battalion commander in Combat Command A of Second Armored Division—"

"I saw the armored division patch," Clete said.

"—Colonel I. D. White commanding," Mattingly went on. "I was visiting him—by then he was a major general and commanding Hell on Wheels—when he had his bridges across the Elbe and was about to head for Berlin. Ike ordered him to hold in place. The general was slightly miffed. He kicked the windows out on his command post—you know, an office on the back of a six-by-six truck."

"Really?"

"Hell hath no fury that remotely compares to I. D. White in a rage," Mattingly said. "But eventually he calmed down a little. Then he looked at me and said, 'I'd really like to know what's going on there, but as I am under a direct order that not one man of Hell on Wheels is to go there, I can't send somebody to find out.

"'But it has just occurred to me, Colonel, that you are no longer under my command. If you asked to borrow one of my Piper Cubs, I would of course make one available to you. And I don't have the authority to tell you where you can or cannot go, do I?'"

"So I said, 'Point taken, General. General, have you got a puddle jumper you could let me use?' And I got in it and flew over Berlin."

"And?"

"One of the first things I saw was Red Army troops—they use Asiatics as assault troops—neatly lined up to gang-rape women in the streets. They are not very nice people, Clete."

"Jesus Christ!"

"When we flew over the Reichstag, there was a large gasoline fire merrily burning in the inner courtyard, outside the Hitler Bunker. I can't be sure, of course, but I suspect I was watching the incineration of der Führer and his bride. Or perhaps the Goebbels family, Mommy, Daddy, and the six children to whom Mommy had just fed cyanide pills. Whoever it was, the sickly smell of burning flesh was without question."

"I'd heard of the burning bodies but not the gang-raping troopers," Clete said, and once again said, "Jesus Christ!"

"At that point three MiG-3 fighters appeared and suggested, by shooting tracers in front of us, that we were not welcome, and we took the hint and flew back across the Elbe."

"They tried to shoot you down?"

"They made it clear they were capable of doing so if we didn't go back where we belonged."

"They're supposed to be our allies, for Christ's sake."

"General Patton suggests that we're going to have to fight them sooner or later, and I suspect he may be right."

"My God!"

"Quickly changing the subject," Mattingly said. "Where we're going now is to the Schlosshotel Kronberg, which—along with this car—I have requisitioned for the OSS. One of my guys had been there before the war, and suggested that since we could use it, we add it to the Don't Hit Under Any Circumstances target list for the Eighth Air Force."

"You had the authority to do that?"

"Ike now likes the OSS. Particularly Allen Dulles, David Bruce, and their underlings, including this one. Yeah, I had the authority to do that. But that's what they call a two-edged sword. If that weren't true, I wouldn't have been saddled with this 'deal with the Russians' business."

"I don't understand," Frade confessed.

"Why don't we wait until we're all together? Let me finish about the Schlosshotel."

"Sure."

"It was built in the 1890s by the Dowager Empress Victoria of the German empire, and named Schloss Friedrichshof. Her husband, Frederick III, was the emperor. Damn the expense, in other words, nothing's too good for Ol' Freddy.

"In 1901, the Empress's youngest daughter, Princess Margaret of Prussia, inherited it from her mother. Margaret married Philip, Prince of Hesse, and the castle was part of her dowry.

"And now, so to speak, I have—or the OSS has—inherited it from His Highness."

He looked at Frade.

"Did I say something amusing?"

"No. I was just thinking you sound like a history professor."

"As a matter of fact, I was a history professor. Sewanee. The University of the South. Actually, I was professor of history and romance languages."

"I'll be damned. How did you wind up as a tank battalion commander?"

"You ever hear that an officer should keep his indiscretions a hundred miles from the flagpole?"

Frade nodded.

"Same thing applies to a professor, particularly one at an institution operated by the Episcopal Church. I solved my problem once a month by driving into Memphis, where I became a second lieutenant in Tank Company A (Separate) of the Tennessee National Guard. Second lieutenants, as I'm sure you remember, are expected to drink and carouse with loose women."

"You were a weekend warrior?" Frade said, laughing.

"Indeed I was. And when we were nationalized, Company A was sent to Fort Knox, Kentucky. They broke it up, and I found myself assigned to the 325th Mechanized Infantry, Major I. D. White commanding. When they assigned him to Second Armored, Hell on Wheels, White took me with him.

"And then one day, in North Africa, Allen Dulles showed up at General White's headquarters—White was then colonel commanding Combat Command A—and he asked me if I would be willing to accept an unspecified assignment involving great danger and parachuting behind enemy lines. I told him I would not. General White said, 'Bob, I won't order you to go, but I think you should.'

"The next thing I knew I was in Scotland learning how to jump out of airplanes and sever the carotid artery with a dagger."

"Why did Dulles recruit you?"

"I speak Russian, German, French, Italian, Spanish,

and a little Hungarian. That had a good deal to do with it. I've got sort of a flair for languages."

"So do I."

"Dulles told me," Mattingly said.

"Did you parachute behind enemy lines?"

"Twice into France and once into Italy."

"That's what those stars on the jump wings mean?"

"Uh-huh. And speaking of uniforms, when we get to the castle, we're going to have to get you some uniforms. You can't run around Berlin looking like a doorman. And we'll have to get you some identification."

They were now out of Frankfurt, moving rapidly down a two-lane, tree-lined highway. The headlights picked out here and there where trees had been cut down to serve as barriers, and where wrecked American and German tanks and vehicles had been shoved off the road.

[FIVE]
Schlosshotel Kronberg
Kronberg im Taunus, Hesse, Germany
1920 19 May 1945

Following Dooley's Mercedes, Enrico steered the Horch around a final corner and suddenly the hotel was visible. The massive structure looked like a castle. It was constructed of gray fieldstone and rose, in parts, five stories high. Lights blazed from just about every window. There was no sign of damage whatever.

"Hermann the butler—I kept him on—tells me that when I ordered the lights turned on, it was the first time they'd been on since September 1939," Mattingly said.

Frade now saw something both unexpected and somehow out of place. An Army sergeant, a great bull of a black man with a Thompson submachine gun hanging from his shoulder, was marching a file of soldiers—all black, all armed with M-1 rifles—up to the entrance. After a moment, Clete realized that the sergeant was changing the sentries on guard.

"Stop right in front, Enrico," Mattingly ordered.

When they got out of the car, the sergeant bellowed, "Ten-hut" and saluted crisply. Mattingly returned it as crisply. Clete, at the last second, kept under control his Pavlovian urge to salute.

People in doormen's uniforms should not salute.

Everybody got out of the two cars and started up the stairs.

As they reached the entrance, a huge door was pulled inward by a very elderly man who had trouble doing so.

"Thank you," Mattingly said in German, then added to Frade, "Faithful retainers. There's about two dozen of them."

"They don't want to leave?"

"We feed them, generously, so there's some they can take home. There's not much food anywhere in Germany."

Mattingly led the party across an elegantly furnished foyer into a well-equipped bar.

Someone in the bar called "Attention" and everybody stood.

"At ease," Mattingly called.

Clete guessed that there were thirty or more men. All but a few were in uniform, half of these adorned with the standard rank and branch insignia. The other half had blue triangles around the letters *U.S.* sewn to the uniform lapels and to the shoulders where unit insignia were normally shown. There were perhaps eight men in civilian clothing, some of it close to elegant, some of it looking like it had come from the Final Reduction racks at Goodwill.

Mattingly led them through the bar to a smaller—but not small—room holding a large circular table and its own bar. There was an elderly man in a white jacket standing behind the bar.

"Would you please ask the general to join us?" Mattingly courteously ordered the barman in German. "And then that will be all, thank you."

He signaled for everyone to take places around the table.

"This room is secure," Mattingly announced. "I have it regularly swept. The result of that is that you'll have to pour your own drinks—Honor System. A quarter for whisky, ten cents for beer. There is a jar on the bar."

He pointed and then went on: "The rule is that when any German enters the room, you stop your conversation in midsentence and don't resume talking until the German has left. And I don't mean that you can change the subject. I mean not a word. Clear?"

He looked around at everybody to make sure he had made the point.

The door opened. A slight, pale-faced man with

sunken eyes, very thin hair, and wearing a baggy, nondescript suit came in.

"What I said before does not apply to this gentleman," Mattingly said to the table, then raised his voice and addressed the man entering the room: "Good evening, sir."

The man walked to where Frade was sitting with Mattingly and wordlessly offered his hand.

"General Gehlen," Mattingly said, "this is Colonel Frade."

Frade hurriedly got to his feet and put out his hand. He was surprised at Gehlen's firm grip as he said, "It's a pleasure to meet you, General Gehlen."

"I understand, Colonel," Gehlen replied, "that you have been taking very good care of my men."

How the hell could he know that?

"I have to tell you, sir," Frade said, "that I have about half of them confined."

"I rather thought you might consider that necessary," Gehlen said. "But you are forgiven, providing, of course, that you've brought the money."

He's making some kind of joke.

Mattingly's face shows he understands the joke.

But what the hell is he talking about?

"Excuse me, General?" Frade asked.

"The money, Clete," Mattingly said. "Graham's half a million dollars. Please don't tell me you don't have it."

Oh, shit!

"I wasn't told to bring any money," Frade said. "And that half a million I signed for—I thought those were funds for other OSS business. My wife's got it put away in the safe in our house in Buenos Aires."

"The best-laid plans of mice and men," General Gehlen said.

"Clete, how soon can you get it here?" Mattingly asked.

"I was about to say on the next SAA flight to Lisbon. But that won't work. The only SAA pilots I'd trust with it on are this rescue-the-diplomats mission."

"Well, then you'll just have to go get it," Mattingly said. "That's what, ten, twelve days at the most? I can have some money flown from London. Not that much. But enough to get started. You do have the money, right? You can get it here?"

Clete nodded, then said, "What's it for?"

"That's something else we'll get into after we have a drink and our supper."

VIII

[ONE]
The Private Dining Room
The Garden Lounge
Schlosshotel Kronberg
Kronberg im Taunus, Hesse, Germany
1930 19 May 1945

"You're not drinking, Clete?" Mattingly asked as he looked around the huge circular table.

Even with "everybody"—General Gehlen, Frade, Stein, Boltitz, von Wachtstein, Rodríguez, Delgano, Peralta, Vega, Dooley, and Mattingly—sitting around the table, there were enough empty chairs for twice that many people.

Clete had the irreverent thought that it looked like only half of the Knights of the Round Table had shown up for King Arthur's nightly briefing.

"When are we flying to Berlin?" Frade responded, and when Mattingly's face showed the answer confused him, he smiled benignly at Dooley and went on: "You'll learn, Dooley, if they ever let you fly big airplanes, like Hansel and me, that it's best to do so clear-eyed and not hung-over."

Mattingly frowned at Frade.

"In the morning," Mattingly said, "you're all going to Berlin—or that's the plan."

"Pour your beer back into the bottle, like a good boy, Dooley," Frade said.

"Kiss my ass," Dooley said.

"I'm going to ask you, Colonel Frade, and you, Colonel Dooley, to try to control your somewhat less than scintillating wit," Mattingly said. "If you can't, I'll stand both of you at attention."

"Yes, sir," Frade said. "Sorry."

"Turning to what happens now," Mattingly said. "The problem of the Russians being difficult in Berlin was already being discussed at SHAEF, and a possible solution thereof had been reached when South American Airlines—more accurately, the Republic of Argentina—was added to the problem.

"The Argentine ambassador in Washington approached the State Department and asked them about flight clearances for their mercy mission. Not being aware of the Russians' mischief, the State Department in effect said, 'Not a problem. We will go to General Marshall and have him tell Eisenhower to take care of it.'

"Marshall's message arrived during a staff conference, at which David Bruce was present and the subject of the Russians was under discussion.

"Eisenhower's first reaction was to quickly decide that

the Argentines would just have to wait until the problem was solved. Beetle Smith—you know who he is? Ike's chief of staff—had another view.

"General Smith didn't think the Russians should be allowed to ban Argentine—or any civilian—aircraft from flying from the American zone of occupation over the Russian zone into the American zone of Berlin any more than they should be allowed to question our right to fly military aircraft in and out.

"David Bruce agreed with General Smith—they usually do agree on just about everything—and then threw something else into the equation, something previously not known to SHAEF.

"South American Airways, David told Ike and Beetle—words to this effect—was an OSS asset, or close to one. Not only that, but the pilot of the Constellation at that moment over the South Atlantic en route to Lisbon was actually the OSS man in charge of the asset, a Marine lieutenant colonel who was held in very high regard by Allen Dulles.

"And there was one more fact bearing on the problem, David Bruce said. The advance element of OSS Europe was already outside of Frankfurt. General Smith asked who was running it, and David Bruce told him, whereupon the Supreme Commander said words to this effect: 'Mattingly used to work for General White, right? He's the officer who flew over Berlin when the Russians were still taking it in one of White's L-4s? The right man, for once, in the right place. Let him deal with this.

"'He might even be able to keep White and Patton

from starting World War Three. Tell the Argentine OSS man to report to Mattingly, and tell the Eighth Air Force to give Mattingly whatever he thinks he needs. Keep me advised. Next problem?'

"Shortly thereafter, David Bruce dumped the problem in my lap.

"Now, there are several reasons that it is important that I deal with this to General Eisenhower's complete satisfaction. Not least among them is that he, so far, has not joined the chorus singing, 'Shut down the OSS now; it's not needed' into President Truman's ear.

"If I—forgive the egotism—if *we* can handle the problem of the Russians trying to keep us out of Berlin, Allen Dulles and/or David Bruce can go to Ike and ask his assistance to keep us alive. He may not give it. Ike unfortunately thinks General Marshall walks on water, but we have to try."

"Sir," Frade said, "how do you plan to deal with it?"

Mattingly's face showed that he appreciated both being called "Sir" and Frade's tone of voice.

"At this moment, Colonel Frade, a small convoy of Air Force vehicles, under the command of a captain, is attempting to drive to Berlin. The convoy consists of two trucks and a jeep. One of the trucks is a mobile aircraft control tower. The other contains supplies.

"There is an autobahn—a superhighway patterned after the New Jersey Turnpike—running between Hanover, which is in the British zone, and Berlin. More specifically, more importantly, to the American zone of Berlin.

"The Soviets have blocked the autobahn at

Helmstedt—at the border between East and West Germany. It's just over one hundred miles—one hundred seventy kilometers—from Helmstedt to the American zone of Berlin. If the Air Force people can get past the Helmstedt roadblock, they can be at Tempelhof in under three hours. Once there, they will immediately put the control tower into operation."

"Sir, what air traffic are they going to control?" Frade asked.

"At first light, Piper Cubs—L-4s—flying between General White's Division Rear, on the Elbe, and Berlin. At about oh-nine-hundred hours, an Air Forces C-54, having flown out of Frankfurt, will contact Tempelhof Air Base and ask for approach and landing instructions. After it discharges its cargo, it will again contact the tower, to file a flight plan back to Rhein-Main. And once it crosses the East/West border, a South American Airways Constellation will be cleared by Rhein-Main to proceed to the U.S. air base at Tempelhof.

"The idea is that not only do we have a right to fly into Berlin, but we are in fact doing it."

"Sir, with respect," Frade said, "it seems that scenario depends almost entirely on this Air Forces captain being able to talk his way past the Russians blocking the highway."

"In other words, 'Is there a Plan B?' Yes, there is. In the event the Mobile Control Tower can't get past the Russians at Helmstedt—it may, as the Air Forces captain is actually one of us, a bright chap, and actually a lieutenant colonel, and we may be lucky—but if we're not, an

Air Forces C-54 will take off at oh-eight-hundred from Rhein-Main and head for Tempelhof. It will have aboard air traffic controllers and their equipment. And me. Once that's up and running, we shift to clearing the SAA Constellation for flight to Tempelhof."

"And what if the Russians shoot down the C-54?" Frade asked.

"We anticipate that—probability eighty percent—they will attempt to turn the C-54 with threatening aerial moves by their fighters. We anticipate that these fighters will be YAK-3s."

Peter von Wachtstein offered: "If you get in a fight with one or more of them, Dooley, get him to chase you in a steep climb, and then, in a steep dive, turn inside him. Try to get his engine from the side; it's well armored on the bottom."

"What makes you think Dooley might get in a fight with them?" Mattingly asked.

"You've fought YAKs?" Dooley asked.

"I was shot down twice by YAK-3s," von Wachtstein said, "before I learned how to fight them. Put your stream of fire into his side."

"I hadn't planned to get into the rules of engagement yet, but since the subject has come up," Mattingly said, "Colonel Dooley, you will select four of your best—and by best, I mean most experienced, levelheaded—pilots and by oh-seven-hundred tomorrow brief them on what is expected of them.

"You will escort the C-54 from the border across East Germany to Berlin. I've got an information packet for you with more details, but briefly here, on takeoff from Rhein-Main, the C-54 will circle the field until attaining an altitude of ten thousand feet and a cruising speed of two hundred twenty-five miles per hour—as fast as a C-54 can fly. General Halebury told me that inasmuch as fuel consumption is not a factor—it's right at two hundred seventy miles from Rhein-Main to Tempelhof—that extra speed would be justified both by reducing flight time and making it easier for the faster P-38s to stay with it.

"The C-54 will then fly northeast on a straight line to Berlin. The compass heading will be forty-eight-point-four degrees.

"This is your call, Dooley, but General Halebury suggested that you place your aircraft two thousand feet above and that far behind the C-54. This will, the general suggests, place you in the best position to interdict any Russian aircraft intending to divert the C-54 from its course or altitude."

"Sir, with respect, General Halebury is not a fighter pilot," Dooley said. "I'd like to go a little higher."

"Well, then fuck him," Frade offered. "What does Halebury know? Do it your way, Dooley."

Mattingly's head snapped angrily to Frade. But when he saw the smile on everyone's face, including that of General Gehlen, he didn't say what he had originally intended to say.

Instead, he said, "I suppose I should have known it was too much to hope that you could contain your wit."

"Did this general have any sage advice as to how

Dooley and his guys are supposed to interdict the YAKs?" Frade asked. "You're talking about bluffing them, right?"

"I think I'd rephrase that," Mattingly said. "What Dooley and his aircraft are going to have to do, presuming the YAKs appear, is make them think it would be ill-advised for them to threaten the C-54 by flying dangerously close to it."

"And the way I'm supposed to do that is fly dangerously close to the YAKs?" Dooley asked.

"I don't see any other way to make them behave, do you?" Frade asked seriously.

"The Russians will be under specific orders," von Wachtstein said. "If those orders are to shoot down the C-54, they'll do just that. Without warning. If their orders are to harass the C-54 with the thought that might make the C-54 pilot turn around, that's all they'll do. Unless, of course, there's someone very senior in one of the YAKs, in which case they would follow his lead."

General Gehlen suddenly spoke up: "I agree with Graf von Wachtstein's assessment of the Russian military mind. And I would suggest further that when they are faced with a force that is capable of causing great damage, they will back down."

"Unless, of course, General," Mattingly said, "they come out to meet the C-54 with the intention of shooting it down to show us how unwelcome we are in Berlin."

"That is true," Gehlen admitted.

"Under what circumstances can I fire at the YAKs?" Dooley asked.

"If they fire at you," Mattingly said. "Or the C-54."

"Or if they even look like they're going to fire at the Connie," Frade said. "Which brings us to that: I might have missed it, but I didn't hear you ask, Colonel Mattingly, if SAA is willing to go along with your plan to give the Russians the finger."

"Are you?" Mattingly asked simply.

"Not my call, Colonel."

"Then whose?"

"Delgano's, both as SAA chief pilot and also—more importantly—as the senior Argentine officer here. Probably the senior Argentine officer in Europe. What about it, *mi coronel*?"

"Oddly enough," Delgano said, getting to his feet, "just before we left Buenos Aires, my general . . ." He paused, looked at General Gehlen, and then went on: "General de Brigada Alejandro Martín, chief of the Ethical Standards Office of the Argentine Ministry of Defense, which is the official euphemism for the Argentine intelligence and counterintelligence service, took me aside and made that point to me.

"He told me that I would be the senior officer of the Ejército Argentino in Europe, and further that inasmuch as the German Reich no longer exists and that Germany is now governed by SHAEF, with which Argentina has no diplomatic relations, the Argentine diplomats in Berlin and those we would bring here have no status beyond that of people with diplomatic passports.

"What I am trying to say is that as I outrank the lieutenant colonel we have as liaison officer to SHAEF, I find myself the senior Argentine officer in Europe period.

"As such, General Martín told me that—no offense intended, Cletus—should Colonel Frade be about to do anything which in my judgment would be detrimental to the interests of my country, I was not only authorized but duty bound to take whatever measures required to keep him from doing it, including placing him under arrest and taking control of the Constellation."

Mattingly made eye contact with Delgano, then nodded and said, "So you don't think you're going to be able to participate in this. I understand your position, Colonel—"

"Please let me continue," Delgano said.

"Sorry," Mattingly said.

"I was having many thoughts as I listened to all this . . ." He paused and smiled, then said: "Including the thought that if I had shot Colonel Frade when I first met him, as I really wanted to, I wouldn't be in this awkward position tonight.

"Among other factors bearing on this situation is that I know General Martín shares your opinion, General Gehlen, of the danger the Soviet Union poses to the world, including Argentina. When I told him that Colonel Frade intended to offer your men sanctuary in Argentina, in accordance with the deal struck by you and Mr. Dulles, his response was, 'Thank God for people like Dulles and Gehlen.'

"And since your people have been in Argentina, my officers and I have had many conversations with them. Primarily with el Teniente Coronel Niedermeyer, but with many others, including some of the Nazis. These conversations convinced us all that the threat posed by the Communists is far worse than we understood.

"For these and other reasons, I have concluded that what you propose, vis-à-vis challenging the Bolsheviks, is in no way inimical to the interests of the Argentine Republic. I will be aboard the SAA Constellation when it flies to Berlin."

"Thank you," Mattingly said.

"However," Delgano added, "I don't think I have the right to order my officers to participate."

Peralta and Vega shot to their feet and stood to attention, obviously waiting for permission to speak.

"Junior officer first," Delgano said, pointing to Vega.

"*Mi coronel*, where you go, I will go. I am surprised there was a question in your mind."

"Thank you," Delgano said. "Mario?"

"*Mi coronel*," Peralta said, "I will consider it an honor to be aboard *Ciudad de Rosario* when we fly her to Berlin."

"Thank you," Delgano said. "Frankly, I expected no less of you. Be seated."

Mattingly then said, "Everybody is aware, right, that there is a real chance you will be shot down?"

"*Mi coronel*," Delgano said. "If that were to happen, and I shall pray that it does not, it would certainly open the eyes of the Argentine people to the threat the godless Communists pose, wouldn't it?"

Frade had a very unkind thought.

The naïve goddamn fool thinks he's Sir Galahad bravely facing a hero's death in the defense of his country.

And the other two are eager to jump on their horses, unsheath their swords, and ride out with him to die nobly while trying to slay the dragon.

The problem is that Delgano and Peralta and Vega have no idea what the dragon really looks like. None of them has ever been shot at, or seen an aircraft enveloped in flames—much less been in one that's on fire—or seen an out-of-control, blazing aircraft turn into a huge ball of flame either before or after it crashed into the ground.

"There is one other factor bearing on our little problem," Frade said sarcastically.

"Which is, Colonel Frade?" Mattingly asked, his tone suggesting he hadn't heard the sarcastic tone or was ignoring it.

"What about the Nazis in Berlin whom some people—including me and the Secret Service—think Argentina's secretary of Labor and Retirement Plans intends to fly out of Berlin to sanctuary in Argentina?"

"Who's the secretary of whatever you just said?" Mattingly asked.

"Tell me about that, please," Gehlen said.

"El Coronel Juan Domingo Perón," Frade explained. "He's behind this rescue-the-diplomats operation, which I don't think has anything to do with rescuing diplomats."

"What do you think the purpose is, Colonel?" Gehlen asked.

"Sir, I believe—and so does, apparently, Secretary of the Treasury Morgenthau—that the purpose of the rescue-the-diplomats mission is to bring some Nazis, probably high-ranking ones, from Germany to Argentina."

"I can't agree that it's the primary purpose," Gehlen said. "But I agree that it has something to do with getting former high-ranking officials of the Third Reich out of Germany. I wasn't aware of Morgenthau's interest. Are you sure about that, Colonel Frade?"

"Yes, sir. Absolutely. When we were at the Val de Cans air base in Brazil, a planeload of Secret Service agents was there waiting for clearance to come here. The commanding general told me that agents had been roaming the base asking junior officers and enlisted men if they'd seen anything that looked like it could be a Nazi smuggling operation. For what it's worth, they were traveling in an Air Forces C-69—a Constellation—the same massive aircraft that I flew over here. The usual means of flying government officials to Europe is by the much slower method of C-54s across the North Atlantic."

"Do you think Mr. Morgenthau has any suspicions vis-à-vis my people, Colonel Frade?"

"I have no reason to think so, sir. But that does not mean we're not operating on the possibility he might."

Mattingly put in: "In other words, he's fishing? The Secret Service agents were fishing?"

"Yes, sir. At this point, that's what I would guess."

General Gehlen said, "When I heard about your flight, Colonel Frade . . . Are you interested in my uninformed scenario?"

"Yes, sir," Mattingly and Frade said, speaking on top of each other.

Gehlen nodded once, then went on: "I wasn't aware of the OSS connection. I wondered what the real purpose of the flight might be. I didn't think it had anything to do with rescuing diplomats. And what I decided was most likely was that since actually taking former Nazi officials aboard the aircraft on its return flight would be dangerous, the Argentine diplomats probably were carrying with them in their luggage a large number of passports."

"Passports?" Clete blurted.

"Yes. Blank passports. Argentine certainly, but probably also Uruguayan and Paraguayan as well. Someone equipped with such a passport wouldn't be afforded the luxury of a twenty-four-hour *flight* to Buenos Aires, but he could make his way to a port in a neutral country—Sweden, for example, or Spain—and there board a ship bound for South America. It would take a little longer, but it would reduce his chances of being questioned."

"Passports never entered my mind," Clete said.

"That's only a possibility," Gehlen said.

"If someone—these Secret Service agents," Mattingly said thoughtfully, and then interrupted himself. "So far as I know—and I would be on the list of people to be notified—Secretary Morgenthau has not told SHAEF he's sending the Secret Service.

"What I was about to say is that if somehow it came out that these Argentine diplomats have, say, two hundred passports with them, they would say, 'Of course, that's what embassies and consulates do, issue passports to their nationals, if the original has expired or been lost.'"

"Well, the passports went right over my head," Clete

said. "But the other thought that I had was that no one—certainly not Argentine customs—is going to go through the luggage of heroic, just-rescued diplomats to see if they might contain a couple of kilos of diamonds."

General Gehlen said: "If we rate my passport scenario on a one-to-ten scale and it's a five, then I would say the transport of valuables—or even currency—is an eight or nine. Allen Dulles told me that, as it became increasingly apparent that Germany was losing the war, the Swiss became increasingly concerned that one could accuse them of helping the Nazis conceal funds."

"Where are Morgenthau's Secret Service agents now, Clete?" Mattingly asked. "Do you know?"

Frade shrugged.

"General Bendick told me they were supposed to be on the ground at Val de Cans only long enough to take on fuel, but then there was a message saying to wait for further orders. They were still there when we took off. I have no idea where they might be."

"There's something about these Secret Service agents that's not right," Mattingly said. "Something that bothers me. It goes without saying that Eisenhower—SHAEF—would do everything possible to keep Nazis from escaping to South America. And SHAEF has the assets to do so."

"And Eisenhower would be unlikely to ask for Secretary Morgenthau's assistance?" Gehlen asked.

"Exactly," Mattingly said.

"And if Morgenthau offered Eisenhower his Secret Service agents?" Gehlen asked.

"Ike would say, 'Thank you just the same, Mr. Secretary, but I can handle this myself.'"

"Which leads us . . . where?"

"I'm not trying to suggest that Ike is in any way lackadaisical about arresting and bringing to trial the Nazis," Mattingly said. "But I don't think it would be unfair to suggest that Morgenthau doesn't think Ike has a passion—the necessary, in Morgenthau's judgment, passion—to deal with the Nazis. Morgenthau's passion is that of a Jew, and God knows they have the right to be passionate."

"So Morgenthau is sending assistance, whether or not General Eisenhower wants it?" Gehlen asked softly.

Mattingly nodded. "I think there would have to be a subterfuge. Morgenthau knows he can't challenge the authority of the Supreme Commander. But some second assistant deputy secretary of the Treasury could take it upon himself to send a planeload of financial experts—who just happened to be Secret Service agents—to look into the financial records of the Third Reich. This would not come to Eisenhower's personal attention, but rather to a one- or two-star in military government, who would presume it was authorized—"

"And some Air Forces brigadier," Frade interjected, "sympathetic to Morgenthau's problem could arrange for the Air Forces Constellation . . ."

"Which would fly via Brazil . . ." Mattingly picked up.

"Once someone in Europe thought it was time—in other words, safe—for the Connie to arrive in Berlin . . ."

"Or Frankfurt . . ."

"Which would explain the 'hold in place' message . . ." Frade said.

"Until SHAEF completes its move to the I.G. Farben building," Mattingly concluded. "When the arrival of one more airplane would not cause comment."

Mattingly looked at Gehlen, who was smiling.

"You're amused, General?"

Gehlen nodded.

"By the way you finish one another's thoughts," Gehlen said. "Otto Niedermeyer and I were—how do I put it?—*smiled at* when we did that at Abwehr Ost."

"You weren't smiling at our scenario?" Mattingly asked.

Gehlen shook his head.

"Actually," he said, "your scenario normally would have wiped away any smile. Despite what Colonel Frade said before, I think we have to consider that somehow Morgenthau has heard of the arrangement I made with Mr. Dulles. Let me go down that path. If Morgenthau has heard of it, I think he would presume that General Eisenhower knows all about it."

"Ike knows nothing about it," Mattingly said.

"Morgenthau would presume he does," Gehlen insisted. "So how can Morgenthau—who I presume you all have heard wants to shoot the senior one hundred Nazis when and where found, and who wants to turn Germany into an agrarian society, and who is not known to be especially critical of the Soviets—stop something he truly believes is evil?

"He would have to go to President Truman, and he

would have to go to him with proof. Since Eisenhower is involved, he would need proof, which Eisenhower is certainly not going to be willing to provide. So he would have to get that proof himself. Thus, the quiet dispatch of the financial experts to look into the finances of the Third Reich."

"How long can we reasonably expect to keep the deal secret?" Frade asked.

"Presuming OSS isn't shut down tomorrow, not for long," Mattingly said. "And if we are shut down, for an even shorter period."

"So what's going to happen?" Frade asked.

"Presuming that OSS is not shut down between now and then, on May twenty-second—which is three days from now—General Gehlen and half a dozen of his officers are going to be found and arrested in Oberusel—not far from here—by agents of the Counterintelligence Corps.

"When he—they—are interrogated—none of them, by the way, are on the Most Wanted Nazis lists—they will report that when defeat became inevitable, they burned all the records of Abwehr Ost and then made their way to refuge in what they knew was going to be West Germany.

"The CIC investigation will be thorough and lengthy, as they will not believe them. Their arrest will be reported to SHAEF, and I suspect that SHAEF will send its own interrogators to Oberusel, and I know the OSS will. The CIC and the OSS and everyone else will ultimately and reluctantly conclude—and so inform SHAEF—that the general and his officers have nothing of value to relate, and further, that since there is no suggestion that they were anything but German officers doing their duty, they are entitled to be treated as such. They will enter the POW system. From which, after having been cleared by the appropriate De-Nazification Board, they will eventually be returned to civilian life.

"While this is going on, the films of all their records, which have been buried in the Austrian Alps, will be recovered by us—the OSS—and moved to Bavaria, to a former monastery called Grünau. The general's men have been told to make their way there. It will be headquarters—if that word fits—of the Gehlen organization.

"The Vatican has very kindly made the monastery available to us without asking any questions—frankly, in return for past services rendered, and in expectation of services to be rendered in the future—but they regrettably can't afford to make the monastery livable and they are not in a position to provide logistical services, such as dining facilities.

"Until earlier this evening, we thought the funds to take care of these expenses would arrive here in your capable hands, Colonel Frade," Mattingly concluded.

"If I had been told . . ." Frade responded, and then stopped. "I should've asked myself what that half million was for, should've thought it through."

"That would have been helpful," Mattingly agreed. "But no lasting harm done, presuming you can get it over here quickly."

"Stein, get word to Buenos Aires to have a Connie

ready to fly back here three hours after we get back," Frade ordered.

"I can't do that until we're airborne tomorrow, Colonel," Stein replied.

"Questions would be asked if you did that, Cletus," Delgano said.

After a moment's thought, Frade said, "You're right. I don't seem to be playing with a full deck, do I?" He paused. "And you and Mario and Vega will be expected to participate in the festivities surrounding the return of the heroic diplomats." He paused again. "So how about this? At the last minute before the next scheduled SAA flight takes off for Lisbon—and I mean the last minute, when the passengers are aboard—Peter and I get aboard. We'll be halfway to Brazil before somebody starts asking questions."

"And then what?" Mattingly asked.

"In Lisbon, we disembark the passengers, take on fuel, and then Hansel and I fly the Connie to Frankfurt, the way we did just now." He paused, then asked, "Why wouldn't that work?"

"Clete, when we get to Berlin, I'm going to Pomerania," von Wachtstein said. "And I don't think, as badly as that money is needed, that you can wait for me to return."

"Excuse me, von Wachtstein," Gehlen said. "What did you just say?"

"I'm going to Pomerania," von Wachtstein said.

"That would be tantamount to committing suicide," Gehlen said.

"I feel duty bound to see my people," von Wachtstein said. "To see what I can do for them."

"I can only infer that you have absolutely no idea what the situation is in Soviet-occupied Germany," Gehlen said.

"Sir, that's what I have to find out," von Wachtstein said.

"Tell him, please, General Gehlen," Mattingly said.

Gehlen looked at Mattingly, obviously collecting his thoughts.

"Why don't you start with what happened to von Stauffenberg?" Mattingly suggested. "To the von Stauffenbergs? And his father? I think everyone would profit from knowing."

General Gehlen thought it over for a long moment.

[TWO]

Finally, after nodding softly, then clearing his throat, General Gehlen somberly began: "When Colonel Claus Graf von Stauffenberg was released from hospital in Munich after recovering from the grievous wounds he suffered when his car was strafed in Tunisia—he lost an eye, his right hand, and two fingers of his left hand—he was assigned to the staff of the Oberkommando der Wehrmacht, the OKW."

Frade and Dooley locked eyes for a moment.

"More precisely," Gehlen continued," he became part of that relatively small number of officers, some senior—Generalleutnant Graf Karl-Friedrich von Wachtstein, for example—and some relatively junior, who had frequent access to Hitler, especially when Hitler was at his East Prussian command post, Wolfsschanze.

"On July twentieth of last year, von Stauffenberg left a bomb in a briefcase under the map table in a small outside building, the Lagebarracke—in other words, not in the Führer Bunker—set the timer, and found an excuse to leave the building.

"He waited until he heard the bomb detonate, then flew to Berlin in a small Heinkel aircraft. He and his adjutant then went to the OKW building on Bendler Strasse, where they learned that while some aspects of the coup had been successful—in Paris, General Carl-Heinrich von Stülpnagel, one of the conspirators, had already arrested most SS officers in the city—the most important facet, the death of Hitler, had not been realized.

"General Friedrich Fromm, one of the conspirators, telephoned Wolfsschanze and spoke with Field Marshal Keitel, who told him Hitler was alive. Fromm, thinking to save his own neck, ordered the arrest of fellow conspirators General Friedrich Olbricht and von Stauffenberg. Instead, they arrested him and locked him in his office.

"Himmler, meanwhile, had contacted Major Otto Ernst Remer, who commanded the Wachbataillon Grossdeutschland in Berlin, told him of the failed assassination attempt, told him that he was now a colonel by order of the Führer, and ordered him to, quote, deal with the traitors at Bendler Strasse, end quote.

"Colonel Remer responded to his orders with enthusiasm. He and his men arrived at Bendler Strasse around twenty-two hundred hours and started shooting. Colonel von Stauffenberg was wounded in the left arm. The conspirators had no choice but to surrender and did so.

"General Fromm, still trying to save his own skin, promptly convened a summary court-martial, which promptly found von Stauffenberg, Olbricht, Colonel Albrecht Mertz von Quirnheim, Colonel-General Ludwig Beck, and Lieutenant Werner von Haeften guilty of high treason and ordered their execution.

"Shortly after midnight, they were led, one by one, before a stack of sandbags in the parking lot and executed by SS submachine-gun fire. Just before his executioners fired, von Stauffenberg shouted, 'Long live our holy Germany.'"

"My God!" von Wachtstein said.

"In a sense, Graf von Wachtstein, they were fortunate," Gehlen said.

Clete noticed that Gehlen had just called von Wachtstein "Graf" and then remembered he had done so before.

"Fortunate?" Delgano asked incredulously.

"The SS immediately began to arrest anyone suspected of being involved," Gehlen went on. "The total was approximately seven thousand people. They missed some of the guilty—"

"Including General Reinhard Gehlen," Mattingly interjected dryly.

"—and arrested many people who were completely innocent," Gehlen went on as if he hadn't heard Mattingly's comment. "Accused officers were denied courts-martial and tried before the Volksgerichthof, whose chief judge was a man named Roland Freisler. Freisler permitted the accused no defense, and usually had the accused standing before the court in uniforms stripped of all insignia, buttons, belts, and braces. They had to try to hold their trousers up with their hands. When Freisler screamed at them to stand to attention, the trousers of course fell down and the accused faced the court in their underdrawers. Not a single person brought before the Volksgerichthof—there were two thousand—was acquitted.

"On August tenth, 1944, three weeks or so after the bomb failed to eliminate Hitler, Graf von Stauffenberg's brother, Berthold, Count von Schulenberg, and three others—including Generalleutnant Graf Karl-Friedrich von Wachtstein—were tried and convicted of high treason and hung with despicable cruelty that afternoon in the execution hut in Berlin-Ploetzensee."

"What does that mean, General?" Delgano asked. "'Despicable cruelty'?"

Clete thought: *For God's sake, Gehlen, don't answer that!*

He glanced at Mattingly, whose face showed he was thinking the same thing.

"They were taken to the execution hut in an inner courtyard of the building," Gehlen went on matter-of-factly, "where they were stripped of the clothing they had been wearing since their arrest. Their hands and feet were bound. Wire—something like piano wire—was looped around their necks, then around hooks—something like the hooks one sees in a butcher's shop—on the wall.

"They then were strangled by their own weight. They took two or three minutes to lose consciousness, whereupon they were revived and the strangulation process begun again. This was repeated four or five times until death finally occurred."

Clete looked at Peter's face. It was white and contorted.

You didn't have to get into the fucking details, you sonofabitch!

"The hangings—strangulations?—were filmed by SS motion picture photographers at the request of Hitler, who wished to see them," Gehlen went on. "I understand he has watched the films over and over.

"All properties of the conspirators and their relatives were confiscated. Just about everybody in the von Stauffenberg family was immediately arrested. Von Stauffenberg's mother, Caroline, was in solitary confinement from July 23, 1944, until the end of the war. Claus von Stauffenberg's widow, Nina, was held in the Alexanderplatz prison in Berlin. She gave birth there, a daughter named Konstanze, in January 1945—"

"Where is Nina—the countess—now?" von Wachtstein interrupted.

"May I suggest, Graf von Wachtstein, that you hold your questions until I finish?"

"Excuse me," von Wachtstein said.

"The third brother, Alexander von Stauffenberg, was brought back from Athens to Berlin. Even when it became apparent that he was not involved in the conspiracy, he was nevertheless arrested and held in various concentration camps.

"Von Stauffenberg's cousin Caesar von Hofacker was condemned to death on August thirtieth but kept alive for interrogation—which was unsuccessful—about Rommel's and Speidel's involvement in the conspiracy, after which, on December twentieth, 1944, he was executed in the manner I described.

"There are other details, but I think I have covered pretty much everything. You had questions, Herr Graf?"

"Where is the Countess von Stauffenberg now? Claus's widow, Nina?" von Wachtstein asked.

"We know only that she escaped both the SS mass execution of the prisoners in Alexanderplatz prison as the Russians drew close and the arrest of the prisoners still living by the Russians when they took the prison. We can only presume—"

"The von Stauffenbergs have a house in Zehlendorf," von Wachtstein said. "Perhaps she is trying to get there."

"*Had* a house, Herr Graf," Gehlen said. "As I said before, all von Stauffenberg property—all the property of all the conspirators, including that of your late father, Herr Graf, was seized by the Third Reich."

He paused to let that sink in.

"The property of the late Admiral Canaris was also seized," Gehlen went on. "His house in Zehlendorf has been requisitioned by General White for the use of the OSS."

"General White, von Wachtstein," Mattingly offered,

"is doing what he can to locate Countess von Stauffenberg and the baby. If they can be found, White will find them. When that happens, she will be taken to the Canaris house and placed under the protection of the OSS."

"How is the OSS going to protect her?" Frade asked. "We have people in Berlin?"

"Did you see Master Sergeant Dunwiddie when we arrived here?" Mattingly said. "That huge black man they call 'Tiny'? He was posting the guard."

Frade nodded.

"He and eight of his men, most of them at least as large as Tiny, will be on the C-54 with me tomorrow," Mattingly said. "Tiny is a very interesting man. His great-grandfather charged up San Juan Hill in Cuba with the Tenth Cavalry. Given the slightest chance, Tiny will tell you the Tenth made it up the hill before Colonel Teddy Roosevelt's First Volunteer Cavalry did."

Gehlen's face showed that he could have done without the history lesson.

"Is there anything else you'd like to know, Herr Graf?" Gehlen asked.

Von Wachtstein seemed to be struggling to find his voice.

Finally, he did, and asked calmly, "General, do you know what happened to the remains? I'd like to take my father's body to Schloss Wachtstein."

"Weren't you listening, Herr Graf, when I told you that the Schloss—all of your land, all your holdings—have been seized?" Gehlen said. "Let me carry that a little further: When the Soviets took the castle—I presume you know it was being used as a recovery hospital for amputees—"

"I knew that, General. I was there."

"—they executed the patients who had not been in condition to leave their beds and flee. The nurses and the doctors who had remained behind to treat them were sent to Russia. After, of course, the nurses had been repeatedly raped."

"With respect, Herr General, my question was regarding the location of my father's remains."

"If you had been in the castle when the Russians took it, Herr Graf, and they learned who you were, you would have been hung by your ankles and your epidermis would have been cut from your body. Your skinned remains would have been left hanging so that the people in the village would get the message that the regime of the aristocracy was over and that the Red Army was in charge."

"They actually skinned people alive?" Clete asked incredulously.

"SS officers and members of the nobility," Mattingly said. "I've seen—what?—maybe *twenty* confirmed reports."

"And my father's remains, Herr General? What can you tell me?" von Wachtstein asked evenly.

"The best information I have, Herr Graf, is that they were taken to the Invalidenfriedhof cemetery and placed in an unmarked pit. They were then burned, some caustic added to speed decomposition, and then, when there were perhaps a hundred corpses in the pit, it was closed.

The reasoning of the SS was that the more corpses in the grave, the harder it would be to identify any individual body if there was later an attempt at exhumation."

After a long moment, von Wachtstein softly said, "Thank you, Herr General."

There was silence in the room. People stared straight ahead, at their hands, at the ceiling, anywhere but at von Wachtstein.

Suddenly, Peter got to his feet and marched to the bar. He stood over it, supporting himself on both arms, his head lowered.

Frade got up and went toward him. Before he reached the bar, Dooley got up and followed him.

The three stood side by side at the bar, Dooley and Frade erect, von Wachtstein still leaning on it.

After a very long moment, von Wachtstein said, without looking at either Frade or Dooley, or even raising his head, "I would really like to have a drink. But if we are flying to Berlin in the morning, I suppose that's not a very good idea."

"Colonel Dooley," Frade said, "if you would be good enough to set brandy snifters on the bar, I will pour that Rémy Martin I see."

Frade poured three-quarters of an inch of cognac into each glass.

"Hansel," Frade said, and after a moment when von Wachtstein raised his head to look at him, Frade held up his glass and proclaimed, "To a fellow warrior I never had the privilege to know: Generalleutnant Graf Karl-Friedrich von Wachtstein."

Von Wachtstein pushed himself erect and looked first at Clete and then at Dooley. Then he picked up his brandy snifter and lifted it.

"And since we get only one of these," Frade said, "I suppose we better include your pal von Stauffenberg in those warriors we never got to know."

"Yeah," Dooley said.

"My father would have liked both of you," von Wachtstein said. "But I'm not so sure about Claus. He was a Swabian, and they're even stuffier than Prussians. I always had the feeling Claus thought fighter pilots should be kept with the other animals in the stables."

He touched the rim of his glass to theirs, and then—simultaneously, as if someone had barked the command *Drink!*—all three raised their glasses to their mouths and drained them.

When they started to return to the table, they saw that everyone at it was standing at attention.

[THREE]
Transient Officers' Quarters
Rhein-Main Air Base
Frankfurt am Main, Germany
2305 19 May 1945

Colonel Mattingly, saying that he wanted to check on what had happened at the Russian roadblock at Helmstedt on the autobahn, dropped Frade, von Wachtstein, Stein, Boltitz, and Rodríguez at the door to the transient officers' quarters, then got behind the wheel of the Horch.

Accustomed to the low-range gears, he pressed heavily on the accelerator as he let out the clutch. The huge Horch, its tires squealing, jumped into motion.

There was a small foyer in the building. There was a window in one wall—now closed by a roll-down metal curtain—behind which a desk clerk had once presided. The room was now sparsely furnished with a small table—on which sat a telephone—and two small wooden armchairs.

Both chairs were occupied by men who rose to their feet when Frade and the others walked in.

They were wearing U.S. Army officer Class A uniforms, a green tunic and pink trousers. Clete first noticed there was no insignia of rank on the epaulets, and that the lapels held only the gold letters *U.S.* but no branch insignia below that.

Something about those gold letters triggered curiosity in Clete's brain. Mattingly, saying they would need them in Berlin, had furnished everybody—from an astonishingly full supply room—with "officer-equivalent civilian employee uniforms" just before they had left Schlosshotel Kronberg. The green tunics had small embroidered insignia—the letters *U.S.* within a triangle within a square sewn to the lapels, and a larger version of that insignia sewn to the right shoulder. They were all stuffed into a U.S. Army duffel bag, which Enrico now carried hanging from his shoulder.

Why do I think the Secret Service has appeared?

"Which one of you is Cletus H. Frade?" one of the men demanded.

Whatever response he expected, he didn't get it. Instead, he found himself looking at the muzzle of Enrico's Remington Model 11 twelve-gauge riot gun and then listening to the metallic *chunk* the weapon made as a double-ought buckshot shotgun shell was chambered.

"Secret Service! Secret Service!" the man said excitedly.

"What?"

"We are special agents of the United States Secret Service!"

"Can you prove it?"

"I have credentials in my pocket."

"Get them. Slowly," Frade ordered, and then pointed at the second man. "And while he's doing that, you drop to your knees and then lock your hands behind your head."

The man, mingled concern and disbelief on his face, hesitated.

Frade snapped, "Are you deaf?"

The man dropped to his knees. The first man carefully took a small leather folder from his breast pocket and slowly offered it to Frade.

Frade examined it carefully, then tossed it to Stein.

"Secret Service, huh? What the hell are you doing in Germany? I thought what you people did was chase counterfeiters."

"We are on a special mission for Secretary of the Treasury Morgenthau," the first special agent said.

"Looking for German counterfeiters?" Frade asked incredulously.

"Looking for German Nazis," the man said.

"Well, they shouldn't be hard to find," Frade said. "There's a bunch of them in Germany."

"These credentials appear bona fide, Commander," Stein said.

"Show them to von Wachtstein," Clete ordered.

"Commander?" the man on his knees asked.

"I don't recall giving you permission to ask questions," Frade said, and then asked, "Are you armed?"

"Yes, of course we're armed," the first special agent said.

"Well, then, very slowly, take whatever you're carrying from its holster, lay it on the floor, and then step away."

"For God's sake, Colonel Frade, I just showed you proof that we're special agents of the United States Secret Service!" the first man said.

He had regained some—but by no means all—of his composure.

"Weapons on the ground, please," Frade ordered. "When you've done that, we'll see if we can make some sense of this."

Each special agent produced a Smith & Wesson revolver and laid it on the floor, then backed away from it. The special agent on his knees did so with more than a little difficulty—it is difficult to back up when one is on one's knees—but finally managed to put six feet between him and his pistol.

Frade then made an imperial gesture, allowing him to stand.

"Pick up their weapons, Stein," Frade ordered, and then, in Spanish, ordered Enrico to take the Secret Service men to his room.

Enrico gestured with the shotgun.

When Frade saw on their faces that neither Secret Service agent understood Spanish, he made the translation.

"I just told him to take you to my room," he said. "I don't want anyone to come across this happy scene. Through the door and up the steps."

Frade sat on his bed and motioned for the Secret Service agents to stand against the wall.

"All right, Colonel Frade," the Secret Service agent who had spoken first and had now recovered his composure said. "Don't you think this charade has now gone far enough?"

Frade smiled at him.

"We know all about you, Colonel . . ."

Somehow, I don't think so.

". . . including, for example, the half million dollars you brought to Germany with you."

Well, I don't think you got that information from anybody else in the OSS except good ol' Colonel Richmond C. Flowers, USA.

That sonofabitch!

"What did you say your name was?" Frade asked.

"Stevenson. Supervisory Special Agent Jerome T. Stevenson."

"Well, Jerome, Boy Scout's honor, I didn't bring a

half million dollars from anywhere. Where'd you get that? What was I supposed to be going to do with all that money? And what makes you think I'm a colonel?"

"You're going to have to turn us loose sooner or later, Colonel Frade," Stevenson said.

"That, or shoot you for interfering with an OSS operation," Frade said.

"Smuggling Nazis into Argentina is an OSS operation? Is that what you're asking me to believe?"

"So, that's what this is all about. What else did that asshole Flowers tell you?"

He saw the look on Stevenson's face.

Bingo! Flowers is the one who ran off at the mouth.

Stevenson said: "You're denying that you are assisting in the escape of Nazis to Argentina?"

Frade replied: "Supervisory Special Agent Stevenson, say hello to OSS Special Agent Stein. Show Supervisory Special Agent Stevenson your credentials, Siggie."

Stein produced his spurious OSS credentials and showed them to Stevenson.

"Now, Jerome, if I told you that Stein is a devout, practicing Hebrew who lost many members of his family to the concentration camp ovens after he barely got out of the Third Reich alive, what would you say the odds are that Siggie would be helping Nazis escape to anywhere?"

Stevenson, who looked more than a little confused, didn't reply.

"Rephrasing the question, Jerome. What would you say the odds are that Special Agent Stein adds a certain enthusiasm to his present tasks that a non-Jew simply couldn't muster?"

"You're suggesting that what you're doing is stopping Nazis from escaping?"

"I'm not suggesting that. I'm telling you that. And what it looks like to me is that you and your pal here are about to screw things up for us. The Secret Service was not on the list of cooperating agencies that SHAEF gave me. Which makes me suspect that you're not telling me the truth, Jerome, which naturally makes me wonder what the hell the truth is."

"The truth, Colonel Frade," Stevenson said, "is that we have been sent here by Secretary of the Treasury Morgenthau to prevent Nazis from escaping to South America."

"Then why didn't SHAEF tell me that?"

Stevenson didn't answer.

"SHAEF doesn't know Morgenthau sent you? Is that what you're telling me—or not telling me, as the case may be?"

Again, Stevenson didn't answer directly. He instead said, "Colonel Frade, when OSS has been disbanded, as I'm sure you know it is about to be, it would be in your interest to have friends in the Secret Service."

"The OSS is about to be disbanded? I never heard that."

"Take my word on it," Stevenson said. "You're about to be homeless, and it is not wise for homeless people to interfere with Secretary Morgenthau."

"I certainly wouldn't want to interfere with Secretary Morgenthau. So I'll tell you what I am going to do: I'm going to move this problem up the chain of command. Do you know what that means?"

Again, Stevenson didn't reply.

"What that means, Jerome, is that we're going to wait here for my boss. He's pretty far up the chain of command at SHAEF, and he's in charge of keeping Nazis from escaping to South America. Maybe he knows something I don't."

Stevenson said nothing.

"He should be here in just a few minutes," Frade said. "And while we're waiting, Jerome, I think you and your pal should take off your shoes and socks and your trousers and underpants."

"What?" Stevenson demanded incredulously.

"That should keep you from trying to run away," Frade said.

"Fuck you!" Stevenson said.

"Well, if you're shy, Jerome, I can have Siggie and Hansel pour water all over you. That would keep you from running, and you and your pal could keep your undersized equipment secret."

"Frade, you're going to pay for this!"

"Siggie, there's a water pitcher under the sink," Frade said, pointing.

Stein had just about filled the water pitcher when Supervisory Special Agent Stevenson started taking off his shoes.

[FOUR]

Colonel Robert Mattingly walked into the room fifteen minutes later. On his heels was Master Sergeant Dunwiddie, now wearing an officer equivalent civilian employee uniform, and with a Thompson submachine gun slung from his shoulder.

Stevenson's eyes widened at the sight of him.

"Good, you're still up," Mattingly said. "The convoy couldn't get past the Russians." He paused and then asked, "What the hell?"

"Sir, the fat one with his hands covering his crotch tells me that he's a Secret Service agent sent here by Secretary of the Treasury Morgenthau to keep Nazis from escaping to South America. You ever hear anything about that?"

"No," Mattingly said. "I haven't."

"Tell the colonel what you told me, Jerome," Frade said.

"Who are you, Colonel?" Stevenson demanded.

"I'm the man asking the questions," Mattingly said. "Question one: Why are you sitting there half naked?"

"That was my idea, sir. In case they decided to run," Frade said.

"Good thinking!" Mattingly said. "Question two: What's this about the secretary of the Treasury sending you over here?"

"We have been sent here by Secretary . . ." Stevenson began.

"If I am to believe you, Mr. Stevenson—and I'm finding it hard to do so, frankly—but what I am to understand," Mattingly said, "is that without seeking the permission of SHAEF, the secretary of the Treasury has sent you here on a private Nazi-hunting operation. Does that about sum it up?"

"May we put our clothing on, Colonel?" Stevenson asked.

Mattingly made a gesture with his hand signaling that that was permissible.

"Thank you," Stevenson said, and reached for his underpants.

"If what you have told me is true," Mattingly said, "this will have to be brought to the attention of General Eisenhower—"

"Who will, I feel sure, be happy to accept, indeed be grateful for, the secretary's desire to help—"

Mattingly silenced him by holding up his hand.

"A word of friendly advice, Mr. Stevenson," Mattingly said. "Those of us who work closely with the Supreme Commander have learned that it is really ill-advised to predict what General Eisenhower will do in any circumstance.

"Now, there are several problems with bringing this situation to the Supreme Commander's attention. One of these is the hour. It's almost midnight. I'm sure the Supreme Commander, wherever he is, is sound asleep."

"Wherever he is?"

Mattingly went on: "SHAEF is in the process of moving here from France, which is another problem. No telling where ol' Ike has laid his head tonight. But the rea problem is that you have arrived at a most unfortunate time. We are in the midst of solving a rather difficult problem . . ."

"What kind of a problem?"

"I'm afraid I can't get into that with you. Suffice it to say, we are acting at the direct order of the Supreme Commander and the action he has ordered cannot be delayed by something like this.

"So, what I'm going to do, Mr. Stevenson, is get the provost marshal over here. What I'm going to tell him is that you—all the Secret Service people—are to be held incommunicado on the base here until seventeen hundred tomorrow. Your aircraft will not be available to you until that hour."

"You can't do that! You don't have the authority."

"Believe me, Mr. Stevenson, I do."

He immediately proved that by picking up the telephone and dialing Operator.

"Colonel," Mattingly said to the Rhein-Main Air Base provost marshal, "if I told you that these two gentlemen and everybody else who arrived with them on that Constellation have to be held incommunicado on the base until either someone from SHAEF comes to deal with them or until seventeen hundred hours tomorrow—whichever happens first—how would you do that?"

"Well, the simplest solution would be to put them in the stockade. Get the others out of the transient officers' quarters and put them with these two in the stockade."

"What, exactly, is the stockade?"

"The Krauts had sort of a police station, a police precinct. It wasn't damaged much, and I took it over. There's enough cells for all these people."

Stevenson spoke up: "Colonel, what if I told you that I'm a supervisory special agent of the United States Secret Service?"

The provost marshal looked at Mattingly. "Is he?"

Mattingly nodded.

"And this man," Stevenson went on, "has no authority whatever to detain us in any way."

The arrogance of Stevenson's tone was not lost on the provost marshal.

"To answer your first question," the provost marshal told Stevenson, "I'd tell you that I don't give a damn. If Colonel Mattingly wants you held incommunicado, you get held incommunicado."

"But we are federal agents!" Stevenson protested.

"I really would rather not put them in cells," Mattingly said. "What about just holding them in the transient officers' quarters?"

"I could put MPs on the BOQ, I suppose."

"And if you took everybody's shoes and socks, trousers and underpants . . ." Frade suggested helpfully.

"I think just the shoes and trousers, Colonel Frade," Mattingly said. "We don't want to embarrass them any more than they already are for having been caught with Secretary Morgenthau's hand in the cookie jar."

"Then just shoes and trousers," the provost marshal said.

"Mr. Dunwiddie," Mattingly said. "Would you go

with the provost marshal while he escorts these gentlemen to their quarters, please?"

"Yes, sir."

With a casual skill that could have come only with a good deal of practice, Dunwiddie shrugged his shoulder, which caused the strap of the Thompson to slide off. Without looking at the submachine gun, he caught it with one hand in midair, then cradled it across his chest as a hunter would a shotgun.

"After you, gentlemen," Dunwiddie said.

"You haven't heard the end of this, Colonel," Stevenson said.

"One more sign of lack of cooperation on your part and you lose your drawers," Mattingly said.

It was only when they were sure the departing party was out of earshot that anyone even chuckled. But then the chuckles turned to giggles, and then—when Frade mocked Stevenson modestly covering his private parts with his hands—became outright laughter.

Mattingly sobered first.

"I can't think of a better solution for the moment to these Secret Service people than the one we just reached," he said. "But did you ever hear 'He who laughs last laughs best'? I think this is probably going to come around and bite us on the gluteus maximus."

Frade then remembered where he had heard the phrase most recently: when Colonel Richmond C. Flowers had given him the half-million dollars in Buenos Aires.

Mattingly then said: "With the Russians having stopped our convoy at Helmstedt, we now turn to Plan B. I think the best thing to do is get our show on the road as early as possible tomorrow morning. Dooley, I want you and your P-38s ready to escort the C-54 at first light. Any problem with you being in the air then?"

"No, sir."

"Know that we do have a communications problem. We have no landlines to Tempelhof. I told the people at Helmstedt to set up the mobile control tower. What I'm hoping is that it will be able to communicate with Dooley's aircraft, and that Dooley and his people can relay to both Rhein-Main and Tempelhof and with the C-54, and—if we get that far with Plan B—with the SAA Connie. We won't know if this will work until we try it, which means there is now a Plan C.

"If things go well, I will depart Rhein-Main—from over Rhein-Main, not takeoff—in the C-54 at oh-seven-forty-five. That should put us on the ground at Tempelhof by oh-nine-hundred. While Dooley's aircraft circle overhead, we will get the mobile control tower that the C-54 will have aboard up and running. I'm told they can do so in thirty minutes; all they need to do is erect some antennae. I'm going to give them an hour. The moment it's up, the C-54 will be cleared to Rhein-Main.

"That should get us back through the Russian zone forty minutes later. The minute that word gets to Rhein-Main, the SAA Connie—which will have been, since ten-thirty hours, circling Rhein-Main at altitude—will then be cleared for departure to Tempelhof, and should arrive at Tempelhof in time for lunch. Got that, Clete?"

"Yes, sir."

"I think we're going to be able to pull this off," Mattingly said. "If not, I'll see you in Siberia, the other side of the Pearly Gates, or, if Supervisory Special Agent Stevenson has any input, at Prisoner Reception at the Fort Leavenworth Prison."

There was laughter, some of it a little strained.

"I will now see Colonel Stevens—the SHAEF military government guy—and tell him to have the diplomats out here to board the SAA Connie . . . when, Clete?"

"Well, if we're going to have to be at ten thousand feet over Rhein-Main by ten-thirty, that means we'll have to take off at, say, ten-fifteen. Tell him to have the diplomats out here ready to go no later than oh-five-thirty."

Von Wachtstein laughed.

"Delgano is right, Cletus. You're evil."

IX

[ONE]
Aboard *Ciudad de Rosario*
Above Rhein-Main Air Base
Frankfurt am Main, Germany
1025 20 May 1945

"We're indicating ten thousand, Hansel," Frade announced. "Commence three-minute three-sixty turn."

"Commencing three-minute circle," von Wachtstein replied.

"And here comes Dooley," Clete said as a P-38 pulled alongside. "Hello there, Little Brother!"

"Why don't you knock that Little Brother shit off, wiseass?"

"Aircraft with your wingtip in my pilot's ear," Frade replied mock-seriously, "be advised you are scaring our passengers."

"Jesus Christ!" Dooley said, disgusted, then excitedly added: "The C-54 just crossed the border!"

"We heard."

Communications had turned out to be much better than anyone had dared hope they would be. The Rhein-

Main control tower could talk to the truck-mounted control tower at Helmstedt, and once the C-54 had landed at Tempelhof and put its control tower in operation, Helmstedt had communication with Berlin.

Whatever Rhein-Main wanted to say to Tempelhof—or vice versa—had to be relayed via Helmstedt, but it was not necessary to relay messages between any tower via aircraft. And, of course, the air-to-ground communications were also far better than expected.

Dooley asked Frade: "Then why did you just begin a turn? Aren't you going to Berlin?"

"This is Rhein-Main. Clear this channel."

"Yes, Mother," Dooley said.

"South American Airways Double Zero Four, Rhein-Main. How do you read?"

"SAA Double Zero Four reads you five by five, Mother."

"Rhein-Main Area Control clears SAA Double Zero Four direct Tempelhof U.S. Army Airfield Berlin on a heading of forty-eight-point-four degrees at ten thousand feet. Visual flight rules. Report to Helmstedt Area Control using Air-Ground Channel Two when crossing U.S.-Soviet zone border. Be advised that there are numerous USAF P-38 aircraft and possibly some Soviet aircraft operating along your route. Exercise appropriate caution. Acknowledge."

Clete repeated, essentially verbatim, the Rhein-Main clearance.

"Double Zero Four, Rhein-Main. Affirmative.

"Mother, SAA Double Zero Four beginning climb to

ten thousand and course change to forty-eight-point-fou at this time."

Since they were already at ten thousand feet, all vo Wachtstein had to do was change course. He made th course correction as a fighter pilot, rather than the captain of an airliner, would—he shoved all four throttle forward as he cranked the yoke just about as far as i would go.

"SAA Double Zero Four, be advised the correct nomenclature of this airfield is Rhein-Main, not Mother."

"Mother, SAA Double Zero Four, say again. Our pilo has been giving our passengers a thrill, and with all tha screaming, I couldn't hear you."

Clete looked out the window at Archie Dooley.

Dooley signaled that he was going to fly ahead. Clet nodded and gave him a thumbs-up.

Dooley's P-38, in a shallow climb, moved out.

Clete was still watching him pull away when he looke out his side window and saw another P-38 pull alongside And then, through von Wachtstein's—the pilot's—sid window, he saw a P-38 out there, too.

"Helmstedt Area Control, South American Airways Zer Zero Four."

"Go ahead, Zero Zero Four."

"Helmstedt, be advised that South American Airway Zero Zero Four, at ten thousand feet and indicating three fifty airspeed on a course of forty-eight-point-four, is departing the American zone at this time. Acknowledge."

"South American Zero Zero Four, Helmstedt acknowledges you making three five zero at ten thousand on a course of forty-eight-point-four and departing American zone. Be advised that both American and Soviet fighter aircraft are operating along your route. Exercise appropriate caution. When possible, contact Tempelhof Area Control on Air-Ground Channel Four."

"Zero Zero Four understands Air-Ground Channel Four."

Frade then experienced a feeling that for a moment he didn't recognize. And then he did.

It was the same emotion he had experienced flying out of Fighter One on Guadalcanal—when, although he couldn't see anything at that moment, he knew that the enemy could appear at any time.

With the great big difference being that then I was flying a Wildcat and could defend myself.

Now I'm flying an aerial bus with absolutely nothing to defend myself.

"All things considered," von Wachtstein announced, "and apropos of nothing at all, I love the Connie. But right now I'd rather be flying a Focke-Wulf. Or even what Archie and his guys are flying."

"Oh, come on, Hansel," Clete said, then looking out ahead blurted, "Oh, shit!"

Three rapidly growing black dots were headed straight for them.

"What are they, Hansel?"

"YAK-3s," von Wachtstein said.

Frade radioed: "Archie, where the hell are you?"

And then they saw something else.

Three P-38s appeared in front of the Constellation, moving so fast that Clete knew they were coming out of a full-power dive, with their airspeed indicator needles pointing to the red tape that meant *If you go any faster than this, the wings will come off.*

The three P-38s lined themselves up with the incoming YAK-3s.

What the hell are they going to do, play chicken? Frade thought, then said, "Jesus, I hope those Russians blink first!"

Suddenly, coming from the rear on both sides of the Connie, there was a burst of tracer fire—four red lines arching across the sky—and then another, and finally a third, single line of tracers, brighter than the first two.

"Ach du Lieber Gott!" von Wachtstein said.

"Not to worry, Hansel," Frade said. "What they're doing is testing their guns."

"For Christ's sake, I know tracers when I see them," von Wachtstein said. "What was the last single burst? The bright one?

"That came from the Hispano-Suiza 20mm machine cannon," Frade said. "The parallel tracer lines came from the four .50-caliber Brownings. You didn't know that?"

Frade looked out his side window. The P-38 pilot who had tested his guns had pulled up next to them. He waved and grinned cheerfully.

Clete could see enough of the YAK-3s now to know that he had never seen one before. He looked at the leading edge of their wings, waiting for the flashes of their weaponry.

They never came.

All of a sudden, the noses of the Russian airplanes lowered and they dived, quickly becoming smaller and smaller dots.

"I think the decision was made not to shoot us down," von Wachtstein said softly.

"They would have had to go through Archie and his guys to do that. I wasn't worried."

I was scared silly, is what I was.

Terrified. About to wet my pants . . .

Frade reached for the radio control panel and switched to Air-Ground Channel Four.

"Tempelhof, this is South American Airways Zero Zero Four."

"Double Zero Four, Tempelhof. I read you five by five. How me?"

Thank you, God!

"Five by five, Tempelhof. We are approximately sixty miles out at ten thousand, indicating three-fifty. Request approach and landing."

"Double Zero Four, maintaining present course, begin to descend to five thousand feet at this time. Report when you have the field in sight."

"Understand descend to five thousand and report when I can see you."

"Affirmative. Be advised there have been reports of Soviet aircraft operating on your course."

"Tempelhof, be advised my Little Brother and his pals chased the bad birds away. Beginning descent to five thousand at this time."

"Tempelhof, Zero Zero Four. At six thousand and I have the field in sight."

"South American Double Zero Four, maintain present altitude until over the field. Then commence descent in ninety-second three-sixty-degree turns. Report when at fifteen hundred."

"Understand when over the field, commence ninety-second circular descent to fifteen hundred."

"Double Zero Four. Affirmative."

"I'm surprised anybody's still alive," Clete said as they slowly descended over the rubble of what was once the German capital. "Jesus, this is worse than Cologne or Frankfurt."

"I don't think Frankfurt or Köln had as many thousand-bomber raids by the Americans in the daytime, followed by English thousand-plane raids at night," von Wachtstein said matter-of-factly. "Hamburg is supposed to be even worse."

"Tempelhof, South American Zero Zero Four at fifteen hundred."

"Tempelhof clears South American Zero Zero Four as Number One to land on Runway Two Seven. Wind is at five from the north. Be advised there is an antiaircraft half-track and an M-4 Sherman tank parked near the threshold."

"Understand Number One on Two Seven."

"Flaps to twenty, gear down," von Wachtstein ordered.

"Flaps at twenty, gear down and locked," Clete replied after a moment, then said: "Try not to bend the bird, Hansel."

"Jesus, that's enormous," Clete said as their landing roll brought them close to the terminal building.

"It's supposed to be one of the twenty largest buildings in the world," von Wachtstein said, and then added, "The last time I saw it, I came in here dead-stick, with oil all over the windscreen of my Focke-Wulf. When I finally touched down, my left gear collapsed."

"I know the feeling, Hansel. You operated out of here?"

"No. So far as I know, we never used it for military operations. When they pulled me out of the Focke-Wulf, a guy asked me if I didn't know I was not supposed to land here."

Frade saw that there were only three aircraft under the arc of the huge building, all of them Piper Cub L-4s and all with the Second Armored Division insignia painted on the fuselage. The engine of one was running, and as von Wachtstein brought the Constellation to a stop and shut it down, that L-4 began to taxi toward the runway.

"There's Mattingly," von Wachtstein said, pointing.

Colonel Robert Mattingly was standing in front of the welcoming party—three other officers and half a dozen soldiers—all of them wearing the triangle patch of the Second Armored Division. Behind them was a small fleet of three-quarter-ton trucks and jeeps.

A strange-looking vehicle appeared from behind the trucks and jeeps and drove up to the rear of the Connie's fuselage.

Von Wachtstein unstrapped himself and then—not without effort—put his head through the small window and looked out.

He pulled his head back in and reported, "It's a hydraulic stairs. I wonder where they found that?"

He took another look, then announced, "Mattingly looks like he's going to come up the stairs."

Clete unstrapped himself, walked through the passenger compartment, and opened the door.

Mattingly loudly announced in Spanish: "Good morning, Captain. I am Colonel Oscar Hammerstein, the civil affairs officer of the United States Second Armored Division. May I address your passengers, please?"

"Yes, of course," Frade said, equally loudly.

The name Oscar Hammerstein rang a bell, but Frade couldn't put a face or anything else to it.

Mattingly came onto the Connie, moved past Clete, stood in the center of the aisle, and loudly said, "If I may have your attention, gentlemen?"

When he had it, he went on: "I am Colonel Oscar Hammerstein, the civil affairs officer of the United States

Second Armored Division. I have the privilege of being your escort during your short visit to Berlin.

"On behalf of General White and the officers and the troopers of Hell on Wheels, permit me to welcome you to Berlin.

"You will now please disembark. You will be taken to the Argentine Embassy under the protection of the Second Armored Division. Your luggage and the supplies will shortly follow. The aircraft crew will remain here at Tempelhof. There is absolutely nothing to fear from the Russians, as we have every reason to believe, despite what you may have heard, that they will respect your diplomatic status.

"I'm sure your diplomatic personnel here will be able to answer any questions you might have before they leave for home, probably about oh-nine-hundred hours—that's nine A.M.—tomorrow.

"I look forward to getting to know those of you who will be staying.

"And now, please begin to debark. Be careful! That ladder was a little unsteady as I came up here. Thank you for your kind attention. Once again, welcome to Berlin!"

Mattingly then quickly made his way up the aisle to the cockpit. Gonzalo Delgano quickly followed him, and on his heels came Vega and Peralta. Frade got there last, and closed the door to the passenger compartment behind them.

"There's a hotel here," Mattingly began, "and—"

There came a knock at the door.

Clete opened it.

Rodolfo Nulder stood there.

"If you don't mind," Nulder said, more than a little arrogantly, "I've got some questions for Colonel Hammerstein. Several, as a matter of fact."

Mattingly said: "And you are, señor?"

"Rodolfo Nulder. I am, so to speak, the person in charge."

"No, Señor Nulder. I am the person in charge, and I just told you to debark. Please do so."

"I protest!"

"Duly noted. Now either stop delaying the movement or sit down and make yourself comfortable. You can spend the night on this aircraft."

"You haven't heard the last of this, Colonel Hammerstein!"

"It's Hammersmith, Felix Hammersmith. I suggest you submit any complaints you might have in writing to SHAEF, after we—*if we*—get you safely out of Berlin. Which is it to be, Señor Nulder—are you going or staying?"

Nulder looked around the cabin. "You all were witnesses to this!" he said, primarily to Delgano, then turned and walked quickly down the aisle to the line of passengers at the door.

Delgano pulled the door closed and said, "Well, at least they'll have something to talk about at the embassy tonight."

"What I really think will happen at the embassy tonight is that your people who were here are going to give a detailed report of the rape of Berlin. Believe me, that will take everybody's mind off Colonel Hammerstein, or Hammersmith, whatever name I used."

"What happens to us now?" Delgado said.

Mattingly looked at Siggie Stein.

"I realized about thirty seconds ago, Siggie, that I should have asked this question yesterday. It is alleged by Mr. Dulles that you are one of the rare people who know how to make a Collins 7.2 work. True?"

"I know the 7.2 pretty well, Colonel."

"Good. We brought one on the C-54. It is now in Admiral Canaris's house in Zehlendorf. Just as soon as the diplomats have driven away and everybody can change into their officer equivalent civilian employee uniforms, we'll go there and you can set it up.

"I suspect everybody from Ike down at SHAEF is wondering how things went this morning, and I don't want to make that report in the clear—the Russians might be listening—over General White's somewhat limited radio network."

"Everybody goes?" Delgano asked.

"Good question, Colonel," Mattingly said. "As I was saying a moment ago, there is a hotel here in the terminal building. Not very damaged. Adequate. It has a mess, which we have also put into operation. They don't serve Argentine beef, of course, but the mess is adequate, too. What I would like to do is put the crew in it overnight, except for one of your officers, your choice, who I suggest should come with us to keep everybody in the loop."

"Mario," Delgano said. "You go. I'll stay here with the others. I'd like to keep an eye on the airplane."

"Sí, mi coronel," Peralta said.

"Colonel Delgano," Mattingly said, "as you climb down that wobbling ladder, you may notice two half-tracks, each mounting four .50-caliber Browning machine guns. They will help you keep an eye on the *Ciudad de Rosario.*"

[TWO]
357 Roonstrasse, Zehlendorf
Berlin, Germany
1335 20 May 1945

The convoy—an M-8 armored car, three jeeps, two three-quarter-ton trucks, and a trailing M-8—had been wending its way slowly through rubble when it suddenly came into a residential area that appeared just about unscathed.

Here and there, some of the large villas and apartment houses showed signs of damage, but most of the buildings were intact.

"Welcome to Zehlendorf," Mattingly announced.

He was driving the first jeep, with Frade sitting beside him and Boltitz and von Wachtstein in the backseat.

"Why is this . . ." Clete wondered aloud.

". . . not bombed into rubble?" Mattingly picked up. "I suppose for the same reason the I.G. Farben building still stands in Frankfurt. Somebody decided we were going to need it and told the Eighth Air Force to leave it alone."

On a side street, they came to a very nice two-story house—as opposed to the preponderance of large, even huge, villas in the area—and stopped. An American flag was hanging limply from a flagpole over the door, and a jeep with two GIs and a pedestal-mounted .50-caliber Browning in it was sitting at the curb.

On the right side of the house, a gaunt man in his sixties was pushing a lawn mower over the small patch of grass that separated Admiral Canaris's house from its much more impressive neighbor.

"That's surreal," Frade said, pointing at him. "That's absolutely surreal!"

As everybody looked, the old man pushed the lawn mower out of sight around the rear of the house.

Tiny Dunwiddie came out the front door of the house and, sounding more like a master sergeant than an officer-equivalent civilian employee, bellowed the suggestion to his men that getting their asses out of goddamned armored cars and helping unload the three-quarter-ton trucks might be a wise thing to do.

Enrico Rodríguez, who had ridden in the third jeep, smiled approvingly as more than a half dozen Second Armored Division troopers erupted from the M-8s and began to carry cartons and crates from the trucks into the house.

"Come on, Siggie," Boltitz said. "I'll show you where to set up the 7.2 before Mattingly starts screaming like that at you."

Stein looked at him, then said, "That's right. You worked for Canaris, didn't you? You've been here before?"

"Yes, I've been here before. The last time just before I became the naval attaché in Buenos Aires."

When Clete, trailed by Enrico, went into the house, he smelled coffee and followed his nose into the kitchen. There Clete found another elderly German man, this one setting out cups and saucers to go with the coffee.

They nodded at each other.

When Dunwiddie walked into the kitchen a minute or so later, Frade saw him take a quick, if thorough, look at Enrico, and then smile at him.

Jesus, how do these guys recognize each other on sight?

"Master Sergeant Dunwiddie, Sergeant Major Rodríguez, retired," Clete said.

Dunwiddie offered his hand.

"You always carry a riot gun, Sergeant Major?"

"Only when I think I may have to shoot somebody," Enrico replied.

"Welcome to Berlin."

"I have been here before, when my colonel was at the Kriegsschule," Enrico said.

"No shit? Small world, isn't it, Sergeant Major?"

"My name is Enrico."

"Tiny," Dunwiddie said, offering his hand again. "Nice to meet you, Enrico."

"I hate to interrupt the mutual admiration society,"

Clete said, "but who are these guys? This one and the one cutting the grass?"

Dunwiddie looked a little uncomfortable.

"Colonel, they knocked on the door just about as soon as I got here. They said they used to work here and would do anything that needed to be done in exchange for food."

"So you put them to work?"

"I never minded shooting the bastards, but watching them starve to death is something else."

"Just so they don't turn out to be some of those Nazis Morgenthau is looking for," Clete joked.

That possibility was immediately put to rest when Boltitz, also following his nose, walked into the kitchen and saw the man setting out coffee cups.

"Gott in Himmel!" Boltitz said. "Max!"

The man setting out the coffee cups popped to rigid attention, and said, "Herr Kapitän."

"Why do I think they know each other, Dunwiddie?" Frade asked. "*Herr Kapitän*, are you going to tell us what's going on?"

"Max was the admiral's chief bosun's mate when he commanded the cruiser *Schlesien*," Boltitz said.

"And the other one?" Frade asked.

"What other one?"

"The one pushing the lawn mower," Clete said, and pointed out the window.

Boltitz looked, then opened the kitchen door. He barked, "Egon!"

The elderly, poorly dressed old man in the backyard

walked quickly—almost ran—to the kitchen door, popped to attention, and said, "Herr Kapitän!" as if he were having trouble using his voice.

"Stand at ease, the both of you," Boltitz ordered. "This is Egon. He was Admiral Canaris's chief of the boat when the admiral commanded U-201 in the First World War."

"And what are they doing here?" Frade asked.

Boltitz looked at them and asked, "Well?"

"Herr Kapitän," Egon said, "we have been keeping an eye on the house for Frau Admiral Canaris since the SS took the admiral away."

"And the Frau Admiral?" Boltitz asked softly.

"The last word we have is that she is with friends in Westertede," Max answered. "The Nazis took their house in Westertede, too. You have heard what they did to the admiral?"

Boltitz nodded. "How come they didn't take you, too?" he asked.

"Every good chief petty officer knows when to be stupid, Herr Kapitän," Egon said. "We told the SS we had heard nothing, seen nothing, knew nothing. After we had told them that fifty times, they put us in the Volkssturm."

"The what?" Frade asked as Dunwiddie opened his mouth to ask the same question.

"As the Russians approached Berlin, every German male from sixteen years old who was not already in uniform was pressed into the Volkssturm," Max said.

"There were boys as young as twelve," Egon said. "And men even older than Max and me."

"And?" Boltitz asked. "When the Soviets came?"

"We deserted," Egon said. "We took three of the younger boys with us, and hid in the ruins of my apartment building until we heard the Americans had come. Then we came here to look after the house for the Frau Admiral."

"And where are you living now?" Boltitz asked.

"In a ruin off Onkel-Tom Strasse."

"What happened to the boys?" Frade asked.

"One of them managed to get home. His mother was still alive. The two other boys are waiting for us to return. Herr Dunwiddie said he would give us some rations. . . ."

"How did you learn what happened to the admiral?" Boltitz asked.

"Herr Kapitän," Max said. "Egon and I served the admiral for most of our lives. We know how to find things out."

"We—the U.S. Army—have buried Admiral Canaris with the honors appropriate to a senior officer," Mattingly announced from behind Frade.

Frade was a little startled; he hadn't heard him walk up.

"That is good to hear, Herr Oberst," Max said. "The admiral did not deserve what the SS did to him."

"I missed the first part of this," Mattingly said, and looked at the elderly Germans. "How is it that you're in the kitchen making coffee and you're cutting the grass in the garden?"

Dunwiddie answered: "They came to me, Colonel, and said they used to work here." He pointed to each and added, "Max and Egon offered to make themselves useful if we fed them."

Karl put in: "They did more than simply work for Admiral Canaris. They served under him."

As he finished giving the details of that, von Wachtstein and Peralta walked into the kitchen.

"I knew I smelled coffee," Peralta said.

"This is Captain Peralta," Boltitz said. "He is an Argentine pilot."

Egon and Max acknowledged Peralta with a nod.

"And this is the Graf von Wachtstein," Boltitz said.

Max and Egon snapped to attention.

"Herr Graf," they said in unison.

"You have heard what happened to Generalleutnant von Wachtstein, presumably," Mattingly said.

They nodded.

"I heard you say before that both of you know 'how to find things out,'" Mattingly said.

Neither Max nor Egon said anything, but both nodded and looked at him curiously.

"Would you be willing to find some things out for us?" Mattingly went on.

Both looked uncomfortable.

"Would you be willing to help us," Mattingly pursued, "by suggesting to whom Boltitz should talk to find out about the submarines that are supposed to be taking high-ranking Nazis to South America?"

"You remember General Gehlen, of course, Max, Egon?" Boltitz said.

"The last time we saw your father, Herr Graf," Egon said softly, "was in this house. There was a small dinner. Your father, Fregattenkapitän von und zu Wacht ing, and Oberst Gehlen of Abwehr Ost. The gentlemen were joined after dinner by SS-Brigadeführer Ritter von Deitzberg, Himmler's adjutant. With the exception of von Deitzberg, all distinguished German officers. Fregattenkapitän von und zu Wachting was tortured and then hung by the SS and then left to rot beside the admiral. I don't know where Oberst Gehlen met his fate. I can only hope it was quicker. . . ."

"General Gehlen," von Wachtstein said, "I am happy to tell you, is alive and well. We had dinner with him last night. SS-Brigadeführer von Deitzberg was sent to hell by one of General Gehlen's officers, Oberstleutnant Niedermeyer . . ."

"The admiral liked Oberstleutnant Niedermeyer," Max said.

". . . who blew von Deitzberg's brains all over the men's room of the Edelweiss Hotel in Bariloche, Argentina. The police found his body in the urinal."

Boltitz began: "Graf von Wachtstein and I, and General Gehlen, are now working with Colonel Mattingly—"

"Herr Kapitän," Egon interrupted him. "If you and I could somehow get to Bremen and talk to some of our old *U-boot* comrades, I think we could learn from them anything they know."

"Bingo!" Clete said.

"Thank you, Egon," Boltitz said.

Clete added, "Now, can I have some of that coffee before it gets cold?"

"I'd forgotten why I came down here," Mattingly said, "but now remember. Stein needs electrical power to get the Collins up and running. What's the status of the generator, Tiny?"

"Generators, plural, two of them, are on the way. I guess my guys waited to pick up what was going to fall off the Constellation."

"What's going to fall off the Constellation?" Frade and Peralta asked together.

"We're not talking about that," Mattingly said.

Tiny Dunwiddie said, "What I'm wondering is what we do with the boys."

"What?" Mattingly asked.

Dunwiddie related the story, then said, "When I had a chance to tell you about Max and Egon, Colonel, I was going to ask if it would be all right if the boys stayed with them on the third floor until we figure out what to do with them."

"Where are your people going to stay?" Mattingly asked.

"I requisitioned the house next door," Tiny said. "That's why we need two generators, so they can have juice, too."

"Okay," Mattingly said after a moment. "That'll work." He turned to Max. "Do you think you could find us a housekeeper? Maybe two? Cook, wash, clean, make beds, et cetera? Both ugly and over fifty?"

Max nodded. "There are tens of thousands of women in Berlin—some young and quite beautiful—who will jump at the chance to work—or do anything else—for food and to be safe from the Russians."

"Get us a couple of the old and ugly ones," Mattingly

ɔrdered. "See if you can do that when you go pick up the ‹ids. Tiny, send Max in one of the M-8s." He paused. "I ‹lon't know how we'll handle two kids around here. How ɔld did you say they were?"

"One is fifteen, the other fourteen," Max said. "Just ɔefore we deserted, the fourteen-year-old, Heinrich, took ɔut a Russian T-34 with a Panzerfaust—"

"With a what?" Frade asked.

"Handheld rocket," Tiny furnished.

"This fourteen-year-old kid killed a Russian tank?" ʼrade asked incredulously.

Egon nodded. "And then Heinrich cried, Herr Oberst, ɪnd wet his pants, and that's when Max and I decided it vas time to desert and try to keep Heinrich and Gerhard ɪlive."

"Jesus Christ!" Frade said, and then asked, "I don't uppose there's anything to drink around here, is there?"

"Patience is a virtue, Colonel Frade," Mattingly said. ʼTry to remember that all things come to he who waits."

THREE]

ʼhe first M-8 armored car that Frade had ever seen was vhen they had landed at Tempelhof. Curious, and want-ng a better look at one, he and von Wachtstein followed ʼiny Dunwiddie out to the street. Tiny was taking Max ɔut to get him a ride to fetch Heinrich, the fourteen-year-ɔld who had killed a T-34, his fifteen-year-old pal Ger-ɪard, and two old and ugly women.

The M-8 had six wheels, like the standard six-by-six

Army truck, and it looked like someone had set the turret of a tank down on top of the truck.

The Second Armored Division troopers were happy to show off their vehicle to the three men in the officer equivalent civilian employee uniforms.

"How about taking me along when you go get these people?" von Wachtstein said.

"Hell, we'll both go," Frade said.

"There won't be room," von Wachtstein said. "Why don't you wait until we come back?"

Frade was about to argue but then saw a three-quarter-ton truck coming down Roonstrasse. It had two of Tiny's men in it. Lieutenant Colonel Archer W. Dooley Jr., USAAF, sat beside the driver.

Frade looked at von Wachtstein and said, "Remember, Hansel, Mattingly said 'old and ugly.' You're now a married man."

Von Wachtstein gave him the finger. The M-8 started to move.

When the three-quarter pulled to the curb, Frade saw what had fallen off the Constellation. In addition to the generators, the truck carried one of the insulated containers holding fifty kilograms of chilled Argentine steak, another insulated container labeled VEGETABLES AND ORANGES, and two wooden cases on which was painted BODEGA DON GUILLERMO MENDOZA CABERNET SAUVIGNON 1944.

"You could have waited for me, hotshot," Dooley said as he climbed out of the truck. "Until I saw Tiny's guys, I was standing on the tarmac with my thumb up my ass."

"Be careful with the wine, Sergeant," Frade ordered. "It's nectar of the gods."

[FOUR]

Tiny's men quickly got one of the generators up and running. Lightbulbs glowed and then came to full brightness. The refrigerator came to life with a screech and several loud thumps.

"Now that we have juice," Mattingly said as he walked out of the kitchen, "Stein will have the Collins up and running, and I will be able to tell David Bruce that we done good." He paused and added, "Don't drink all the wine before I get back."

Tiny pulled the cork from a bottle of the Cabernet with what looked like the corkscrew accessory on a Boy Scout knife. Clete put his hand out and after a moment Tiny took his meaning. He laid the knife with the Boy Scout insignia on it.

"'Be Prepared'!" Tiny said. "You never heard that, Colonel?"

"You're speaking to Eagle Scout Clete Frade, Troop 36, Midland, Texas," he said with a knowing grin, then flashed the Scout sign with his right hand.

Frade's grin faded quickly when von Wachtstein walked into the kitchen followed by Max, who had his hands on the shoulders of two gaunt, pale-faced boys wearing tattered, ill-fitting remnants of German army uniforms.

Jesus H. Christ!

The little one has to be Heinrich.

The one who killed a T-34 with a Panzerfaust, then pissed his pants.

"Hello," Frade said. "You're Heinrich, right?"

The boy came to attention.

"The war is over, Heinrich," Frade said. "You don't have to do that anymore."

Max walked to a corner of the kitchen and picked up two waxpaper-wrapped cartons labeled C-RATION.

"With your permission, Herr Dunwiddie?"

"You don't have to ask, for Christ's sake," Tiny snapped.

He pulled chairs out from the kitchen table and motioned for the boys to sit in them. When they had done so, he used his Boy Scout knife to open the C-rations.

He took a *Bar, Chocolate, Single, Hershey's,* from each and tore the corners off and handed them to the boys.

"It's all right," Max said in German, "It's chocolate."

Both boys took a small bite, then smiled shyly.

"Is that the best we can do for them, C-rations?" Frade asked. He realized his voice sounded strange.

"In just a minute, Colonel, I'm going to open that"—he pointed to one of the insulated containers that had fallen off the Constellation—"and see if I can find them an orange."

"They're also going to need a bath and some clothes," Frade said. "What can we do about that?"

"Now that we have electricity, Herr Oberst," Egon said, "there will be hot water in half an hour."

"And can we buy them something to wear? Have we got any German money?"

"German money is useless, Colonel," Tiny said. "So, for that matter, is American. But I think Max can get them some clothing by trading a couple of C-rations and packs of Lucky Strikes. I also have Nescafé."

He pulled open a kitchen cabinet door. The cabinet was stuffed with cartons of cigarettes and Nescafé.

"Like I said, Colonel—'Be Prepared.'"

He walked back to the table, where he showed the boys how to open small, olive-drab tin cans labeled STEW, BEEF, W/POTATOES.

Clete saw that tears were running down Heinrich's and Gerhard's cheeks.

Frade took a swallow of the Don Guillermo Cabernet Sauvignon 1944. It didn't taste as good as he expected it to.

Then he looked at Lieutenant Colonel Archer W. Dooley Jr. and saw that tears were running down his cheeks, too. *Suboficial Mayor* Enrico Rodríguez, retired, wasn't crying, but he looked as if he was about to.

"You going to drink all that wine by yourself, hotshot, or do I get some?" Dooley asked.

Mattingly came into the kitchen.

"Pay attention," he said. "There is a message from the Supreme Commander. Quote. Pass to all OSS and Air Forces personnel involved. Well done. Eisenhower. General of the Army. Close quote."

"You're welcome, Ike," Frade said. "We're always happy to do what we can."

"The significant part of the Supreme Commander's message, Colonel Frade, is that Ike is grateful to the OSS. That just may buy us some time."

"Point taken," Frade said.

"And then, when David Bruce had finished delivering Ike's thank-you, he dropped the other shoe. 'Get the Argentine diplomats and their airplane out of Berlin as soon as possible.' He was more than a little disappointed that we couldn't leave this afternoon. But first thing in the morning . . ."

[FIVE]
357 Roonstrasse, Zehlendorf
Berlin, Germany
0715 21 May 1945

Breakfast was prepared by the two women Max had brought to the house late the previous afternoon, when he returned from his bartering expedition to get the boy clothing.

The women were neither old nor ugly.

Clete saw that their eyes, however, were empty. They were sexless.

Neuter, Clete thought. ***Zombies in skirts.***

It was hard to guess even how old they were. Somewhere, Clete gauged, between his own age and fifty.

Both wore wedding rings, but Clete suspected their husbands were no longer part of their lives.

Frade, when able to do so quietly, gave in to the temptation to ask Egon if he thought they had been raped.

"They told me, with great hesitation," Egon reported, "that the Asiatics had Giesela for most of a week. And Inge for four days. That meant Giesela had been repeatedly raped for most of a week, but Inge for 'only' four days."

"Jesus H. Christ!"

"It happened all over, Herr Oberst," Egon said. "Women. Young girls. Grandmothers. Boys. It would have happened to Gerhard and Heinrich, too. Except that when the Asiatics finished with boys from the Volkssturm, they killed them. That's why Max and I took Heinrich and Gerhard with us."

Von Wachtstein came into the kitchen. His officer equivalent civilian employee uniform had been replaced by clothing that looked only a little cleaner and less tattered than what the boys had been wearing.

Frade knew immediately what that meant, but had a hard time accepting the reality of it.

Shit!

"Have a nice flight, Clete," von Wachtstein said. "I'll see you when you come back with the money."

"Didn't you hear what Gehlen said, you goddamn fool? The Russians are going to crucify you upside down, because you'll be easier to skin that way."

"That presumes the Russians catch me. I'm going to try very hard to see that doesn't happen."

"Well, you're not going, so get rid of those clothes and put on your uniform. We're about to leave for Tempelhof."

As if to make the point that it was time to go to the

airport, Peralta came into the kitchen, followed by Stein, Mattingly, and Boltitz.

Mattingly's, Boltitz's, and Stein's faces showed that they also knew the meaning of the clothing and didn't like it either.

Peralta's face showed complete disbelief.

"Hansel," Frade went on, "you're going back with us if I have to have Tiny and his guys tie you up and throw you on the airplane."

"You could of course do that, Clete. But all that would do is delay my departure for Pomerania and increase the chances I'll be caught by the Russians."

"You're out of your fucking mind!" Clete said.

"It is my duty to our people."

"What about your duty to your wife and child? Don't try to feed me that noblesse oblige bullshit. I don't buy it, Herr Graf! It's a crock of shit!"

"I'm sorry you don't understand, Cletus. It is a matter of honor."

"Where's the honor in getting skinned like a fucking Christmas turkey?"

That's stuffed like a turkey, jackass!

"You know how much of the von Wachtstein assets are in Argentina, Cletus. How could I live with myself in Argentina if I didn't use them to help what are now my people?"

"How are you going to help them, Herr Graf, your royal fucking majesty, if you're nailed skinless and upside down to the fucking castle door?"

"What I am going to do, Cletus, is let my people know—"

"You sound like Moses, for Christ's sake. You should hear yourself! 'Let my people go!' Jesus!"

"Moses said, 'Let my people go.' What I said was that I intend to let my people *know* that the Graf von Wachtstein has not deserted them and will do everything in his power . . ."

"There's that regal fucking third person! Mattingly, do you believe this?"

". . . everything in his power to get them out from under the Communists and to a new life in Argentina."

"Send them a fucking telegram!"

"They have to see me. Once they have seen me, and I have spoken with them, I will come here."

"Just for the sake of argument, let's say that doesn't work. What am I supposed to tell your wife?"

"If something should happen to me, my dear friend, I would want you to tell the Countess von Wachtstein that I loved her as I have never loved any other woman, and that I regret that she must now assume the responsibilities that come with the title. And remind her that if I am no longer alive, our son is the Graf von Wachtstein."

Clete looked at him but, feeling his throat constrict and knowing his voice simply wasn't going to work, said nothing more.

"I have treasured your friendship, Cletus," von Wachtstein said. "Will you not shake my hand and wish me luck?"

Peter put out his hand.

After a long moment, Clete took it.

Their eyes met. The handshake turned into an embrace.

When Colonel Robert Mattingly and Lieutenant Colonel Archer W. Dooley Jr. heard Frade, his voice breaking, say, "You better come back, you crazy Kraut sonofabitch, or I'll come to that goddamn castle of yours and kick your ass all the way back to Argentina," they averted their faces and dabbed at their eyes with their handkerchiefs.

[SIX]
Tempelhof Air Base
Berlin, Germany
1005 21 May 1945

"Tempelhof Departure Control. South American Airways Double Zero Four on the threshold of Twenty-seven."

"Tempelhof Departure Control clears South American Airways Zero Zero Four as Number One for takeoff on Runway Two Seven. South American Double Zero Four is cleared Direct Rhein-Main Air Base. On takeoff, when on course two-three-two-point-two degrees, climb to twenty thousand feet. When possible, change to Helmstedt Area Control on Ground-Air Channel Two. Be aware, P-38 aircraft are, and Soviet aircraft may be, active on your route. Acknowledge."

Clete repeated the clearance.

"Takeoff power, please," Chief Pilot Delgano ordered.

"Tempelhof," Clete reported a moment later. "South American Double Zero Four Rolling."

"Helmstedt Area Control, South American Double Zero Four," Frade radioed.

"Double Zero Four, Helmstedt reads you five by five. How me?"

"Helmstedt, also five by five. South American Double Zero Four at twenty thousand indicating three-fifty on a course of two-three-two-point-two. Leaving Soviet zone and entering American zone at this time."

"Helmstedt understands Zero Zero Four has entered American zone."

"Affirmative. Helmstedt, South American. En route change of destination. Please close out my Rhein-Main flight plan, and note that we are changing course to two-three-seven-point-three at this time. Direct ultimate destination Lisbon, Portugal."

"Double Zero Four, I'm not sure you can do that."

"Don't be silly," Frade said. "Of course we can."

Dooley's voice then came across Frade's headset: "Hey, hotshot. Try not to run into the Pyrenees."

"Little Brother," Frade replied, "I wondered where you were."

"I've been covering your ass from above and behind."

Sixty seconds later, Colonel Dooley demonstrated this by suddenly appearing—coming out of a high-speed dive—in front of the *Ciudad de Rosario*. Then he twice rolled the Lockheed Lightning and made a steep descending turn out of their path.

"So long, hotshot!" Dooley said. "Write if you find work."

When Dooley was out of sight, Frade said, "Gonzo, when Dooley gets out of the Air Forces after the war, I was thinking he'd make a fine SAA pilot."

"Is that an order or an observation?"

"Right now, just an observation."

"In that case, I quite agree," Delgano said, then his tone softened as he added: "Clete, Mario told me about Peter von Wachtstein."

"And?"

"I knew when we had dinner with General Gehlen that Peter was going to Pomerania, and that there was nothing you or anyone else could do to stop him."

"You're pretty perceptive. Maybe you should consider giving up driving airplanes and becoming, oh, I don't know, maybe an intelligence officer."

X

[ONE]

4730 Avenida Libertador General San Martín
Buenos Aires, Argentina
1900 25 May 1945

It is times like this, Cletus H. Frade thought as he surveyed the scene taking place in the library, *that I very much miss my father.*

And that I curse those goddamn Nazi bastards for taking him away from me . . . from us . . . from this.

Clete felt his throat constrict.

Damn it! He would've been so proud.

Doña Dorotea Mallín de Frade stood beside him as they watched her mother, la Señora Pamela Holworth-Talley de Mallín, formerly of Huddersfield, Yorkshire, and Clete's "mother," Mrs. Martha Howell of Midland, Texas. The two grandmothers were playing with Dorotea and Clete's sons—Jorge Howell Frade, eighteen months old, and five-month-old Cletus Howell Frade Jr.

Also watching them were Miss Beth Howell and Miss Marjorie Howell, and Clete suspected his "sisters" were daydreaming of adding offspring to the family.

Clete looked over at the svelte woman in her fifties with gray-flecked hair who was standing near the girls. She was Doña Claudia Carzino-Cormano, who was one of Argentina's wealthiest women and who had lived for decades with el Coronel Jorge Frade until he'd been assassinated. She held a small child on her hip. He was known as Karlchen, which meant "Little Karl" in German—and not as Carlito, which meant the same thing in Spanish. His mother—Countess Alicia von Wachtstein, the former Señorita Alicia Carzino-Cormano—had insisted on that.

As General Gehlen had so graphically described, Karlchen's grandfather and namesake, Generalleutnant Graf Karl-Friedrich von Wachtstein, had died in August of 1944 after hanging for twenty-three minutes from a meat hook by piano wire wrapped around his neck.

Allen W. Dulles had agreed to get Clete a copy of the motion pictures SS photographers had made of the executions of those involved in the failed 1944 bomb plot so that Adolf Hitler could watch them over and over.

Clete had intended to give von Wachtstein the films.

But not now. Not ever.

His mind went off at a tangent: *I suppose now that his father is dead, Hansel is the Graf von Wachtstein, Gretel is the Gräfin, and Karlchen is the baron.*

I wonder why I never thought of that before?

Then Karl-Friedrich Baron von Wachtstein made a face and threw up on the neck and bosom of his grandmother.

"Oh, Karlchen!" his mother said, and rushed to take the child.

Holding the infant at arm's length—Karlchen now was screaming—she ordered that towels and water be brought to clean up the mess.

After everyone was cleansed of Karlchen's present, Alicia announced, "Mother, shouldn't we be getting back so we can prepare for your cocktail?" She scanned the crowd and said, "Everybody is coming, right? Everyone except, of course, my missing husband."

"And me," Cletus said.

"Cletus, are you sure you don't want to come? You'll be missed."

"Not if my Tío Juan and Señor Rodolfo Nulder are there," Clete said. "I'll pass, thank you."

"What am I supposed to say when people ask about Peter? And they will."

"When all else fails, Alicia, tell the truth. Peter stayed in Germany to take care of some family business."

Alicia nodded. Then she went to Dorotea, who had Karlchen on her lap, took him, kissed Dorotea and Clete, and walked out of the library.

Dorotea walked to the window and looked out to see that Alicia actually got into her mother's Rolls-Royce.

Then she walked to where her husband was sitting in a brown leather armchair and holding a glass dark with Chivas Regal. She sat in the matching armchair.

"It is now truth time, my darling."

"You sure you want to hear this?"

"I'm sure I want to hear everything."

Clete took a healthy swallow of the Chivas Regal.

"We had dinner, with General Gehlen, in a castle belonging to the Prince of Hesse. General Gehlen told Peter—in great detail—how his father had died. Peter said he wanted to go to Schloss Wachtstein in Pomerania. General Gehlen told him that if the Russians caught him, they would nail him to the wall and skin him alive.

"We then went to Berlin, where we met, among other people, two women who had been repeatedly raped for days by the Russians—actually, some kind of Asiatics in the Red Army; they use them as assault troops—and a fourteen-year-old boy named Heinrich who had killed a Russian tank with a rocket grenade and then wet his pants.

"All of this convinced Peter that the Russians would indeed skin him alive if he went to Pomerania and they caught him."

Dorotea inhaled.

"And he went anyway," she said.

"Don Cletus did everything he could to stop him, Doña Dorotea," Enrico said.

"Oh, my God!"

"Yeah, oh, my God," Clete said.

"Why?"

"Noblesse oblige, sweetheart. Hansel, Graf von Wachtstein, is doing his duty. The stupid sonofabitch."

"You don't think he'll be coming back?"

"I've always had a lousy memory, baby, but for the rest of my life I will remember every goddamned word Peter said just before we left Berlin."

Dorotea made a *go ahead* signal with both of her hands.

"'If something should happen to me, my dear friend, I would want you to tell the Countess von Wachtstein that I loved her as I have never loved any other woman, and that I regret that she must now assume the responsibilities that come with the title. And remind her that if I am no longer alive, our son is the Graf von Wachtstein.'"

When she saw her husband's chest heave, and the tears form, Doña Dorotea got out of her chair, knelt beside his, and pulled his head to her breast.

A long moment later, she asked, "When are you going to tell her, darling?"

"Not until I see a picture of the sonofabitch nailed to the wall of his goddamn castle," Clete said, his voice unsteady. He cleared his throat. "Miracles happen. You ever hear that God takes care of fools and drunks? The sonofabitch Hansel qualifies on both counts."

"You're not going back to Berlin?" Dorotea asked incredulously.

Clete met her eyes and nodded. "The next SAA flight to Lisbon is on the twenty-eighth. Enrico and I will be on it."

"Oh, God!"

"We're taking with us that half million dollars. That's needed to set Gehlen and his people up."

"I wondered what that money was for."

"And a suitcase full of clothes for a couple of teenage boys, which Enrico is right now going to go out and buy."

"*Sí*, Don Cletus."

[TWO]
Tempelhof Air Base
Berlin, Germany
1635 1 June 1945

Immediately after Cletus Frade and Enrico Rodríguez had gotten off the Douglas C-47 that had flown them from Rhein-Main, they'd been ushered into the presence of a U.S. Army Military Police officer of the Second Armored Division. Frade announced: "Major, we're going to need a ride to Roonstrasse in Zehlendorf."

"With respect, Colonel, what you're going to get is a ride back to Rhein-Main. Nobody gets into Berlin unless they're on orders and cleared by SHAEF. You don't have any orders, and there's no Marine officer or civilian employee on my list. I can't believe that Gooney Bird pilot let you two on his aircraft."

"Maybe because I showed him this," Frade said, and handed him the spurious credentials identifying OSS Area Commander Cletus H. Frade.

"Some of Colonel Mattingly's people, huh? I should have guessed. What else could a Marine lieutenant colonel and a civilian with a riot gun and carrying a briefcase be but the OSS?"

"We were hoping you'd think we were the Salvation Army," Frade said.

The MP officer chuckled and picked up his telephone.

"Send a jeep over here," he ordered, then hung up. "I don't suppose you're going to tell me what's in those bags that's so important that you need to guard it with a riot gun?"

"Would you believe me, Major, if I told you that one contains clothing for the orphanage Colonel Mattingly is running and that there's half a million dollars in the other one?"

"I've learned to believe just about anything I've heard about Colonel Mattingly and the OSS. But that one's stretching it a little too far."

Frade found the commanding officer of OSS Europe Forward in the garden behind the house. He was sitting at a table and drinking a glass of wine that Frade suspected had fallen off *Ciudad de Rosario* the last time he was in Berlin.

"May I say that you look dashing in your Marine Corps suit, Colonel Frade?" Mattingly announced by way of greeting. "You could be on a recruiting poster."

"If you're not nice, you don't get the half million," Frade said.

"I think I would kill for that half million," Mattingly said. "And now that I've said that and thought it over, you may take that literally. We need it bad, and I was getting worried that they'd found you before you could get it back over here."

"Who they?"

"Sit down and have a glass of this excellent grape the Argentine diplomats graciously shared with us, and I will bring you up to date on what's happened. Good news and bad news. Mostly bad."

"Don Cletus?" Enrico asked, holding up a duffel and nodding toward it.

"Go ahead," Frade said.

"What's he got in the bag?"

"Clothing for Heinrich and the other one."

"Gerhard's the other one. On that subject, Siggie Stein says that if we can get them to Argentina, he knows a nun that'll take care of them until better arrangements can be made. Good idea?"

"Damn good idea, Bob. I even know the nun. But how are we going to get them to Argentina?"

"Through the compassion of the Vatican, Clete. They owe me a couple of big favors, so for once the pitiful orphaned German children getting off the airplane to find succor in Argentina will actually be pitiful orphaned children. And I really want to get them out of here. I don't think the trouble we're getting from the Russians is going to stop. It's probably going to get much worse."

"Is that the bad news?"

"That's the good news, Clete. The bad news is that David Bruce told me he had a private chat with the Supreme Commander. Ike told him that when he talked with General Marshall about keeping the OSS alive, Marshall told him that President Truman has decided to shut us down. Further, Ike told Bruce that he told Marshall that he wanted to bring up keeping us alive to Truman himself, whereupon Marshall told him to butt out, or words to that effect."

"Does Ike know about Gehlen?"

"He does now. David said he felt he had to tell him."

"And?"

"Reduced to basics: He's not going to tell Marshall. If we get caught, Ike will have to own up, which would blow the entire Gehlen project out of the water."

"So?"

"We need a sacrificial lamb."

"Whose name is Frade?"

Mattingly nodded.

"This was less a callous decision on the part of Dulles, Graham, and myself than the fact that the secretary of the Treasury is already on your case. Remember what I told you about he who laughs last?"

"I didn't hear me volunteering to be a sacrificial lamb."

"And you don't have to be, Clete. You are perfectly free to tell Morgenthau's people whatever they want to know."

"And that's who's looking for me?"

Mattingly nodded.

"You can fess up and say that all you were doing was obeying orders."

When Frade didn't reply, Mattingly said: "'All I was doing is obeying my orders' is really the last refuge of the scoundrel. I never thought of that until I started reading the first interrogation reports of some really despicable Nazis. They admitted gassing people—how could they deny it?—but said all they were doing was obeying orders. If it works for them, it would follow that it would work for you."

"And what are my other options?"

"You really don't have any. They're going to find you sooner or later. As a practical matter—because of your dual citizenship, your Navy Cross, and Cletus Marcus Howell—there's a good chance it will never get as far as a court-martial."

"Oh, now that is good news!" Frade blurted sarcastically.

"What Morgenthau is after is two things. He wants the Nazis in Germany and he wants to make an example of somebody so that no one else will be tempted to be nice to the Nazis."

"Oh? Why shouldn't I like Nazis? I mean, all they did was murder my father and try to murder me on several occasions. Not to forget they strangled my best friend's father to death."

Mattingly shrugged. "You were involved in getting Nazis to Argentina, and that's all Morgenthau will care about. And so far as he's concerned, every German you helped get to Argentina is as bad as Himmler."

"Well, I'm not going to give up people like Niedermeyer," Frade said. "Or Boltitz. Or von Wachtstein. Speaking of whom . . . ?"

"Not a word, Clete. I'm sorry."

"Can we find out?"

"Gehlen's working on that for you."

"Boltitz?"

"He went to Bremen, with Max, to work on the U-boat intel. Stein went with them. I think that will prove to be valuable."

"So, what do you want me to do?"

"About the best thing you can do is stall for a while, give me some time to hide Gehlen and his people."

"Okay. I'll stall in Argentina. They'll never find me in Argentina."

"What I have to say to you now is delicate, Clete."

"So be delicate."

"Dulles believes, and Graham concurs, and I do, too, that you should let the Secret Service—Morgenthau—find you."

"What's the reasoning behind that idiot notion?"

"If they can't find you, they'll go after other members of Team Turtle. And they may reveal things we don't want them to know."

"No fucking way. They're good people. They'll keep their mouths shut."

"Think that through, Clete. No one's questioning their courage. But are they up to dealing with all the pressure Morgenthau and the Secret Service can throw at them? Threats of going to Leavenworth, et cetera?"

Frade didn't immediately reply.

Mattingly went on: "One scenario is that if they have you, they won't spend much effort in looking for people you're hiding in Argentina. When they break you, you'll tell them where they can be found."

"In a pig's ass I will."

"If you can stall them, Clete, it will give us time to work out the Gehlen problem. Bruce has begun vague talks with the Brits, with MI6."

"So, what do I do? Go to Washington, knock on Morgenthau's door, and say, 'I understand you're looking for me'?"

"The military attaché in Buenos Aires, whom I believe you know, has told the Secret Service that he also believes you have been involved with helping Nazis get to Argentina. He also told them that you have received large amounts of money—more than six million dollars—from Colonel Graham, which you have refused to discuss with him, and that he suspects this is somehow connected with finding refuge for Nazis in Argentina. These charges are to be investigated by Naval Intelligence."

"Jesus H. Christ!"

"The military attaché, his name is Flowers—"

"Richmond C. Flowers. I know the miserable bastard's name."

"—as the OSS station chief in Buenos Aires will be ordered by Director Donovan to present you with orders issued by the Navy Department to board the next U.S. Navy vessel calling at Buenos Aires—it will be a destroyer, the USS *Bartram Greene*, due to arrive in Buenos Aires June ninth—for transport to the Naval Air Station at Pensacola, Florida, where the charges laid against you will be investigated to determine if a court-martial is appropriate."

"How the hell do you know all that?"

"While you will indeed be hanging in the wind, Colonel Frade, you will not be entirely alone."

"That's pretty fucking cryptic. It sounds like you don't entirely trust me."

"This is one of those situations where the less you

know about friends of the OSS, the safer it will be for them."

"What about Donovan? What does he know about Gehlen?"

"Dulles and/or Graham is going to have to tell him, if one of them hasn't already."

"The destroyer ride is to kill time, right?"

"Every hour I have to hide Gehlen and his people, the better," Mattingly said. "By the way, the general has been arrested by the CIC and is currently undergoing interrogation. Just as soon as I can tear myself away from the duties here, I will go to Oberusel and interrogate Gehlen myself. Slowly and thoroughly."

"And the reason you're in Berlin, not in that castle, is because you need permission—and a reason—to come to Berlin, and the Secret Service doesn't want to come out and say they want to come to Berlin to interrogate you—the head of the OSS—about the OSS helping Nazis to get to Argentina?"

"Oh, you can be clever, can't you, Colonel Frade?"

XI

[ONE]
Executive Officers' Quarters
USS *Bartram Greene* DD-201
River Plate Estuary, Argentina
1900 12 June 1945

There came a knock at the stateroom door. Lieutenant Colonel Cletus H. Frade, USMC, who was lying on the bunk, called, "Come!"

A very tall, very thin, ascetic-looking lieutenant commander opened the door and entered the stateroom.

Frade put down his copy of that day's *Buenos Aires Herald* and looked at him.

The visitor said evenly, "Correct me if I'm wrong, Colonel, but I believe naval courtesy requires that all naval personnel come to attention when the captain of a man-o'-war enters a living space, even when said captain is junior."

Frade chuckled and pushed himself off the bunk.

"Until just now, Commander, I didn't know you were the captain."

"I have that honor, sir. My name is R. G. Prentiss, and I am the captain."

Frade nodded.

Captain Prentiss said: "Colonel, we have a somewhat awkward situation here. I have been ordered by COMMATL—"

"By who?"

"Commander Atlantic," Captain Prentiss furnished, "has ordered the *Greene* to transport you to NAS Pensacola. Colonel Flowers has informed me that you are the subject of an investigation by Naval Intelligence. Is that your understanding of the situation?"

"That pretty much sums it up."

"Under these circumstances, Colonel, while you will be afforded the courtesies to which your rank entitles you, there are several conditions I feel necessary to impose."

"Shoot," Frade said. "Figuratively speaking, of course, Captain."

"You will mess with the officers in the wardroom. Pushing that button"—he pointed—"will summon my steward, who will take care of your laundry, et cetera, and bring you, if you wish, coffee and doughnuts from the galley. You will not engage in conversation with the ship's company—the sailors—at any time, and will converse with my officers only when I or my executive officer is present."

"That's that sort of roly-poly lieutenant who brought me down here when I came aboard?"

"His name is Lieutenant John Crosby, Colonel. You

are not permitted to leave 'officers' country'—do you know what that means, Colonel?"

"I'd hazard a wild guess that's where your officers hang out."

Prentiss nodded. "And you are not permitted to be on the bridge. You may, should you desire, go to the flying bridges on either side of the bridge itself."

Frade waited for him to go on.

"I think I've covered everything. Any questions, Colonel Frade?"

"I guess I missed supper, huh, Captain?"

Captain Prentiss turned and left the cabin without speaking.

[TWO]
Executive Officers' Quarters
USS *Bartram Greene* DD-201
South Atlantic Ocean off Brazil
0805 15 June 1945

Captain Prentiss knocked at the door, was given permission to enter, and did so.

Frade, who had been sitting at the fold-down desk, stood.

"I had hoped to see you at breakfast, Colonel."

"It's a little chilly in there for me, Captain."

"I had planned to read this aloud to the wardroom," Prentiss said, and handed Frade a sheet of paper. "That was transmitted in the clear, Colonel."

```
FOR SLATS FROM LITTLE DICK
POPPA SAYS YOUR SUPERCARGO REALLY GOOD
GUY
TREAT HIM ACCORDINGLY
```

Frade handed the paper back without comment.

"My roommate at Annapolis," Captain Prentiss explained, "Colonel J. C. Wallace, was called 'Little Dick.' He called me 'Slats.'"

"I understand why people could call you Slats, Captain. But it would not behoove me as a field-grade Marine officer to ask why you called your roommate Little Dick."

Prentiss grinned. Then he said: "Actually, one of the reasons was because his father, Vice Admiral Wallace, is called Big Dick."

"Oh."

"Colonel, you now have freedom of the ship, including the bridge. And I would be pleased if you would join me now for breakfast. I assure you, it will be much warmer in the wardroom than it has been."

"Thank you."

"All of my officers, and me, have been wondering exactly what it was that caused you to give Colonel Flowers the finger as we let loose all lines."

[THREE]
Navy Pier
Pensacola, Florida
0915 25 June 1945

Captain Prentiss and Lieutenant Colonel Frade were standing on the flying bridge of the USS *Bartram Green*, DD-201 as she was being tied up to the pier. Frade was in a Marine summer uniform he'd never worn before.

"I would hazard the guess, Clete, that that's your welcoming party," Prentiss said, nodding toward an officer standing beside a Navy gray Plymouth sedan on the pier.

"I'm crushed, Slats. I was expecting a brass band and a cheering crowd."

"I've been meaning to ask," Prentiss said, tapping the Navy Cross on Frade's chest, "where you got that."

Frade glanced down at it, then replied: "In a hockshop on Bourbon Street in New Orleans. I bought a pair of those"—he tapped the binoculars hanging from Prentiss's neck—"and the hockshop guy threw that in for free. I thought it looked nice, so I pinned it on."

"Is that also where you got the Wings of Gold? In a New Orleans pawnshop?"

"No. A very long time ago, in another life, I got those here."

"I'll walk you to the gangway," Prentiss said.

"Thanks for the ride, Slats."

"In other circumstances, Clete, I would have been delighted to have you aboard."

Prentiss and Frade reached the gangway just as it was lowered into place. The Navy officer—they were close enough for Frade to be able to see that he was a spectacles-wearing, mousy-looking lieutenant commander, with the insignia of the Judge Advocate Corps where the star of a line officer would be, above the stripes on his sleeve—now stood waiting to come aboard.

Frade said: "I don't see any reason I can't get off, do you?"

Prentiss shook his head.

"Permission to leave the ship, sir?" Frade said.

"Granted."

Frade saluted Prentiss, then the colors flying aft.

Prentiss offered his hand.

"Good luck, Clete."

"Thank you, Captain."

The JAG officer saluted as Frade stepped off the gangway.

Frade returned it.

"You are Lieutenant Colonel C. H. Frade, sir?"

"Guilty—for lack of a better word."

The JAG officer ignored that. He said, "I'm Lieutenant Commander McGrory, Colonel. I have been appointed your counsel."

He offered his hand. Frade was not surprised that McGrory's grip was limp.

"We have a car, sir," McGrory said.

A sailor opened the rear door of the Plymouth and Frade got in. As the car started down the pier, Frade saw that Prentiss was standing on the deck of the *Greene* watching them drive away.

When they were on Navy Boulevard, which would take them to Main Side, Naval Air Station, Pensacola, Frade said, "Exactly what are you going to counsel me about, Commander?"

"Certain allegations have been laid against you, Colonel . . ."

"What kind of allegations?"

". . . and naval regulations provide that you are entitled to counsel while you are being interviewed with regard to these allegations."

"In other words, you're not going to tell me?"

"The specifics of the allegations will be made known to you in formal proceedings, Colonel."

"And when are these formal proceedings going to take place?"

They were now at the gate to Main Side, Naval Air Station, Pensacola.

A perfectly turned-out Marine corporal took a look at the Plymouth, popped to attention, saluted, and bellowed, "Good morning, Colonel! Pass."

Clete returned the salute, remembering the first time he'd come through this gate.

Life had been much simpler then.

All Second Lieutenant Frade, USMCR, had to do was learn how to fly the Marine Corps' airplanes—and that wouldn't be hard, as he had been flying since he was age twelve—then go to the Pacific and sweep the dirty Japs from the sky, whereupon all would be well with the world and he could go back to Big Foot Ranch, Midland, Texas, and get on with his life.

The Plymouth entered Main Side.

"What about the formal proceedings, Commander?" Frade asked.

"Inasmuch as no charges have been laid against you, Colonel, your status is that of a Marine officer returning from service abroad. Regulations prescribe certain things must take place for all returning officers. We will deal with that first."

Two hours later, the medical staff of Naval Hospital, Pensacola, after a thorough examination of his body, determined that Lieutenant Colonel Frade not only was free of any infectious diseases—including sexual—that he might have encountered in his foreign service, but also that his general condition was such that he could engage in flight.

An hour after that, the Disbursing Office, NAS Pensacola, determined that inasmuch as he had not flown for more than three years the minimum four hours per month that was necessary to qualify for flight play, and inasmuch as on several occasions he had been paid flight pay in error, that flight pay would have to be taken from the amount of pay he was now due.

As would $102.85, the cost to the government of one *Watch, Wrist, Hamilton, Naval Aviator's Chronometer,* which had been issued to First Lieutenant C. H. Frade, USMCR, VMF-221, on Guadalcanal and never been returned.

He left the Disbursing Office $1,255.75 richer, most of it in new twenty-dollar bills. It made quite a bulge in his tunic pocket.

The Housing Office, NAS Pensacola, took three of the twenties as a deposit against damage to Room Twenty-three, Senior Officers Quarters, and another twenty as a deposit for a telephone that they hoped to connect within seventy-two hours.

The Housing Office also required him to sign a statement acknowledging he understood that the presence of female guests in his quarters at any time was proscribed, and that violation of the proscription could result in court-martial or such other disciplinary action as the base commander might elect to impose.

Thirty minutes after that, Lieutenant Commander McGrory, sitting at his desk in a spotless office, said, "We have a little problem, Colonel."

"I'm breathless with anticipation, Commander."

"Your home of record is Big Foot Ranch, RFD Number 2, Box 131, Midland, Texas. Is that correct?"

Well, some people think I live on Estancia San Pedro y San Pablo outside Buenos Aires, but what the hell!

"That's correct."

"Unfortunately, that's outside the twenty-four-hour zone."

"What the hell is the twenty-four-hour zone?"

"Officers in your status cannot be placed on leave to any address from which he cannot return, when so ordered, to NAS Pensacola within twenty-four hours. Hence 'twenty-four-hour zone.'"

"Am I going on leave?"

"Officers returning from overseas service are automatically granted a thirty-day leave. Providing, of course, that their leave address is within the twenty-four-hour zone. Perhaps you might consider going to one of the fine hotels or motels on Pensacola Beach and having Mrs. Howell join you there. The beaches here are absolutely beautiful."

"Mrs. Howell?"

"Mrs. Martha Howell, your adoptive mother, of the Midland address, is listed as your next of kin. Isn't that correct?"

I have a wife and two children, but I don't think this is the time to get into that.

"That's correct. Tell me, Commander, how far is it, timewise, from here to New Orleans?"

"You have a family member in New Orleans, Colonel?"

"My grandfather."

And who is the last person in the world I need to see right now.

If the Old Man hears what's going on with me—and I would have to tell him—ten minutes after that two senators and his pal Colonel McCormack of the Chicago Tribune *will be coming to my rescue.*

"I'll need his name and address, Colonel. And his telephone number."

What the hell, I'll call the house and see if the Old Man is there.

If he is, I'll hang up. If he's not . . .

"The address is 3470 Saint Charles Avenue, New Orleans. My grandfather's name is Cletus Marcus Howell. I don't know the phone, but I'm sure it's in the book."

"And your grandfather is sure to be there?"

"Absolutely. At his age, getting around is very difficult."

Please God, let the Old Man be in Washington, Venezuela, Dallas, San Francisco—anywhere but on Saint Charles Avenue.

"You understand, Colonel, that I am taking your word as a Marine officer and gentleman about your grandfather and that address?"

"I understand, Commander."

"Well, then, I happen to know there is a three-forty train to New Orleans. You'll just have time to make it."

[FOUR]
3470 Saint Charles Avenue
New Orleans, Louisiana
1955 25 June 1945

"The Howell Residence," Jean-Jacques Jouvier said when he picked up the telephone. He was an elderly, erect, very light-skinned black man with silver hair. He wore a gray linen jacket. He had been Cletus Marcus Howell's butler for forty-two years.

"No, Mister Cletus, he's in Venezuela."

He took the telephone from his ear and held it in his hand and looked at it.

Then he looked at the pale-skinned blond woman standing at the door to the library.

"That was Mister Cletus, Miss Dorotea," he said.

"Where is he? What happened? Why did you hang up?"

"I didn't hang up, Miss Dorotea. Mister Cletus did. When I told him that Mister Howell was in Venezuela, he said, 'Get out the Peychaux's Bitters, the rye, and crack some ice. I'll be right there.' And then he hung up."

"I have no idea what you're talking about, Jean-Jacques," Dorotea said.

"Mister Cletus—and Mister Howell—really like a Sazerac or two before dinner, Miss Dorotea. It's a cocktail. Rye whisky . . ."

"And something bitter and cracked ice," Dorotea said. "While you crack the ice, Jean-Jacques, I'll change into something suitable to welcome our boy home."

[FIVE]
Arnaud's Restaurant
813 Bienville Street, New Orleans, Louisiana
2145 25 June 1945

"I can't believe you ate two dozen of those things," Doña Dorotea said to Don Cletus.

"They call them oysters, my love, and I ate two dozen of them because the oysters in Argentina are lousy. And as to the two dozen? You know what they say about oysters. . . ."

Dorotea confessed she didn't know what was said about oysters, so he leaned over and whispered in her ear what magical qualities were said about oysters.

"I really hope that's true," Dorotea said. "Will they give you back your money if they don't work?"

"Somehow I suspect all of these will work just fine."

"And afterward?"

"I think I'll sleep."

"You know what I mean, Cletus."

"I honest to God don't know, sweetheart. You know what Mattingly told me. You told me that Team Turtle is out of reach of the Secret Service. Mattingly said there will be friends to help. I was treated like an admiral on the *Greene*—I told you—after there was a radio message from some friend of somebody.

"I don't know what to think about that Navy lawyer in Pensacola, McGrory. He could be a friend who put me on leave to hide me, or he could just be a pencil-pusher who put me on leave because the book said that's what to do. The only thing I know for sure is that I have to stay out of the clutches of the Secret Service for as long as I can to give Mattingly the time to get General Gehlen and his people set up."

"Eventually, darling, they are going to have you in their clutches. Then what?"

"I will lie to them as convincingly as I can for as long as I can."

"You realize you sound like Peter? You're going to do your duty, no matter what?"

"There's a slight difference between Peter and me

While I don't think Secretary Morgenthau likes me very much, dear, I really can't see him skinning me alive."

"What are your chances of going to prison?"

"I really don't think it will go that far."

"You'll forgive me if I don't think that's very encouraging."

"It's the best I can do, sweetheart."

The waiter appeared.

"May I bring you another Sazerac, madam? Sir?"

"Not for me, thank you," Dorotea said. "I've already had too many of them."

"I'll have another, thank you," Cletus said and, looking at Dorotea, added, "Actually, those are my plans for the indefinite future. Drink lots of Sazeracs and eat lots of oysters."

The waiter smiled. "Sounds like a good plan, sir."

"It's the only one I have," Clete said, looking at Dorotea.

"That being the case," Dorotea said, and turned to the waiter. "Bring me another, too, please. No oysters. But a broiled white fish of some kind."

"May I suggest the trout Pontchartrain?"

"Just so long as it's broiled and white," Dorotea said.

[SIX]
3470 Saint Charles Avenue
New Orleans, Louisiana
1715 18 July 1945

"I'll get it, Jean-Jacques," Dorotea called out in the house. "I'm at the door."

She pulled it open. A tall and muscular Navy commander stood there, a thick silver cord hanging from his shoulder.

"Mrs. Howell?"

"No, I'm Mrs. Frade. Mrs. Howell is my mother-in-law. Please come in, Commander." She then raised her voice. "I think you had better come out here, darling. I think the other shoe has just dropped."

"Mrs. Frade, I'm looking for Lieutenant Colonel Cletus Frade. Your brother, perhaps?"

"No, he's my husband, something he's been keeping a dark secret from the U.S. government for reasons he hasn't elected to tell me."

Clete appeared at the library door, carrying one of his sons in his arms and holding the hand of the other one.

"Colonel Frade?"

"Guilty."

"My name is Portman, Colonel. I'm Rear Admiral Sourer's aide-de-camp. The admiral's compliments, Colonel. The admiral desires that you attend him immediately. In uniform, please, Colonel, and bring with you sufficient uniforms for a week."

"And those are the Colonel's children," Dorotea said.

"Something else I suspect he hasn't told the Marine Corps."

"Have I walked into a family argument?" Commander Portman asked.

"Whatever gave you that idea?" Dorotea said.

"She's been drinking Sazeracs," Clete said. "They make some women romantic and some belligerent."

"You have no complaints in the romantic department," Dorotea said. "Even if you're hiding me from the goddamn Marine Corps."

"What happened, Commander, is that I told her when they checked my records at Pensacola, there was no record of our marriage—"

"Or of the boys," Dorotea furnished.

"You really should look into it, Colonel," Commander Portman said. "Your wife and children are entitled to dependent status. A monthly check comes with that."

Frade looked askance at Portman, and thought, *You sonofabitch, you're enjoying this!*

"And you know how we need the money," Dorotea said. "Oysters by the dozen aren't cheap. Can I offer you a Sazerac, Commander?"

"Well, perhaps while Colonel Frade is getting into his uniform. Thank you."

"Where are we going, Commander?" Frade asked.

"Sorry, I can't get into that, sir."

"I thought if we're headed for Pensacola, I could get my records fixed."

"We're not going to Pensacola. I can tell you that. Colonel, the admiral doesn't like to be kept waiting."

There was a Navy Chevrolet staff car at the curb. From it, the last thing Clete saw was Dorotea standing on the porch, holding one of their sons in her arms and holding the hand of the other. The older boy was crying.

"Okay. She can't hear. Where are we going?"

"To the airport. I can tell you that much."

There was a Constellation at the airport, with U.S. NAVY on the fuselage and wings, and blue plates with the silver stars of a rear admiral in holders beside the pilot's window and the passenger door.

Portman waved Frade up a set of stairs ahead of him.

A white-jacketed steward got out of a seat and motioned for Clete to enter the passenger compartment.

"Welcome aboard, sir," he said.

The interior of the passenger compartment was unlike any Clete had ever seen. It looked more like a living room than anything else, with chairs and couches facing in both directions, and tables scattered between them. There was even a small bar, tended by another white-jacketed steward.

Clete remembered hearing that "admiral" meant "prince of the sea."

"Colonel Frade?"

Clete found himself facing an erect, middle-aged man in a white shirt, collar open and tie pulled down, no jacket, and wearing suspenders.

Clete came to attention.

"Sir, Lieutenant Colonel Frade reporting to the admiral as ordered."

"Welcome aboard, Colonel. I'm Admiral Sourer."

"Sir, may I ask the admiral where we're going?"

"No. But as soon as my junior aide gets back from Arnaud's with our dinner, we're going wheels-up for there. Sit down, Colonel, enjoy the ride."

"Yes, sir. Thank you, sir."

The first stop was Boston. When they took off from Boston and headed just about due east, Clete first thought they were headed to Europe.

Probably Prestwick, Scotland. That's within the Connie's range.

Hell, the Connie could make it direct to Berlin.

Are we headed to Berlin?

Why the hell would a two-star admiral be going to Berlin?

[SEVEN]
Tempelhof Air Base
Berlin, Germany
1445 19 July 1945

"Stay on board, Colonel," Admiral Sourer said, "until we get through this arriving VIP nonsense. I'll send Portman to fetch you."

"Aye, aye, sir."

There was a squad of senior Army brass waiting at the foot of the stairs, and an Army band. One of the Army officers was an erect, tough-looking two-star, and Clete decided he was looking at the legendary General I. D. White.

He looked for Mattingly but didn't see him.

Frade still had no idea what was going on. Admiral Sourer had quizzed him skillfully and at length on the flight to Boston, but had not made any accusations. Or threats of Leavenworth, either, if Clete didn't fess up that he was smuggling Nazis from Germany to Argentina.

Admiral Sourer trooped the line of Hell on Wheels tankers, shook hands with the tough-looking two-star Clete was now pretty sure was I. D. White, and then climbed into a 1940 Packard limousine and, preceded and followed by M-8 armored cars, roared off the tarmac.

Commander Portman appeared at the passenger door and waved for Clete to debark.

A car—an Opel Kapitän, a Chevrolet-sized sedan now bearing U.S. Army markings—was waiting for them.

"Can I ask now if we're going to Berlin?"

"Yes."

"Can I ask where we're going?"

"To Potsdam. To a place called Sans Souci. It means 'without care.' It belonged to Crown Prince Wilhelm of the Hohenzollern dynasty."

"Can I ask why we're going to 'care less'?"

"I think that means more 'care free' than 'care less.' And, no, you can't ask why we're going there."

It was about a twenty-minute drive from Tempelhof to Potsdam, through areas that were about equally utter destruction and seemingly untouched in any way.

They crossed a very well-guarded bridge, then entered an equally well-guarded area. Finally, they were at sort of a palace. The palace seemed surrounded by heavily armed troops.

A full colonel very carefully examined both Portman and Frade, and their identity cards, then passed them to a captain, who led them into the building and then into a small room that looked as if it had at one time been some medium-level bureaucrat's office.

Admiral Sourer was alone in the room, sitting on a hard-backed chair by a small desk.

"That'll be all, Jack, thank you," Sourer said.

"I'll be outside, sir."

He had no sooner closed that door than another door opened and a middle-aged man walked in.

"How was the flight, Sid?" the man asked.

"Eleven hours nonstop from Boston, Mr. President. You really should have taken the Connie when Hughes offered it to you."

Harry S Truman looked at Cletus Frade.

The President said: "So, this is the guy who's got Henry in a snit?"

"Lieutenant Colonel Frade, Mr. President," Sourer said.

"Do you drink, Colonel?"

"Yes, sir, Mr. President."

"Good, because the admiral is a teetotaler, and I really

want a drink—I have really earned a couple of drinks in the last couple of hours—and I don't like to drink alone. Bourbon all right, Colonel?"

"Yes, sir, Mr. President."

"Ask the steward outside, please, Sid, if we have a time problem."

"Certainly."

The President looked at Frade. "I don't have time to skirt around the edges of this, Colonel. So getting right to it: If I told you that yesterday afternoon I took Marshal Stalin aside and told him the United States has new bombs, each with the explosive power of twenty thousand tons of TNT, and I couldn't detect an iota of surprise in him, what would you say?"

"Sir, Mr. President, what you told him wasn't news to him. There are Soviet spies all over the Manhattan Project."

"Where'd you get that?"

"From General Gehlen, sir."

"From what I understand, Colonel, General Gehlen is a Nazi sonofabitch about as bad as any other, and worse than some."

"Sir, I respectfully suggest you have been misinformed."

"A lot of people try to misinform me. Don't you try it when you tell me what you know of the deal Allen Dulles made with Gehlen."

Admiral Sourer returned with a whisky glass in each hand.

"I like it neat," the President said as he took the glass. "Is that all right with you, Colonel?"

"Yes, sir, that's fine."

"Sid, he's going to tell us what he knows of the Dulles-Gehlen deal," Truman said, and gestured for Frade to start.

After a slight hesitation, during which he realized, almost as a surprise, that if any man had the right to know everything, it was the President of the United States, Clete related everything he knew about the deal.

The President, when Clete finished, nodded thoughtfully.

"Colonel," he then said, "for years now—back to when I was in the Senate, I mean—officers—good, senior, experienced officers—have been coming to me to help them get the OSS shut down. When I became President, the pressure on me really built. Finally, I decided that all those officers couldn't be wrong. I really admire General Donovan, but the bottom line was that it was Donovan versus just about every senior officer except Eisenhower. And you couldn't call Ike an *enthusiastic* supporter.

"So I decided the OSS had to go. On September twentieth, an Executive Order will be issued disbanding the OSS—"

"With all possible respect, Mr. President, that'd be a terrible mistake," Clete blurted.

"Hold your horses, son. Even 'with all possible respect,' lieutenant colonels are not supposed to volunteer to their commander in chief that he is about to make a terrible mistake."

Clete didn't reply.

"Even when you're right, Colonel," Truman said. "Now, the minute the word got out that I was shutting down the OSS, that terrible organization that wasn't worth the powder to blow it up, a funny thing happened. Just about everybody from J. Edgar Hoover to the secretary of the Treasury, Henry Morgenthau, got me in a corner and let me know they'd be happy to take the OSS organization under their wing.

"So that started me to think. If the OSS was so useless, why did they want it? I had an idea, and I took it to Sid—Admiral Sourer—here and asked him. We're old friends. He's not career Navy. Like me, he was a weekend warrior in the Navy Reserve when I was making my way up to colonel in the National Guard. The admiral told me what I was beginning to suspect on my own. All the generals and admirals and diplomats and bureaucrats didn't hate the OSS. They hated Wild Bill Donovan, and the reason they hated Donovan was that he was independent. They couldn't control him.

"And now they want to absorb the OSS into their little empires because they think that will make them stronger.

"Well, Colonel Frade, that's not going to happen. I am now convinced—especially because of the trouble the goddamn Russians are certain to cause us . . ."

He paused, then went on: "Let me go off on a tangent on that one. At one o'clock this afternoon, I told

General Marshall to shut off all aid to the Soviets immediately, today."

"Jesus, Harry!" Admiral Sourer said.

"The sonsofbitches have to be taught they can't push Harry Truman around the way they pushed poor sick FDR around."

"And that Bess isn't Eleanor?" Sourer asked innocently.

"Bess keeps her nose out of politics, and you know she does," Truman said. "And we're getting off the subject. Getting back to it. A month or so after the OSS is shut down—as soon as I can—I am going to set up an organization, call it the Intelligence Agency or something like that, that will take the place of the OSS.

"Now, since I can't name Wild Bill Donovan, Alec Graham, and Allen Dulles to run it, for the obvious reasons, I had to find somebody else. He didn't have to be too smart—"

"Go to hell, Harry," Sourer said dryly.

"—so I settled on Rear Admiral Sidney W. Sourer, United States Naval Reserve, to head the new agency. Which brings us to you, Colonel: Allen Dulles has convinced me we can't afford to lose General Gehlen and his intelligence assets. One sure way to lose him is for Morgenthau to lay his hands on you or any of your people or—especially—any of the Nazis you have smuggled into Argentina. I want the truth now. Can you prevent that from happening in the next few months with damned little—no—help from anybody until Sid—Admiral Sourer—is up and running with the new agency?"

"I'll do my best, Mr. President. I really think I can."

Truman looked at him for a long moment.

"So do I. I really think you can," the President said. Then he laughed. "When I heard you made the Secret Service take off their trousers . . . what did I say, Sid?"

"You said, 'That young officer is apparently capable of anything.'"

"That's what I said, and that's what I meant."

He put out his hand to Clete.

"Thank you, Colonel Frade. I hope to see you again, and soon." The President paused. "But right now, the thing to do is get you back to Argentina and out of sight. Sid, can we send him in that fancy airplane of yours? Can that make it to Argentina?"

"Not a problem, Mr. President."

"Then it's done. Sid, you can come back to Washington with me on *The Independence*."

"There's a couple of problems with that, Mr. President, as far as I'm concerned," Frade said. "The first is that your Connie can take us only as far as one of our air bases in Brazil; it would cause too much attention in Argentina."

"And what else?"

"The military attaché in our embassy in Buenos Aires is not one of my admirers."

"You're speaking of Colonel Richmond C. Flowers?" Admiral Sourer asked. "I know a good deal about him."

"Yes, sir. And if he finds out I'm back in Argentina, it'll be all over Washington in a matter of hours."

"Sid?" President Truman asked.

"By the time you get to Buenos Aires, Colonel Frade," Admiral Sourer said, "Colonel Flowers will be en route to his new assignment. Nome, Alaska, comes to mind."

"Anything else, son?" the President asked.

"My wife and sons are in New Orleans."

"We can't have that," the President said. "Sid . . ."

"By the time you get to Brazil, Colonel, I think your family will also be there," Admiral Sourer said.

"Is that it?" the President asked.

"Yes, sir."

"Have a nice flight, Colonel," the President of the United States said.

He turned and, sipping his bourbon, walked out of the room.

[EIGHT]
357 Roonstrasse, Zehlendorf
Berlin, Germany
1710 19 July 1945

"They're in the garden, Colonel," one of Tiny's men said when Frade walked into the house.

Clete was afraid to ask just who that meant, and didn't.

Then he saw Karl Boltitz, Siggie Stein, and Heinrich and Gerhard sitting at a small table. With Graf von Wachtstein.

Hansel's back!

Thank you, God!

Frade announced: "Okay, everybody up. We have a plane to catch."

"Says who?" Stein asked.

"Since you asked, says the President of the United States. Our orders are to hide in Argentina from the Secret Service until things settle down a little."

"Why do I think he's telling the truth?" von Wachtstein asked.

"Why is it you still have skin?"

"Because I am smarter than anyone thought I am."

"How did you do in Bremen, Karl?"

"Pretty well, Clete," Boltitz said. "So far as the subs are concerned, the sooner I get to Argentina the better."

He looked at the boys, then back at Clete, and asked, "How much time do we have?"

"None. Let's go."

The men all stood.

Heinrich and Gerhard remained in their seats, their gazes glued to the table.

"You guys don't want to go to Argentina and meet Uncle Siggie's nice nun?" Clete asked.

The boys looked up at each other.

Then Heinrich looked at Clete and said, "Excuse me? We can go?"

"Of course you can go," Frade said.

"Can you do that, Cletus?" von Wachtstein asked.

"What? Of course I can! I am the world's greatest expert in smuggling Germans into Argentina. If you don't believe me, just ask the secretary of the Treasury."